PYRA KILONOVA

Joseph McRae Palmer

PYRA KILONOVA

www.josephmcraepalmer.com

This book is a work of fiction. The characters, incidents, and dialog are drawn from the author's imagination and are not to be construed as real. Any resemblance to actual events or persons, living or dead, is fictionalized or coincidental.

ISBN (paperback) 978-1-961782-34-1

ISBN (ebook) 978-1-961782-33-4

Cover design: Donna Cunningham@BeauxArts.design

Prologue

So, you're back for more of my questionable life choices? I'm flattered, really. Most people hear about my run-ins with space empires and ancient cosmic entities and decide that's enough secondhand disaster for one lifetime. But here you are, ready for another round of "How Kory Drake Nearly Got Himself Killed This Time." I guess there's no accounting for taste. Pull up a chair—or whatever you're sitting on in your century—and let me tell you about the time I went hunting for a prison that contained a god.

Before we dive into this particular catastrophe, let me catch you up, in case you picked up this volume without reading the previous installment of my memoirs. Though honestly, skipping around in my life story is probably safer for your mental health. Not everything I've done is worth remembering—just ask any of my former commanding officers.

Last time, I told you about Sofia's injury. Sofia Kohl—my partner, both professionally and personally. At least, she was my personal partner back then. But I'm getting ahead of myself. Sofia took a devastating head injury when our previous ship, the *Inferis,* was ripped apart in the battle of

Virelia. I watched her brain bleed inside that escape pod, helpless, while the woman I loved slipped away. Even now, my hands shake remembering it. The desperate escape, Queen Zeta's rescue, and then the mad scramble across western North America looking for someone who could put Sofia's brain back together.

You wouldn't think "brain surgeon shopping" would be on the resume of an insurgent starship captain, but life has a way of expanding your skill set in the most unwelcome ways possible. One minute you're planning battle tactics against Kergan destroyers, the next you're bribing informants in bombed-out Sacramento for leads on neurologists who haven't been captured or killed.

"Your girlfriend needs a miracle," one particularly unhelpful doctor said. "And miracles are in short supply these days." I wanted to tell him I'd already used up my lifetime allocation of miracles simply by surviving to adulthood on the streets of San Jose, but I didn't have time for philosophical debates on probability.

The trail led us to Dr. Chen—brilliant, steady-handed, and unfortunately in Kergan custody, in what was left of Sacramento. The *Thunder*'s crew, bless their collection of misfits and malcontents, pulled off what I still consider one of our finest rescue operations. Picture this: a precision insertion, a silent infiltration of a Kergan military hospital, and an extraction so clean that the guards didn't realize she was gone until we were halfway back to base. Well, mostly clean. Don't let the dozen bodies we left behind convince you otherwise. The Kergans are probably still cleaning that mess up.

Dr. Chen looked at Sofia's scans and did that thing doctors do—pursed lips, furrowed brow, the subtle head shake that makes your stomach drop through the floor.

"I can save her," she finally said, "but there's a

complication."

In my experience, whenever someone says "complication," they really mean "horrible thing I don't want to tell you about directly." This particular complication came in the form of a Kergan neural implant—the only technology advanced enough to repair the damage to Sofia's synaptic pathways.

"You want to put enemy tech in her brain?" I asked, my voice climbing to a pitch I hadn't hit since puberty.

Dr. Chen looked at me like I was a particularly slow student. "I want to save her life. The implant is just a tool."

Turns out, it wasn't just a tool. After the surgery, when Sofia finally woke up—a moment where I felt like I could breathe for the first time in weeks—strange things started happening. She'd freeze mid-conversation, her eyes going distant, then snap back with information she couldn't possibly know. Kergan troop movements. Dominion security protocols. Classified research initiatives involving something called a "Noble Phylactery."

"It's like having a library downloaded directly into my brain," Sofia told me one night, her face ghostly in the dim light of our quarters. "But I can't control when the books open."

The implant wasn't just regulating her neural functions—it was packed with encrypted Kergan intelligence. A database some analyst probably thought was safely hidden behind layers of security, now sitting in the head of my partner. I've never been a big believer in luck, but even I had to admit that was a windfall. Dangerous as all hell, but a windfall nonetheless.

Around that same time, Wolf Jaw Base—our hidden headquarters in the Sierra Nevada mountains—became compromised. A Kergan scout patrol got too close for comfort, and then a force of Kergans and human collaborators attacked. Nothing kicks an insurgent operation into high gear like the threat of imminent annihilation. The evacuation was organized chaos—equipment packed, personnel assigned to transports, and priority data secured in record time.

We needed a new home, some place the Kergans wouldn't think to look. That's where 1036 Ganymed entered the picture—a 37-kilometer chunk of rock and metal drifting in near-Earth orbit. "The Rock," as we affectionately call it, became our new base of operations. Building a functional headquarters on an asteroid with practically no gravity was exactly as difficult as it sounds. Every tool had to be tethered, every step had to be calculated, and the constant risk of decompression meant that even minor construction errors could be fatal.

"Just like renovating an apartment," I joked to my chief engineer, "except the security deposit is your life."

She didn't laugh. Engineers rarely appreciate my humor when we're balancing on the knife-edge of catastrophic structural failure.

It was during the Ganymed construction that Sofia's random information downloads started focusing on something specific—the Noble Phylactery. At first, it was just fragments: ancient Primordian technology, containment protocols, sydereal energy signatures. But gradually, a complete picture emerged, and it was the kind of picture that makes you want to go back to bed and pull the covers over your head.

The Noble Phylactery isn't just an artifact—it's a prison. A highly sophisticated, multi-dimensional cage designed to hold something that shouldn't be caged: Nekufima, an Astral Titan. If you're not familiar with the cosmic hierarchy, Astral Titans are essentially gods—glyphshades so massive and powerful that they can reshape reality through sheer force of will. They exist primarily in the Syderealium, that infinite plane of consciousness that underpins our physical universe.

To put it in perspective: I'm six foot four, and I've been told I have an intimidating presence when I want to. An Astral Titan makes me look like an ant confronting a supernova. Not even a particularly impressive ant, at that.

"Why would anyone want to release something like that?" Destiny asked when we briefed the senior crew.

"Power," Sofia answered simply. "Whoever controls the Phylactery could theoretically harness Nekufima's abilities."

"Or become a puppet for a pissed-off cosmic entity," I added helpfully.

The intelligence from Sofia's implant made it clear: both the Kergan Empire and Arctis's rebel faction of the Collective Dominion were actively hunting for the Phylactery. The race was on, and we couldn't afford to let either side win. The thought of either the Kergans or Arctis with the power of an Astral Titan at their disposal was enough to give me cold sweats.

So that's where our new story begins—*Thunder*'s trek across the galaxy in search of the Noble Phylactery. I promise you'll get the full tour: Primordian ruins where the air itself seems to whisper ancient secrets; Kergan museums with security systems that would make ancient Earth's Fort Knox look like a child's piggy bank; star systems where the laws of physics take creative liberties; and my personal favorite, a gas giant with atmospheric storms so beautiful they've driven people mad just from looking at them too long.

All while dealing with a crew stretched to breaking point.

Sofia and I were sleeping in separate quarters by this time, our conversations limited to mission parameters and tactical assessments. Professional to a fault, that's us. Nothing says "relationship difficulties" quite like discussing ammunition supplies with someone who used to know exactly how you take your coffee.

The strain wasn't just personal. Everyone on *Thunder* was feeling it—the constant pressure of knowing that two of the most powerful forces in the galaxy were hunting the same prize we were, with vastly superior resources and manpower. We were the underdogs, as usual. I've spent so much time as an underdog that I sometimes forget what it's like to have the advantage. Probably involves less frantic improvisation and desperate gambles, but where's the fun in that?

And then there was Nekufima herself. I mentioned facing a literal demon, and I wasn't being melodramatic for once. The closer we got to the Phylactery, the more I started experiencing... let's call them "visitations." Dreams that didn't feel like dreams. Whispers when I was alone. A constant sense of being watched by something ancient and amused, like a cat that's spotted a particularly entertaining mouse.

"You're hearing voices in your head, and your solution is to get closer to the thing causing it?" Sofia asked when I finally admitted what was happening.

When she put it that way, it did sound remarkably stupid. But that's been my approach to most problems in life—head straight toward the danger and figure out a solution on the way. It's not the healthiest strategy, I'll admit, but it's gotten me this far. Though "this far" includes multiple near-death experiences, political exile, and a romantic relationship currently on life support, so take my advice with an appropriate amount of skepticism.

What follows is the true account of our hunt for the Noble Phylactery—the triumphs, the disasters, the moments of brilliance and idiocy that defined our mission. I won't pretend I made all the right choices. Anyone who claims they always make the right choices is either lying or hasn't made enough choices to know better. But I tried my best with the information I had, and sometimes that's all you can do when you're up against impossible odds.

So brace yourself for tales of daring space battles, archaeological puzzles, tense standoffs, and the occasional existential crisis. I promise this story has it all—humor in the darkest moments, loyalty tested to breaking point, and the questionable wisdom of antagonizing a being who existed before our sun was born.

Ready? Good. Let me take you back to where it all began: a cramped planning room on an asteroid base, with a desperate crew and a captain who was about to learn that some prisons are meant to stay locked—especially when they contain gods who've had millions of years to plan their revenge.

1

I was drowning in light.

Not water—something worse. A flood of raw awareness, colors too vivid, sensations sharp enough to bleed. My body floated in nothingness, weightless and unbearably heavy at the same time, like I'd slipped free of gravity and landed in the deep end of a god's fever dream.

This wasn't a dream, though. I'd had those—plenty. Dreams had rules, limits, the reassuring promise you'd wake up in a cold sweat and maybe punch your pillow. The Syderealium didn't come with that kind of safety net. It *expanded* you—stretched your thoughts until they weren't entirely yours anymore.

I could feel colors brush my skin, soft as silk and sharp as regret. Memories whispered past—not mine. Moments from lives I'd never lived, emotions like echoes from someone else's soul.

"Great," I muttered into the void. "Another cosmic acid trip. Can't wait to fill out the after-action report for this one."

My words didn't echo. They *unfolded*—rippling through the airless dark in fractals I could *see*, geometric waves of meaning that exploded beyond what I actually said. And that's when the presence noticed me.

It didn't arrive. It had always been here—just hadn't been looking at me until now. But when it did, I *felt* it. Like every cell in my body snapped to attention. Like something older than stars had just locked eyes with an insect.

The dark deepened. Not darker, but *denser*—soaked with intention, humming with intelligence.

The space twisted. Symbols swirled out of the void—*energlyphs,* like Zeta's, but older, wilder, unstable. They spun faster, contracting into shape. First abstract. Then humanoid. Then *her.*

A woman, if you could call something made of shadow and radiation a woman. She was light and gravity and ancient fury in the shape of a smile.

"You're more coherent than most," she said, her voice threading through my skull like silk and static. "Most of your kind just... drown."

"Nekufima," I said, the name coming to me from nowhere and everywhere at once.

The figure paused, and I felt a cold curiosity emanating from her. "You know my name. How... interesting." The light comprising her form rippled with what might have been amusement. "Most entities require an introduction. Or several."

As she spoke, her appearance continued to transform. The abstract patterns of energlyphs resolved into a more solid feminine form—naked, perfect, and clearly designed to appeal to human desires. Long, flowing hair made of darkness and starlight framed a face of impossible beauty. She moved with liquid grace, each gesture both innocent and deeply seductive.

"Is this form more comfortable for your limited perception?" she asked, her voice now honey-smooth, with just enough of an edge to slice through any illusions I might harbor about her true nature.

"I've seen the smoke-and-mirrors routine before," I said, aiming for nonchalance despite the unnerving effect she was having on me. "Though I'll admit your production values are higher than most."

She laughed, and the sound made my chest tighten with a mixture of desire and dread. "Such bravado from something so young, so temporary." She floated closer, circling me like a shark. "You remind me of them, you know. The ones who thought they could chain infinity."

I tried to move away, but in the Syderealium, intent didn't always translate to action. "Look, I'm flattered by the attention, but I'm already in a committed relationship with someone who doesn't speak in riddles and existential threats."

"Oh, Kory Drake." She said my name like she was tasting it, each syllable a delicacy to be savored. "You mistake my interest for choice. Bonds form in the Syderealium without permission or consent. Your little consciousness brushed against mine, a mote of dust disturbing a hurricane."

She reached out, not with a hand but with tendrils of darkness that brushed against my face. The touch burned cold and hot simultaneously, sending spasms of pleasure and pain through my nervous system. "I've been alone for so very long," she whispered, her voice suddenly vulnerable, intimate. "Imprisoned while stars were born and died. Can you imagine such solitude?"

Despite knowing better, I felt a stab of sympathy. "That sounds... difficult."

Her expression hardened, beautiful features twisting into something predatory. "Don't patronize me, child. Your pity is as meaningless as your resistance." The tendrils of darkness withdrew, then shot forward again, wrapping around my throat. I couldn't breathe, but since this wasn't my physical body, I didn't need to. Still, the sensation of choking was convincingly unpleasant.

"I could crush your consciousness right now," she hissed, her face inches from mine. "Extinguish your little spark and feast on the energies released." The pressure increased, and spots danced in my vision. "But that would be... wasteful."

As suddenly as it had begun, the assault stopped. The tendrils unwound from my throat, transforming into gentle caresses that trailed down my chest. The sensation was disturbingly pleasurable, sending unwanted heat through my body.

"We are connected now, you and I," she said, her voice a seductive murmur. "What a fascinating accident of probability. Your consciousness vibrates at just the right frequency to resonate with mine."

"Lucky me," I managed, trying to ignore the way her touch affected me. "Do all your relationships start with strangulation, or am I special?"

She smiled, and there was genuine amusement in it. "Oh, you are special, Kory Drake. More than you know." Her form moved closer, pressing against me in ways that sent confusion and unwanted arousal through me. "You carry something of mine, though you don't realize it yet."

I tried to pull away, but she moved with me, her body of light and shadow conforming to mine. "I have nothing of yours."

"Not yet," she agreed, "but you will." Her lips, cool and

burning at once, brushed against my ear. "You will find me where twin death-light burns, or I will find you in the spaces between your thoughts."

"That's not cryptic at all," I said, struggling to maintain my composure as her hands—were they hands? They felt like hands—traced patterns on my skin that left trails of fire in their wake. "Could you be a little more specific? Like, I don't know, coordinates? A planet name?"

She laughed again, the sound both beautiful and terrible. "Where would be the fun in that? Besides, you'll know it when you see it. The pull between us will only grow stronger." Her expression turned serious, almost sad. "You should come to me willingly, Kory Drake. The alternative will be... unpleasant for both of us."

"Thanks, but I've already got plans. Command a starship, protect Earth, maybe catch up on some reading."

Her eyes flashed with anger, but it was quickly replaced by something worse—patience. The kind of patience only something truly ancient could possess.

"Your defiance is amusing, but ultimately futile." She floated back slightly, her perfect form beginning to dissolve at the edges, breaking down into those strange symbolic patterns again. "Time moves differently for me. I've waited millions of years. I can wait a little longer."

The Sydereal ium around us began to pulse, the colors shifting toward red. I felt a pulling sensation, as if reality was trying to reclaim me.

"Our connection is new, still forming," Nekufima said, her voice now coming from everywhere at once. "But it will strengthen. Every time you sleep, every time your mind wanders, I'll be there, waiting in the shadows."

Tendrils of darkness shot out from her dissolving form, hundreds of them, reaching for me like hungry serpents.

They didn't grab me this time but instead brushed against my consciousness, leaving impressions—fragments of memories, sensations, knowledge that wasn't mine.

"A parting gift," she whispered as she faded into the swirling chaos of the Sydererealium. "A taste of what awaits."

The tendrils touched my forehead, and pain detonated behind my eyes—not physical pain, but the searing overload of too much knowledge forced into a human mind. Images surged through me in an unrelenting tide: a ring-like megastructure orbiting twin stars that pulsed with sick, warped light; a crystalline container brimming with volatile, swirling energies; civilizations rising, thriving, and vanishing in the span of heartbeats.

"Twin death-light burns eternal," her voice echoed, not in my ears but within the deepest part of my consciousness, as the Syderealium began to unravel around me. "Find me before I find you, Kory Drake. For both our sakes."

The last thing I saw before reality pulled me back was her face—no longer beautiful, but ancient and monstrous, her eyes alight with the cold fury of dying stars.

Then everything went black.

And I fell—not asleep, not unconscious, but into something worse.

Into memory.

Into her.

2

I woke up like I'd been shot out of a cannon, my body launching upright before my brain had fully engaged. Sweat soaked the sheets around me, my heart hammering so hard I half expected it to burst through my ribcage like one of those movie aliens. The dream—no, not a dream, something far worse—clung to me like a second skin, Nekufima's voice still echoing in the corners of my mind. I gasped for air, each breath shallow and insufficient, as if the room's oxygen had been replaced with something thinner, less substantial.

"Twin death-light," I whispered, the words tasting wrong in my mouth.

Beside me, Sofia slept on, her breathing deep and regular. The dim red night lighting cast her face in shadow, highlighting the sharp angle of her cheekbone and the soft curve of her lips. Her naked scalp begging to be caressed, one arm flung out toward my side of the bed as if reaching for me even in sleep.

A surge of desire hit me unexpectedly, my body responding with embarrassing enthusiasm. For a moment, I considered waking her, pulling her warm body against mine to drive away the chill that had settled in my bones. My hand hovered over her shoulder.

And then I stopped, disgust replacing arousal as I realized what was happening. This wasn't my desire—it was an echo of Nekufima's manipulation, a phantom sensation left behind like the memory of a touch. Using Sofia to scratch that particular itch felt wrong on every level.

"Get out of my head," I muttered, carefully sliding from the bed to avoid disturbing Sofia. My legs wobbled like they belonged to a newborn giraffe, forcing me to grab the edge of the nightstand for support.

The captain's quarters aboard *Thunder* weren't exactly spacious—more like a closet that had aspirations of someday growing up to be a proper room. In the night-cycle lighting, the space looked even smaller; the shadows compressing the walls inward. Our meager personal belongings sat in neat, regulation-approved storage containers. Sofia's influence, not mine. Left to my own devices, my organizational system consisted primarily of "that pile over there."

I checked the time on the wall display: 0300 hours. Still the dead of ship's night, with four hours before my scheduled bridge shift.

"Just stress," I told myself, running shaking hands through my sweat-dampened hair. "Battle fatigue. Too much caffeine. Something you ate. Definitely not an ancient cosmic entity invading your dreams."

Even as I listed the possibilities, I knew none of them were true. The Syderealium experience had been too real, too different from ordinary dreams. I'd had nightmares before—plenty of them since taking command of *Thunder*—but they faded upon waking, details dissolving like sugar in hot coffee. This remained crystal clear, every moment carved into my memory with painful precision.

I stumbled to the small sink in my quarter's small private head, splashing cold water on my face. The shock of it helped ground me in reality, but when I looked up at the mirror, I barely recognized the man staring back. My face looked like it had been carved from wax and left too close to a heater—pale, drawn, with dark circles under my eyes that resembled bruises. My brown hair stuck up at odd angles, and my eyes held a haunted look I'd seen before—in soldiers who'd seen too much combat, in refugees fleeing war zones.

"You look like hell, Drake," I told my reflection, which offered no argument.

I tried lying back down, closing my eyes and focusing on Sofia's steady breathing beside me. But every time I approached the edge of sleep, I saw Nekufima's face, felt those shadow tendrils brushing against my skin. After thirty minutes of this torture, I gave up.

Sleep wasn't happening. Not tonight.

I dressed silently in the dark, pulling on my uniform with practiced efficiency. Sofia stirred once, murmuring something unintelligible before rolling over. I paused at the door, watching her for a moment. Whatever was happening to me, I didn't want it touching her. She'd been through enough already with the Kergan brain implant and the classified information it kept feeding her.

The corridors of *Thunder* were eerily quiet during the night cycle. The lighting was dimmed to simulate evening, creating pools of shadow between the soft amber guide lights along the floor. My footsteps echoed against the metal deck plating, each sound seeming unnaturally loud in the stillness. Most of the crew was asleep, save for the night shift, keeping the ship running.

I nodded to a pair of engineers heading back from some

midnight repair job, their coveralls stained with lubricant that looked black in the low light. They straightened when they saw me, surprise evident in their quick salutes.

"At ease," I said automatically. "Just taking a walk."

They relaxed marginally, exchanging glances that clearly communicated, "Why is the captain prowling around at three in the morning?" but were too professional to ask aloud.

The bridge doors hissed open as I approached, revealing the night shift at their stations. Unlike the daytime bridge, with its constant activity and chatter, night operations had a cathedral-like hush—quiet conversations, the soft beeping of instruments, the occasional clink of a coffee mug being set down.

Five heads turned simultaneously as I entered, expressions ranging from surprise to concern. Lieutenant Okafor, the night watch officer, rose from the command chair so quickly he nearly spilled his coffee.

"Captain on the bridge!" he announced, his rich Nigerian accent adding weight to the words.

"As you were," I said, waving them back to their duties. "Just thought I'd get an early start today."

Okafor hesitated, dark eyes assessing me with the careful scrutiny of a man responsible for noting anything out of the ordinary. At six-foot-two, he nearly matched my height, his broad shoulders filling out his uniform impressively. Unlike me, he looked alert and composed, despite being five hours into a night shift.

"Is everything alright, sir?" he asked quietly, falling into step beside me as I moved toward the main viewscreen.

"Fine, Lieutenant. Just couldn't sleep." I attempted a casual shrug that probably looked more like a nervous spasm. "Figured I'd check some navigational calculations for tomorrow's departure. No point staring at the ceiling."

"Of course, sir." His tone was perfectly respectful, but I didn't miss the skepticism in his eyes. "We've just completed the pre-departure checklist. All systems are nominal. Engineering reports full power available, and weapons systems are on standby."

I nodded, grateful for his professionalism. "Good work. How are the supplies from Ganymed Base integrating with our systems?"

"The ammunition for the railguns has been stored, and the new medical supplies have been inventoried. Doc Montana signed off on them personally." He paused. "There was one irregularity with the chromatic batteries. PO Gunnison can brief you on that."

A young woman at the engineering station straightened in her chair. "Just a minor calibration issue, sir. The radon concentration was slightly below our optimal range. Engineering adjusted the transducers to compensate."

"Good initiative," I said, settling into the captain's chair as Okafor stepped aside. The seat was still warm from his body, a strange intimacy that momentarily distracted me.

The main viewscreen showed a stunning vista of space, with Earth a distant blue marble against the black void. Ganymed's irregular surface took up the right portion of the screen, its craggy terrain cast in sharp relief by the sun's light. The asteroid's slow rotation meant the view changed gradually, stars sliding across the screen in a stately procession.

I tucked my hands under my thighs, hiding the persistent trembling that refused to subside. The physical reaction bothered me more than the dream itself—I'd faced down alien enemies, survived battles in space, and once had to give a speech to the entire SWS faculty with my fly open.

My hands hadn't shaken then.

Around me, the night shift went about their duties with quiet efficiency. The navigation officer plotted our departure vector for tomorrow's journey to Jupiter, her fingers dancing across the control panel with practiced ease. The communications specialist monitored the low-level chatter from Ganymed Base, acknowledging routine status updates with brief responses. The tactical station remained largely quiet—this far from occupied Earth, there was little need for constant weapons monitoring.

It should have been calming, this routine, this normalcy. Instead, every shadow on the bridge seemed to move when I wasn't looking directly at it. Every quiet beep from a console made me tense, expecting Nekufima's voice to somehow emanate from the speakers. The recycled air felt too thin, insufficient for my lungs despite the environmentals reading normal on all displays.

Fragments of the encounter kept flashing through my mind—her face morphing from beauty to terror, the sensation of those shadow tendrils against my skin, the cryptic warning about twin death-light. I'd dealt with the Syderealium before, both during my training, and frequently in combat. But this had been different, more intimate and invasive.

"Captain?" Okafor's voice pulled me from my thoughts. "The final supply load from Ganymed Base is requesting permission to unload. They're ahead of schedule."

I blinked, focusing on the tactical display. "Grant permission. Let's get everything loaded, so we're ready for departure at 0800."

"Yes, sir." He returned to his station, issuing the necessary orders.

Tomorrow we'd leave the relative safety of near-Earth

orbit, heading to Jupiter to fill our reactor fuel tanks with helium-3 before departing for a nearby Lagrange point and veilspace. So far, our ultimate destination was unknown. All we knew was that we needed to find the Noble Phylactery before either Ban'ach or Arctis did. If the enemy got their hands on Nekufima—a god-like Astral Titan trapped in this plane—and learned how to manipulate her, we could all be doomed.

So why did I feel like we should already know where we were going?

I stared out at the stars, my mind returning to Nekufima's words despite my best efforts. Twin death-light. What the hell did that mean? Binary stars maybe? There were plenty of those in the galaxy, nothing specific enough to narrow down a location.

A shiver ran down my spine as another possibility occurred to me. What if it wasn't a place at all? What if it was a warning? Or a threat?

The stars continued their slow march across the viewscreen, indifferent to my concerns. One of them seemed to pulse slightly, drawing my attention. Just a visual trick, I told myself. Stars don't pulse like that out her in deep space.

But as I watched, I could have sworn it winked at me.

And somewhere, in a place that wasn't quite in my head but definitely wasn't outside it either, I heard the faint echo of Nekufima's laughter.

3

I watched Zeta float before me, her plasma form pulsing with a calm intensity that never failed to remind me how out of my depth I was. The Queen's octahedral capsule hovered at perfect attention, while I slouched in my captain's chair like a kid playing dress-up in a uniform two sizes too important. The recessed lighting of my ready room cast everything in that perfect military blue-white glow that was supposed to make you feel authoritative. It mostly made me feel like I was perpetually under examination.

"Zeta wishes to express her gratitude for your crew's continued loyalty during these trying times," she said, her luminous form shifting in patterns that reminded me of solar flares dancing across a star's surface.

"Just doing my job, Zeta." I straightened my posture, feeling the familiar twinge in my lower back—a souvenir from our mission to rescue Dr. Chen. The holographic displays surrounding us showed *Thunder*'s current status: weapons systems green, engines operating at peak efficiency, crew complement at one hundred three percent.

All the numbers looked good. So why did my stomach feel like it was trying to escape through my boots?

"Queen Zeta must return to the Collective Dominion," Zeta continued, her formal third-person speech pattern unchanged. "The royalist faction requires direct leadership if we are to successfully challenge Arctis's illegitimate claim to power."

I nodded, processing what this meant. "I understand. I wish *Thunder* could accompany you."

"*Thunder* will continue its mission to locate and secure the Noble Phylactery." The plasma inside her containment field swirled with increased intensity. "Zeta has the utmost confidence in your abilities, Kory."

Great. The exiled queen of an interstellar empire had the "utmost confidence" in a former street kid from San Jose. The universe had a twisted sense of humor. I'd gone from scrounging for food in dumpsters to commanding a warship on a mission that could determine the fate of civilizations. If my old acquaintances could see me now, they'd laugh themselves into hernias.

"I appreciate the vote of confidence," I said, keeping my face carefully neutral. My jaw tightened involuntarily. "But I'm not sure my Officer Training School courses covered 'Hunting Ancient Cosmic Artifacts 101.'"

A ripple passed through Zeta's form that I recognized as amusement. "Zeta believes your... unorthodox background provides perspectives that traditional officers lack."

Translation: I was unpredictable enough to be useful. Fair assessment.

The holographic display shifted to show Jupiter—our next destination. We needed to fuel *Thunder's* helium-3 tanks from the giant planet's upper atmosphere. But from there, we still didn't know where we were going.

"The Queen must emphasize something of grave importance." Zeta's tone shifted, the formal cadence taking on a weight I rarely heard. "The Noble Phylactery is not a prize, but a prison."

I leaned forward, elbows on my knees. "A prison for Nekufima. We've covered this in the briefings."

"But perhaps not with sufficient warning." The light from Zeta's form intensified, casting elongated shadows across the ready room. "Nekufima is ancient beyond comprehension, a primordial entity who has witnessed billions of years of cosmic history. Her imprisonment is not an injustice to be corrected, but a necessary containment."

A fleeting smirk crossed my face. "So we're not mounting a jailbreak?"

"This is not a matter for levity, Kory." The temperature in the room seemed to drop several degrees. "Nekufima cannot be trusted. Ever. She will speak to you through the sydereal bond the Phylactery creates, and every word will be calculated to secure her freedom."

I rubbed the back of my neck, feeling a phantom itch where Nekufima had touched me last night. "And if she's freed?"

"The consequences would be... unpredictable. And in cosmic matters, unpredictability rarely favors organic life." Zeta's capsule rotated slightly. "Nekufima's consciousness exists partially within the Syderealium itself. She perceives reality in ways we cannot comprehend."

"So secure the Phylactery, don't free the cosmic horror. Got it." I stood, feeling the weight of command settling onto my shoulders like an ill-fitted coat. "Is there anything else about our mission parameters that's changing with your departure?"

"Negative. Your primary objective remains retrieval of

the Phylactery before Arctis's or Banach's forces can claim it." Zeta began moving toward the door. "The Queen will now prepare for departure."

I followed her into the corridor, where the blue-white light of my ready room gave way to the more utilitarian illumination of *Thunder*'s main passageways. The ship's familiar hum vibrated through the deck plates beneath my boots—a constant reminder that we were living next to chromatic batteries with enough charge to power the entire Earth for several days.

Crew members we passed snapped to attention, offering respectful nods to Zeta. They'd grown accustomed to the presence of royalty aboard, but that didn't diminish the awe she inspired. An igna queen was a rare sight even in the Collective Dominion; out here, on the fringes of explored space, she was practically mythological.

I caught Lieutenant Phoebe Brooks's eye as we passed the tactical operations center. The slight widening of her pupils told me the news of Zeta's departure was already circulating. No surprise there—ships ran on gossip as much as they did on battery charge.

"*Thunder* has served the Queen well," Zeta said as we approached the docking bay. "It is a vessel worthy of its name."

"High praise coming from someone who rules planets." The words slipped out before I could filter them, another bad habit from my street days.

But Zeta merely pulsed with that ripple of amusement again. "Zeta finds your directness refreshing, Lieutenant Commander. It is a quality too often sacrificed in pursuit of political advantage."

The docking bay doors slid open with a pneumatic hiss. Through the massive viewport, I could see Zeta's sleek yacht, the *Luminara*, waiting in the void. Its recently repaired hull gleamed against the backdrop of distant stars, the faint shimmer of its bolsters barely visible. Flanking it were two Royal Guard frigates, their distinctive armor plating catching the light from a distant star. Their presence was both reassurance and reminder—Zeta might be in exile, but she was still a queen, still protected by those sworn to her service.

"Your escort looks ready," I observed, trying to ignore the hollow feeling spreading in my chest. I'd grown used to having Zeta aboard, her ancient wisdom just a comm call away.

"Yes. The time for decisive action approaches." Zeta turned her capsule to face me directly. "Lieutenant Commander Drake, Zeta wishes to offer final words of caution regarding your quest."

Here it comes, I thought. The royal version of "don't screw this up."

"The Noble Phylactery has existed for millions of your years, yet its purpose remains only partially understood. It was created by beings whose civilization had already reached its zenith when mammals first appeared on Earth."

"No pressure there," I muttered.

"When you locate it, you will feel drawn to it. This is by design. The Phylactery seeks a bond partner for Nekufima—a mind through which she can speak, influence, perhaps eventually control and find her freedom."

I swallowed hard. "That part wasn't in the briefing materials."

"Because Zeta hoped it would not become relevant." Her form pulsed with what might have been regret. "The Queen had intended to handle this aspect of the mission personally. But circumstances have changed."

"They always do." I squared my shoulders. "What else should I know?"

"Trust your instincts, Commander. They have served you well thus far." Zeta's capsule began moving toward the airlock that would take her to the *Luminara*. "And remember that ancient beings measure time differently than we do. What seems urgent to Nekufima may have waited millennia; what seems trivial may be of cosmic significance."

"So everything matters and nothing matters. Helpful." I managed a half-smile.

"Indeed." Zeta paused at the airlock. "Zeta will return as soon as circumstances permit. Until then, the Queen entrusts *Thunder* and its mission to your capable hands."

The airlock cycled open, and Zeta's luminous form entered her vessel without another word. I watched through the viewport as her octahedral capsule was secured in what I assumed was the *Luminara*'s equivalent of a bridge.

The yacht's engines engaged with no visible light—only the slightest vibration from gravitational wave emissions registered on *Thunder*'s sensors. The small formation pulled away with elegant precision, accelerating before receding into the distance.

And just like that, I was alone. Well, as alone as one could be on a warship with a crew complement of nearly two hundred.

I made my way to the command deck, acknowledging salutes with nods that I hoped conveyed confident authority rather than the "what the hell am I doing?" panic that threatened to bubble up from my gut.

"Course laid in, sir?" asked PO Rivera from the helm station.

"Standby," I replied, keeping my expression neutral despite the hollow feeling that had expanded from my chest to encompass most of my torso. "We won't lift until logistics clears the final loadouts."

"Aye, sir. Preflight nav solution is plotted. We're ready to launch on your word."

I settled into the command chair—my chair entirely, with Zeta gone and no one to defer to. The bridge crew worked through the pre-departure checklists with professional efficiency, but I still noticed the sideways glances, the subtle hesitations, the unspoken question: where was the captain taking us?

Thunder felt different already.

The next few hours passed in a blur of inspections, crew arrivals, final briefings, and readiness drills. I found myself staring at the space Zeta used to occupy in the ops center, catching myself turning to ask her opinion before remembering she wasn't just absent—she was gone.

"Nicobe believes the power lines are operating at peak efficiency," reported Nicobe during the engineering update. The igna Heliacal Templar's crimson dodecahedron capsule hovered at shoulder height, pulsing faintly as she spoke. "Though Nicobe must confess a certain melancholy has affected the harmonization rituals without Her Majesty's resonant frequencies."

Translation: she missed Zeta too.

"We'll manage," I said, scrolling through the maintenance reports on my tablet. "How's the bolster generator calibration coming?"

"Nicobe has overseen three complete recalibration cycles. The bolsters will hold against conventional weapons fire and physical stress." Her speech, though formal, carried subtle markers of loss. "Nicobe wonders if the Captain has given thought to our destination once the refueling operation at Jupiter is complete?"

I hadn't, not really.

"Working on it," I lied. "I'll have something for the senior staff by 0800 tomorrow."

Nicobe's capsule dipped in the closest thing she had to a nod. "Nicobe stands ready to assist in any capacity required."

After she left, I sat alone in my ready room, surrounded by holographic displays of everything we knew about the Noble Phylactery. It wasn't much. Allegedly the prison of a cosmic entity so dangerous the Primordians had thrown it into the equivalent of a sydereal max-security prison.

I played back one of Zeta's recordings, her voice crisp and regal: "She cannot be trusted. Ever."

Yet here we were, getting ready to fly straight toward the thing she warned us about. Don't trust the ancient evil—but go get the box it's trapped in. What could possibly go wrong?

I rubbed my eyes, feeling the fatigue of command settling into my bones. Two years ago, my biggest concern was finding somewhere dry to sleep in San Jose. Now I was making decisions that could shift the fate of galactic civilization.

The universe had a hell of a sense of humor.

I closed the holo displays with a flick of my hand and made my decision. We would continue as planned. Find the Phylactery. Secure it. Bring it back. Simple. Clean. Suicidal.

"Just following the glowing breadcrumbs into the cosmic oven," I muttered. "What's the worst that could happen? Oh, right—unleashing an ancient evil that's been imprisoned for millions of years. Tuesday stuff."

But as I sat in my chair, staring at the dull glow of the

overhead lights, I couldn't shake the feeling that Zeta had left something out.

Something crucial.

Something about why Nekufima had been imprisoned in the first place.

4

Jupiter loomed in *Thunder*'s viewscreen like a massive, swirling bullseye, its bands of orange and cream hypnotic in their eternal dance. I'd seen the gas giant in countless vids, but they didn't capture the sheer intimidation factor of the real thing—2.5 times Earth's gravity waiting to crush us like bugs, atmospheric pressures that could flatten our hull like an aluminum can, and radiation that would microwave our insides if our magnetosphere shields failed. Yet here we were, about to dip into that cosmic nightmare to siphon off some helium-3, because apparently suicidal mining operations were now part of my captain's job description. I rolled my shoulders, already feeling phantom weight pressing down on them. Three days in Jupiter's gravity well. My spine compressed just thinking about it.

"Approaching optimal insertion vector, Captain," Lieutenant Park announced from the helm, her voice tight with the same tension I felt.

I nodded, eyes fixed on the swirling chaos of Jupiter's upper atmosphere. "Begin deceleration sequence. Let's ease her in nice and gentle."

Our new fusion reactor was a technological marvel, a gift from Queen Zeta before she'd departed for the Collective Dominion. It promised independence—the ability to recharge our own chromatic batteries without limping back to a friendly port every time we needed a top-off. The catch? We needed helium-3, and lots of it. Jupiter was our gas station, and we were about to pull up to the pump.

"All hands," I spoke into the shipwide comm, "prepare for gravity increase. We're beginning our descent into Jupiter's atmosphere in five minutes. Secure all loose equipment and engage your braces."

I looked across the bridge at Destiny Austin, who sat at the tactical station, her fingers dancing across the holographic interface. My street sister, and now my executive officer, second in command of *Thunder*. She had been my family for seven years now, ever since I met her in San Jose soon after escaping the orphanage.

She caught my glance and rolled her eyes. "Three days of feeling like an elephant's been bench-pressing my lungs," she muttered. "Exactly how I dreamed of spending my week."

"Could be worse," I said, forcing a grin. "We could be shoveling snow off Saturn's rings."

She gave me a look. "There's no snow in space, Kory."

"Exactly. That's why it would be worse."

The first tendrils of Jupiter's upper atmosphere brushed against our hull, and *Thunder* shuddered slightly. I felt the artificial gravity compensators kick in, but they could only do so much. Our technology could increase gravity just fine, but negating external forces was another matter. As our velocity dropped, the weight settled onto me gradually, like someone was stacking bricks on my shoulders one by one.

"Beginning atmospheric insertion," Park announced, her voice already strained. "Activating collection arrays."

Thunder was equipped with specialized scoops designed to filter helium-3 from the hydrogen-dominant atmosphere. In theory, it was simple—dip in, collect, process, store, get out. In practice, it meant flying through a gravity well that wanted to suck us down to pressures that would crush us into a ball of exotic metals.

By the time we reached optimal collection depth, every movement required deliberate effort. I could feel my heart working harder, my skin being tugged down. My muscle braces helped, compressing my lower body to prevent blood from pooling, but nothing could fully counter 2.5 times the gravity the human body was designed for.

"Collection arrays at full capacity," Nicobe reported engineering. Her voice was steady, professional. "Estimated collection time for optimal quantities: seventy-two hours."

Three days. Three days of this crushing pressure. I nodded, the simple movement requiring more effort than I cared to admit.

"Prepare for sustained collection operations," I ordered. "Rotating shifts. Nobody stays on duty longer than four hours at a time."

Day one was manageable, in the way that a mild case of the flu is manageable. It sucks, but you can function. The crew moved with deliberate care, conversations muted by the effort of simply breathing. Every step felt like wading through wet cement. Even the ship seemed to groan under the strain, creaks and settling sounds I'd never heard before echoing through the corridors.

I made my rounds, checking on each department. Engineering had it worst—Phoebe Brooks, *Thunder*'s assistant engineer, and her team constantly adjusting the collection arrays, crawling through maintenance tubes that suddenly felt half their normal size.

"How's it holding up?" I asked, leaning against the doorframe of the engineering bay more heavily than I wanted to admit.

Phoebe looked up from her console, sweat beading on her forehead. Her usual amiable smile was strained.

"The arrays are performing above specs," she said, brushing a strand of hair from her face with a motion that seemed to take tremendous effort. "But the gravity is hell on the hydraulics. We're having to cycle the pressure relief valves every hour instead of every twelve."

I nodded. "Do what you need to do. This helium-3 is worth the strain."

Her eyes lingered on me a beat longer than necessary. "Always impressed by your stamina, Captain."

I chose to ignore the comment, chalking it up to the stress of our situation. "Keep me updated on any issues."

By the end of my shift, my legs felt like they were made of lead, and my spine was sending sharp complaints with every movement. I made it to my quarters and collapsed onto my bunk, not even bothering to remove my uniform. The weight of my own body pinned me to the mattress like a specimen in a collection.

Sleep came in fits and starts, my body too aware of the crushing pressure to fully relax.

Day two arrived with a symphony of aches I hadn't felt since my most brutal days at Officer Training School. Muscles I'd forgotten existed screamed in protest as I forced myself upright. My uniform felt ten kilos heavier as I pulled it on. Looking in the mirror, I noticed the strain around my eyes, the way my cheeks seemed to sag slightly under the increased gravity.

I regretted mining Jupiter's atmosphere. We should have gone to Saturn instead. I knew it would have added a week to our schedule, but at least the gravity would have been close to one gee.

"You look like hell," Destiny commented when I entered the bridge. Despite her words, she didn't look much better—her normally perfect posture compromised by the invisible weight on her shoulders.

"Good morning to you too," I replied, lowering myself carefully into the command chair. "Status report?"

"Collection proceeding at ninety-four percent efficiency," she said. "We've reached approximately forty percent of our target quantity."

I nodded, the simple motion requiring conscious effort. "Good. How are the storage tanks holding up?"

"Pressure within acceptable parameters," she replied. "But we've got a problem with cooling array three. The increased gravitational stress is causing the circulation pumps to work harder than designed."

Of course, there was a problem. There was always a problem. That was the captain's job—problem-solving, while feeling like your organs were being compressed into paste.

"Options?" I asked, massaging my temple where a headache was forming.

"Phoebe says we can reroute coolant through the secondary system, but it'll mean taking array three offline for six hours."

I considered this. "Do it. Better to lose some collection efficiency than risk a coolant rupture."

Destiny nodded and turned to relay the orders. As she

did, I caught a glimpse of her profile, the determined set of her jaw despite the physical strain. A wave of appreciation washed over me. Everyone on this ship was pushing through their own private hell of aches and compressed organs, all because I'd decided we needed this helium-3.

The problem with cooling array three turned into an ordeal that ate up most of the day. The repair crew moved like they were underwater, tools slipping from fingers that felt twice as heavy as normal. Simple tasks became endurance events. I joined them at one point, holding a flashlight steady (which felt like hoisting a dumbbell after ten minutes) while Chief Engineer Nicobe supervised the replacement of a circuit board that had literally been crushed by its own weight under the increased gravity.

By the time I staggered back to my quarters that evening, my body felt like one massive bruise. I found Sofia already there, sprawled on the bed in a way that suggested she'd simply fallen there.

"I think my kidneys have migrated to my knees," she mumbled into the pillow.

I laughed, then winced at how it made my ribs ache. "Pretty sure that's anatomically impossible."

"Give it another day in this gravity."

I carefully lowered myself beside her, every joint protesting. "One more day. Then we'll have enough helium-3 to power *Thunder* for weeks without stopping for a recharge."

She turned her head to look at me, her blue eyes tired but determined. "Worth it. But I'm demanding a massage when we're back in normal gravity."

I kissed her forehead, even that small movement an effort. "Deal."

* * *

Day three dawned with the particular cruelty reserved for the final stretch of any ordeal. My body had moved beyond simple pain into a state of comprehensive rebellion. My spine felt permanently compressed, my legs barely responding to commands. Getting out of bed was an Olympic event.

"Captain to the bridge," Destiny's voice came over the comm, strained but urgent.

I dragged myself to the bridge, each step a negotiation with gravity. "Report."

"We've got company," Destiny said, gesturing to the tactical display.

A small blip had appeared in Jupiter's orbital plane, moving on an intercept course with our position. Not immediately threatening, but concerning.

"Identification?" I asked, easing into the command chair.

"Registered as a private Kergan mining vessel," Sofia reported from the intelligence station. "The *Ryzaju Sakemy*. Independent operator."

I frowned. "What are they doing here?"

"Same as us, probably," Destiny said. "Helium-3 is valuable stuff."

I nodded. "Keep an eye on them. If they approach within five thousand kilometers, hail them."

The rest of the day unfolded in a grueling crawl. The helium-3 collection continued, our tanks slowly filling, while the crew moved like zombies through their tasks. Every action required deliberate focus. Dropping a tool meant staring at it on the deck, calculating if retrieving it was worth the effort of bending down and standing back up.

The *Ryzaju Sakemy* maintained a respectful distance, apparently content to stay in the other hemisphere. Smart of them—Jupiter was big enough for multiple mining operations, but proximity in these conditions added unnecessary risk and the possibility of being discovered by Kergan military units.

By the time our tanks reached ninety-eight percent capacity, I felt like I'd aged ten years. Muscles I didn't know I had ached in ways I couldn't describe. My vision occasionally blurred from the pressure on my eyeballs. Even breathing felt like an accomplishment.

"Prepare for extraction sequence," I ordered, my voice rough. "Let's get the hell out of this gravity well."

The crew moved with renewed energy despite their exhaustion, the promise of relief lending strength to leaden limbs. *Thunder*'s engines roared to life, fighting against Jupiter's pull. The ship shuddered, straining against the invisible chains of gravity.

For a moment, I feared we wouldn't break free—that we'd slide deeper into Jupiter's embrace until the pressure crushed us. Then I felt the subtle shift as we began to ascend, the gravity gradually, blessedly, decreasing.

"Extraction successful," Destiny announced, her voice cracking with relief. "Ascending to safe orbital distance."

A ragged cheer went up across the bridge. I didn't reprimand them—they'd earned it. As *Thunder* pulled away from Jupiter's atmosphere, the crushing weight began to lift. It wasn't immediate—our artificial gravity compensated gradually to prevent physiological shock—but even that incremental relief felt like floating.

"Collection operation complete," Nicobe reported. "Total yield: ninety-nine point four percent of maximum capacity."

A smile cracked through Sofia's professional facade. "We did it."

I nodded, feeling the first hints of pride breaking

through the exhaustion. "Well done, everyone. Once we're at a safe distance, secure from collection operations and prepare for transit."

As the bridge crew acknowledged the orders, I allowed myself a moment of satisfaction. The helium-3 we'd collected would power *Thunder*'s new fusion reactor for weeks, giving us the range and independence we needed for the mission ahead. Worth three days of crushed organs and compressed spines? I'd know better once the aches subsided.

For now, I was content to sit in my command chair as Jupiter receded behind us, its massive gravity no longer reaching out to pull us down into its depths. *Thunder* had what she needed, and soon, so would we all—a good meal, a hot shower, and the blessed relief of normal gravity.

"Set course to the closest Lagrange coordinates," I ordered. "It's time to plan our next move."

5

The briefing room felt smaller than usual. Six of us crammed around a table designed for eight, but currently feeling like it was meant for four. Two hours removed from Jupiter's crushing gravity, and we were all still moving like arthritic octogenarians. Destiny sat with her spine unnaturally straight, as if she'd replaced it with a metal rod. Clemen Busto—CO of *Thunder*'s Marine Detachment, or MARDET—kept rolling his massive shoulders, his face twitching each time something popped back into place. Nicobe's crimson dodecahedron hovered slightly lower than its usual position, perhaps her gravitational stabilizers still recalibrating. Sofia's normally perfect posture had given way to a slight slouch, though she straightened whenever she caught me looking. And Phoebe—well, Phoebe somehow managed to look fresh and poised despite the ordeal, which was either impressive or suspicious. I, meanwhile, felt like I'd been disassembled and put back together by a blindfolded mechanic with trembling hands.

"Let's get started," I said, tapping the table to activate

the holodisplay. "First, I want to acknowledge everyone's hard work during the Jupiter operation. Three days at 2.5 gees isn't something they prepare you for during bootcamp."

"Speak for yourself, Captain," Busto grunted, massaging his neck. "Marines train for high-g insertions. Though usually not for seventy-two consecutive hours."

"Nicobe's internal fluid pressure is still normalizing," the igna's crimson dodecahedron bobbed slightly. "Nicobe calculates another twenty-four hours before optimal function resumes."

"At least we're all vertical," Destiny said. "More or less." She winced as she sat. "Although I think one of my lungs are now part of my lower intestine."

"Biologically improbable," Sofia said, though a smirk betrayed her amusement.

"Coming from the woman who spent yesterday walking like she'd just wrestled a grav-sled and lost."

I cleared my throat. "The good news is that the helium-3 we collected has been successfully transferred to *Thunder*'s new fusion reactor. We're now operating at full capacity with the ability to recharge our own chromatic batteries. Our operational range has increased by an order of magnitude."

"Worth three days of feeling like my skeleton was trying to compress into a diamond," Phoebe said, stretching her arms above her head in a way that emphasized her figure. Her eyes caught mine as she did it, holding contact a beat too long. "Though some of us handled the pressure better than others."

I looked away, uncomfortable with the suggestion in her tone. "That brings us to the main purpose of this meeting. Now that *Thunder* has extended range, we need to determine our next destination." I nodded to Destiny. "Lieutenant Commander Austin has been researching potential leads on the Noble Phylactery."

"Before we dive into treasure hunting," Busto interrupted, leaning forward with a grimace that suggested his back was still protesting movement, "I'd like to revisit the wisdom of this mission." He looked around the table, his gaze settling on each of us in turn. "We're basically headed on a quest to find a genie in a lamp before the wicked witch gets it first."

"That's an oversimplification, Lieutenant," I said.

Busto wasn't deterred. "Is it, though? We're chasing a mythical containment device holding an ancient entity with godlike powers, based on intelligence that's sketchy at best." He thumped his fist on the table, making Destiny jump slightly. "Meanwhile, Earth is still under Kergan occupation. People are dying every day. Our time would be better spent staying home and fighting the enemy we can see."

I understood Busto's frustration. The former Marine Raider had been ready to fight when the Kergans invaded, only to watch helplessly as Earth fell. But his perspective was limited by his training—direct action against visible enemies was his comfort zone.

"Nicobe respectfully reminds Lieutenant Busto that the threat posed by Nekufima falling into enemy hands vastly outweighs conventional military considerations." The igna's dodecahedron glowed slightly brighter as she spoke. "Nicobe has observed the destructive capabilities of unbound Astral Titans firsthand."

"So you keep saying," Busto replied, not unkindly. "But we're operating on information from a regime that kept humanity in the dark. Pardon my skepticism about Dominion boogeyman stories."

Nicobe's capsule pulsed with the igna equivalent of indignation. "Nicobe assures this gathering that Nekufima is no 'boogeyman.' The historical record is quite clear about the devastation caused during the Titan Wars."

I caught Sofia's eye across the table. She gave me a subtle nod—a signal to let them air their arguments before stepping in. This wasn't the first time we'd had this discussion, but with new information potentially changing our course, it was worth revisiting.

Destiny was rubbing her temples. "Can we please skip the recap debate? My vertebrae are still realigning from Jupiter, and I don't have the patience for Round Twelve of 'Should We Chase the Cosmic Horror.'"

"The stakes warrant repetition," Nicobe's tone was firm. "Whoever controls Nekufima will possess unprecedented sydereal capabilities. Mind control of entire populations. Planetary crust fracturing. Potentially even stellar manipulation, resulting in supernova events."

Busto whistled low. "So why don't the Kergans already have this super-weapon? They seem to be doing just fine conquering the galaxy without it."

"Because they haven't found it yet," Phoebe interjected. She leaned forward, her movement bringing her shoulder against mine, seemingly accidental but lasting longer than necessary. "But they're looking, just like Arctis's rebels are looking. The race is on." She turned to me, her expression earnest but her eyes holding something else. "Right, Captain?"

I shifted slightly, putting a few more centimeters between us. "That's correct. And it's a race we can't afford to lose." I looked around the table, meeting each person's gaze. "I understand the desire to focus on Earth's immediate situation. But we've already agreed on this course of action. Queen Zeta left under that assumption, and we gave her our word."

"And *Thunder* always keeps its promises," Destiny added, the corner of her mouth lifting in a half-smile.

"Exactly." I straightened in my chair, ignoring the twinge in my lower back. "The crew of *Thunder* follows through. It's what separates us from other ships, other captains. We keep our word, and we finish what we start."

As I spoke, I was acutely aware of Phoebe's gaze, her eyes tracing my face, my hands, my shoulders. It wasn't my imagination—she'd been different lately. More attentive, more forward. Brushing against me in corridors, finding reasons to visit my ready room, standing just inside my personal space during conversations. I'd known Phoebe for two years. She'd always been friendly, occasionally flirtatious in a general way. But this targeted attention was new, and it made me deeply uncomfortable.

"Nicobe supports Captain Drake's position," the igna said. "Our commitment to Queen Zeta remains binding. Additionally, Nicobe calculates a sixty-seven percent probability that locating the Noble Phylactery will create strategic opportunities beneficial to Earth's liberation."

Busto sighed, his broad shoulders slumping slightly. "Fine. I've said my piece. I'll follow orders, as always." He shot me a rueful grin. "Just don't expect me to be happy about chasing ghost stories across the galaxy."

"Noted," I replied with a small smile of my own. "Now, let's hear what Destiny has found."

Destiny activated her datapad, linking it to the room's holodisplay. A three-dimensional star map materialized above the table, rotating slowly to show our position in the solar system and a highlighted route stretching into the distance.

"With Nicobe's help, I've been sifting through Dominion

archives for information about the Phylactery," she began. Her fingers moved across the datapad, zooming in on a specific region of the map. "I've found three independent references to an artifact labeled 'PYRA.' All three sources place its last known location in a system called Xar's Veil."

The map zoomed further, revealing a binary system with several planets. One star glowed with an ominous, dark purple hue.

"Xar's Veil is a black hole system in the Sagittarius Arm, approximately twelve thousand light-years from our current position," Destiny continued. "Travel time would be around two weeks with our current drive capabilities."

"A black hole system?" Sofia leaned forward, her professional interest piqued. "That's an unusual place to store a valuable artifact."

"Maybe that's the point," I mused. "Hide something where few would dare to look."

Destiny nodded. "The black hole is part of a binary system with a main sequence star. There are seven planets, including two gas giants. According to the records, PYRA is located on a moon designated Xar-a5e, which orbits the second gas giant."

She manipulated the display again, highlighting a small moon in the system. "Information about PYRA itself is limited. One record describes it as a 'ruined structure,' possibly some kind of research facility or archive."

"Any information on defenses, indigenous life, or environmental hazards?" Busto asked, his tactical mind already at work despite his reservations.

"Minimal atmospheric composition, cold surface temperatures, no recorded indigenous life," Destiny replied. "As for defenses, the records don't mention any. But they're also at least several centuries old."

"And you believe this PYRA structure contains information about the Noble Phylactery?" Sofia asked.

Destiny shrugged, then winced at the movement. "I can't say for certain. But all three references connect PYRA to historical records of the Phylactery. It's the strongest lead we have."

Phoebe had been unusually quiet during Destiny's presentation. Now she spoke up, her voice carrying a lightness that didn't match the seriousness of the discussion.

"So we're traveling across half the galaxy to visit some ruins that might have information about another thing that might contain a cosmic horror?" She glanced at me, a smile playing at her lips. "I love how you always find us the most exotic vacation destinations, Captain."

The comment wasn't inappropriate in itself, but something in her tone and the way her eyes lingered on me made it feel loaded.

"What exactly are we hoping to find at this PYRA?" Phoebe continued, shifting slightly closer to me. "Ancient maps? A cosmic treasure hunt with 'X marks the spot'?"

"We don't know yet," Destiny replied, a note of irritation creeping into her voice. "That's why we need to go and search."

"Seems like a lot of effort for a 'maybe,'" Phoebe said, her fingers brushing against the table near mine. "But if anyone can make it worthwhile, it's our captain." She gave me another lingering look that sent uncomfortable prickles up my spine.

Sofia had been watching this exchange, her expression growing increasingly hard. I could see the muscles in her jaw tightening.

"Perhaps if you spent more time analyzing engineering

reports and less time analyzing the captain's every word, you'd have more useful input for this meeting, Lieutenant Brooks," Sofia said, her German accent becoming more pronounced as it always did when she was angry.

The room went silent. Phoebe's cheeks flushed red, her easy smile vanishing.

"I was just asking a legitimate question about the mission," she replied, but the embarrassment in her voice betrayed her.

The tension in the room thickened. Busto suddenly became very interested in examining the holographic display. Nicobe's dodecahedron rotated slowly, her equivalent of an uncomfortable shuffle. Destiny looked between Sofia and Phoebe with raised eyebrows.

I cleared my throat. "Let's stay focused on the task at hand. Destiny, what's your assessment of the risk-reward ratio for this expedition?"

Destiny seemed grateful for the redirect. "Given our extended range thanks to the Jupiter operation, we can reach Xar's Veil without requiring resupply. The system's proximity to a black hole presents navigational challenges, but nothing *Thunder* can't handle. If PYRA contains even fragmentary information about the Phylactery's location, it would significantly advance our mission objectives."

I nodded, deliberately keeping my eyes on the holodisplay and away from both Sofia and Phoebe. "I agree. It's our best lead, and we need to pursue it."

"Nicobe concurs," the igna said. "The probability of useful intelligence at PYRA exceeds alternative search patterns by a factor of three."

"Then it's settled," I said. "We'll set course for Xar's Veil immediately." I looked around the table. "Any other concerns before we adjourn?"

Busto raised a hand. "Just one. Any chance we could adjust the artificial gravity to about point nine for another day or two? My spine would appreciate it."

"Seconded," Destiny said immediately. "I'd like my organs to find their original positions sometime this century."

I smiled, grateful for the break in tension. "I'll have engineering make the adjustment. Consider it a recovery period before our journey."

"Nicobe expresses gratitude," the igna said. "Fluid equilibrium will be restored more efficiently at reduced gravity."

"Great." I stood, trying not to wince as various parts of my body protested. "We leave in twenty-four hours. Prepare your departments accordingly. Dismissed."

As the meeting broke up, Sofia lingered, her eyes following Phoebe as the engineer left the room. Once everyone else had filed out, Sofia turned to me.

"We need to talk about her," she said quietly.

I sighed. "I know."

"She's becoming more obvious by the day. The touches, the looks, the comments. She's making a play for you, Kory."

I ran a hand through my hair. "I've noticed. I thought I was imagining it at first, but..."

"You're not imagining it," Sofia's voice was tight. "And I don't appreciate it."

"I don't either," I assured her. "I'll talk to her—make it clear that her behavior is inappropriate and needs to stop."

Sofia studied my face for a moment, then nodded. "Good." She hesitated, then added, "I trust you, Kory. It's her I don't trust."

I took her hand, squeezing it gently. "You have nothing to worry about. But I will address it."

Some of the tension left her shoulders. "Thank you."

As we left the briefing room together, I found myself dreading the conversation I needed to have with Phoebe. Commanding a starship through Jupiter's killing gravity was one thing. Navigating the treacherous waters of inappropriate attraction from a crew member was another challenge entirely—one they definitely hadn't covered in Officer Training School.

But first, we had a two-week journey to a black hole system and a mysterious ruin called PYRA. Whatever secrets it held about the Noble Phylactery and the ancient entity Nekufima, I had a feeling they would make our current problems seem trivial by comparison. The hunt was on, and *Thunder* was committed to seeing it through.

6

The Sydereallium flowed past *Thunder*'s hull like luminous oil, patterns of energy rippling across dimensions I couldn't name. Two weeks into our journey toward Xar's Veil, and I still found myself marveling at how a ship that had once been little more than a glorified fighter had transformed into this beast of war. My command. My responsibility. My home. But right now, with Sofia's warm body curled against mine, the weight of commanding nearly two hundred souls felt pleasantly distant.

Thunder cut through the higher dimensions on a trajectory only I could see. The Marauder-class refit had changed everything—quadruple the range, enough firepower to make planetary defense systems think twice, and armor that could shrug off hits that would have vaporized the old hull. The United Human Confederacy Armada might be in shambles back home, but out here, we were the sharp end of humanity's stick. A terrifying machine of war with me at its heart.

Sofia stirred slightly beside me, her breath warm

against my chest. Her eyelids flickered in some dream I wasn't privy to, and I found myself studying the curves of her face in the dim light of our quarters. The sheets had slipped down to our waists, leaving her shoulders bare, her skin pale against the dark fabric of our bed.

Her shaved scalp caught the light. Her blonde hair had first been removed for the emergency brain surgery that saved her life—an urgent operation to relieve the pressure from a subdural hematoma she suffered during our chaotic escape from the Dominion flagship *Inferis*. That had been over a month ago, yet Sofia still shaved her scalp, refusing to let her beautiful hair grow back. The scar was faint now, just a thin pink line tracing the curve of her skull—barely visible, but impossible to forget.

I traced my fingers gently along the outline of her jaw, careful not to wake her. She needed the rest. We both did, though sleep was proving elusive for me tonight. We'd made love with the desperate intensity that never seemed to diminish between us, as if each time might be our last. In our line of work, it very well could be.

The thought made my chest tighten. I'd almost lost her. The memory of her unconscious form, blood seeping from her ear as the escape pod tumbled through space, still visited me in nightmares. Dr. Chen had worked miracles with that Kergan implant, but it had been touch and go for days.

I pressed my lips against her forehead, breathing in the scent of her—that familiar mix of standard-issue soap and something uniquely Sofia. What would I have done if she hadn't pulled through? If the woman who had returned to me was just a shell of who she had been?

"I'd have loved you anyway," I whispered to her sleeping form, answering my own unspoken question.

But I was grateful beyond words that I hadn't needed to

find out. That her strength had carried her through. That she was here, whole and sharp as ever, despite the occasional headaches and the strange flashbacks from the Kergan implant's stored data. She never complained, but I noticed the moments when her eyes would unfocus, accessing memories that weren't hers.

My body relaxed into the mattress, Sofia's warmth against me a comfort I never took for granted. But as my mind drifted toward sleep, an unwelcome thought surfaced —Phoebe.

I still hadn't talked to her about the advances, the lingering touches, the looks that lasted too long. I'd been putting it off for weeks now. Sofia hadn't asked if I'd handled it yet, but I knew she was waiting. The guilt sat in my stomach like a cold stone.

Phoebe was my friend. Had been since before Sofia and I became partners. She was smart, capable, and an essential part of *Thunder*'s engineering team. The thought of confronting her, making things awkward between us, potentially fracturing our friendship—it made me wince. What would I even say? "Hey, could you stop looking at me like you want to tear my clothes off? My partner's noticed, and it's making things uncomfortable."

I shifted slightly, careful not to disturb Sofia. The truth was, I understood Phoebe better than I wanted to admit. She was young, beautiful, and alone. Life aboard a warship didn't offer many romantic opportunities, especially for someone as brilliant as her. The crew respected her too much to make passes, and most were too intimidated by her intelligence to try.

And yet, she'd fixated on me. Me, who was so obviously taken, so clearly committed to the woman sleeping beside me. There was a desperation to Phoebe's attention that made me sad for her. Maybe that's why I couldn't bring myself to shut her down—because beneath the inappropriate flirtation was a loneliness I recognized all too well from my own years on the streets.

So I'd convinced myself to wait. To see if the situation resolved itself without my intervention. Maybe she'd get over her infatuation naturally. Maybe she'd find someone else among the crew. Maybe I was overreacting to innocent friendliness.

The excuse sounded hollow even in my own head.

Sofia shifted against me, her arm tightening around my waist as if she could sense my disquiet even in sleep. I forced myself to relax, to push thoughts of Phoebe aside. Tomorrow would bring its own problems. For now, I had this—the woman I loved safe in my arms, a ship worthy of her protection around us, and a mission that might help secure humanity's future.

It would have to be enough.

I closed my eyes and synchronized my breathing with Sofia's, letting the gentle rise and fall of her chest lull me toward sleep. *Thunder* continued its silent passage through the dimensional folds of the Syderealium, carrying us toward whatever waited at Xar's Veil.

But for these few hours, I allowed myself to exist solely in the space between heartbeats—between breath and dream, fear and hope—where the war couldn't reach, and the weight of command momentarily slipped from my shoulders.

In that quiet, I wasn't a captain. I was just a man holding on to what mattered.

Xar's Veil unfolded before us like a cosmic magic trick—a binary system dominated by an active black hole, the two celestial bodies locked in a gravitational tango that shouldn't have been stable but somehow was. The black hole's accretion disk glowed with a sickly purple-blue light, casting long, distorted shadows across the system's planets. I'd seen renderings in the briefing materials, but they'd captured the reality about as well as stick figures capture the human form.

"Dropping out of veilspace in three... two... one..." My hands danced across the control interface as *Thunder* transitioned fully into normal space. The light conduits running throughout the ship pulsed once, bright blue, then settled into their standard operational glow.

"All systems nominal," reported the tactical officer. "No signs of hostile presence in-system."

I nodded, but kept my attention on the navigational display. Xar's Veil wasn't just visually spectacular—it was a navigational nightmare. An M-class star orbited a stelar-mass black hole that was currently in an active feeding phase. Six planets traced complex orbital patterns through the system, their paths warped by the N-body gravitational fields into something that looked more like a child's scribble than proper elliptical orbits.

"Destiny, you seeing this?" I asked.

My XO stood at the tactical station, her dark eyes reflecting the purple-blue glow of the display. "Yeah. It's... something."

"That's one word for it." I adjusted our course toward the second gas giant—a Jupiter-sized monstrosity of swirling orange and red bands with a particularly nasty radiation signature. According to our intel, its fifth moon, designated Xar-a5e, was where we'd find PYRA.

"What's our ETA to the target moon?" Destiny asked.

"Eighteen hours at standard approach," I replied. "We could push it to twelve, but I'd rather keep some reserve charge for whatever we find there."

"Agreed." She tapped her console. "I'll have the survey team prepare their equipment. We don't have exact coordinates for PYRA, so we're looking at a full surface scan."

"Joy," I muttered. Nothing like searching for a needle in a haystack when the haystack is an irradiated moon circling a gas giant that's flirting with a black hole.

The next eighteen hours passed in a blur of system checks, briefings, and snatched moments of sleep. By the time we achieved orbit around Xar-a5e, the entire crew was humming with a mixture of anticipation and anxiety.

The moon itself was unremarkable at first glance—a cratered, barren rock about half the size of Earth's moon, its surface a patchwork of impact scars and what looked like ancient lava flows. What made it remarkable was the radiation. The gas giant's magnetosphere, interacting with the black hole's relativistic particle emissions, bathed the moon in a soup of radiation that would cook an unprotected human in minutes.

"Beginning surface scan," announced the sensor operator. "Pattern Alpha-Three, high resolution."

And so began the tedious work. Hour after hour, *Thunder* traced perfect orbital lines above the moon's surface, our sensors probing every crevice and crater. The crew rotated through shifts, catching sleep when they could. I stayed on the bridge longer than I should have, finally retreating to my quarters when Sofia commed to inform me that I was "being a stubborn ass" and needed rest.

She wasn't wrong.

Three days into the search, fatigue had settled into everyone's movements. Even Destiny's usual sharp banter had dulled to occasional grunts. We'd scanned nearly 80% of the moon's surface with nothing to show for it except increasingly creative curses from the sensor team.

"Maybe the intel was wrong," Busto suggested during our morning briefing on the fourth day. The lieutenant's perpetual scowl had deepened to something approaching geological. "Wouldn't be the first time we chased ghost stories."

"The intel's solid," Destiny insisted. "PYRA is here. We just haven't found it yet."

I was about to weigh in when the bridge comm chirped. "Captain, this is Sensor Station Two. We've got something."

Four hours later, I was easing *Thunder* into a landing approach, aiming for a flat expanse about half a kilometer from what appeared to be our target. The "something" turned out to be a massive crater, almost perfectly circular, with strange crystalline structures jutting from its center. According to the readings, it had to be PYRA.

"Atmospheric pressure negligible. Radiation levels at 380 rems-per-hour and climbing," Sofia reported from the environmental station. "Surface temperature negative one-twenty Celsius."

"In other words, a balmy day at the beach," I quipped.

"If the beach were in hell," Destiny muttered.

The landing struts connected with the lunar surface with a gentle thud that resonated through the ship. I shut down the main engines, leaving only the essential systems running.

"Undercarriage secure. *Thunder* is grounded," I announced formally. "Commence surface operations."

Phoebe was already at the drone control station, her fingers dancing over the interface with practiced ease. "Launching Scout One," she said, her voice crisp and professional.

The small probe detached from *Thunder*'s hull with a pneumatic hiss, visible on the main screen as it arced gracefully toward the crater. Phoebe guided it with micro-bursts from its thrusters, her face illuminated by the soft blue glow of the control panel. The concentration on her features made her look almost sculpted—her long brown hair pulled back in a tight ponytail, her lips slightly parted as she focused.

I caught myself staring and quickly looked away, only to find Sofia watching me with an unreadable expression. She raised an eyebrow slightly before turning back to her station. My stomach knotted. I needed to fix this situation, and soon.

"Entering the crater now," Phoebe announced, pulling everyone's attention back to the main screen.

The drone's camera revealed a landscape that belonged in a fever dream rather than on a moon in our universe. The crater walls were unnaturally smooth, as if melted and then instantly frozen. At the center stood what could only be PYRA—a structure that defied simple description.

It resembled a massive crystalline prism, but one that couldn't quite decide on its geometry. Its surfaces rippled like liquid metal despite clearly being solid, catching and distorting the dim light from the distant stars. Deep crimson pulses traveled across its exterior in patterns that seemed almost deliberate—like a heartbeat, or perhaps a language written in light.

"That's... not natural," Busto said, stating the obvious in his trademark deadpan.

"No kidding," Destiny replied. "Nicobe, any ideas?"

The crimson dodecahedron hovering near the tactical station rotated slightly. "Nicobe recognizes the architecture. This is indeed a Primordian construct, though one of unusual configuration. The temporal distortion patterns suggest it may be considerably older than most Primordian sites we have encountered."

As the drone circled the structure, we could see that part of it had been damaged—a large hole punched into one side, revealing darkened chambers within. Scans indicated the damage was ancient, likely from a meteor impact millions of years ago.

"Can the drone enter through the breach?" I asked.

Phoebe nodded. "I think so. The opening is large enough, and I'm not detecting any active defenses that would target it."

"Proceed," I ordered, but even as Phoebe guided the drone toward the opening, I felt something—a familiar tingle at the edges of my consciousness.

I closed my eyes, letting my awareness expand into the Syderealium. The physical world faded, replaced by the multidimensional landscape of energy patterns and information. And there, where PYRA stood in the physical world, I could see a complex knot of sydereal energies—ancient but still active, pulsing with purpose.

"There's a sydereal lock on the main entrance," I said, opening my eyes. "The facility can only be accessed by a flairsparked."

"How convenient," Destiny said dryly.

The drone's camera now showed the interior of the breach—darkened corridors with walls made of the same shifting material as the exterior. Strange geometric shapes floated in various chambers, orbiting invisible points like miniature solar systems.

"I'm picking up power signatures," Phoebe reported, excitement creeping into her voice. "This place is still running, after what must be millions of years."

"Nicobe is detecting warning glyphs," the igna announced suddenly. Her crimson shell pulsed as she processed the information coming from the drone. "They appear to be security notifications. One moment while Nicobe translates."

We waited, the bridge silent except for the soft hum of equipment. Finally, Nicobe rotated toward me.

"The glyphs are quite explicit. No armed personnel are permitted within the facility. The defensive systems will activate if weapons are detected, resulting in, to quote directly, 'dimensional inversion of intruders.' Nicobe does not recommend testing this claim."

"Dimensional inversion?" Busto growled. "What the hell does that mean?"

"Nicobe suggests it would be unpleasant to experience firsthand."

I exchanged a look with Destiny. "So we need to go in unarmed. That complicates things."

"We?" Sofia asked, a sharp edge to her voice.

"Someone has to," I replied, turning to face the command crew. "And since I'm the only flairsparked on board, I have to be one of them. The question is, who comes with me?"

A brief strategy session with Destiny and Busto on the command deck crystallized our options, none of them ideal. The team needed to be small, given the confined spaces we'd seen in the drone footage. We needed technical expertise to access whatever information PYRA contained. And we needed to move fast—the longer we stayed on this radiation-soaked rock, the greater the risk to *Thunder* and her crew.

"I'll take Nicobe," I decided. "Her knowledge of Primordian technology is essential."

"You'll need an engineer," Destiny pointed out. "Someone

who can interface with systems that Nicobe identifies."

"I volunteer," Phoebe said immediately, stepping forward from her station.

"I was thinking of taking you," I admitted. "Your expertise with hybrid systems would be valuable."

"What about the radiation?" Sofia interjected. "The surface exposure would be too dangerous for a standard EVA."

"We'll take the Captain's Gig," I replied. "It's small enough to fit through that breach in the structure, and it'll shield us from the radiation until we're inside."

"The Gig only has room for two humans and Nicobe," Destiny noted.

"Then it'll be me, Nicobe, and Phoebe," I concluded.

Sofia's voice cut through the discussion. "Lieutenant Brooks isn't trained for direct field operations. Her expertise is in starship engineering, not alien archaeology. I suggest Ensign Gifuwabi from our kavreni contingent instead."

I turned to look at Sofia, recognizing the manufactured concern for what it was. Gifuwabi was competent, sure, but nowhere near Phoebe's level with adaptive systems. Sofia's eyes met mine, challenging, and beneath the professional mask, I could see it—the real reason. She didn't want Phoebe alone with me in a confined space for hours.

"Gifuwabi's in medical with that virus that's been going around the kavreni crew," Destiny pointed out. "Phoebe's our best option."

A flicker of frustration crossed Sofia's face, quickly replaced by her professional mask. "Then perhaps I should go instead. I have field training and enough technical background to be useful."

"You're our chief intelligence officer," I countered gently. "We need you coordinating from here, especially if something goes wrong."

The subtle tension humming between us was probably invisible to most of the crew, but Phoebe noticed. A small, satisfied smile played at the corner of her mouth before she smoothed it away.

"I'll prepare the equipment," Phoebe said, turning to leave the command deck.

"Nicobe will assist," the igna added, floating after her.

When they were gone, Sofia approached me, her voice low. "This is a mistake, Kory."

"It's the right call tactically," I replied, equally quiet.

"That's not what I mean, and you know it."

I sighed, running a hand through my hair. "I know. And I'll handle it. But right now, the mission comes first."

Her blue eyes searched mine for a moment, then she nodded once, curtly. "Fine. But when you get back, we're having a conversation about this."

I watched her walk away, her back rigid with suppressed frustration. Caught between the mission, Sofia's justified concern, and Phoebe's increasingly obvious advances, I felt like I was trying to navigate a minefield with a broken scanner.

All I wanted was to do my job—explore PYRA, find whatever the Primordians had left behind, and get my crew home safely. Instead, I was trapped in some romantic drama I never asked for.

"Captain?" Destiny's voice snapped me back to the present. "The Gig will be ready in twenty minutes."

I nodded, pushing personal concerns aside. "Tell Phoebe and Nicobe to suit up. We're going in."

7

The Captain's Gig was never designed for comfort. A stubby, utilitarian craft with just enough room for a pilot and two passengers. It had all the charm of a supply closet with engines. I strapped myself into the pilot's seat, painfully aware of Phoebe settling into the passenger seat directly behind me, close enough that I could feel her breath on the back of my neck. Nicobe's dodecahedral form hovered in the other passenger spot, the crimson glow of her shell casting everything in a bloody light. The Gig's cockpit suddenly felt about three sizes too small.

"Pre-flight checks complete," I announced, more to break the silence than out of necessity. "Depressurizing hangar."

The comm crackled with Destiny's voice. "*Thunder* to Gig. You're clear for departure. Maintain radio contact at all times."

I caught the hint of concern beneath her professional tone. "Copy that, *Thunder*. We'll keep the line open."

The hangar doors peeled apart, revealing the desolate, crater-pocked surface of Xar-a5e. Beyond, the massive form of PYRA rose from the center of its crater, crimson pulses traveling across its crystalline surface like slow-motion lightning.

"Here we go," I muttered, engaging the thrusters.

The Gig slipped from *Thunder*'s hangar with a gentle lurch, the craft's maneuvering pods creating interesting eddies in the moon dust that hung suspended in the low gravity before settling back to the surface. The journey was almost comically short—barely five hundred meters across the lunar surface. Under different circumstances, we could have walked it in minutes. But not in this kind of radiation.

"Approaching the breach point," I reported, guiding the Gig toward the jagged hole in PYRA's side. "Structure appears stable."

Phoebe leaned forward, her arm brushing against mine as she pointed through the viewport. "The opening is large enough. We've got at least three meters of clearance on all sides."

I nodded, trying to ignore the lingering warmth where her body had pressed against mine. "Entering now. Switching on lights."

The Gig's exterior floods snapped on, illuminating the breach as we glided through. The hole opened into what might have once been some kind of storage bay—a cavernous space now open to vacuum, its contents long since destroyed or removed. What remained were fragments of structures that resembled shelving units, their surfaces covered in the same rippling, almost liquid-metal appearance as the exterior.

I set the Gig down gently in a clear area, the landing struts connecting with the ancient floor with a dull thud that resonated through the small craft.

"We're down," I reported to *Thunder*. "Commencing EVA

to locate internal access point."

"Copy that," Destiny's voice replied. "Remember, two-hour window or we're coming in after you."

"Understood."

Phoebe was already deploying her protomatter helmet, the black nanobots flowing to form a seamless seal with her armor. I did the same, the familiar cool sensation washing over my face as the helmet materialized.

"Comms check," I said, switching to the suit's internal system.

"Signal's clear," Phoebe confirmed.

"Nicobe acknowledges," came the igna's serene voice.

The three of us cycled through the Gig's tiny airlock and stepped out onto the floor of the breach. Without atmosphere to carry sound, our movements were eerily silent, visible only as vibrations traveling through the structure beneath our feet. Nicobe's crimson dodecahedron floated beside us, untroubled by the vacuum.

I activated the suit's built-in lights, sweeping the beam across the damaged chamber. The scale of the place was impressive—easily fifty meters across, with a ceiling that soared at least twenty meters above us. The walls curved organically, lacking the right angles and flat surfaces I associated with human architecture.

"We need to find a door," I said, scanning the perimeter. "Something that would have connected this space to the rest of the facility."

"Sensor sweep in progress," Phoebe replied, waving a compact scanner over the nearest wall. "I'm picking up power fluctuations behind this section."

We worked our way along the curved wall, following the energy readings. After about fifteen minutes, we found what we were looking for—a recessed panel that seemed to shimmer slightly, as if not quite in phase with the rest of the structure.

"This is it," I confirmed, reaching out with my sydereal senses. "I can feel the lock mechanism."

"Nicobe concurs," the igna added. "This appears to be an emergency access point designed to activate in case of primary entrance failure."

Phoebe ran her gloved hand along the edge of the panel. "We'll need to establish an airlock before we open it. My readings show atmosphere on the other side."

She unpacked a compact device from her equipment pouch—a temporary airlock kit developed for exactly this kind of exploration. With practiced efficiency, she attached the device to the wall around the panel, the built-in protomatter seals adhering to the strange material of PYRA.

"Impressive," I commented as the field generator sprang to life, creating a shimmering barrier that would hold atmosphere once the door was opened.

Phoebe smiled behind her helmet visor. "Just doing my job, Captain."

The way she said "Captain" made me uneasy—just a touch too familiar, too intimate. I turned away, focusing on the task at hand.

"Nicobe, what are the atmospheric readings beyond the door?"

The igna hovered closer to the panel. "Composition is 82% nitrogen, 18% oxygen, with trace gases consistent with human habitability. Temperature is 19 degrees Celsius. Radiation levels are minimal. The environment appears to be maintained by internal systems."

"After millions of years?" Phoebe asked, incredulous.

"Primordian technology was designed for extreme durability," Nicobe replied. "Many of their systems incorporated self-repair mechanisms powered by dimensional energy taps. This facility appears to be drawing power directly from sydereal dimensional flux."

"Convenient," I muttered. "Alright, I'm going to open the lock. Stand back."

I closed my eyes, extending my awareness into the Sycerealium. The physical world fell away, replaced by the intricate multi-dimensional landscape of energlyphs and information patterns. The lock glowed in this realm—a complex knot of ancient energlyphs arranged in a pattern I'd never seen before. Not a simple key, but something more like a puzzle.

I concentrated, studying the pattern, feeling for the solution. After several minutes of mental probing, I found it—the energlyphs needed to be rotated through a specific sequence of dimensional orientations, like a combination lock with an infinite number of possible positions.

Carefully, I manipulated the energlyphs, rotating them through the required sequence. The lock resisted at first, ancient and stiff from disuse, but gradually yielded to my pressure. With a final mental push, the pattern aligned, and the lock disengaged.

In the physical world, the panel slid aside with a hiss of equalizing pressure. Air rushed into Phoebe's temporary airlock, creating a momentary fog as moisture condensed in the temperature differential.

"Door's open," I reported, both to my companions and to *Thunder* over the radio. "We're establishing atmosphere and preparing to enter."

"Copy that," Destiny replied, her voice slightly distorted by interference. "Clock's ticking."

The readings on my suit confirmed Nicobe's assessment—the air was breathable.

"We can remove our helmets," I said, retracting my own protomatter helmet, the nanobots flowing back into the collar of my suit. The air had a slightly metallic taste, but was otherwise fresh—remarkably so for a sealed environment millions of years old.

Phoebe followed suit, shaking out her long brown hair as her helmet retracted. "Much better," she smiled, running a hand through her locks. "Those things get stuffy after a while."

We stepped through the doorway into PYRA proper, and I stopped short, momentarily stunned by what I saw. The corridor before us was intact and fully functional—soft, diffuse lighting emanated from the walls themselves, illuminating a passageway that stretched at least a hundred meters before curving out of sight. The rippling, liquid-metal appearance of the exterior continued here, but with more structure and purpose. Geometric patterns flowed across the surfaces like slow-motion waves, occasionally forming what looked like glyphs before dissolving back into the general pattern.

"It's beautiful," Phoebe breathed beside me.

"The state of preservation impresses Nicobe," the igna commented. "This facility appears to have been maintained in near-perfect condition despite its age."

I toggled my radio. "*Thunder*, are you getting this? The facility is active and intact."

Destiny's reply came back with more static than before. "Copy... signal's... deteriorating... Keep... updates..."

"We're encountering interference," I reported. "Continuing with exploration. Will maintain contact as able."

We proceeded cautiously down the corridor, passing several sealed doorways that resisted my attempts to open them. The architecture was unlike anything I'd seen before —spaces that seemed to shift subtly as we moved through them, perspectives that didn't quite align with Euclidean geometry.

"There should be a central control area," Phoebe suggested. "Based on the power distribution I'm reading, I'd guess it's below us."

"Nicobe concurs," the igna said. "Primordian facilities typically centralized their computational systems in lower levels for thermal management."

We found a descending passageway that spiraled gently downward. As we descended, the radio signal deteriorated further, until all we could hear from *Thunder* was occasional bursts of static.

"We're losing contact," I noted. "The facility must be shielded somehow."

"Or it's the black hole's magnetic fields," Phoebe suggested. "The deeper we go, the more distortion we might encounter."

After descending what felt like several stories, we emerged into a vast chamber that could only be described as a high bay. The ceiling soared twenty meters above us, and the room stretched at least fifty meters in each direction. Industrial-looking equipment lined the walls—machines whose purpose I couldn't begin to guess, covered in the same flowing, metallic material as everything else in PYRA.

Most striking were the robots—dozens of them, lined up along one wall like silent sentinels. They resembled abstract sculptures more than machines, their forms suggesting humanoid shapes without directly mimicking them. Each stood in what appeared to be a charging station, soft lights pulsing across their surfaces.

"Maintenance drones," Nicobe observed. "They are likely responsible for the facility's continued upkeep."

At the center of the chamber stood what had to be the central computer—a column of crystalline material that rose from floor to ceiling, surrounded by floating control interfaces that hovered at various heights.

I tried the radio one more time. "*Thunder*, do you copy? We've located what appears to be the central computer system."

Nothing but static answered me.

"We're out of contact," I informed my companions. "If we don't report back within two hours from departure, Destiny will send in the Marines."

"That gives us..." Phoebe checked her chrono, "about an hour and thirty minutes before they come looking."

I nodded, turning to Nicobe. "Can you interface with this system?"

The igna floated closer to the central column. "Nicobe believes so, yes. The architecture is complex but recognizable."

"I'm surprised the Kergans, or the Dominion, didn't strip this place ages ago," I commented, running a hand along one of the floating interfaces. It rippled under my touch like liquid, then reformed.

"The facility is likely protected by defensive systems beyond those we have already observed," Nicobe replied. "Additionally, its location in this particular star system would make prolonged operations difficult because of the radiation and gravitational anomalies."

"Can you access the data? Find out what this place was for?"

"Nicobe will attempt to do so." The igna extended several cable-like appendages from her crimson shell, connecting them to various points on the central column. "This may require time. Nicobe will need to establish basic protocols before attempting data extraction."

"How long?" I asked.

"Uncertain. Possibly minutes, possibly longer. Nicobe must caution that she may appear unresponsive during the interface process. This is normal and no cause for concern."

"Understood."

"Nicobe will transfer any critical data to portable storage for analysis aboard *Thunder*." With that, the igna's shell dimmed slightly, the pulsing patterns of light slowing as she focused her processing power on the interface.

That left Phoebe and me standing in awkward silence amid the alien machinery. I walked a few paces away, examining one of the maintenance robots to give myself something to do. The silence stretched uncomfortably.

After a few minutes, Phoebe approached Nicobe and nudged her gently. "Nicobe? How's it going?"

The igna remained unresponsive, her shell dim except for occasional pulses of light that traveled across its surface.

"She did warn us," I remarked.

Phoebe turned toward me, and the look in her eyes made my stomach tighten. It wasn't subtle—raw and unmistakable, the kind of hunger that had nothing to do with food and everything to do with the fact that we were completely alone, out of contact with *Thunder*, and Nicobe still eerily unresponsive.

8

The ancient Primordian computer hummed softly, the only sound in the cavernous room besides our breathing. Nicobe's crimson shell had dimmed to a dull glow as she interfaced with the system, leaving Phoebe and me effectively alone. The realization hit me like a punch to the gut—we were completely cut off from *Thunder.* No comms, no backup, and the one buffer between us was currently lost in a digital trance. The weight of Phoebe's gaze pressed against me more insistently than any physical touch could have.

I pretended to study the maintenance robots, analyzing their alien geometry with forced interest. But I could feel her approaching, her footsteps light on the metallic floor. When I finally turned, she was standing closer than comfortable, her brown eyes locked on mine with an intensity that made my chest tighten.

"Need something, Lieutenant?" I asked, deliberately using her rank, trying to reestablish the professional boundary between us.

Phoebe smiled—not the polite, professional smile of a crew member, but something more intimate, as if we shared a secret. "Just thinking about how strange it is to be here. Millions of years of history around us, and it's just you and me experiencing it."

"And Nicobe," I added pointedly, nodding toward the igna.

"She's not exactly present at the moment," Phoebe replied, taking another step closer. I fought the urge to step back. "Does it ever overwhelm you, Kory? The responsibility of it all? Leading *Thunder,* making decisions that affect so many lives?"

The switch to my first name wasn't subtle. "It comes with the job," I said, keeping my tone neutral. "Everyone on *Thunder* has responsibilities."

"But yours is different." She was close enough now that I could smell her—that clean, slightly floral scent that somehow persisted despite our environment. "You carry it all, ultimately. I've watched you, you know. How you handle it, how you never let the pressure show. It's impressive."

"Just doing my job," I echoed her earlier words, uncomfortable with the admiration in her voice.

"No," she shook her head, "it's more than that. It's who you are. And it's why you deserve better than what you have."

The conversation had veered into dangerous territory. "I'm not sure what you mean."

Her lips curved into a sad smile. "Yes, you do. Sofia is... fine. She's capable, she's smart. But she doesn't understand you, not really. Not like I do."

I took a deliberate step back. "Lieutenant Brooks, this conversation is inappropriate."

"We're alone, Kory. No ranks here." She moved forward again, erasing the distance I'd created. "I've cared for you since we met. Back at Wolf Jaw, when you first came aboard —I knew then there was something special about you."

"I'm in a relationship," I said firmly. "A committed one. And I don't appreciate the advances you've been making lately. It's making Sofia uncomfortable, and frankly, it's making me uncomfortable too."

A flash of irritation crossed her face. "I don't care what she feels," Phoebe said, her voice hardening. "She latched onto you when you were vulnerable, when you needed someone. But that doesn't mean she's right for you."

She closed the gap between us again, and this time, her armor pressed against mine. Despite the layers of protective material, the protomatter transmitted tactile sensations with uncanny fidelity. I could feel the warmth of her body, the slight pressure where her chest met mine. It was uncomfortably intimate.

"Phoebe," I warned, my voice low. "Stop this. Now."

"Why? Because you're afraid you might feel something back?" Her eyes searched mine, looking for confirmation. "I see how you look at me sometimes, when you think no one's watching. I know you're not indifferent."

I couldn't deny that Phoebe was attractive—anyone with functioning eyes could see that. Her long brunette hair framed a face that belonged on recruitment posters, and she moved with a fluidity that drew attention. But attraction wasn't commitment, and it sure as hell wasn't love.

"What I feel is loyalty to Sofia," I said, my voice firmer now. "And respect for the relationship we've built."

Phoebe's expression softened, but the determination in her eyes remained. "Did I ever tell you about the dream I had? It was last year, while you were trapped on Astrithon during your trial."

The abrupt change of topic threw me. "Dream?"

She nodded, her eyes never leaving mine. "It was so vivid, Kory. Like living another life. We were together—not just as colleagues or even lovers, but partners in every sense. We'd grown old together, built a life after all this war and chaos was over."

Her voice took on a dreamy quality, disturbingly sincere. "We had a home—a real one, on Earth, overlooking the Pacific. You'd wake up early to watch the sunrise, and I'd bring you coffee on the porch. We had children, Kory. A boy with your eyes and a girl with my smile. They grew up strong and brave, like their father."

The intensity of her fantasy unsettled me. This wasn't just attraction or a crush—this was something deeper, more concerning.

"We'd sit together in the evenings, your hand in mine, watching our grandchildren play in the yard. And the way you looked at me—like I was the answer to every question you'd ever had." Her voice cracked slightly. "I woke up crying because it felt so real, and then it was gone."

I didn't know what to say. The dream she described was so specific, so detailed, it bordered on obsession.

"Ever since then, I've known that we're meant to be together," she continued. "Maybe not now. Maybe you need to be with Sofia for a while—maybe she's part of your journey. But eventually, you'll realize what I already know."

"Phoebe," I said gently, "it was just a dream."

Her eyes flashed. "It was more than that. It was a vision. And I don't care how long I have to wait. I know what's in my heart."

Before I could react, she leaned forward, her intention clear. Her lips were inches from mine, her eyes beginning to close—

I stepped back and placed my hands firmly on her shoulders, holding her at arm's length. "No," I said, the word quiet but absolute. "This isn't happening, Phoebe. Not now, not ever."

Hurt flashed across her features, followed quickly by anger, then a forced composure. "You don't mean that."

"I do. I'm committed to Sofia. I love her. And even if I didn't, this—whatever this is—isn't healthy. You've built an entire fantasy around an idea of me that isn't real."

She stiffened under my hands. I was searching for the right words to continue, something that would definitively end this without destroying our professional relationship, when salvation came from an unexpected source.

"Nicobe has completed the data retrieval," announced the igna, her shell brightening suddenly as she disconnected from the Primordian computer. "Nicobe has discovered information of significant importance regarding PYRA's original purpose. The data has been transferred to portable storage for analysis aboard *Thunder*."

If Nicobe noticed the tension between Phoebe and me, she gave no indication. Her crimson dodecahedron rotated slightly as she surveyed the room. "Has Nicobe been unresponsive for long?"

"Over an hour," I replied, relieved at the interruption. "We should head back before Destiny sends in the cavalry."

Phoebe stepped away from me, her face a careful mask. "I'll gather the equipment," she said, her voice professionally neutral, though I could hear the strain beneath it.

We made our way back up through the facility in uncomfortable silence. When we reached the level where we'd entered, I was relieved to find that our radio contact with *Thunder* had reestablished.

"—repeat, *Thunder* to away team. Do you copy?" Destiny's voice crackled through the static, tight with concern.

"Away team to *Thunder,* we copy," I responded. "Mission successful. We're on our way back now."

"About damn time," came the relieved reply. "You were two minutes from having Busto and a squad of Marines busting down your door."

"Sorry for the radio silence. The facility's structure blocked communications. We're all fine."

"Understood. See you back home."

As we cycled back through the temporary airlock and resealed our helmets for the journey across the vacuum section, I caught Phoebe watching me. The look in her eyes told me this wasn't over—not by a long shot. Whatever fantasy she'd constructed about our future together wasn't something she'd give up easily.

The walk back to the Gig felt longer than it should have. Once inside, I strapped myself into the pilot's seat, painfully aware of Phoebe sitting directly behind me again. The confined space of the small craft seemed to amplify the tension between us.

The flight back to *Thunder* took less than five minutes, but it felt like hours. As we approached the hangar, I could see Sofia waiting on the deck, her face tight with concern. The sight of her made my chest loosen slightly. Whatever mess I'd gotten myself into with Phoebe, I knew where my heart belonged.

But as I guided the Gig into its docking cradle, the weight of the unresolved situation settled over me. Nicobe had her data. The mission was a technical success, but the personal complication had only grown more tangled. The calm, controlled life I'd been building was threatening to unravel, and I had no one to blame but myself for letting it get this far.

I needed to fix this, and soon. Before the fantasy in Phoebe's head became a problem that even I couldn't talk my way out of—or worse, before it took something real and shattered it beyond repair.

9

The corridor leading from the hangar to the main deck of *Thunder* felt twice as long as usual, with Phoebe trailing three steps behind me like we'd established some unspoken minimum safe distance. My hands were numb from gripping the equipment case too tight, but I felt a warmth in my chest, an uncomfortable heat that I recognized as guilt—which was stupid, because technically I had done nothing wrong. But in relationships, technicalities were usually the first casualty of emotional artillery.

"I can take that to engineering," Phoebe said, her voice carrying that forced lightness people use when trying to paper over a crater-sized awkwardness.

"I've got it," I replied, the words coming out sharper than intended.

She fell silent again. Our footsteps echoed in mismatched rhythm—mine quick and driven, hers hesitant. The PYRA excursion had been productive from a mission standpoint, but Phoebe's confession—her hand on my arm, the look in her eyes as she told me she'd "always felt something" between us—had transformed our professional relationship into a minefield. The return flight to *Thunder* had been an exercise in aggressive avoidance, with both of us studying readouts that didn't need studying and adjusting settings that were perfectly calibrated.

We passed a pair of junior officers who snapped to attention, then exchanged glances after we walked by. Great. The crew already sensed something was off. Nothing travels faster than rumor on a starship—except maybe the hurt feelings of your partner when those rumors reach her.

The officer's wardroom door slid open, and there was Sofia, standing by the tactical display with a data tablet in hand. Her shaved head shining in the lights, but something about the rigid set of her shoulders told me she wasn't just reviewing intelligence reports. Her eyes lifted to mine, then shifted to Phoebe, narrowing slightly before returning to the tablet.

"Lieutenant Brooks," Sofia said, her German accent more pronounced—a sure sign she was upset. "I trust your presence on the ground team didn't distract from the mission's objectives."

Phoebe cleared her throat. "Chief Engineer Nicobe requested technical assistance with the data extraction."

"I'm aware," Sofia replied coolly, eyes still on her tablet. "I was simply under the impression your expertise was in propulsion diagnostics, not artifact interface protocols."

I set the equipment case down on the nearest table. "We've got some promising leads from the—"

"Lieutenant Commander Drake," Sofia interrupted, the formal title sharp as a scalpel, "I require your input on these intelligence assessments when you're available." She still didn't look up.

"Sure," I said, feeling the temperature in the room drop

several degrees. "Phoebe, why don't you get started on the technical analysis?"

Phoebe hesitated, her eyes darting between Sofia and me. "Yes, sir," she finally said, taking the equipment case and almost fleeing the wardroom.

As the door closed behind her, Sofia set down her tablet with deliberate care. For several seconds, the only sound was the ambient hum of *Thunder*'s systems. Then she turned to face me fully.

"What did that woman do?" The question came out flat, direct, each word carefully controlled.

My mouth went dry. The correct answer—"She confessed feelings for me, but I shut it down immediately"—should have been simple to produce. Instead, my brain short-circuited, cycling through responses like a malfunctioning targeting computer.

"Nothing happened," I said, which was both true and completely inadequate.

Sofia's face went pale, the color draining away like someone had pulled a plug. "That is not what I asked," she said, her voice so quiet I had to strain to hear it. "If nothing happened, you would have answered differently."

"Look, we need to focus on the mission," I said, the words tasting sour as they left my mouth. Classic deflection. I was making this worse with every second. "Nicobe found something important in the Primordian data archives. I need you to look into it with Destiny."

Sofia's expression hardened into something I'd never seen directed at me before—professional courtesy layered over profound hurt.

"And this cannot wait long enough for you to answer a simple question?" she asked.

I ran a hand through my hair. "Phoebe said some...

inappropriate things. I shut it down immediately. That's all."

"I see." Two words that contained multitudes of disbelief.

"It meant nothing," I insisted. "We've got bigger concerns right now."

"Yes," Sofia said, picking up her tablet again. "The mission. Always the mission."

"This could be our breakthrough," I pressed on, desperate to move past the moment. "I need your expertise on this. You and Destiny working together."

"Fine." Sofia's posture straightened even further, if that was possible. "I will coordinate with Commander Austin."

"Thank you." I reached for her hand, but she subtly shifted her position, putting the tactical display between us.

"She should never have gone on the excursion," Sofia said, her tone flat. "She wasn't needed. Any communications specialist could have handled the data extraction."

"It was Nicobe's call," I said, knowing how weak it sounded. "As chief engineer, she selected who she thought was the best technical person for the job."

"Of course." Sofia nodded stiffly. "I will begin work on the data immediately, Lieutenant Commander." She moved toward the door, each step precise and measured.

"Sofia—" I started.

"Is there anything else required for the mission, sir?" she asked, her back to me, voice crisp and professional.

"No," I said quietly, defeat settling over me like a heavy blanket. "That's all for now."

She left without another word, the door hissing shut behind her with disturbing finality. I stood alone in the wardroom, the weight of command suddenly heavier than usual on my shoulders. I'd faced down alien threats and hostile fire with less fear than I felt watching my partner retreat into formal protocol.

The worst part was, I couldn't even blame her.

Thunder sat on the lunar surface like a tired predator, her landing struts sunk several inches into the gray regolith. Two days we'd been here, waiting on a breakthrough that seemed increasingly unlikely. I paced the corridors between the bridge and the data lab where Destiny, Sofia, and Nicobe hunched over terminals like archaeologists trying to piece together a civilization from three pottery shards and a broken comb. With each hour that passed, I felt the weight of command pressing down harder on my shoulders, made heavier by the chilly silence that had replaced Sofia's usual warmth.

"Any progress?" I asked, leaning against the doorframe of the data lab for what must have been the twentieth time that day.

Destiny looked up, dark circles under her eyes testament to her lack of sleep. "Define 'progress.' We've eliminated sixteen different encryption protocols that don't work."

Sofia didn't look up from her terminal. She wore a black uniform jacket buttoned to the throat despite the lab's warmth, her posture rigid as a training officer's. Since our confrontation, she'd addressed me exclusively as "Lieutenant Commander" or "sir," each syllable precise and cutting.

"Nicobe believes we are approaching an optimal decryption matrix," the crimson dodecahedron hovering near Destiny announced. "The Primordian data structures are most peculiar in their architecture. They fold inward upon themselves in ways Nicobe finds both elegant and frustrating."

I nodded, trying to look like I understood more than every third word. "Keep at it. Let me know if—"

"Sir," Sofia interrupted, her voice flat, "might Nicobe's efforts be better supported if Lieutenant Brooks were to assist? This is, after all, her area of expertise." The question was technically addressed to me, but her eyes flicked toward Destiny, a silent communication passing between them.

Destiny's mouth twitched. "We're managing fine."

I recognized the subtext. Sofia was pointedly reminding everyone that Phoebe should be here doing the technical work that supposedly required her presence on the PYRA mission. I cleared my throat. "Carry on. I'll check back in an hour."

That pattern repeated itself through the rest of the day, and into the next. Brief check-ins, technical updates I barely understood, and Sofia's penetrating silence. After forty-eight hours, they finally had something to show for their efforts—though "something" was being generous.

"The Sovereign Archive for Deep Matter Compliance," Destiny read from the display, "and the Ossuary Ring." She looked up at me with a grimace. "That's it. No coordinates, no description, no helpful 'X marks the spot' on a star chart."

"Both are associated with the Phylactery," Sofia added, still not meeting my gaze. "But the nature of the association remains unclear, other than the fact that the Ossuary Ring seems to be the location of the Phylactery. But we cannot find any references to this Ring in any other records. No coordinates. No description. Nothing."

I ran a hand through my hair. "So we've got two names that might as well be 'Place You Don't Know' and 'Other Place You Can't Find.'"

"Nicobe apologizes for the inadequacy of the extracted

data," the floating dodecahedron bobbed slightly. "The PYRA facility was more damaged than initially assessed."

The unspoken reality settled over me like a shroud: we'd risked everything for nothing. I'd have to report back to Zeta that we'd taken *Thunder* deep into enemy territory and returned with two meaningless phrases. Worse, I'd have to live with knowing I'd failed my crew, the mission, and potentially humanity itself if the Kergan threat was as serious as we believed.

"We keep digging," I said with more confidence than I felt. "There has to be something—"

Sofia gasped, her hand flying to her temple. Her eyes unfocused, staring at nothing, her lips moving silently.

"Sofia?" I was at her side in an instant, protocol forgotten. "What is it?"

Her breathing was rapid, shallow. "I'm... seeing it again. The implant..."

The Kergan brain implant that had saved her life was also a ticking time bomb of classified information, triggering unpredictable flashbacks. I held her shoulders, steadying her as her eyes darted back and forth, reading data only she could see.

"The Sovereign Archive for Deep Matter Compliance," she whispered. "It's a repository... Primordian records kept in a Kergan facility." Her eyes snapped back into focus, bright with revelation. "The Celestial Heritage Vault. A museum on Trenak-Zul."

"Trenak-Zul?" Destiny leaned forward. "That's deep in Kergan territory."

"8,000 light-years," Sofia confirmed, her professional mask slipping for the first time in days as excitement overtook her. "The implant had coordinates, security protocols—it's all fragmentary, but it's there."

I squeezed her shoulders gently before stepping back. "Destiny, call the command staff to the briefing room. We need to plan our next move."

Thirty minutes later, I stood at the head of the briefing room table, looking at the faces of my senior officers. Sofia sat to my right, Destiny to my left. Nicobe hovered near Destiny's shoulder. Phoebe sat at the far end, her usual animated energy subdued, eyes darting occasionally toward Sofia. Busto sat at her side.

"We've identified our target," I began. "The Celestial Heritage Vault on Trenak-Zul contains the information we need about the Phylactery. The problem is that it's 8,000 light-years deep in Kergan space, and we don't have detailed intelligence on the facility's defenses."

"We could request additional resources from Zeta," Phoebe suggested. "A dedicated infiltration team with specialized equipment."

Sofia's posture stiffened. "That would delay the mission by weeks, at a minimum. The intelligence value could be compromised by then."

"I'm just saying we shouldn't rush in unprepared," Phoebe countered, a defensive edge in her voice.

"Unlike some people," Sofia said coolly, "I prefer thorough analysis before suggesting courses of action. The Vault's security systems appear to be standard Kergan protocols. Nothing we haven't dealt with before."

Phoebe's cheeks flushed. "With all due respect, Chief Kohl, I've been studying Kergan systems longer than you've been with the UHC. Their museum security isn't 'standard' anything."

"Ladies," I cut in, "let's focus on solutions."

"I am focused," Phoebe snapped. "But it's hard when

certain people let personal feelings cloud their judgment."

The room went silent. Sofia's eyes narrowed to dangerous slits.

"Lieutenant Brooks," I said, my voice dropping an octave, "that comment was inappropriate and unproductive." I hated doing this publicly, but I couldn't let it slide. "Sofia's analysis is sound. We'll proceed with the information we have."

Phoebe's face fell, embarrassment replacing anger. "Yes, sir. I apologize."

Sofia didn't acknowledge the apology, but I saw the smallest hint of satisfaction in the set of her jaw. I felt like I'd been maneuvered into taking sides in their personal conflict, which was exactly what a commander shouldn't do—but I also couldn't fault Sofia's tactical assessment.

"Here's the plan," I continued, pushing past the awkwardness. "We'll take *Thunder* to Trenak-Zul under stealth systems. We observe, gather intelligence, and improvise from there. I'm not going to sugarcoat this—we're heading deep behind enemy lines with minimal intel and a high-value target. This is going to be dangerous, even by our standards."

I looked around the table, seeing determination mixed with apprehension on every face. The mission was clear, the stakes enormous. But as I dismissed the staff to prepare for departure, I couldn't shake the feeling that I was leading my ship—my family—into a trap we might not escape.

10

I didn't remember falling asleep in my ready room. One moment I was reviewing tactical approaches to Trenak-Zul, and the next I was standing in a space that wasn't space—a realm where direction had no meaning and distances were measured in consciousness rather than meters. The Sydereaium. The dimensional texture around me rippled like dark silk shot through with threads of impossible colors. I'd been here enough times to recognize when I was being summoned rather than wandering, and the silhouette forming before me confirmed my suspicion. Nekufima was fishing for me again, casting her line into my mind and reeling me in while I was vulnerable.

"Captain Drake," she purred, her voice somehow both in my ears and inside my skull simultaneously. "How lovely of you to join me!"

The energlyphs that composed her being coalesced into the form she'd chosen for our interactions—a voluptuously beautiful human woman, naked and glowing with an inner light that accentuated every curve. Her hair floated around her face in tendrils of liquid shadow, her eyes two dark stars pulling at my attention.

"Cut the crap, Nekufima," I said, forcing my gaze to remain on her face. "I didn't 'join' you. You dragged me here."

She smiled, gliding closer. "Such hostility. Is that any way to treat the being who holds the key to your mission's success?" Her fingers reached for my face, stopping just short of touching my skin. I could feel the energy radiating from her—not heat, but something more primal, a tingling awareness of power barely contained.

"What do you want?" I asked, knowing the answer but needing to hear her say it.

"The same thing I've always wanted, Kory." My name in her mouth sounded different—intimate and somehow corrupted. "Freedom. Partnership. The chance to reshape this dull universe into something more... interesting." Her form shimmered, the light within her pulsing in rhythm with her words. "And I want you to be the one who frees me."

"Why me?"

"Because you're special," she whispered, circling me like a predator. "You have potential few mortals possess. Together, we could rule over all of creation. Every star, every world, every soul would know your name. I would serve you, guide you, elevate you."

I laughed, the sound harsh against the ethereal backdrop. "Right. An ancient entity with godlike powers wants to 'serve' me. Try again."

Her expression shifted to something resembling hurt, though I knew better than to believe it was genuine. "You doubt my sincerity? How disappointing." She moved closer, her form radiating sensuality like a weapon. "Is it so hard to believe I might desire a partner after eons of solitude? Someone to share my... everything with?"

"I love Sofia," I said firmly. "I'm devoted to her."

Nekufima waved a dismissive hand, trails of light following her gesture. "Your little soldier? I have no problem with her being in the picture, Kory. She can join us. You can have all the companions you want." Her smile turned knowing. "The engineer who desires you, perhaps? The one with the wandering eyes and the convenient technical skills? Phoebe, isn't it?"

I felt a flash of anger. "First of all, there's only one woman I care about. Second, you're not a woman. You're not even human. You're trying to manipulate me by appealing to base instincts, but it won't work."

Her beautiful facade flickered momentarily, revealing something ancient and terrible beneath. "You speak as though your 'base instincts' aren't the core of what you are," she hissed. "As though you're more than the animal impulses that drive you to mate, to feed, to survive. You're not special, Kory Drake. You're meat and electricity, temporarily conscious."

"And what are you?" I challenged. "Just another prisoner rattling her cage."

Darkness flashed in her eyes, and the surrounding Syderealium dimmed in response. "Be careful, little captain. If I escape this prison without your help, you'll be the first I consume. I won't forget your indifference to my plight."

"Threats now?" I shook my head. "You're getting desperate."

"I'm getting impatient," she corrected, her form stabilizing again into seductive beauty. "What must it be like, I wonder, to be so fleeting? To know your brief candle will sputter out before the universe has completed even a single breath?"

"What's it like to be an immortal god-like being with a lifespan of billions of years?" I countered. "Do you even remember what it means to be afraid? To know that your actions have consequences you'll actually live to see?"

She laughed, the sound like crystal breaking. "Perspective is everything, Captain. When you're as old as I am, a billion years is nothing. A heartbeat. A blink." She drifted closer again. "But loneliness? Loneliness is eternal."

"Spare me the tragic backstory," I said. "I'm tired of your manipulations and your malevolence. I'm ending this projection."

"Before you go," she said quickly, her tone shifting to something more businesslike, "you should know I've been watching you. Your little excursion to PYRA was quite illuminating."

I froze. "What are you talking about?"

"The Celestial Heritage Vault," she continued, satisfaction clear in her voice. "Quite the formidable target. The Kergans don't take kindly to thieves, especially those interested in Primordian artifacts."

"How could you possibly know about that?" I demanded.

Her smile was triumphant. "I have my ways. My prison may limit me, but it doesn't blind me." She paused, letting the implication sink in. "I could help you, you know. I could tell you exactly how to infiltrate the Vault, where to find what you seek."

"I don't trust you," I said flatly. "And even if I did, you're trapped in a phylactery. There's nothing you can do to change events."

"I have more power than might appear," she replied, her voice dropping to a seductive whisper. "I have the power of knowledge, Kory. Knowledge that spans billions of years and countless civilizations."

I shook my head. "Not interested."

"You'll change your mind," she said confidently. "When you understand the difficulty of infiltrating the Vault—and you will, soon enough—you'll come back to me. You'll beg for my guidance." Her form began to dissipate around the edges. "And I'll be waiting."

"Don't hold your breath," I said, focusing my will on breaking the connection.

"I don't breathe, Captain," she laughed as her image faded. "That's one of many advantages I have over you."

The Syderealium collapsed around me, reality rushing back like water filling a vacuum. I gasped, jerking upright in my chair, heart hammering against my ribs. The ready room was exactly as I'd left it—tactical displays glowing softly, coffee gone cold beside my hand. But the lingering sensation of Nekufima's presence clung to me like smoke, her final words echoing in my mind.

I rubbed my face, trying to scrub away the memory of her manufactured perfection and the temptation she embodied. The worst part wasn't her threats or her seduction attempts—it was the seed of doubt she'd planted. How did she know about our mission? And if she was right about the Vault's defenses, could we afford to ignore whatever help she offered, no matter how poisoned the source?

I shook my head. Those were thoughts for another time. Right now, I had a ship to command, a mission to plan, and a relationship to repair—if Sofia would still let me try.

11

I leaned back in the command chair, the synthetic leather creaking under my weight like it was complaining about my existence. The bridge of *Thunder* hummed with the quiet efficiency that follows a mission gone right—screens glowing with navigation data, status indicators all green, crew movements precise and unhurried. We'd gotten what we came for at PYRA, but there was an itch between my shoulder blades, a persistent little voice whispering that when things go too smoothly, that's usually when the universe is winding up to punch you in the teeth.

"Plotting course to the Trenak-Zul jump point," PO Mazari said from the navigation station, her fingers dancing across the holographic interface. "Transit time approximately four hours at standard acceleration."

"Acknowledged," I said, rubbing my jaw. "Keep us on minimal emissions. No sense advertising our exit."

Thunder's engines thrummed with restrained power beneath us. We were cutting through the darkness of Xar's Veil with all the subtlety I could manage, which, admittedly, wasn't my strong suit. But when you're piloting a military vessel through hostile territory, sometimes subtlety is the difference between getting home and becoming an expanding cloud of very patriotic debris.

Destiny's voice cut through my thoughts. "Kory, I'm picking up something... odd." She was hunched over her console, brow furrowed, the blue light from the display painting shadows across her face.

I straightened in my chair. "Define 'odd,' XO."

"Passive UV sensors are showing anomalous diffraction patterns at bearing 047, elevation plus 12. Intermittent glints and movement that's... well, it's not space dust or asteroids." Her fingers tapped across her interface, adjusting parameters. "Pattern matching suggests a Kergan long-range scout."

The casual atmosphere on the bridge evaporated like water on a hot plate. Everyone's movements became more deliberate, more focused. Chief Rykov at tactical swiveled his chair toward me, already pulling up weapons systems without being ordered to.

"Distance?" I asked.

"Approximately 12,000 kilometers and closing," Destiny replied. "They're on an intercept trajectory, though I don't think they've spotted us yet."

I considered our options. Kergan scouts were small and agile, designed for reconnaissance rather than combat. They carried no weapons—their defense was speed and the ability to transmit intel faster than you could shut them up.

"Specifications on Kergan scouts?" I asked, though I already knew the answer. Sometimes saying things out loud helped crystalize my thoughts.

Sofia, our intelligence officer, answered from her station behind me. "Fast, unarmed, but they're equipped with high-grade sydderealdyne transceivers. If it spots us, the entire Kergan fleet will know our position within seconds."

"Then it can't spot us," I said, making my decision. "Rykov, power up weapons systems, but keep them on standby. No active targeting. Mazari, plot an intercept course, but keep our emissions profile low—minimum thrusters, passive cooling only."

I turned to Destiny. "How close do we need to be for a guaranteed railgun hit?"

She checked her calculations. "Given their evasion capabilities and our current munitions... 800 kilometers or less."

"Then that's our target. Slow and steady, people. We're going fishing."

The next several minutes were an exercise in restraint. *Thunder* slid through space on a carefully calculated course, using minimal thruster burns timed to coincide with the scout's sensor sweeps. We kept our power emissions low enough that we might as well have been a slightly oversized asteroid. The bridge was quiet, the tension building with each passing minute. Only the soft beeps of consoles and the occasional whispered update broke the silence.

I could feel sweat gathering at my hairline despite the bridge's climate control. My eyes flicked between the tactical display and the main viewscreen, watching as the distance between us and the scout gradually decreased. 11,000 kilometers. 10,000. 9,000.

Destiny's voice was barely audible. "They're still running standard sweep patterns. No indication they've detected us."

I nodded, not trusting myself to speak. My fingers drummed silently on the armrest of my chair, the only outward sign of my impatience. The minutes stretched like taffy, thick and slow.

5,000 kilometers.

"Weapons status?" I murmured.

"Railguns charged and ready," Rykov replied. "Missiles prepped in magazine one."

3,000 kilometers.

"They've adjusted course," Destiny reported. "Still no indication it's in response to us. Routine patrol pattern variation."

2,000 kilometers.

My muscles were tensed like I was physically holding the ship's emissions in check. *Thunder* was a predator stalking its prey, and every instinct I had was screaming to pounce, but I held back. Patience. We needed to be sure.

1,200 kilometers.

"Preparing active targeting," Rykov said, his fingers hovering over the controls.

1,000 kilometers.

"Almost there," I whispered, more to myself than anyone else.

900 kilometers.

"Range optimal in fifteen seconds," Destiny announced.

850 kilometers.

"Establish weapons lock," I ordered.

Rykov activated the targeting systems, a series of concentric circles appearing on the main viewscreen as *Thunder*'s computers calculated firing solutions.

820 kilometers.

"Firing solution acquired," Rykov reported. "Railguns locked."

"Fire on my mark," I said, leaning forward. "Three... two..."

The scout suddenly veered sharply off its patrol route,

accelerating at a rate that made our interceptors look arthritic.

"They've spotted us!" Destiny's hands flew across her console. "They're initiating evasive maneuvers and—damn it—they're powering up their syderealdyne transceiver!"

"Fire railguns!" I ordered. "Full spread!"

Thunder shuddered as the electromagnetic accelerators sent tungsten slugs hurtling toward the Kergan scout at a significant fraction of the speed of light. But the scout's sudden course change had thrown off our carefully calculated firing solution. The railgun rounds passed through empty space where the scout had been milliseconds before.

"Missiles, fire!" I barked. "Maximum thrust!"

Four anti-ship missiles burst from *Thunder*'s launch tubes, their engines flaring bright in infrared as they accelerated toward the fleeing scout. The viewscreen automatically dimmed to compensate for the glare.

The scout performed a series of burns that seemed to defy the laws of physics, each one more unpredictable than the last. It twisted and rolled, using its thrusters in short, powerful bursts that changed its vector faster than our targeting computers could recalculate.

"How the hell is it moving like that?" I growled.

"Kergan scouts have thrust-to-weight ratios four times higher than our missiles," Sofia provided. "And their pilots are... unconventional."

One by one, our missiles detonated harmlessly in the void, their proximity fuses triggered but finding nothing but vacuum where the scout should have been.

"Recalculate and fire another railgun volley!" I ordered, frustration evident in my voice.

Again *Thunder* shuddered as the railguns fired, and

again the scout performed an impossible maneuver that left our ordinance passing through empty space.

"Their transceiver is at 70% charge," Destiny reported, her voice tight. "Transmission imminent."

I slammed my fist against the armrest. "Target their projected course! Don't aim where they are—aim where they'll be!"

Rykov adjusted the targeting parameters, his fingers flying across the holographic interface. "Firing solution recalculated. Firing!"

A third volley of railgun rounds streaked across space. The scout performed another evasive maneuver, but this time Rykov had anticipated it, leading the target just enough to—

Nothing. Another miss.

"90% charge," Destiny said.

My stomach felt like it was filled with ice water. We were moments away from the entire Kergan fleet knowing exactly where we were and what we'd been doing. The element of surprise we'd been counting on was about to vanish.

"Fire everything we've got!" I ordered. "Saturate their projected path!"

Thunder trembled as all her railguns fired simultaneously, followed by another salvo of missiles. The space between us and the scout lit up with explosions and streaking projectiles.

"Transceiver discharge detected," Destiny announced, her voice falling flat. "They've transmitted."

A collective exhalation of defeat passed through the bridge crew. The scout had done its job. Whatever data it had on us was now propagating through Kergan command networks.

Then, almost as an afterthought, one of our railgun rounds connected with the scout's midsection. The small vessel crumpled, atmosphere and debris venting into space as it spun out of control. A secondary explosion—probably its power core—finished the job, leaving nothing but an expanding field of wreckage.

The bridge fell silent. A hollow victory if I'd ever seen one.

"Confirm transmission contents," I said quietly.

Sofia analyzed the data. "Standard contact report. Position, heading, vessel class identified as Dominion. They may not know it was us, Kory."

I sat back in my chair, feeling a warmth in my chest, an uncomfortable heat that I recognized as frustration mixed with the first stirrings of fear. The Kergans now knew somebody was in their territory, knew we'd been to Xar's Veil, maybe even knew about PYRA. Whatever advantage we'd gained from our mission was at least partially compromised.

"Well," I said, trying to keep my voice light, "I guess the cat's out of the bag. Or whatever the Kergan equivalent of a cat is. Probably something with too many legs and a bad attitude."

No one laughed. Tough crowd.

"PO Mazari," I said, straightening my shoulders, "plot the fastest course to the jump point. Maximum burn. No point in being sneaky now."

"Aye, sir," she replied, already inputting the commands.

I turned to Destiny. "How long until we reach the jump point at maximum acceleration?"

"One hour, seventeen minutes," she replied after a quick calculation.

I nodded. "And how long until the nearest Kergan

response force could intercept?"

Sofia answered from her station. "Based on known Kergan patrol patterns... approximately two hours, assuming an immediate response to the scout's transmission."

"So we've got a forty-three minute cushion," I said, forcing a grin. "Plenty of time. Practically a vacation."

Destiny rolled her eyes. "Only you would call a high-speed escape through enemy territory a vacation."

"I have simple needs," I replied. "Not getting blown up is high on my list of leisure activities."

The tension on the bridge eased slightly. Not much, but enough. Sometimes that's all you can ask for.

Thunder's engines roared to full power, pushing us back into our seats as we accelerated toward the jump point. The stars on the viewscreen stretched slightly as our velocity increased. We'd destroyed the scout, but the damage was done. The Kergans knew somebody was here.

And now we would have to ensure they didn't find our trail.

12

Time moves differently in veilspace. Ten days felt like ten years as *Thunder* carved its way through the dimensional folds, our course set for Trenak-Zul. I'd spent most of the journey avoiding the two women who were slowly terraforming my life into an emotional minefield—Sofia with her glacier-cold silences, and Phoebe with her absence that somehow managed to be louder than presence. The guilt I carried was a constant companion, like a stowaway that had snuck aboard sometime between my first lie and my latest mistake.

My daily routine had devolved into a predictable pattern: wake before Sofia, shower, dress, and slip out of our quarters like a thief escaping a crime scene. Ten hours on the bridge, staring at the swirling non-colors of veilspace through the viewports until my eyes burned. Meals taken in my ready room, reports reviewed until the words blurred together. It wasn't exactly the heroic captain's life they romanticized in the recruitment vids.

"Still hiding?" Destiny asked on day six, cornering me in

the mess hall during the ship's artificial night cycle, where I'd snuck in, hoping for solitude and a cup of synthetic coffee.

"Tactical retreat," I corrected, lifting my mug in a mock toast. "There's a difference."

"Sure there is." She slid into the seat across from me, her curly black hair pulled back in a tight knot. "And I'm just here for the stimulating conversation, not to tell you you're being an idiot."

I snorted. "Add it to my list of accomplishments. I'm building quite the resume."

Her dark eyes narrowed. "You can't avoid them forever, Kory. This ship isn't that big."

"Watch me try." I took a sip of coffee, wincing at the bitter aftertaste. "Besides, Phoebe's doing her part by keeping clear."

"And Sofia?"

The question hung between us like a live grenade with the pin pulled. I set down my mug. "Sofia's... Sofia. We share a bed but might as well be in different star systems."

Destiny didn't respond, just shook her head slightly. The motion reminded me of how we'd been doing this dance for years, since we were hungry kids on the streets, her looking out for me even when I was determined to self-destruct. Some things never changed.

Nights were the worst. I'd return to our quarters well after Sofia had gone to bed, slip beneath the covers, and maintain a careful buffer of empty space between us. The centimeters might as well have been light-years. I'd lie there, listening to her measured breathing, wondering how someone could be physically so close and yet so utterly unreachable. Sometimes I'd feel her shift, just slightly, increasing that invisible boundary between us by another millimeter. I'd pretend to be asleep, and she'd pretend to believe it, and we'd both pretend this was fine.

By day eight, even Busto had noticed something was off, which meant things had deteriorated beyond the point of salvaging. The marine officer caught me in the corridor outside the armory, his buzz cut looking freshly maintained even in deep space.

"With respect, sir," he said, his voice gruff but concerned, "the crew's picking up on the tension."

"And here I thought I was being discreet," I replied, running a hand through my hair, which, unlike his, had grown shaggy during our journey.

"About as discreet as a fusion core breach." His expression didn't change, but I caught the flicker of concern in his eyes. "Whatever's happening between you and Chief Kohl—"

"Is between me and Chief Kohl," I finished firmly.

He nodded once, military-crisp. "Understood, sir. Just remember, a ship's only as stable as its command structure."

I wanted to tell him that my command structure currently had all the stability of a house of cards in a hurricane, but kept that particular insight to myself.

On day ten, the veilspace drive wound down with a familiar sequence of thrums and groans, like an old man settling into a chair. The viewport filled with normal space once more—stars sharp and clear against the void, and hanging before us like a massive sapphire, Trenak-Zul.

"Position confirmed," our navigator announced. "One million kilometers from Trenak-Zul. Stealth systems active."

I stepped forward, studying the ocean world that rotated slowly on its axis. It was larger than Earth by half, its surface a continuous expanse of deep blue broken only by the occasional weather system swirling white across its face.

"Magnify grid BG401482," I ordered, and the main viewport zoomed in on a cluster of surface structures.

The Kergan architecture became visible then—massive structures rising from beneath the waves like the spines of ancient sea monsters. Some buildings pierced the surface completely, their upper levels reaching toward the sky while their foundations remained anchored to the ocean floor. Lights glimmered from underwater sections, giving the impression of a civilization that had made peace with the depths rather than conquered them.

"Pretty," Destiny commented, appearing at my side. "If you like the whole 'city under the sea' aesthetic."

"I'm more concerned with what's inside one particular building than how it looks," I replied, eyes still fixed on the alien world. Somewhere down there, locked away in the Celestial Heritage Vault, was our objective—and with it, perhaps, some answers about Nekufima and her games.

"Stealth field holding at ninety-seven percent efficiency," the tactical officer reported. "We're effectively invisible to planetary sensors."

I nodded, allowing myself a moment's satisfaction. We'd made it this far without incident. Now came the hard part.

"Establish high orbit," I ordered. "And let's find out what we're really dealing with down there."

13

Nicobe worked at her station with the single-minded focus of someone defusing a bomb. Her crimson dodecahedron capsule pulsed with subtle light as the igna inside manipulated the streams of data flowing through *Thunder*'s communication arrays. I watched the holographic displays above her workstation flicker with Kergan symbols and diagrams, a language I could barely comprehend, but that she parsed with effortless precision. We'd been in orbit for six hours, and so far, our information harvest was about as bountiful as an asteroid field farm.

"Nicobe is finding the Kergan security protocols... intriguing," she commented, her dodecahedron rotating slightly as she spoke. The formal third-person way she referred to herself never failed to amuse me, even in tense situations. "Their public networks are surprisingly forthcoming about mundane matters, yet strategically silent on anything of actual importance."

"So we've got museum opening hours but no floor plans," I said, leaning against the bulkhead. "Wonderful."

"Nicobe would not describe our situation in such pessimistic terms," she replied, a hint of playfulness in her otherwise measured voice. "The Celestial Heritage Vault presents itself as a prestigious cultural institution. Its official description boasts of housing 'the finest collection of Primordian artifacts in the Kergan sphere of influence,' with special mention of the Sovereign Archive as its most treasured collection."

I studied the rotating three-dimensional image of the Vault that Nicobe had pieced together from public tourism databases. The structure resembled a massive inverted cone, with its widest point at the surface of the ocean and its narrowest extending deep into the oceanic abyss. The upper levels that breached the water's surface were shaped like overlapping circular platforms, resembling a stack of discs that some cosmic sculptor had artfully arranged.

"What about access points?" I asked.

Nicobe's capsule dimmed slightly—the equivalent of a frown. "Limited. The primary entrance is here," a section of the hologram highlighted, "at the water's surface. Secondary entrances appear to exist underwater, but their exact locations are not documented in public records. Security details are similarly elusive."

"So we're flying blind," I muttered.

"Not entirely blind. Perhaps merely severely myopic," Nicobe corrected, with that dry humor that made her invaluable beyond her technical skills.

I stared at the hologram, as if glaring at it might intimidate it into revealing more secrets. "We need more. We can't infiltrate with this little to go on."

The unspoken option hung in the air between us. Nicobe's capsule rotated toward me, the equivalent of a pointed look. "Nicobe senses the captain is contemplating a course of action he has previously deemed inadvisable."

"That's a diplomatic way of saying I'm about to do something stupid," I replied with a grimace.

"Nicobe would never be so direct," she said, but the slight brightening of her capsule betrayed her amusement.

I straightened up. "Keep digging. I'm going to... consult an alternative information source."

"Nicobe wishes the captain good fortune in his negotiations with the entity," she said, turning back to her console. "And suggests that the captain remember who truly holds the power in such exchanges."

I stopped mid-step, pulse spiking. "Wait—what did you just say?"

Nicobe didn't turn. "Nicobe assumes the captain would not have formed such a bond lightly."

"You know?" I asked, lowering my voice. "How long have you known?"

There was a pause, just long enough to be deliberate. "Nicobe observes patterns. And she listens."

I moved closer. "You could've said something sooner."

"Nicobe did not think it her place to question a captain's internal dialogues," she replied evenly. "But she advises caution. Such voices rarely whisper without a cost."

I stared at her, but she was already immersed in her displays again, the conversation clearly over.

"Yeah," I muttered, turning toward the lift. "That's what I'm afraid of."

Back in my quarters, I sat cross-legged on the floor, my back against the bed that had become a battleground of silent hostilities. The irony wasn't lost on me that I was seeking solace in the Syderealium—home to an entity who'd made psychological torment an art form—to escape the emotional minefield of my personal life.

I closed my eyes, focusing on my breathing while mentally reciting the flairspark techniques I'd learned. The transition was never comfortable—like being turned inside out while simultaneously being compressed into a pinpoint of consciousness. The physical world fell away, replaced by the vast, multidimensional expanse of the Syderealium.

Here, thought and existence were interchangeable currencies. My consciousness manifested as a familiar pattern of energlyphs—symbols of light and information that comprised my sydereal signature. Around me, the infinite realm stretched in directions that had no name in normal space, populated by echoes and fragments of countless consciousnesses.

And waiting for me, as if she'd been expecting my visit—which she probably had—was Nekufima.

Unlike the physical realm's holographic projections, Nekufima's presence in the Syderealium was overwhelming. Her form was a constant cascade of shifting energlyphs, arranged in patterns that hurt to look at directly—like trying to comprehend a language that predated the concept of comprehension itself. The beauty and horror of her existence were inseparable, a reminder that I was dealing with something that had witnessed the birth and death of stars as casually as I might observe raindrops on a window.

"The wayward captain returns," her voice echoed through my consciousness, each word simultaneously a caress and a paper cut. "How predictable you are, little flairspark."

"I'm not here for games," I projected, keeping my thoughts focused and sharp. "We need information about the Celestial Heritage Vault."

Her energlyphs rippled in amusement. "Always so direct. No pleasantries? No 'how have you been since our last chat, ancient one?'"

"You know exactly why I'm here," I countered. "You could simply tell us where your phylactery is located."

"And where would be the entertainment in that?" Her form expanded and contracted, a cosmic heartbeat. "You wish to prove yourself worthy of wielding my power. I merely provide the opportunity for you to do so."

Frustration bubbled up within me, manifesting as disruptive patterns in my own energlyphic signature. "This isn't a game. Real people—my people—are at risk."

"Your concern for your little collection of temporary beings is... quaint." Her tone shifted slightly, becoming both mocking and oddly contemplative. "Very well. I shall provide you with a morsel, a crumb from my infinite table of knowledge."

"I'm listening," I managed, swallowing my anger.

"The Vault receives a private shipment in two cycles of your rotation measurement," Nekufima's energlyphs pulsed with each word. "A vessel designated 'Kergan Mercantile Transport *Vox-Tellus*,' registry KMT-117893, will deliver artifacts to the Vault's private receiving dock beneath the water's surface."

I hadn't expected such specific information. "What kind of artifacts?"

"The kind that opens doors," she replied cryptically, then continued. "The vessel will arrive at the coordinates I am now placing in your consciousness at precisely what you would call 0300 hours, Confederacy Standard Time."

Numbers and coordinates flowed into my mind, burning themselves into my memory.

"Why are you being so helpful suddenly?" I asked, suspicious.

Her form condensed, energlyphs swirling closer to my

consciousness—too close for comfort. "Perhaps I grow weary of waiting. Perhaps I wish to speed up our inevitable reunion. Or perhaps..." her presence seemed to smile, though she did not show her face, "I simply enjoy watching you dance to my tune, never quite certain whether you're being helped or manipulated."

"Both, I imagine," I said dryly.

"Perceptive for a brief flicker of existence," she replied. "The information is accurate. What you do with it determines whether you are truly worthy of what you seek."

Before I could press further, her presence began to fade. "Until next time, little flairspark. I'll be watching your performance with great interest."

The transition back to physical reality was jarring, like being dumped from a warm bath into an ice-cold stream. I opened my eyes to find myself still sitting on the floor of my quarters, a thin sheen of sweat covering my forehead. The conversation had lasted only minutes in real-time, but my mind felt like it had run a marathon.

I stood up, legs stiff, and moved to the comm panel. "Drake to bridge. Assemble the command team in the briefing room. I've got something."

14

The briefing room felt like a pressure cooker set to explode. I stood at the head of the table, watching as my command team filed in one by one, each bringing their own particular flavor of tension to the mix. Destiny slid into her chair with the effortless grace of someone who'd learned to make herself comfortable anywhere. Busto entered with military precision, datapad tucked under his arm like a rifle ready for inspection. Nicobe's dodecahedron hovered into position above her designated seat, pulsing quietly. Then came the real fun—Sofia's ice-cold entrance, her eyes sweeping past me as if I were just another piece of ship equipment, followed moments later by Phoebe, who studied the floor with the intense focus of someone trying to become invisible. Just another day in the dysfunctional family business of interstellar espionage.

"Let's get started," I said, activating the holo-projector in the center of the table. The image of the Kergan freighter appeared, rotating slowly above our heads. "I've obtained intelligence on our best way into the Vault."

Sofia's eyebrow arched slightly. "Obtained from where, exactly?" Her German accent was always more pronounced when she was irritated, the consonants sharper, cutting like tiny blades.

I met her gaze, keeping my expression neutral. "From Nekufima."

The temperature in the room seemed to drop by several degrees. Sofia's expression hardened, her lips pressing into a thin line.

"You went into the Sydereal ium? Alone?" Destiny leaned forward, concern etched across her features. "Kory, we talked about this. That entity is—"

"I know what she is," I interrupted. "But we needed information, and she provided it."

Sofia made a sound somewhere between a scoff and a laugh. "Of course. Another meeting with another woman. You collect them like souvenirs." The words were delivered with clinical precision, designed to draw blood.

Beside her, Phoebe's cheeks flushed crimson. She stared intently at her datapad, as if it contained the secrets of the universe, her discomfort radiating outward like heat from an overtaxed engine. The guilt I'd been carrying around gained another few pounds, settling heavier on my shoulders.

I cleared my throat. "If we're done with the personal commentary, I'd like to focus on the mission." I tapped the controls, and the freighter image expanded, revealing registry information. "This is the Kergan Mercantile Transport *Vox-Tellus*. In approximately 48 hours, it will be delivering a shipment of artifacts to the Vault. According to Nekufima, it will approach from vector 117.3-delta-003.8 and dock at an underwater receiving port."

Nicobe's capsule brightened. "Nicobe has cross-referenced this information with the partial schematics we've obtained. The underwater port appears to be located here." The hologram shifted to show a section of the Vault, with a highlighted area beneath the waterline. "This delivery represents an optimal insertion vector."

"So we intercept the freighter before it reaches Trenak-Zul," Destiny said, leaning back in her chair, fingers drumming against the table's edge. "Take control, then impersonate the crew for the delivery."

Busto nodded, his expression thoughtful. "My MARDET teams are ready for a boarding action. We've been running drills specifically for Kergan vessel layouts." He pulled up additional schematics on his datapad. "This class of freighter typically carries a crew of twelve, minimal security. If we hit them fast with shock tactics, we can secure the vessel with minimal resistance."

"And minimal casualties," I added pointedly. "We're not looking to start an interstellar incident."

"Non-lethal takedown protocols are standard, sir," Busto replied with a slight nod. "Stun charges and neurological suppressors only."

Sofia leaned forward, her professional demeanor temporarily overriding her personal feelings toward me. "What about communication protocols? The Vault will expect standard authentication from the freighter crew."

"That's where Nicobe comes in," I said. "She'll slice their comm systems and replicate the necessary codes."

"Nicobe finds this challenge well within her operational parameters," the igna confirmed, her dodecahedron rotating with enthusiasm.

"Once we're in," I continued, "we'll need a small team to infiltrate the Vault itself while the rest secure the freighter. Our window will be tight—probably less than two hours before someone realizes something's amiss."

"I should be on that team," Destiny said immediately. "I've got experience with similar infiltrations, and I can read Kergan script better than most of you."

"I need you on *Thunder*," I countered. "If things go sideways, someone I trust needs to be in command."

Her expression suggested she didn't buy my explanation for a second, but she didn't push it. Not here, anyway. I knew I'd get an earful in private later.

"I should go," Phoebe spoke up for the first time, her voice quiet but firm. "The artifacts will need technical assessment to determine which might be connected to what we're looking for. That's my specialty."

Sofia's gaze flicked toward her, then back to me, a silent challenge in her eyes. I could almost hear her thoughts: Of course you'll take her, won't you?

"I've made my decision on the team composition," I said, deliberately not looking at either woman. "Myself, Nicobe, Busto, and a fireteam from his MARDET. We need combat capability and technical expertise, and we need to keep the team small."

Phoebe looked like she wanted to object, but thought better of it. Sofia's expression didn't change, but I caught the slight relaxation in her shoulders—a small tell that betrayed her relief.

"Nicobe is pleased to be included in this exciting adventure," the igna said, breaking the tense silence. "Though Nicobe wonders if the captain has considered that her capsule is somewhat conspicuous among Kergan personnel."

That earned a few chuckles around the table, easing the tension slightly.

"We'll figure something out," I said. "Maybe a nice hat."

"I'll select my most qualified personnel," Busto said, already scrolling through his roster. "We'll be ready for departure at 0200 hours."

I nodded, glancing around the table. "We intercept the freighter twenty million kilometers out from Trenak-Zul. That gives us plenty of distance from their sensor nets. Questions?"

There were none—or at least, none related to the mission. The personal questions simmering beneath the surface would have to wait.

"Dismissed," I said, and watched as they filed out in roughly the same order they'd entered. Sofia left without a backward glance. Phoebe hesitated at the door, looking like she wanted to say something, then thought better of it and hurried out.

Only Destiny lingered, arms crossed, giving me the look she'd perfected since we were teenagers—the one that said I was being an idiot, but she was going to help me, anyway.

"Not a word," I warned.

"Wasn't going to say anything," she replied, headed for the door. "But for what it's worth, I think you made the right call about the team."

Small victories, I supposed. Now all we had to do was intercept a Kergan freighter, commandeer it without raising alarms, infiltrate one of the most secure facilities on the planet, find the coordinates for the Ossuary Ring, and get out alive.

Simple.

15

I gripped *Thunder*'s control yoke with steady hands, feeling the subtle vibrations of the ship's systems flow through my fingertips like a familiar song. The command deck hummed with the quiet intensity of professionals at work—the soft murmur of status reports, the blue glow of tactical displays painting shadows across concentrated faces. We were hunters waiting in the dark, positioned along the vector connecting the L5 Lagrange point with Trenak-Zul. All to intercept a rectangular box of a freighter that had no idea it was about to have a very bad day.

"Status of the jamming systems?" I asked, eyes fixed on the tactical display where our intercept coordinates glowed like a promise.

Sofia's voice came from her station, precise and cool as ever. "Jammers prepped and ready, Kory. Range optimized for freighter-class communications arrays."

That slight German accent of hers still did things to me, even in the middle of an operation. I nodded, tamping down the distraction.

"Any word from Busto?" I swiveled my chair slightly, scanning the command deck. Twenty-one Marines were about to risk their necks on my orders. The weight of command never got lighter, no matter how many times I'd carried it.

Destiny, standing at the tactical station with her usual composed intensity, gave me a half-smile. "He says his Marines are 'ready to dance.' His words, not mine."

"Let's hope it's a waltz and not a mosh pit," I muttered, earning a snort from my XO.

The minutes ticked by with excruciating slowness. I'd never been good at waiting—a character flaw honed to razor sharpness during my years on San Jose's streets. My fingers drummed against the control panel, a staccato rhythm of impatience that I forced myself to stop.

"Contact," announced the sensor officer. "Freighter signature matching *Vox-Tellus* parameters approaching from designated vector."

Right on schedule. I leaned forward, watching as the blocky silhouette of the freighter materialized on our main viewscreen. *Vox-Tellus* was nothing special to look at—a rectangular utilitarian transport with cargo modules clustered along its spine like barnacles. The kind of unremarkable vessel that moved unremarkable cargo through unremarkable space. Except today, its cargo manifest included artifacts bound for the Celestial Heritage Vault—and soon, us.

"Confirm identity," I ordered.

"Transponder signals match *Vox-Tellus* registry," Sofia reported. "Crew complement registers as eleven marac."

I nodded, feeling a familiar tightness in my shoulders. "Initiate communications blackout. Lieutenant, execute jamming protocols."

The tactical officer's fingers danced across his console. "Jamming active. They won't be calling home about our surprise party."

"Destiny, inform Busto he has a green light."

Destiny relayed the order through her headset, her voice carrying the cool authority that had once intimidated street thugs twice her size. The same voice that had once talked me out of a knife fight when we were just kids on the streets. Now she was using it to launch a military assault.

Life takes strange turns.

On the tactical display, I watched two indicators detach from *Thunder*'s outline—our Albatross assault shuttles, each loaded with Marines and enough firepower to ruin anyone's day. The shuttles' trajectories curved gracefully toward the freighter, which continued its steady course, oblivious to the threat.

"Talon Flight is away," Destiny confirmed. "ETA to contact, three minutes."

Those three minutes stretched like taffy. I monitored the freighter's systems through *Thunder*'s sensors, watching for any sign they'd detected our approach or broken through our communications jamming. Nothing. Just the steady pulse of their engines, the regular cycling of their life support systems.

"Talon One docking," reported the tactical officer on the status of the first assault shuttle. "Clean approach. No defensive measures detected."

I allowed myself a small exhale. "Shuttle Talon Two?"

"Docking... confirmed. Both assault teams are attaching to external airlocks."

Now came the truly dangerous part. I closed my eyes briefly, visualizing Busto leading his Marines through the airlock, weapons ready, facing whatever waited on the other side.

"Breaching teams reporting entry," Destiny said, one hand pressed to her earpiece. "Vandal Team moving toward bridge. Breaker Team securing engineering."

The tactical display showed our Marines as blue indicators spreading through the freighter's schematic like water through channels. I watched their methodical progress, listened to the clipped professionalism of their communication relays.

"*Thunder,* this is Vandal Actual, bridge secured," came Busto's voice through the comm. "Crew complying. No casualties."

Something tight in my chest uncoiled slightly. "Engineering status?"

"This is Breaker Actual, engineering secured," replied Rowbottom's voice. "All systems under our control."

I nodded to Destiny, who gave me a small smile of acknowledgment. "Sweep the rest of the ship," I ordered. "I want every compartment checked, and every marac accounted for."

The next ten minutes were a blur of status reports and confirmations as Busto's two teams systematically secured the freighter. When the final all-clear came through, I finally allowed myself to relax back into my chair.

"*Thunder,* Vandal Actual," came the lieutenant's voice, gruff with satisfaction. "*Vox-Tellus* is ours. No distress signals transmitted. Crew is detained and cooperative."

I looked around at my command crew, seeing the same mix of relief and professional pride I felt myself. "Well done, everyone. Now for the fun part." I turned to Destiny. "Prepare the away team equipment. We have a delivery to make."

Sometimes plans actually worked. It was an unsettling

feeling for someone with my background, where survival usually meant improvising through disasters. Maybe I was getting better at this captain thing after all. Or maybe the universe was just setting me up for something worse down the line.

With my luck, probably the latter.

The shipping crate smelled like synthetic packing material and Busto's tactical deodorant, which was failing spectacularly under the circumstances. I lay curled in a fetal position that would've earned me a blanket and a corner spot back on the streets of San Jose, my protomatter armor the only thing preventing my spine from permanently adopting the shape of a question mark. This, apparently, was what command looked like at the lieutenant commander level of the UHC Armada—being packaged like discount merchandise with an elbow in my gut and someone else's boot obscuring my limited view of absolute darkness.

"Busto," I whispered, "is that your elbow, or are you just happy to see me?"

"Sorry, sir," came his gruff reply, though he didn't sound sorry at all. "Limited real estate in here."

"Rowbottom, I can identify your foot by smell alone now. That's a level of intimacy I wasn't prepared for on this mission."

"Compliments to my bootmaker, sir," Rowbottom replied with deadpan professionalism, but made no attempt to move his foot away from my face.

We'd planned this operation down to the minute. The marac crew of *Vox-Tellus* was still at the helm, but with armed Marines standing behind them, ensuring their cooperation. The freighter would make its scheduled delivery to the Celestial Heritage Vault, following normal routines and procedures, while we hid among the cargo like expensive stowaways.

Everyone on the away team—except Nicobe—was sealed into protomatter tactical armor, the material conforming to our bodies with a second-skin perfection that made the cramped conditions marginally more bearable. Flechette guns and laser pistols were strapped against our bodies, digging into uncomfortable places with every subtle shift of the freighter. In the crate's darkness, I couldn't see them, but I could feel every hard edge.

Nicobe had outdone herself, as usual. While the rest of us were playing sardines, she'd fabricated a disguise that made her crimson dodecahedron look like just another cargo-handling drone. She'd also planted devices in our crates that mimicked the signature of inert organic material and fossilized artifacts—exactly what the Vault would be expecting to receive.

Back on *Thunder,* Destiny was in command, with Phoebe and Sofia backing her up. I'd seen the look in Sofia's eyes when I'd explained the plan—a mixture of professional assessment and personal concern that made my chest tight. "Don't get yourself killed in a box," she'd said, her icy demeanor relaxing momentarily as she pecked me. "It would be an undignified end."

"Freighter's moving," Busto murmured, as we felt the subtle shift in momentum.

"Everyone steady," I whispered, though it was unnecessary. The four Marines packed into adjacent crates were professional enough to stay silent without my reminder. But giving orders helped me feel less like cargo and more like a commander.

The freighter's departure from orbit started smoothly enough—a gentle push that shifted my position slightly closer to Busto's elbow. Then came the vibrations of the thrusters engaging for descent, rattling through the metal floor of the crate and into my already-numb legs.

"Atmospheric entry in approximately three minutes," I whispered, more to mark time than to provide information anyone needed.

"Sir," Rowbottom's voice came from the darkness, "your left leg is cutting off circulation to my—"

"If the next word is what I think it is, lieutenant, we're going to pretend this conversation never happened," I interrupted.

The first turbulence hit like a sucker punch, slamming us against each other and the crate walls. My head smacked against metal, and despite my helmet, stars exploded behind my eyes. Someone—I think it was Busto—swore creatively enough to make a veteran spacer blush.

The shaking continued as we entered Trenak-Zul's atmosphere, the freighter's hull heating with the blackbody radiation of the compressed gases of reentry radiating into our crates. Sweat trickled down my back, pooling uncomfortably at the base of my spine. The protomatter armor adjusted its thermal properties, but nothing could completely counteract the rising temperature.

"This is still better than that time in Nuevo Laredo," Busto muttered, his voice barely audible over the roar of atmospheric entry.

"Which time?" asked Rowbottom.

"The time with the shipping container and the goat."

"You never told me about a goat," I said.

"There's a reason for that, sir."

Before I could press for details—and I desperately wanted details—the freighter suddenly decelerated, pushing us all forward in our cramped spaces. My face pressed against something I hoped was Rowbottom's backpack and not any part of his anatomy.

Then came the strangest sensation of all—the subtle damping of external noise as we hit the ocean surface. The rattling vibrations of atmospheric flight transformed into the smoother, swaying motion of submersion. Water sounds—muffled, pressurized—replaced the howl of atmosphere against the hull.

"We're underwater," I whispered, unnecessarily.

"No shit, sir," came Busto's reply, followed by a grunt as the freighter tilted slightly, sending us sliding against each other in new and inventive configurations.

The descent continued for what felt like hours, but was probably only minutes. The pressure in my ears built and then equalized as the freighter's environmental systems adjusted to the increasing depth. Finally, we felt the distinctive bump and scrape of docking procedures.

"Docking clamps engaged," I murmured, picturing the massive underwater structure of the Celestial Heritage Vault connecting to our stolen freighter. "Everyone stay frosty. Unloading should begin soon."

The wait for unloading was worse than the flight. At least during descent, the constant movement had distracted from the cramping pain of immobility. Now, in the stillness, every compressed muscle screamed for relief. I focused on my breathing, using techniques I'd learned at the Space Warfare School to manage discomfort.

When the crates finally moved, it was with an abrupt jolt that sent Busto's elbow even deeper into my abdomen. I bit back a curse as we were lifted, turned, and placed onto what I assumed was a cargo transport. The motion sickness was immediate and intense—being moved while unable to see outside was like the worst carnival ride ever designed.

After more jostling, sliding, and one particularly alarming drop of about half a meter, the movement ceased. The silence that followed was profound.

"Warehouse secure," came Nicobe's voice, muffled through the crate. "Nicobe has confirmed crew departure. Extraction safe to proceed."

I've never been so happy to hear third-person speech in my life.

The crate lid lifted away, and light stabbed into my eyes like needles. I unfolded myself with all the grace of an arthritic giraffe, every joint popping in protest. Beside me, Busto emerged from our shared container with a groan that suggested he might be reconsidering his career choices.

"Next time," I said, rubbing my neck as I surveyed the massive warehouse filled with crates and artifacts, "I'm sending Destiny."

Rowbottom straightened his uniform with military precision, despite having been folded like origami for hours. "Admit it, sir—you'll miss our quality time together."

"Like I'd miss a root canal," I replied, but couldn't help smiling as I checked my weapons. "Alright, people. We're in. Let's not waste the opportunity."

Around us, the Celestial Heritage Vault's warehouse stretched vast and shadowed, filled with the accumulated treasures of a thousand worlds. Somewhere in here was what we'd come for—and all we had to do was find it, take it, and get out without getting caught or killed.

Just another day at the office.

16

I tucked my too-long body behind the shipping crate and tried not to breathe too loudly, which is harder than it sounds when your heart's doing its best impression of a railgun on full auto. The receiving area of the Vault gleamed with sterile, unfriendly light. We were barely five minutes into the infiltration, and I already had that familiar itch between my shoulder blades—the one that usually means someone's about to shoot me in the back or, worse, catch me doing something monumentally stupid. This time, it was option B.

The distinctive scrape of a marac translation pod against polished floor tiles reached my ears. Not part of the plan. Not even close.

I held up a fist—universal military sign for "freeze or die"—and our team went statue-still. Rowbottom's eyes locked with mine from his position two crates over, his expression tight but controlled. Between us, Busto's weathered face had turned to granite, his hand already hovering near his sidearm. The four Marines spread around our perimeter might as well have become part of the floor.

Through a hairline crack in my crate's paneling, I watched the marac enter. Its translation pod glided across the receiving dock with an eerie smoothness that always made my skin crawl. Twelve tentacles extended from the bulbous central body, each moving with unnatural precision. Four glossy eyes swiveled independently, scanning the recent shipment—our shipment—with methodical attention. One tentacle adjusted what looked like archival glasses perched above its eyes.

An archivist. Doing an early inspection. Fantastic.

My mouth went desert-dry. I'd faced down Soul Ravagers and survived the battle of Virelia, but somehow the sight of this bookish marac with its clipboard equivalent had my intestines performing gymnastics routines that would make Olympic judges weep.

So, Kory Drake, tactical genius, what's your backup plan for the backup plan that just imploded? I thought. *Oh right, you didn't have one because Sofia's implant data said the initial receiving inspection wouldn't happen until 0900 tomorrow.*

The archivist's tentacles reached our crate first, tracing the seams with delicate precision. I could practically count the suckers on its appendages through the crack. My muscles tensed so hard they screamed, ready to either fight or flee—neither of which would end well in a high-security Kergan facility housing their most precious artifacts. The archivist made a bubbling sound—the marac equivalent of humming to oneself—as it prodded the seal on Rowbottom's crate.

We exchanged glances across the floor. Rowbottom's eyes widened a fraction—an entire paragraph of panic from someone as controlled as him. Diaz, the youngest Marine with a face that suggested she'd rather be anywhere else, had gone pale as a dead star.

That's when Nicobe made her move. The crimson dodecahedron of her capsule had been perfectly integrated into the chassis of what appeared to be a standard Kergan cargo-handling drone—one of many scattered throughout the receiving bay. With barely a whir of servos, she activated, the drone's limbs extending as she rose from her charging station.

The marac archivist glanced her way, but Nicobe had matched the movements of the other automated systems perfectly. She glided toward a nearby terminal, her dodecahedron pulsing almost imperceptibly as she interfaced with the Vault's surveillance network. The light patterns shifted on a nearby monitor, drawing the archivist's attention for a crucial moment.

"Maintenance diagnostic in progress," announced the terminal in the clicking Kergan language. "Please verify the cargo manifest on bay terminal three."

I didn't waste the opportunity. With a subtle hand motion, I signaled the team to disperse. We slipped from our hiding spots, moving with the careful precision that comes from training—or in my case, years of avoiding people who wanted to kill me.

The receiving chamber offered plenty of new cover. I slid behind an ancient stone monolith covered in scripts I couldn't begin to read, its surface radiating a faint cold that penetrated my uniform. Rowbottom found a position behind a stasis field containing what looked like the preserved remains of some massive, tentacled creature—probably a distant cousin to our marac friend, I thought grimly.

Busto and two Marines took cover behind a series of deactivated devices that hummed with latent energy despite supposedly being powered down. The artifacts in this place gave me the creeps—too many dead civilizations represented in one room, too many warnings about what happens to species that reach too far.

The remaining Marines positioned themselves behind shipping containers marked with Kergan glyphs warning of extreme danger—which was either the perfect hiding spot or the absolute worst, depending on whether those warnings were accurate.

The archivist hovered at the terminal Nicobe had directed it to, tentacles working furiously across the interface. I caught Busto's eye across the chamber. The former Marine Raider pointed deliberately toward an environmental control panel on the far wall, then made three quick hand gestures I recognized from our planning sessions.

Create distraction. Advance to target. Two-minute window.

I nodded once. My hands weren't numb, but I felt a weight in my chest—not quite guilt, more like the dense anticipation that comes right before the shooting starts. The kind that reminds you that no plan survives first contact, especially when that contact is a twelve-limbed alien archivist with an inconvenient work ethic.

Busto moved like he was made of shadows and bad intentions. For a guy built like a combat refrigerator, he could glide across a floor without making a sound—a talent I'd seen save our lives more times than I could count. I tracked his progress toward the environmental control panel, counting seconds in my head, while the marac archivist continued cataloguing shipments with the methodical patience of a creature that had nothing but time. Twelve limbs working in perfect coordination—it was almost hypnotic. If you could forget those limbs belonged to a member of the species currently occupying Earth.

The lieutenant reached the panel and positioned himself as if performing routine maintenance. His fingers flew across the keypad with a confidence that came from hours of Sofia drilling the sequence into our heads during mission prep. The code—extracted from her Kergan implant's data cache—was a complex string of numbers and symbols that would trigger an emergency environmental breach protocol.

"Three," I mouthed silently, watching Busto's hands. "Two. One."

The effect was instantaneous. Klaxons erupted throughout the facility, their wailing so piercing I felt it in my molars. Emergency lights pulsed an angry red, bathing the pristine white walls in a hellish glow that made the shadows dance. The facility's automated system barked evacuation orders in Kergan, its clicks and whistles nearly drowned out by the alarms.

"Environmental containment breach! All personnel evacuate immediately! This is not a drill!"

The marac archivist's reaction was almost comical—if you found panic in a twelve-limbed alien amusing. Its tentacles flailed in all directions at once, like someone had dropped a live wire into a bucket of snakes. The translation pod jerked upward, then sideways, knocking into a stack of inventory tablets that clattered to the floor. The archivist didn't even pause to right them, which told me everything I needed to know about how seriously Kergan facilities took environmental breaches.

Throughout the receiving area, other staff members appeared from adjoining rooms, their movements harried and rushed. Two more marac in scientific attire burst from a nearby office, tentacles frantically securing specimen containers. A handful of bipedal aliens—collaborators from conquered worlds, judging by their subservient postures—

rushed to secure artifacts and seal preservation units.

Papers flew in the artificial wind created by suddenly activated emergency ventilation systems. Safety barriers dropped with hydraulic thumps around particularly valuable displays. Some kind of preservative mist sprayed automatically over a collection of biological samples, creating a momentary fog that provided perfect cover.

"Move," I hissed, catching Rowbottom's eye.

Our team converged from various hiding spots, forming up with practiced efficiency. Rowbottom fell in beside me, his face flushed with adrenaline, but his movements controlled. Nicobe detached from the terminal and rejoined us, her crimson capsule pulsing with satisfaction.

"Nicobe has disabled the secondary security protocols," she announced in her formal third-person manner. "We have approximately seven minutes before system reset."

We moved deeper into the facility, the corridors eerily empty—cleared out by evacuating personnel. No one remained to give us a second glance, which was just as well; we were clearly not authorized maracs. Beyond the receiving area, the hallways narrowed, their walls lined with secured display cases filled with artifacts from across the galaxy.

One container held what appeared to be a primitive stone tool, unremarkable except for the fact it was made of a material that subtly shifted colors as we passed. Another housed what looked like a musical instrument constructed from bones that were never meant to belong to the same creature. A third contained nothing but a small metal cube that somehow hurt to look at directly—my eyes slid away from it no matter how I tried to focus.

I led the way, following the mental map Sofia had burned into my brain during our endless preparation sessions. Her implant data had finally yielded the exact layout of the Vault, right down to the locations of security checkpoints and personnel stations.

"Left at the next junction," I murmured. "Two guards usually posted. Should be evacuated now."

Busto and his Marines formed a protective perimeter around us as we moved, their weapons concealed but ready. The youngest Marine—Chapman, I remembered—had his hand inside his uniform jacket, likely gripping his sidearm with white knuckles. I couldn't blame him. Breaking into the most secure Kergan facility in this sector would make anyone twitchy.

The checkpoint appeared exactly where Sofia had said it would be. The guard station was empty, abandoned during the evacuation, screens still glowing with security feeds. I slipped behind the console and entered the override sequence Sofia had extracted from her implant.

"Evacuation Protocol Override Alpha-Seven," announced the system. "Emergency access granted."

The reinforced security doors slid open, revealing another corridor—this one lined with even more valuable and dangerous acquisitions. We passed display cases containing weapons that predated human civilization, preserved specimens of extinct alien species, and data crystals purportedly containing the complete cultural archives of worlds the Kergans had conquered.

"Two more checkpoints," I reminded the team as we moved efficiently through the empty halls. "Then we hit the Sovereign Archive."

We encountered the second checkpoint—this one featuring an automated defense turret that swiveled toward us as we approached. I froze mid-step, but Nicobe floated forward confidently, probes reaching out from her capsule to touch some kind of scanner. After a tense moment, the turret powered down.

"Thirty seconds to pass," she whispered. "The system will register anomalous access after that."

We slipped through like ghosts, the Marines covering our six with professional vigilance.

The final checkpoint featured a full-body scanner that would normally detect any non-marac biorhythms. Nicobe interfaced with it directly, her crimson dodecahedron flashing rapidly as she fed it falsified data. The barrier disappeared, and we found ourselves facing a massive reinforced door marked with Kergan glyphs that shimmered with an inner light.

"Sovereign Archive—Authorized Personnel Only," I translated, thanks to the crash course in Kergan script Sofia had given me. The door loomed before us like an ultimate challenge, its surface etched with warning symbols and access protocols. Beyond it lay the information that might just save Earth—if we could get to it in time.

The klaxons continued their mournful wail, but I noticed with growing concern that the interval between alarms was shortening. They'd discover the false breach soon.

17

I ran my fingers over the security panel, inputting the exact sequence Sofia had drilled into me. The symbols felt alien under my touch—literally—but my muscle memory didn't care. Each keystroke sent a small shiver down my spine, like I was pressing my fingertips against something alive rather than a machine. The panel flickered from red to green, and the massive door released with a pneumatic hiss that made my ears pop. We'd breached the heart of Kergan intelligence, the repository of closely guarded secrets. And judging by the heavy security, whatever waited inside was definitely not something they wanted humans to find.

The door slid open with the smooth precision of expensive engineering, revealing a circular chamber that could have been lifted straight from one of the more budget-conscious sci-fi movies I'd watched as a kid. Data terminals ringed the perimeter, their surfaces glowing with scrolling Kergan script. The center of the room housed a raised platform where holographic displays projected star charts and expedition logs in three dimensions, shifting and rotating in a dance of light and information.

Rowbottom moved in first, his eyes scanning for threats with practiced efficiency. "Clear," he murmured, though his voice held a note of awe I rarely heard from him.

The Marines filed in after him, taking up defensive positions near the entrance while Busto stationed himself at the door, his back to us, eyes focused on the corridor beyond. His hand rested on his concealed weapon, fingers twitching slightly—the only sign he was as tense as the rest of us.

"Nicobe requires direct access to the central terminal," our igna engineer announced, her capsule floating toward the platform at the room's center. "Time is of limited quantity."

I nodded, checking my chronometer. The evacuation alarm had been blaring for nearly five minutes now. Soon, someone would realize it was a false alarm, and security would come looking for intruders.

"Do your thing," I told her. "We need those coordinates yesterday."

Nicobe settled onto the central terminal, her dodecahedron interfacing directly with the Kergan technology. It was always unsettling to watch—her crimson shell would partially merge with the alien tech, creating an interface that was neither fully Collective Dominion nor fully Kergan. Data pathways illuminated the air between them, visible streams of information flowing like luminescent rivers.

I stood back, watching her work. Nicobe was normally playful in her own subdued way, prone to dropping dry observations that caught you off balance just when you thought you had her figured out. But now, connected to the Kergan system, all that playfulness vanished. Her capsule pulsed with steady, methodical rhythms as she sifted through what must have been terabytes of classified information.

"Accessing expedition logs," she announced, her voice flatter than usual. "Sorting by relevance to Ossuary Ring parameters."

A holographic display expanded above the terminal, showing expedition route patterns through an unfamiliar sector of space. Star systems flashed and disappeared as Nicobe filtered through them with machine precision.

"This might actually work," I muttered to Rowbottom, who had moved to stand beside me. His face was illuminated in the pale blue light of the holograms, making him look ethereal and somehow distant.

Suddenly, Nicobe's dodecahedron flashed erratically, pulsing in patterns I'd never seen before. The data flow stuttered, then resumed at twice the previous speed.

"Nicobe has found something disturbing," she announced, her formal speech pattern somehow more ominous for its lack of emotion.

A new hologram materialized above the terminal—a log entry, judging by the timestamp and classification markings. The image resolved into a video feed showing what appeared to be the interior of a Kergan science vessel. A marac scientist occupied the center of the frame, but something was terribly wrong. Its normally precise tentacles moved spasmodically, and dark fluid—blood, I realized with a jolt—streamed from its four eyes. Behind it, equipment lay shattered, and what looked like calculation surfaces were covered in frantic, nonsensical scrawls.

"You cannot bring her out!" the marac scientist screamed in Kergan, Nicobe translating for us. "The ring is a door, and she waits on the other side! The binary stars are her eyes! You cannot—" The feed cut to static with the abruptness of an execution.

A silence fell over our team, broken only by the distant wail of the evacuation alarm.

"What the hell was that?" Busto asked from his position by the door, his professional composure momentarily cracked.

"That was the last transmission from Expedition Vessel *Trk'ash*," Nicobe responded, her capsule still pulsing irregularly. "The first Kergan expedition to the Ossuary Ring. Nicobe has located the coordinates—a binary neutron star system in quad 87-Delta."

The hologram shifted to display a star chart with a highlighted route. Additional data scrolled alongside it—research notes, observations, and warning markers.

"The second expedition returned with all crew members exhibiting signs of extreme psychological trauma," Nicobe continued, extracting the information rapidly now. "Three subsequent expeditions were dispatched. None returned. The survivors of the second expedition committed ritual suicide within twenty standard cycles of return."

"Charming vacation spot," I muttered, feeling a cold weight settle in my stomach. "Can you download all of it?"

"Transfer in progress," Nicobe confirmed. "Including research notes describing the Ring's theoretical properties as a space-time anomaly capable of—" She paused. "The Kergan term does not translate directly. The closest approximation would be 'dimensional breach point.'"

Busto's hand gripped my arm suddenly, his fingers digging in with surprising strength. "We need to go," he said, his voice tight. "Security override protocols are being initiated. The system knows we're here."

As if on cue, the alarms changed pitch, becoming more

urgent.

"Download complete," Nicobe announced, detaching from the terminal. Her capsule seemed to shudder as it separated from the Kergan technology.

"Fall back to extraction point," I ordered, and the team moved with practiced efficiency. The Marines formed a protective formation around Nicobe—our most valuable asset now that we had the data.

We retraced our steps through the facility, but the evacuation that had provided our cover was shifting to a security response. Twice we had to duck into side corridors to avoid security teams moving in formation, their weapons drawn.

By some miracle—or more likely, thanks to Nicobe's ongoing interference with the security systems—we reached the receiving bay without confrontation. Our entry point, disguised as a maintenance access, remained uncompromised.

"Move fast, stay low," Busto instructed as we slipped through the access port and into the adjacent docking port where our stolen freighter waited. The civilian vessel looked laughably out of place among the sleek Kergan ships, but right now, its nondescript appearance was our best asset.

We boarded silently, and I sealed the hatch behind us with hands that remained surprisingly steady despite everything. Busto ordered our captive crew to start departure sequences.

The freighter lifted off with a gentle rumble, joining a stream of vessels evacuating because of the "environmental emergency." We maintained radio silence, just another ship following evacuation procedures, until we were safely beyond the facility's immediate sensor range.

Only when the Vault had shrunk to a distant speck

behind us did I allow myself to exhale. Soon we'd rendezvous with *Thunder,* and then we'd have to decide what to do with the information we'd stolen—information that had driven its discoverers insane.

I glanced at Nicobe, her dodecahedron now restored to its normal, steady pulse. "So," I said, forcing a lightness into my voice that I didn't feel, "about this 'she' who's waiting on the other side of the Ring..."

No one laughed. Some jokes even I couldn't sell.

18

We'd been back aboard *Thunder* for only two hours when alarms hit like a hammer to the skull—piercing, insistent wails that transformed *Thunder*'s bridge from ordered chaos to controlled panic in less than a heartbeat. My fingers were already flying across the command console before conscious thought caught up. Proximity alert. Kergan patrol vessel. Range closing. The holographic tactical display splashed crimson warnings across my field of vision as the enemy ship's profile sharpened, its sensor arrays obviously focused on the security breach we'd just created at the Vault.

"They've backtracked the freighter's trajectory," Destiny announced, her voice tight but steady. "They know we're here."

My mouth went dry. The math wasn't complicated: one Kergan patrol ship was manageable. What followed would not be. I made the call in the space between heartbeats.

"Weapons, lock main batteries. Fire as soon as you have a solution."

No hesitation. No dramatic countdown. Just the subtle

vibration beneath my boots as *Thunder*'s railguns spat hyperaccelerated slugs toward the patrol vessel. On the tactical display, the enemy ship bloomed into an expanding cloud of superheated gas and debris.

"Direct hit," reported the tactical officer, his voice flat. "Target destroyed."

I didn't feel the surge of victory I should have. Instead, my stomach knotted as I watched the data stream from our long-range sensors. "Did they get a transmission out?"

Destiny's fingers danced across her console. "Affirmative. Burst transmission, encrypted. Full system alert protocols detected across all Kergan frequencies."

"Well, shit." I dragged a hand through my hair. "So much for the stealthy approach. Dump the captive freighter."

“Let them go?” Destiny asked.

“Yes, they're no good to us now, and we're not murderers.”

The tactical display transformed before my eyes, new signatures blossoming like malignant flowers, as the captured freighter—now free—fled from *Thunder* as fast as its weak translation pods would push it. Two Kergan frigates, sharp-edged and predatory, accelerated from their patrol routes. Behind them, the massive bulk of a battlecruiser emerged from behind the system's gas giant, its weapon ports already cycling open.

My hands weren't numb, but I felt a warmth in my chest, an uncomfortable heat that I recognized as fear, not for myself, but for my crew. For Sofia, who had just entered the bridge and strapped into her jump seat, her eyes meeting mine with grim understanding.

"Time to veilspace capability?" I asked, keeping my voice level.

"Eighteen minutes to full charge," Nicobe's voice came through the ship's comms, her formal tones somehow comforting in their precision. "Nicobe regrets the delay, but the drive requires proper calibration after our recent transit."

I nodded, though she couldn't see it. "Set course for the L4 Lagrange point, maximum acceleration. Deploy chaff and thermal decoys on five-second intervals."

The tactical display updated, showing our projected course and the intercept vectors of the Kergan vessels. The numbers scrolled past—relative velocities, weapon ranges, time-to-intercept calculations. None of them told a story I wanted to read.

"The battlecruiser is a Ravager-class," Destiny said quietly. "Specifically designed to kill ships like *Thunder*."

"Thanks for that morale boost," I replied dryly. "I was worried this might be too easy."

She snorted, the familiar sound somehow making the flashing red alerts seem less apocalyptic. "Just keeping you informed, Captain."

Captain. Not Commander. She only called me that when things were truly dire. The gesture touched me even as it confirmed what the tactical display was already screaming: we were catastrophically outgunned.

The battlecruiser alone carried enough firepower to reduce *Thunder* to its component atoms. The frigates were just overkill. Standard Kergan battle doctrine—never use one hammer when three will do.

I studied their formation, noting how they'd spread out to trap us in a classic pincer maneuver. Textbook. Effective. But maybe just a little predictable.

"Tactical, give me a firing solution on the port-side frigate," I ordered.

The tactical officer glanced up, confusion evident. "Sir, they're well outside effective range."

"I'm aware." I tapped the display, highlighting the frigate's projected course. "I don't need to hit it. I need to make it change course."

Understanding dawned in his eyes. "Forcing them to break formation."

"Exactly. Calculate for maximum spread. I want that space between us and them filled with so much metal they'll have no choice but to alter vector."

Sofia caught my eye from her jump seat. "Risky. If they don't take the bait—"

"Then we're no worse off than we are now," I finished. "And if they do..."

"We might buy enough time to reach the jump point," she concluded with a tight nod.

The tactical officer worked his console with precision, born of countless drills. "Solution plotted. Ready to fire on your command."

I felt the weight of every eye on the bridge. The tension had moved beyond the red alert klaxons, beyond the flashing warnings on every display. It lived in the space between breaths, in the subtle tremor of fingers hovering over consoles.

"Fire."

Thunder shuddered as the railguns unleashed their payload, the massive electromagnetic coils accelerating tungsten slugs to a significant fraction of light speed. On the tactical display, I watched our desperate gambit unfold in real-time—dozens of projectiles racing toward the void where, if our calculations were correct, the Kergan frigate would eventually be.

Destiny's eyes never left her display. "Kergan vessels

adjusting formation. The frigate is altering course to avoid the projected impact zone."

I allowed myself a tight smile. "And the others?"

"Compensating. Formation integrity compromised. Estimated interception time now twenty-two minutes."

Not enough, but better than what we'd had. I leaned forward in my command chair, eyes fixed on the escape route that might, with enough luck and skill, get us out of this mess alive.

"Maintain course for the L4 point. Prepare for evasive maneuvers on my mark." I paused, then added, "And someone find me a way to make this veilspace drive charge faster, or we're going to have a very short and explosive reunion with our Kergan friends."

The first missile exchange was almost beautiful—like some deadly choreographed dance of light and shadow against the void. Our laser point defense blisters lit up the darkness, tracing luminous webs as they tracked and fired. The Kergan ships responded in kind, their own countermeasures blooming against the blackness. For a brief, surreal moment, I almost forgot we were fighting for our lives. Then reality crashed back as *Thunder* shuddered around me.

"Multiple missile launches detected! Kergan frigates have entered optimal engagement range," Destiny called out, her fingers flying across her tactical station. "Twenty-plus anti-ship missiles inbound, multiple vectors."

I kept my voice steady despite the adrenaline surge that threatened to crack my composure. "Launch intercept missiles, pattern delta. All LPD systems to automatic targeting."

Thunder's defense systems roared to life. Intercept missiles streaked from our launch tubes, rushing to meet the incoming Kergan ordnance. The LPD blisters tracked with mechanical precision, their targeting algorithms identifying threats faster than human reflexes ever could.

Kergan missiles died in spectacular flashes, torn apart by our interceptors or burned through by precision laser fire. But war is a numbers game, and the Kergans had numbers to spare.

"Missile lock breaking through port quarter!" the tactical officer shouted.

I opened my mouth to order evasive maneuvers, but the impact came first—a violent judder that slammed through *Thunder*'s frame and threw me against my restraints. The bridge lights flickered, and for one terrifying heartbeat, I thought we'd lost power completely.

"Direct hit to stern section!" someone called through the ringing in my ears. "Tractor pod three is compromised. Stern bolsters damaged."

I tasted blood where I'd bitten my cheek. "Status of veilspace drive?"

"Functional," Nicobe replied, her voice somehow maintaining its composure. "But stern damage has reduced power flow efficiency by twenty-two percent. Recalculating charge time."

The ship had barely stopped shaking from the first hit when the second missile struck. This time the impact came from above, a hammer blow that sent several unrestrained crew members sprawling. Warning indicators flooded my display—a constellation of red and amber alerts that told a story of a mounting crisis.

"Dorsal impact," reported the damage control officer. "Heat exchanger array has taken severe damage."

Sofia gripped her jump seat with white knuckles, her expression focused despite the chaos. Our eyes met briefly across the bridge—a moment of connection amid the madness—before duty pulled my attention back to the tactical display.

"Engineering reports partial system heat overload," Destiny announced, her voice tight. "Veilspace jump preparation extended to fourteen minutes."

Fourteen minutes. The tactical display told me we wouldn't survive that long on our current trajectory. The Kergan battlecruiser was closing the gap, its weapons systems fully charged and ready to deliver the killing blow.

"New course," I ordered, pointing to a small object near the L4 Lagrange point. "Take us toward that Trojan asteroid."

Around me, the bridge had transformed into a vision of controlled hell. Warning lights bathed every surface in pulsing red and amber. The acrid smell of overheated systems stung my nostrils, mixing with the metallic tang of blood and sweat. Through the overhead comms, I heard the controlled chaos of damage control teams rushing through corridors, their urgent calls punctuated by the hiss of fire suppression systems.

My uniform clung to my skin, soaked with sweat that felt ice cold despite the rising temperature. I ignored the tremor in my hands—the aftermath of adrenaline and fear—and kept my expression neutral. The crew didn't need to see their commander rattled, even as calculations of our diminishing survival odds played through my mind like a morbid mathematics exam.

"Destiny," I called, "prepare cluster mines. Standard dispersal pattern."

She nodded, already programming the deployment sequence. "Mines ready on your mark."

The asteroid grew larger on our forward displays—an

irregular lump of rock and ice, utterly unremarkable except for its potential as temporary cover. Not much, but in space combat, even momentary protection can mean the difference between life and death.

"Status of pursuing vessels?"

"First frigate has closed to seven thousand kilometers," Destiny reported. "Second frigate at eight thousand and adjusting course to cut off our projected path. Battlecruiser has increased thrust, now twelve thousand kilometers and closing."

I wiped blood from my lip with the back of my hand. "Helm, prepare for maximum thrust on my mark. We're going to whip around that rock and reverse course for two seconds."

The helmsman's eyes widened slightly, but he nodded. "Understood, sir."

"Destiny, set mines to proximity detonation, three-second delay after trigger. Target the second frigate's projected course."

The asteroid loomed larger, its cratered surface filling our forward view. I waited, counting down in my head, feeling the weight of seconds stretching into agonizing eternities.

"Mark!"

Thunder's remaining tractor pods fired at maximum thrust, hurling us around the asteroid in a slingshot maneuver that strained both the ship's structural integrity and my body's tolerance for g-forces. For a brief moment, we faced directly back toward our pursuers.

"Deploy mines! Now!"

The cluster mines spat from *Thunder*'s deployment tubes, spreading outward in a deadly cloud just as we reversed course again, accelerating away from the asteroid. On the tactical display, I watched the second Kergan frigate barrel into our trap, unable to alter its course quickly enough to avoid the minefield.

The detonation was spectacular—dozens of explosions rippling across space as the proximity triggers activated in sequence. The frigate disappeared momentarily in a blinding flash, then reappeared, tumbling badly, atmosphere and debris venting from multiple hull breaches.

"Direct hit," Destiny confirmed, a grim satisfaction in her voice. "Second frigate is crippled. Life support failing. They're launching escape pods."

"The battlecruiser?" I asked, already knowing we couldn't celebrate yet.

"Diverting to avoid debris field. They've lost approximately thirty seconds on intercept time."

Thirty seconds. Not victory, not even close, but a breath of space we desperately needed. I looked around the bridge—at the damage, the exhausted faces, the determination that somehow persisted despite everything—and made myself ignore the fatigue trying to claim my limbs.

"Reset course for the jump point," I ordered. "Maximum sustainable thrust. Let's make those thirty seconds count."

As *Thunder* leaped forward again, I caught Sofia's gaze. She wore the expression of someone calculating odds and finding them wanting, but she gave me a slight nod, anyway. It wasn't confidence—we were both too realistic for that—but it was solidarity. In that moment, it was enough.

19

The Kergan battlecruiser grew on our displays like a mechanical predator, its silhouette bristling with weapon ports and sensor arrays. We were achingly close to the jump point—that invisible coordinate in space where *Thunder* could slip into the Syderealium and escape—but the mathematics of our situation had turned brutally simple: they would reach us before we could jump. Another spread of missiles erupted from the battlecruiser's launch tubes, the deadly projectiles spreading into an inescapable net.

"Multiple missile launch detected," Destiny announced, her voice maintaining that impossible steadiness. "Tracking twenty-plus inbound, spread pattern alpha."

I leaned forward in my chair. "All LPDs to active tracking. Launch remaining intercept missiles."

Thunder's defenses activated with practiced precision. Laser point defense blisters swiveled and fired, creating a web of coherent light that sliced through vacuum toward the incoming threats. Our last intercept missiles streaked outward, their drives burning hot as they rushed to meet the Kergan ordnance.

The tactical display updated in real-time, showing kills as our defenses eliminated missile after missile. Sixteen down. Eighteen. Nineteen.

But not all.

"Impact imminent!" the tactical officer shouted.

"Brace!" I called, my knuckles white on the arms of my command chair.

The missile struck precisely where we were most vulnerable—the already damaged stern bolster. The impact wasn't just a physical shock; it was like *Thunder* itself had screamed. Metal tore, systems failed, and the ship bucked violently beneath us. I was thrown against my restraints hard enough to knock the wind from my lungs, stars exploding across my vision as my head snapped forward, then back.

Through the ringing in my ears, I heard the worst possible sound: the high-pitched whine of the veilspace drive cycling down.

"Drive core has automatically shifted to safe mode," Nicobe reported, her formal tones somehow cutting through the chaos. "Safety protocols have detected critical feedback in the sydereal resonator."

I tasted copper and realized I'd bitten my tongue. "Can you override?"

"Nicobe is already implementing emergency bypass procedures."

On the engineering station, Nicobe's crimson dodecahedron capsule pulsed with internal light as she interfaced directly with *Thunder*'s systems. Tendrils of energy extended from her geometric shell, linking with the ship's sydereal conduits in ways that human engineers couldn't manage.

"Time to veilspace jump: six minutes," Destiny announced, her eyes fixed on her display. "Cruiser ETA: four minutes."

Four minutes. The bridge fell silent for a heartbeat as everyone processed the simple math of our destruction.

"They're moving into railgun range," the tactical officer reported, breaking the silence. "Targeting systems active."

I watched the display, mind racing through options that dwindled with each passing second. *Thunder* was bleeding momentum, our damaged tractor pods unable to maintain full acceleration. Conventional tactics would get us killed. Standard evasive maneuvers would only delay the inevitable.

Sofia caught my eye from her jump seat. She didn't speak, but I read the question in her gaze: Do you have anything left?

I nodded slightly, though my insides clenched at what I was about to attempt. As an officer of the UHC Armada, I had a duty to try every option, no matter the personal cost.

"Maintain course for the jump point," I ordered, my voice steady despite the fear curling through my gut. "Full thrust on remaining pods."

Then I closed my eyes and reached—not with my hands, but with my consciousness—into the Syderealium. The transition was never easy, especially in the middle of a battle with adrenaline flooding my system. The dimensional realm overlapped with physical space in ways that defied conventional geometry, its infinite layers shimmering with the conscious energy of all beings, living and dead.

I felt my body strain as I extended my awareness, creating a dimensional bubble between the battlecruiser and *Thunder*. Sweat beaded on my forehead, then turned cold as my muscles trembled with effort. Something warm trickled from my nose—blood, though I couldn't spare the concentration to wipe it away.

My vision narrowed to a tunnel, the edges darkening as I forced more of my consciousness into maintaining the dimensional construct. Through it, I could sense the battlecruiser's railguns cycling to full charge, preparing to fire.

"Captain," Destiny's voice seemed to come from very far away. "Your nose is bleeding."

I couldn't respond. Every ounce of my focus was bent on shaping the bubble, giving it the precise properties I needed. The battlecruiser fired multiple railgun slugs—hyperaccelerated metal aimed directly at *Thunder*'s most vulnerable sections.

The slugs passed into my dimensional bubble. With a mental twist that felt like tearing muscle from bone, I reshaped the bubble's dimensional properties, inverting its relation to normal space-time. The railgun slugs' trajectories bent, curving back toward their origin.

One reflected slug struck the battlecruiser midship. The impact triggered a catastrophic secondary explosion—likely a ruptured power conduit or ammunition cache. The massive vessel shuddered, then began drifting out of control, emergency systems flaring across its hull.

I released the dimensional bubble, collapsing back into my body with a gasp that felt like surfacing from deep water. My muscles screamed in protest, and my head pounded with each heartbeat. Warm blood continued to trickle from my nose, and my vision swam with dark spots.

"The veilspace drive is back online," Nicobe announced, her capsule pulsing triumphantly. "Ready to initiate jump sequence."

"Full thrust to the jump point," I managed, my voice

hoarse. "Tactical, prepare a full reverse salvo. Anti-ship missiles, railguns, chaff, thermal decoys—everything we have left. Fire on my mark."

The tactical officer blinked in surprise. "Sir, we'll be firing backward while accelerating forward?"

"Exactly." I nodded, fighting to keep my head clear. "Pivot the translation pods to maintain forward acceleration. I want to saturate the battlespace behind us as we make the jump."

Understanding dawned across the bridge. We would jump into veilspace while leaving a deadly farewell gift—a wall of ordnance and countermeasures that would buy us precious seconds if the Kergan vessel recovered faster than expected.

"The battlecruiser is restabilizing," Destiny warned. "Power signatures increasing. They're coming back online."

"Mark!" I ordered.

Thunder shuddered as our remaining weapons emptied in a final defiant gesture—missiles streaming backward, railguns firing their last salvos, chaff and thermal decoys spreading in a confusing cloud. Simultaneously, the veilspace drive engaged, the familiar disorienting sensation washing over us as the fabric of reality shifted around *Thunder*.

The last thing I saw on our sensors was the Kergan battlecruiser, damaged but functional, beginning to move again—just as *Thunder* slipped into the dimensional realm beyond normal space, leaving our pursuers and their weapons behind in real-space.

We had escaped. By the narrowest of margins.

Veilspace enveloped *Thunder* in its strange embrace, swallowing the chaos of battle in an almost eerie silence. The viewports, once filled with the hard black of realspace, now shimmered with currents of color that defied description—not quite light, not quite energy, but something between matter and thought.

I slumped in my command chair, every muscle aching, the metallic taste of blood still sharp on my tongue. The shift from mortal peril to sudden safety felt jarring, almost disorienting.

Around me, the command deck was hushed. The alarms were silenced, the flashing warnings reduced to steady amber indicators—damage reports, not death sentences. Crew members moved with the slow, shaky precision of people just past the breaking point, exhaustion creeping in now that survival was no longer in doubt.

I wiped my nose. My hand came away streaked with drying blood. The sydereal exertion had cost me more than I'd admit out loud. My vision still swam with dark spots, and my limbs felt hollow, filled with lead.

A shadow fell across me. Busto stood at parade rest beside my chair. His normally grim expression softened—barely. For him, it was practically a smile.

"That was some fancy flying, Commander," he said, voice gruff but tinged with something rare: respect.

I managed a tired smirk. "Just your standard 'reflect-railgun-slugs-with-your-mind-while-bleeding-from-the-face' maneuver. They're teaching it at Space Warfare School now. Real crowd-pleaser."

Busto's mouth twitched—possibly an attempt at a smile. "They don't teach that in the Raiders. Creative. Effective." A beat. "Insane, but effective."

"High praise from a Marine," I said, trying to sit straighter. "I'll take it."

As he returned to his station, Destiny approached with

a datapad. Her uniform was rumpled, a dark bruise blooming on her forearm, but her gaze was steady.

"Damage report," she said, handing me the pad. "We're banged up, but still flying."

I scanned the list: tractor pod three offline. Stern bolster wrecked beyond onboard repair. Heat exchanger is down to sixty percent. Hull breaches sealed, but stress fractures remained. The report read like a ship that had come within a hair of disintegration.

Amazingly, there were no crew casualties.

Through the veiled light of the viewport, I glimpsed *Thunder's* scarred exterior—blackened plating, twisted metal, and repair patches glinting like fresh scabs across the hull.

Sofia unstrapped from her seat and crossed to me, her steps careful in veilspace's disorienting inertia. She offered me a clean cloth. Our fingers brushed—brief, but grounding. The spark wasn't static; it was something deeper, something earned.

"You pushed too hard," she said, her accent stronger with fatigue.

I dabbed at my face. "Didn't have much choice."

"I know." She paused. "It was impressive. Terrifying—but impressive."

Around us, the bridge hummed with low activity. Systems stabilizing. Crew regrouping. The strange veilspace glow playing over the damaged interior gave it all a surreal, dreamlike feel—like we weren't just between stars, but between realities.

"Nicobe confirms veilspace transit is stable," Destiny called. "ETA to destination: fourteen hours."

Fourteen hours to patch the worst of the damage. To regroup. To prepare. Because the mission had changed. We weren't covert anymore. We'd crossed a line.

Busto spoke without looking up. "They'll be hunting us now. Everywhere."

I nodded. "Then we'll need to be faster. Smarter." I sat forward, ignoring my body's protests. "Begin repair protocols. Rotate damage control teams. Prioritize life support, then weapons, then propulsion."

Sofia eyed me. "And you, Commander?"

"I'll manage." I stood, swaying slightly. "Have Doc Montana meet me in my quarters in an hour. I'll clean up. Then gather the senior staff—we need a plan."

As I headed for the bridge exit, I glanced back. The crew—exhausted but alive, rattled but focused—moved with quiet purpose. The veilspace currents cast otherworldly hues across their faces, making them seem momentarily unreal… before snapping back to the people I trusted with my life.

We'd survived—barely. And the mission had never been more dangerous.

But watching them now, I felt something unexpected. Not confidence in the odds—we'd never have that. But confidence in them.

I paused at the threshold. The bridge lights flickered in time with the veilspace currents, and *Thunder* drifted on through dimensions beyond comprehension.

For now, we were safe.

20

Hours into veilspace transit, en route to a remote star system where we could refuel and patch *Thunder* back together, I sat alone in my ready room, staring at repair reports I'd already read twice. The letters blurred. Another headache was forming—slow, insistent, the kind that made every syllable feel like a weight.

The room felt smaller than usual tonight. The walls of command inching inward. *Thunder* hummed steadily beneath my boots, a low reminder of everything still on my shoulders—ship, crew, Sofia.

I rubbed my temples and sighed. Two more reports, then maybe I could call it a night. Assuming the universe didn't crash through the bulkhead and demand something new. It usually did.

The door chimed, and I straightened in my chair, pulling the captain's mask back over my exhaustion.

"Enter," I called, voice steadier than I felt.

Phoebe Brooks slipped through the doorway like water finding its path, her brown hair loose around her shoulders instead of in the usual regulation bun. She shut the door behind her with a soft click that somehow sounded like trouble.

"Lieutenant," I acknowledged, trying not to notice how her standard-issue coveralls hugged her curves in ways they didn't on other crew members.

"Captain," she replied, smiling in that way that made the corners of her eyes crinkle. "I have the engineering report on the stern bolsters."

She handed me a datapad, our fingers brushing. A tiny electric jolt ran up my arm—static electricity from the dry ship air, nothing more—but it made my stomach tighten all the same. I gestured to the chair across from my desk.

"Have a seat," I said, then immediately regretted it. The rumors were already swirling through the ship. Lieutenant Commander Drake spending too much time alone with his pretty engineer. I could already picture Destiny's raised eyebrow, the knowing looks from the crew. But I was the captain, goddammit. I needed to meet with my officers.

Phoebe settled into the chair, crossing her legs in a fluid motion that drew my eyes before I forced them back to the report.

"The repairs are progressing well," she said, leaning forward slightly. "We've reinforced the primary coupling on the port side, but the starboard section is showing more stress fractures than we initially detected."

I nodded, grateful for the technical discussion. "Timeline for completion?"

"That's the issue, sir." She tucked a strand of hair behind her ear. "We can patch it for now, but for a complete repair, we'll need to land somewhere with suitable materials. Deploy the nanoforge."

I scrolled through the schematics. "How urgent?"

"We can manage another two jumps without risk, but after that..." She shrugged, the motion making her collarbones peek out of her not-quite-zipped coverall. "I wouldn't recommend pushing our luck."

"I'll talk to Sofia about potential landing sites, see what intel she has," I said, setting the datapad down.

Something flickered across Phoebe's face at the mention of Sofia, there and gone so quickly I might have imagined it.

"Is there something else, Lieutenant?" I asked, sensing she wasn't ready to leave.

Phoebe's eyes softened. "I was thinking about when we first met. Did I ever tell you about where I was before *Thunder*?"

I shook my head. "Wolf Jaw, wasn't it?"

"My family was living in the woods outside town." She stared past me, into some private memory. "When food got scarce, I'd sneak into town alone. There were these refugee men who started following me one day."

My chest tightened. I'd seen enough of humanity's darker instincts during my own time on the streets.

"What happened?" I asked quietly.

"I led them into an abandoned warehouse," she continued, a grim pride in her voice. "Set up a trip wire by the exit, then climbed out through a vent in the ceiling. When they fell, I got away." Her eyes returned to mine, suddenly present and intense. "That's why I was so happy to join your team after you arrived in town. Needed to feel safe."

"I'm sorry that happened to you," I said, meaning it.

"Don't be. Made me stronger." She uncrossed her legs and leaned closer. "There are only two men I've ever felt completely safe with. My father, and you, Kory."

The use of my first name sent warning signals flashing.

This wasn't a captain-lieutenant conversation anymore.

"I should probably—" I began, but stopped as Phoebe stood up.

"You know what else I was thinking about?" she asked, stepping around the edge of my desk with deliberate, swaying movements. She ran her hands slowly up her sides, tracing the contours of her body. "How good it feels to finally not be afraid."

My mouth went dry. I should say something, do something, stop this—but my body betrayed me, rooting me to my chair as she circled behind me. I could smell her—engine oil and something sweet, floral.

"Phoebe, this isn't appropriate," I managed, the words sounding hollow even to my own ears.

She came to a stop beside me, perching on the edge of my desk, her thigh inches from my arm. Her hand dropped casually to my knee, burning through the fabric of my uniform.

"Do you know how much the crew respects you?" she asked, her fingers tracing idle patterns. "How they talk about Lieutenant Commander Drake—the man who wounded a Soul Ravager in combat?"

I couldn't take my eyes off her, couldn't move away from her touch. My heart pounded in my chest, blood rushing in my ears.

"Those shoulders," she continued, her gaze drifting over me like a physical touch. "The way you stand on the bridge. Those kind eyes that see everything. And your hair..." Her free hand hovered near my face. "I've dreamed about running my fingers through it."

The ready room shrank around us, the air heavy and charged. I felt a familiar warmth in my chest, an uncomfortable heat that I recognized as guilt, but it competed with something else—something primal that I hadn't let surface in a long time.

"Lieutenant Brooks," I said, my voice a strangled approximation of command. "I think this conversation has gone far enough."

Her hand squeezed my knee, and her smile told me she didn't agree at all.

My eyes betrayed me, following her hand as it slid up the front of her coveralls. My mouth went sandpaper dry as her fingers found the zipper tab and began to pull it downward with agonizing slowness. The metallic whisper of the teeth separating seemed to echo in the ready room like a siren's call, each centimeter revealing more of what I knew I shouldn't be seeing. The rational part of my brain screamed at me to stop this, but my body had apparently staged a mutiny, refusing to move as Phoebe's coverall parted like curtains on a show I had no business attending.

A triangle of pale skin appeared, then more. She wasn't wearing the regulation sports bra, but something else entirely—white lace that pushed her breasts up like offerings on an altar. The zipper continued its journey downward, revealing a flat stomach and then matching underwear, equally non-regulation. The heavy utility fabric fell open, framing her lingerie-clad body like a portrait.

"Phoebe," I managed, my voice a croak.

She leaned closer, the scent of her skin filling my lungs. "I've wanted this for so long," she whispered, her breath warm against my ear. She took my hand and guided it toward her exposed skin. "Feel how my heart is racing for you."

I snatched my hand back as if burned. Our fingers brushed, and I felt a spark, a physical shock that finally cut through the fog of arousal.

Sofia's face flashed in my mind—her blue eyes, her honey-blonde fuzz she had finally started growing out again, the trust we'd built together. What the hell was I doing?

Phoebe misinterpreted my hesitation, licking her lips as she perched on the edge of my desk. "All I want," she purred, "is for you to lean me over this desk and have your way with me." She ran a hand down her exposed body. "No one has to know. It'll be our secret."

The spell broke. I stood up so quickly my chair rolled backward and hit the wall.

"Stop. Now." My voice found its command tone again. "Put yourself back together, Lieutenant."

Confusion crossed her face, quickly replaced by a seductive smile. "Why?" She trailed a finger along the edge of her lace bra. "We're both adults. Nobody will know." She reached for my hand again. "It's just us, Kory. I want to be with you. Don't you want me, too?"

I stepped back. "I'll know. Sofia will know, even if I don't tell her." I gestured at her state of undress. "And I would tell her, because that's what partners do. The guilt would eat me alive, Phoebe."

Something flashed behind her eyes—anger, desperation. I couldn't tell. She slid off the desk and moved toward me with swaying hips, her coverall hanging open like an invitation.

"Then let me ease your guilt," she said, reaching for my waist as she attempted to settle onto my lap.

I caught her by the shoulders, holding her at arm's length. "That's enough." I kept my voice firm but low, aware of how thin *Thunder*'s bulkheads could be. I pushed her back toward the other side of the desk, my hands firm but not rough.

Her eyes lit up at my touch. "Oh," she breathed, a flush rising to her cheeks. "You like it this way? You can do whatever you want to me, Kory. I'm yours."

I released her and stepped back around my desk, putting the furniture between us like a shield. "Lieutenant Brooks, I want you to pull yourself together and report to Doc Montana tomorrow."

The seductive mask fell away, replaced by indignation. "What?"

"This isn't healthy behavior, Phoebe. Something's wrong, and I want you to get help."

Her face contorted with anger. "There's nothing wrong with me! This isn't some mental breakdown—it's my heart speaking!" She yanked her zipper up with a violent motion. "I'm just trying to show you how I feel. My body is the only language you seem to notice."

"That's not true. I—"

"Save it." She cut me off, her eyes bright with unshed tears. "I get it. I'm not good enough for the great Lieutenant Commander Drake."

Before I could respond, she stalked to the door and slammed her palm against the release. The portal slid open with a hiss that sounded like disappointment.

I followed her out, needing to explain, to find some way to salvage this situation before it tore the crew apart. I emerged from my ready room just in time to see Sofia rounding the corner of the corridor, a datapad in her hand. Her steps faltered as she saw Phoebe storming away from my door, face flushed, hair disheveled.

Sofia's eyes met mine, confusion morphing into something harder as she pieced together the scene. I started toward her, mouth opening to explain, but she turned sharply and walked in the opposite direction, her back rigid with the particular kind of military posture that conveyed more anger than a shouting match ever could.

"Sofia, wait—" I called, but she didn't turn around.

Perfect. Just perfect.

"You look like something the cat dragged in, spit out, then dragged back in again," Destiny said six hours later when I finally emerged from an emergency meeting with the navigation team.

I grunted in response, reaching for the coffeepot in the officers' mess. The liquid inside looked like it had been brewed during the first interstellar war, but I poured a cup, anyway.

"Trouble in paradise?" she asked, sliding into the seat across from me.

I raised an eyebrow. "What have you heard?"

Destiny gave me her patented you-can't-be-that-stupid look. "What haven't I heard? The ship's not that big, Kory." She lowered her voice. "Half the crew thinks you're banging our assistant engineer, the other half thinks you're just about to start, and everyone's waiting to see if Sofia's going to space you without a suit."

I choked on my coffee. "It's not—I didn't—"

"Save it." She held up a hand. "I know you better than that. But perception is reality on a ship this size." She leaned forward. "You need to fix this before it tears *Thunder* apart. Sofia's hurt, Phoebe's telling anyone who'll listen that you called her crazy, and morale is headed for the airlock."

I stared into my coffee cup, watching the sludgy surface ripple with the vibrations of the ship. Destiny was right. This wasn't just about my relationship with Sofia anymore. This was about the cohesion of my crew, the functionality of my command.

"I know," I said finally. "I have to do something."

Destiny's expression softened slightly. "For what it's worth, I believe you. But belief doesn't count for much against good gossip."

I nodded, feeling the weight of command pressing down on my shoulders like a physical burden. Relationships on a starship were complex enough without adding this kind of drama. If I didn't find a way to resolve this, the rift between these women would tear *Thunder* apart more effectively than any battlecruiser ever could.

21

I rapped twice on Busto's door — not a formal knock, just enough to say, "It's me."

The door hissed open, and there he was, standing like he was personally holding the bulkheads together. His expression didn't shift much, but his eyes flicked over me, reading me like a checklist. He stepped aside without a word.

"Didn't realize we were having a party," he said as I stepped in.

"Just needed some oxygen," I said. "And maybe something stronger."

He gave a grunt that might've passed for a laugh. "Depends how much you're willing to pretend you saw nothing."

I blinked as he moved to the far corner of his room—right past the perfectly regulation bunk and the painfully neat desk—and popped open a ventilation panel with the ease of long practice. From inside, he pulled out a dented old canister and two battered cups.

I raised an eyebrow. "Hiding contraband in the life-support systems? That feels counterproductive."

Busto poured a measure of shimmering, angry-smelling liquid into each cup. "They check lockers. They don't check breathing vents."

He handed me a cup, and I caught a whiff of whatever reactor-grade solvent he'd managed to ferment.

"Should I be filing a report?" I asked, mock-serious.

"You should be forgetting this conversation exists." His mouth twitched into the ghost of a smirk.

We clinked cups without ceremony and drank.

It hit like an orbital strike. I coughed hard enough to see spots, earning a raised eyebrow and a look that clearly said, Marine up, Commander.

"You sure this stuff's safe for human consumption?" I rasped.

He shrugged. "Depends on your definition of 'safe.' If you don't grow a third arm, it's a win."

We drank again, and finally, the tension started to bleed out of me. I leaned against the wall, cup dangling from my fingers. He settled onto the edge of his bunk, casual in a way few people ever saw.

"You wanna talk about it?" he asked eventually, like a man who already knew the answer.

I nodded, staring at the swirling liquid in my cup. "It's a mess, Busto."

"Understatement of the cycle."

I huffed a dry laugh, and for a minute, we sat in silence. Good silence. The kind you only got with someone who knew when to leave the space alone.

Finally, I said it out loud: "I thought I could keep it under control. Sofia. Phoebe. The crew."

"You can't seal a hull breach with good intentions," he

said.

Another drink. Another burn.

"Brooks is circling you like a missile lock," Busto said, voice still casual, but the weight behind it pressing down. "Kohl's retreating into her own head. Destiny's already mapped out succession plans, just in case."

I winced. "Destiny?"

He nodded. "Smart kid. Smarter than you give her credit for."

I stared at the floor, the guilt climbing my ribs like vines.

Busto leaned forward, elbows on his knees. His voice dropped lower. "You want a Raider story?"

I grunted. "Always."

He took a long drink before starting.

"Had a CO in the Raiders. Man was a damn legend. Could out-think a Syrian fireteam blindfolded and drunk." He shook his head, something sad flickering in his eyes. "Then he fell for his logistics officer. Good woman. No complaints there. But love doesn't give a damn about your mission orders."

Busto toyed with the rim of his cup as he talked.

"Got bad on a drop in the Rift. We were supposed to hit an ammo cache and evac clean. But when she got pinned, he froze. Diverted extraction teams to pull her out. Left our flank wide open."

He didn't have to finish the story. I already knew.

"Eight good people dead," he said anyway. "Including her. Whole op collapsed inside three minutes."

Silence stretched between us.

"You're not him," Busto said after a while. "But you're walking closer to that line than you think."

I rubbed my face, the hooch and the memories and the

guilt knotting in my stomach.

"So what? I cut everyone out? Live like a monk?"

Busto snorted. "Nah. You just stop being a question mark."

I blinked at him.

"Make a choice," he said. "Make it clear. Make it final. You hesitate, we die."

He poured one last measure, just a splash. We clinked cups again without a word.

"Ships can break from enemy guns," he said, voice quiet and certain. "But they can also break from inside. From hairline cracks no one notices until the hull comes apart."

He finished his drink and stood. Big, solid, immovable Busto.

At the door, he clapped me once, heavy on the shoulder.

"It's not the enemy's shot you don't see that kills you," he said.

"It's the hesitation when you should've pulled the trigger."

I nodded, the truth heavier than the alcohol in my blood.

As I stepped into the corridor, the thought stuck with me, colder than the recycled air:

I needed to make a choice.

And I needed to do it before the next shot came.

22

The science lab was sealed tighter than a miser's credit account. It took two separate identity checks before the pneumatic doors finally sighed open, releasing a puff of filtered air tinged with ozone and overwork.

Inside, the atmosphere crackled with tension and the faint hum of overlapping holographic displays. Primordian data fragments floated in the air like pieces of a shattered cosmic puzzle, each one demanding interpretation no one was qualified to give.

Sofia, Destiny, and Nicobe had been locked in here for nearly eighteen hours, and it showed. They moved around each other in a fatigued ballet of stubborn determination, their usual camaraderie hollowed out into brisk, quiet efficiency.

Sofia stood closest to the center, her honey-blonde fuzz now long enough to catch the light like a halo. She hadn't noticed me enter—or pretended not to. Her eyes were locked on a sequence of slowly rotating glyphs, fingers dancing through the air with surgeon-like precision. But her posture told a different story: stiff shoulders, clenched jaw, the subtle tension of someone carrying more than just professional strain. She'd been withdrawing for days now, retreating behind walls I couldn't breach, and I was starting to wonder if she'd let me try.

Destiny wasn't faring much better. Her usually animated face was set in lines of frustrated concentration. She paced back and forth between workstations, muttering calculations under her breath, occasionally shooting irritated glances at Nicobe's crimson dodecahedron hovering silently in the corner.

"Nicobe believes the sequential pattern suggests a gravitational constant," Destiny said to no one in particular, "but the tertiary alignment is completely inconsistent with standard Primordian numerical systems."

"Nicobe maintains that the inconsistency is itself the key," the igna's melodic voice replied from her floating capsule. "The ancient ones often encoded warnings through mathematical discordance."

That explained the tension. Nicobe had been interfacing directly with the Sovereign Archive we'd recovered, and the cognitive load was taking its toll. Ignae didn't experience mental fatigue the way humans did, but prolonged exposure to alien thought systems could cause what Nicobe called "conceptual dissonance." From the slight wobble in her capsule's hovering pattern, she was struggling.

"Lieutenant Commander Drake has arrived," Nicobe announced, a formal note in her voice that wasn't usually there. "Nicobe welcomes the commander's presence."

Sofia's fingers paused momentarily on the holographic interface, then resumed their work without acknowledging me. Destiny turned, her exhaustion momentarily masked by a flash of her old sarcastic grin.

"Well, well. The captain graces us with his presence," she said, but there was no genuine heat in the words. "Come to check if the science geeks have magically solved all your problems yet?"

"Just making the rounds," I replied, trying to keep my tone light. "Any progress worth reporting?"

The look that passed between Destiny and Sofia was brief but loaded with meaning I couldn't decipher. Their fingers brushed as Sofia passed a data tablet to Destiny, and they both flinched.

"We've been cross-referencing the Primordian cipher fragments," Sofia said, finally meeting my eyes. Her voice was professional, distant. "There are... concerning implications about the Ossuary Ring's structure."

"Concerning how?" I moved closer to the central holotable, where a three-dimensional model of the Ossuary Ring orbited a binary neutron star system. The detail was impressive—you could see the intricate honeycomb structure of the megastructure, the twin neutron stars pulsing with deadly radiation. *"Where twin death-light burns..."* I whispered, remembering Nekufima's words in my vision.

Destiny stepped forward, tablet in hand. "I think you should sit down for this one, Kory."

I remained standing. "Just give it to me straight."

She tapped the tablet, and the holographic display shifted, zooming in on a section of the Ossuary Ring. A pulsing red point appeared, labeled in both Standard and Primordian script.

"The Phylactery isn't just stored there," Destiny said, her voice uncharacteristically grave. "It's integrated into the structure. According to these specifications, it's a gravitational linchpin—part of the system that keeps those two neutron stars in stable orbit."

I stared at the display, not fully comprehending. "You're saying we can't remove it?"

"Nicobe is saying," the igna's capsule drifted closer, its crimson surface reflecting the holographic light, "that removing the Phylactery will destabilize the delicate balance between the neutron stars."

Sofia stepped in, her professional demeanor never slipping despite the enormity of what she was explaining. "The Primordians didn't just hide Nekufima away—they built her prison into the fundamental structure of the Ossuary Ring. The Phylactery acts as a sydereal anchor point, maintaining the precise gravitational equilibrium between the stars."

"So we find a way to replace it," I suggested, but the grim expressions facing me said there was more.

Nicobe's capsule pulsed once, projecting a new set of calculations into the air. "Nicobe has confirmed through independent analysis. The Phylactery's removal will trigger an irreversible gravitational cascade."

"In plain English," Destiny translated, "pull out the Phylactery, and both neutron stars go nova."

"Critical orbital decay would begin immediately," Sofia said, pulling up a simulation that showed the twin stars spiraling toward each other. "The gravitational waves might tear the Ossuary Ring apart within hours. Full stellar collision would follow within hours."

I watched the simulation play out, the neutron stars drawing inexorably together, their gravitational fields warping and merging until they triggered a cataclysmic explosion that engulfed the entire system in blinding light before the simulation abruptly ended.

"That," Destiny said quietly, "is a kilonova. Almost as

powerful as a standard supernova."

"A kilonova," Nicobe began, her capsule bobbing slightly as her voice took on the lecturing tone she used when explaining complex concepts, "is not merely a stellar explosion. It is the catastrophic collision of two neutron stars—the compressed cores of dead suns, each containing the mass of our sun crushed into a sphere no larger than one of your human cities." The holographic display shifted, showing two impossibly dense spheres circling each other in a death spiral. "When they merge, the results are... spectacular and horrifying."

The hologram expanded, showing the simulated collision in slow motion. The neutron stars, rendered in false color—one blue, one red—distorted as they approached each other, their surfaces elongating like liquid pulled by impossible tides.

"Neutron stars are the densest objects in the universe besides black holes," Nicobe continued. "A teaspoon of neutron star material would weigh approximately one billion tons on Earth. When two such objects collide, the energy release is... difficult for organic minds to comprehend."

The simulation showed the stars touching, then merging in a blinding flash that sent concentric rings of energy outward through the virtual space of the hologram. The light was so intense that the lab's automatic dimming systems engaged, casting strange shadows across our faces.

"The collision produces a brief gamma-ray burst," Nicobe's voice continued through the simulated cataclysm, "releasing more energy in seconds than your sun will produce in its entire lifetime. The explosion ejects neutron-rich material at nearly the speed of light, which rapidly decays into heavy elements—gold, platinum, uranium."

"The universe's most violent jewelry store," Destiny

muttered, but her usual sarcasm fell flat in the face of the simulated apocalypse playing out before us.

"The gravitational waves produced by such an event," Nicobe added, "are powerful enough to distort space-time across light-years. Nicobe's people first detected your humans using such waves."

Sofia stepped forward, her fingers moving through the holographic interface with practiced precision. The simulation reset, this time focusing on a time-lapse from the perspective of our ship's position relative to the Ossuary Ring.

"I've been reviewing the findings with the navigational data we have," she said, her voice clinically detached. "The timeline from triggering collapse to system-wide destruction is alarmingly brief." She highlighted a section of scrolling calculations. "Three to four hours from the moment the Phylactery is removed until total system annihilation."

"Four hours isn't enough time to clear the system," I said, the implications sinking in. "Even at maximum burn, we'd need at least seven to reach a safe distance."

"Seven hours, twenty-three minutes, and approximately twelve seconds," Sofia confirmed, not looking at me directly. "Assuming optimal engine performance, which we currently don't have after the damage sustained during our escape."

The weight of this revelation settled over the lab like a physical pressure. I could see it in the tight set of Destiny's shoulders, in the way Sofia's fingers tensed against the edge of the console, in the subtle fluctuations of Nicobe's capsule illumination.

"So the Phylactery is unretrievable," I said, trying to keep my voice steady. "Mission scrubbed."

"Not necessarily unretrievable," Destiny countered,

though she didn't sound particularly enthusiastic about whatever alternative she was considering. "Just unretrievable without sacrificing whoever goes to get it."

"Unacceptable," I snapped, the word coming out harsher than I intended. "We don't leave people behind. That's not how we operate."

"The mission parameters may require reevaluation," Sofia said quietly, still not meeting my eyes. "The importance of obtaining the Phylactery—"

"Doesn't outweigh human lives," I cut her off. "What I want to know is why anyone—Primordian or otherwise—would design such a suicidal trap in the first place? What's the point of a security system that kills everyone, including the ones trying to access the thing being protected?"

Nicobe's capsule drifted to the center of our small circle, her crimson surface reflecting our tired faces like a distorted mirror. "Nicobe has formulated a hypothesis based on the fragmentary data recovered. It is... disturbing."

"More disturbing than a star-destroying booby trap?" Destiny asked.

"The Primordians were not careless engineers," Nicobe said. "Their technological sophistication far exceeded even the current Collective Dominion standards. If they created a system designed to trigger mutual destruction, it was not by accident or oversight."

"They meant for it to happen," Sofia concluded, her analytical mind following Nicobe's logic.

"Correct." Nicobe's capsule pulsed once, projecting a small fragment of Primordian text that rotated slowly in the air. "This glyph sequence, when properly interpreted, suggests not a warning but a purpose. Nicobe believes the Phylactery's occupant—Nekufima—was considered so dangerous that the ancient builders decided the only acceptable outcome of any rescue attempt was mutual annihilation."

"What could be so dangerous," I asked, "that destroying an entire star system was considered a reasonable containment measure?"

"The Primordians were not given to overreaction," Nicobe replied. "If they deemed this necessary, then Nekufima represents a threat category beyond standard classification."

"Fantastic," Destiny threw up her hands. "So we're either abandoning the mission or committing suicide to retrieve an entity so dangerous that an advanced civilization thought blowing up two stars was a proper security system."

"There may be alternatives we haven't considered," Sofia said. Her voice was measured, professional, but I could see the exhaustion pulling at her. "We need to analyze the structural design more thoroughly. Perhaps there's a way to stabilize the system while removing the Phylactery."

"Nicobe considers this unlikely," the igna responded. "The integration appears deliberate and fundamental."

As they debated, something strange happened. A sound —no, not even a sound, more like the suggestion of a sound —whispered at the edges of my awareness. At first, I dismissed it as fatigue, the kind of auditory hallucination that comes from too much caffeine and too little sleep.

But it persisted, growing incrementally stronger with each passing second. A whisper that seemed to originate not from the room around me, but from somewhere inside my own mind. Sydereal echoes, similar to what I'd experienced in the Syderealium, but more focused, more... intentional.

"Kory?" Destiny's voice seemed to come from very far away. "You okay? You zoned out for a second there."

I blinked, realizing I'd been staring at nothing. "Did you hear that?"

"Hear what?" Sofia asked, suddenly alert, her personal distance temporarily forgotten.

The whisper came again, clearer this time. A voice that slid through my consciousness like silk over steel. Female, ancient, amused. Saying my name, calling to me from across impossible distances.

"Nothing," I lied, shaking my head. "Just tired."

But as the debate resumed around me, the voice came again, unmistakable now:

Come to me...

I felt cold, not from fear but from certainty. Nekufima, an entity dangerous enough to warrant a stellar self-destruct mechanism, was reaching out across space—reaching specifically for me.

We needed to keep her out of the hands of the Kergans and the Dominion rebels.

But she was too dangerous to keep to ourselves.

Maybe the best thing we could do—the wisest action—was to trigger the kilonova and allow it to destroy the Phylactery and Nekufima together.

23

The M-type star hung in the viewport like a dying ember, casting a dull crimson glow across Thunder's battle-scarred hull. I'd chosen this forgotten system precisely because no one would think to look for us here—just a scattering of dead rocks and a gas giant, ideal for hiding, refueling, and licking our wounds.

We'd spent five long days anchored to a miserable little asteroid, the nanoforge humming nonstop as it rebuilt our shattered stern bolster. Five days of waiting, watching, half-expecting a Kergan gunship to drop in uninvited.

But now the repairs were finished. We were mobile again. I should've been able to breathe.

I was wrong.

"Nanoforge operations complete, Lieutenant Commander," Nicobe announced from her engineering station, her crimson capsule hovering with an almost smug air of efficiency. "Nicobe has confirmed optimal integrity restoration of the stern bolster. Structural integrity now at ninety-seven percent of design specifications."

"Only ninety-seven?" I asked, rubbing my gritty eyes.

"Nicobe reminds the captain that perfection is an asymptotic value," she replied, the edges of her geometric form pulsing with amusement. "Given our limited resources, this outcome should be celebrated rather than questioned."

I snorted. "Fair enough. Let's move to phase two."

The gas giant loomed ahead, its swirling bands of amber and copper growing in our viewports as *Thunder*'s tractor pods pushed us forward. The planet was a treasure trove of helium-3, exactly what we needed to top off our fusion reserves. Standard procedure: dip into the upper atmosphere, extend the scoops, fill the tanks, get out. Textbook stuff, which was why I had mixed feelings about having all my senior officers on the bridge at once.

Destiny stood at tactical, her fingers dancing across the holographic interface with practiced precision. Sofia monitored comms and sensor arrays, her face a mask of concentration that couldn't quite hide the shadows under her eyes—another night of Kergan-implant-induced nightmares, I suspected. And then there was Phoebe, who'd volunteered to assist with the engineering controls despite it not being her scheduled duty. She kept finding excuses to brush past my station, each time leaving behind the faint scent of some floral soap that definitely wasn't standard UHC issue.

I guided *Thunder* into a gentle descent vector, the first tremors of atmospheric contact humming through the deck plates beneath my boots. "Prepare to extend collection scoops on my mark."

The planet's gravity pulled at us, but it was only about the size of Saturn—just over one gee. Comfortable enough. A far cry from the 2.5 gees Jupiter once tried to crush us with.

"Scoops prepped and ready," Phoebe confirmed, throwing me a smile that lingered a beat too long.

"Atmospheric density within optimal parameters," Sofia added, her voice clipped, her eyes flickering briefly toward Phoebe with unmistakable irritation.

The tension between them had not decreased at all. I wasn't an idiot—I knew exactly what was happening. Phoebe's interest in me wasn't exactly subtle, and Sofia's patience with it was wearing thinner by the day. I'd been hoping they'd sort it out professionally, but the glacial looks passing between them suggested otherwise.

"Mark. Extend scoops."

The ship shuddered slightly as the massive collection arrays unfurled from *Thunder*'s flanks, reaching out to gulp hydrogen and helium from the gas giant's atmosphere. From there, *Thunder's* enrichment plant would extract helium-3. The readouts showed a steady trickle into our reserves—all nominal, all routine.

Until my comm panel lit up with an internal transmission from the officer's wardroom, flagged urgent.

"Bridge, this is CPO Rayburn." The voice sounded strained. "Sir, Chief Kohl and Lieutenant Brooks are having... an altercation. It's getting heated."

I glanced up to see both women had vanished from their stations. Fantastic timing.

Destiny caught my eye. "How did they both slip out? I didn't—"

"Doesn't matter. We need them back at their posts. Now." I kept my voice level despite the surge of anger. "Go get them, Des."

She nodded sharply and headed for the exit at a quick jog.

"And tell them this isn't a goddamn cocktail party they

can just wander away from!" I called after her.

The door hissed shut, leaving me alone on the bridge with Nicobe's hovering form for company and a few enlisted spacers. I sighed and turned back to the helm controls. Thunder rode the atmospheric currents like a surfer on a gentle wave, the collection readouts showing we were at 13% capacity already.

The first alarm caught me mid-yawn.

A yellow caution indicator flashed on the fuel intake panel—just a minor imbalance between port and starboard scoops. I tapped a correction into the system, expecting the light to go green.

It didn't.

Instead, a second alarm joined the first—tractor pod power fluctuation. Then a third: forward pitch warning.

"Nicobe, what am I looking at?" I asked, keeping my voice steady even as my pulse kicked up.

"Analyzing," she replied, her crimson form pulsing more rapidly. "Detecting irregular pressure variation in the starboard collection scoop. Compensating."

A violent shudder ran through the deck plates. Not the gentle vibration of atmospheric entry—this was the ship fighting itself.

"Starboard tractor pod experiencing power fluctuations," Nicobe reported, her normally measured tone accelerating. "Nicobe is detecting—"

Thunder lurched suddenly, the nose dipping sharply toward the planet. My stomach dropped with it as I grabbed the console to stay upright.

"Nicobe is reporting catastrophic failure of starboard tractor pod!" Her form flashed urgently. "The starboard scoop backpressure has created a surge in the intake manifold. *Thunder* is experiencing severe destabilization of forward trim."

My fingers flew across the helm controls. "Retract the starboard scoop!"

"Nicobe cannot comply. The backpressure has physically jammed the actuator mechanism."

Another violent tremor, stronger than the first, and the ship's nose pitched further downward. Warning lights cascaded across every panel on the bridge. The viewscreen showed nothing but the swirling depths of the gas giant's atmosphere, growing denser and more turbulent as we plunged deeper.

"Reinitializing helm control," I barked, fighting the stick that suddenly felt dead in my hands. The ship wasn't responding—not to automated commands, not to manual override. Every correction I attempted resulted in a negligible response from the remaining tractor pods.

"Atmospheric pressure increasing beyond operational parameters," Nicobe warned. "Hull stress indicators approaching yellow line. Drag coefficient increasing exponentially."

The deck angled more steeply beneath my feet as *Thunder* accelerated into the gravity well. Sweat beaded on my forehead despite the climate controls. We were falling—not drifting, not descending, but falling—into a planet that would crush us like an empty beer can.

"Where the hell is Destiny?" I muttered, frantically trying another override sequence. "Where is everybody?"

But I knew the answer. They were dealing with a petty argument while our ship dove toward oblivion.

The primary display showed our depth and velocity in stark, unforgiving numbers. At this rate, we had less than three minutes before we hit crush depth.

I slammed my fist on the all-ship comm. "All hands to

emergency stations! This is not a drill!"

My voice echoed through empty corridors as *Thunder* continued its deadly plunge.

The hull integrity alarm had a special way of turning your spine to ice. Not the standard warning tones we'd all grown used to—this was a primal scream of tortured metal, the sound of Thunder telling us she was being crushed alive. Red emergency lighting bathed the bridge in the color of blood as localized heating warnings flashed across my console. Somewhere below, on deck nine, crew members were running for their lives as the gas giant's asphyxiating atmosphere leaked in at high pressure. I had maybe ninety seconds before critical structural failure turned us all into a smear of organic material compressed into a ball the size of my fist.

"Confirmed hull breaches, Decks Nine and Ten!" the damage control officer's voice crackled over the comm, straining above the blare of alarms. "Bulkheads are sealed, but we're losing structural integrity in Compartments Two-Three through Two-Seven!"

The ship groaned—not the familiar sound of a vessel under stress, but something deeper, more primal. The sound of something dying.

"Sixty-four seconds to critical atmospheric crush," Nicobe announced, her crimson form pulsing rapidly. "Nicobe suggests immediate ascent is imperative for crew survival."

"No shit," I muttered, hands dancing across controls that might as well have been decorative for all the response I was getting.

The bridge door slid open with a hydraulic hiss, and Destiny burst in, hair wild, eyes wide. She took one look at the emergency lights and the steep angle of the deck and snapped into action.

"What the hell's happening?" she demanded, lunging for her station.

"Starboard scoop jammed open, starboard tractor pod dead, and we're diving into crush depth," I answered, clipped and fast. "Where are Brooks and Kohl?"

"Busto's got them. He's read them the riot act—they're heading to emergency stations." She didn't look up from her console. "Dammit, the automatic responses are too slow. The system's still trying standard protocols."

The ship lurched again, throwing me against my restraints. Another warning appeared on my display—the forward hull temperature was spiking as we plunged deeper into the denser atmosphere.

I took a deep breath and did what I was trained to do—I took command.

"Override the automated response systems," I ordered, my voice finding a clarity I didn't know I possessed. "Reroute all available power to the remaining tractor pods. We need maximum thrust at a seventy-degree vector from our current heading."

Destiny's fingers flew across her console. "The safety interlocks won't let me allocate that much thrust differential —"

"Override them. Authorization Drake-Alpha-Three-Seven."

"That's going to strain the structural integrity even more—"

"We're dead anyway if we don't get out of this dive." I stabbed at my comm. "Nicobe, I need more power to the working pods. Whatever you've got."

"The chromatic batteries are already at one hundred and three percent of rated output," her voice replied.

"Pushing beyond current thresholds will result in system damage—"

"I don't care if they explode afterward. We need power now!"

A moment of silence, then: "Nicobe acknowledges. Bypassing safety protocols. Chromatic battery output now at one hundred and twenty percent and rising. Thermal warnings indicated."

The deck vibrated beneath me as the overtaxed power systems dumped energy into the remaining tractor pods. The nose of the ship started to respond, trying to pull up against the planet's relentless pull.

But we were still falling too fast.

"Busto," I called into the comm. "I need that starboard scoop retracted or we're dead. Tell me you've got something."

His voice came back strained, with the sounds of shouting and metallic banging in the background. "We're at the control junction, sir. The actuator's completely jammed—pressure differential's too strong. We can't move it manually."

I felt sweat trickling down my spine despite the climate controls. "Then un-jam it. Whatever it takes."

"Sir..." There was hesitation in his voice. "We could use a breach charge. Blow the whole assembly free."

"That'll cause more structural damage," Destiny warned.

I glanced at the countdown timer. Forty-three seconds. "Do it, Busto. Now!"

The moments stretched as we waited. The ship continued to groan, metal stress sounds becoming more pronounced. A secondary alarm joined the chorus—power fluctuations throughout the ship as Nicobe pushed our systems beyond their limits.

"Fifteen seconds to charge placement," Busto reported. "Clear the adjacent compartments!"

I turned to Destiny. "We need to lose mass. Dump the primary water tank."

Her eyes widened. "That's three days of reserve—"

"Dump it. Now."

She hit the commands, and somewhere below us, thousands of liters of water were jettisoned into the atmosphere, instantly vaporizing in the heat and pressure.

The ship jerked upward slightly, but not enough.

"Breach charge in three... two... one... FIRE IN THE HOLE!"

The deck shuddered as a controlled explosion ripped through the outer hull. For a sickening moment, everything went silent.

Then: "Actuator assembly destroyed! Scoop is retracting!" Busto's triumphant voice filled the bridge.

"Thrust now!" I shouted, slamming the controls forward.

The remaining three tractor pods screamed in protest as they pushed against the enormous pressure. The ship's nose began to rise, the angle of our descent finally shifting.

"Structural integrity at thirty-seven percent and falling," Nicobe warned. "Chromatic batteries experiencing critical thermal events. Shutdown imminent."

"Hold them together just a little longer," I pleaded, watching as our trajectory slowly, painfully curved upward.

The viewscreen showed the swirling gases beginning to thin as we clawed our way back toward space. I felt the ship shuddering around us, pieces of the outer hull tearing away in the violent ascent. Alarms continued to sound, but they were changing character—no longer warning of imminent crush depth, but of system failures and damage.

"Come on, baby," I whispered to *Thunder.* "Just a little more."

The stars appeared in the viewscreen—first one, then dozens, then the blackness of space spreading across our view. The violent shaking subsided as we pulled free of the planet's atmosphere, a trail of escaping gases streaming behind us from the hull breaches.

I sagged in my chair, suddenly aware that I'd been holding my breath. Around me, the bridge crew exhaled in unison.

"We've cleared the upper atmosphere," Destiny confirmed, her voice hoarse. "Stable orbit established."

"Damage report," I managed, my mouth dry as dust.

"Hull breaches on decks seven through ten, sections 19 through 31," Nicobe reported. "Starboard tractor pod destroyed. Chromatic batteries at fourteen percent capacity and requiring full replacement. Life support functioning at reduced efficiency. Nanoforge will require approximately fifty-two hours to affect critical repairs."

I nodded slowly, the adrenaline beginning to ebb from my system, leaving behind a bone-deep exhaustion.

"And the casualty report?" I asked, dreading the answer.

"Three injuries reported. No fatalities," Destiny said, a note of wonder in her voice. "It's a miracle, Kory."

Not a miracle—just a crew that performed when it mattered most, despite everything. I looked around the battered bridge, the lighting dimmed to emergency levels, damage indicators flaring like warning beacons across *Thunder's* wounded frame.

Flying inside a gas giant always felt like tempting fate. There was no solid ground to crash into—just endless pressure waiting below, growing denser with every meter. If anything failed—if propulsion cut out, if stabilization systems buckled—the planet wouldn't hesitate. It would just pull us down, dragging the ship into its crushing depths until we were nothing but compressed vapor and scattered molecules. Every second inside that atmosphere was a calculated risk. And this time, we'd cut it too close.

"Begin damage control procedures," I ordered, my voice steadier than I felt. "And when we're stable... I want to see the command staff in the briefing room."

Thunder limped through the upper layers of the gas giant, trailing atmosphere like blood in water.

But we were alive. For now, that was enough.

24

The briefing room felt like a funeral parlor as my command staff filed in one by one. I stood at the head of the table, back straight as a rifle barrel, jaw clenched tight enough to crack walnuts. My uniform collar chafed against my neck like a reminder of the responsibility weighing on my shoulders. *Thunder* hummed beneath my feet, alive and whole despite our best efforts to become space debris in the atmosphere of a gas giant that, frankly, wouldn't have even noticed our passing.

I'd spent the last hour rehearsing this speech in my head, trying to find the balance between "terrifying commander" and "disappointed parent." Neither felt particularly comfortable, but comfort wasn't a luxury any of us could afford right now. The blue glow from the idle holo display cast everyone in the same cold light as they took their seats around the conference table.

No one spoke. That was a first.

Sofia entered last, her honey-blonde fuzz still damp from a shower, her face an expressionless mask that I'd come to recognize as her professional default. She sat as far from Phoebe as the table would allow, which wasn't saying much in *Thunder*'s compact briefing room. Phoebe's eyes flickered between me and Sofia, her fingers tapping a nervous rhythm on the polished surface of the table.

Destiny slouched in her chair, dark eyes darting around as though plotting multiple escape routes. As my XO, she knew exactly what was coming. I caught her gaze for a moment, and she gave me the tiniest nod. At least someone was on my side.

"I'll keep this brief," I said, the words falling into the silence like stones down a well. "We're currently en route back to the asteroid where we performed repairs, where we'll undergo *additional* repairs that will set us back at least a week." I paused, letting that sink in. "A week we don't have."

A few shifting bodies, a cleared throat, but no one interrupted. Smart.

"I've reviewed the logs from our little adventure in Balthazar's atmosphere." I leaned forward, placing my palms flat on the table. "Here's what I found: at 0743, the fuel scoop system reported an anomaly. Lieutenant Brooks was notified but was delayed in responding because she was engaged in what the log euphemistically calls 'a heated discussion' in the wardroom."

Phoebe's face flushed, but to her credit, she maintained eye contact with me.

"This discussion," I continued, "was with Chief Kohl, who was supposed to be monitoring sensor feeds for potential threats in the region."

Sofia's posture stiffened, her hands clasped so tightly her knuckles whitened.

"Commander Austin," I said, turning to Destiny, "left her

station on the bridge to intervene in this... discussion. During her absence, the automated alarm systems failed to register increasing pressure in the fuel manifolds because of a software patch that had been improperly installed during our rebuild."

The room temperature seemed to drop a few degrees. I wasn't imagining the shame that flashed across several faces.

"By the time anyone noticed the cascading failures, we had penetrated too deep into the atmosphere. The gravitational shear nearly tore our port stabilizers off. The heat damaged our sensor array. The pressure crushed our external comms relay." I ticked off each item like I was reading a grocery list, though inside my stomach was churning with the memory of how the ship had bucked and screamed around us.

"We didn't almost die because of malfunctioning fuel scoops," I said, my voice dropping lower, forcing them to lean in. "We almost died because personal conflicts interfered with duty. Because a ship can't function when its officers are too busy with their own drama to do their jobs."

I looked at each of them in turn. Sofia studied her tablet with sudden fascination. Phoebe found something interesting about her fingernails. Even Busto, who had nothing to do with the incident, couldn't quite meet my eyes.

"Let me be perfectly clear," I continued, the edge in my voice sharp enough to draw blood. "*Thunder* doesn't belong to me. It doesn't belong to any one of you. It belongs to all of us. And more importantly, we belong to it. When you put on that uniform, you made a promise that you would put this ship and its mission above your personal bullshit."

My hands were steady, but I felt a familiar heat rising in my chest—not quite anger, more like the disturbing clarity that comes when you realize just how close you came to death. I'd felt it before, in the streets of San Jose when I was younger. I'd felt it in the Syderealium facing Ban'ach. And now I felt it here, looking at my command staff—my friends—and knowing that their actions had nearly killed us all.

"The cascade of failures that followed our initial problems shouldn't have happened. Not on my ship. Not with this crew." I straightened up, my voice finding a dangerous calm. "We have been through too much together to end up as a cautionary tale in someone else's briefing room."

No one moved. No one spoke. The only sound was the steady hum of *Thunder*'s systems, oblivious to the human drama playing out within its hull.

I pushed away from the table and began a slow circuit around it, making eye contact with each officer as I passed. My boots made soft thuds against the deck plating, marking time like a metronome. I'd never been one for the theatrical aspects of command—the dramatic pauses, the carefully timed silences—but sometimes you need to let the moment breathe. Sometimes you need to let the weight of what almost happened settle onto shoulders that had gotten too comfortable.

"I'm not interested in apologies," I said, continuing my slow orbit of the table. "I'm not interested in explanations or excuses or who started what. What I'm interested in is making damn sure this never happens again."

Continuing, I said, "Personal conflicts are to be handled off-duty. Period." The words came out level, measured, but with an edge that even I could hear. "I don't care if you love each other, hate each other, or feel nothing at all. I don't care if you're sleeping together or can't stand to be in the same room. When you're on duty, you're officers of this ship first, and everything else second."

I completed my circuit and returned to my place at the head of the table, placing my palms flat on its surface and leaning forward.

"I don't care what's happening between any of you," I stated, making sure to look each of them in the eye, "but I will not allow it to endanger this ship or its crew again."

The silence that followed had weight to it. A few nodded. Some couldn't meet my gaze. Destiny's face showed approval, while Sofia's remained carefully neutral. Phoebe stared at her hands, her usual seductive confidence nowhere to be seen.

"Let me be clear about the consequences," I continued. "Any future incidents of this nature will result in formal disciplinary hearings. I will not hesitate to remove anyone from this ship—regardless of rank, position, or personal relationship—if they prove to be a liability rather than an asset."

I straightened up, clasping my hands behind my back. "Any crew member behaving in such a manner would deserve punishment, but for senior officers to be caught conducting themselves this way is unforgivable."

I let that word hang in the air for a moment. Unforgivable. Strong word. Maybe too strong. But I needed them to understand.

"You set the tone for the rest of the ship," I said, softening my voice just a fraction. "The crew looks to you not just for orders, but for examples. If you can't manage to put aside your differences when lives are on the line, what message does that send?"

Around the table, I saw different reactions playing out. Busto nodded slowly, his weathered face grim with agreement. Destiny glanced between Sofia and Phoebe with a clinical detachment that suggested she'd already diagnosed their interpersonal condition and found it terminal.

"I'm not asking you to be perfect," I added. "God knows I'm not. But I am asking—no, I'm requiring—that you be professionals. That you remember what it means to wear that uniform and serve on this ship."

I took a deep breath. "Dismissed."

They rose as one, the scrape of chairs against the deck breaking the spell that had fallen over the room. I watched them file out, noting the rigid set of Sofia's shoulders, the slight drag in Destiny's step.

Phoebe was the last to reach the door. She hesitated for just a moment, turning back as if to say something, then thought better of it and left.

The door hissed shut, leaving me alone with my thoughts, which were about as pleasant as a spacewalk without a suit. The decision I'd been avoiding since we limped away from the gas giant crystallized in my mind: Phoebe needed to go. Not because she wasn't good at her job—she was brilliant—but because the dynamic between her, Sofia, and, by extension, me had become toxic to the ship's function.

It wasn't a decision I wanted to make. It wasn't even one I was sure I had the right to make. But as I stood there in the empty briefing room, I knew it was necessary. The safety of my ship and crew had to come before any individual, including someone I'd once considered a friend.

My stomach churned at the thought of the conversations to come. I rubbed my face, feeling the stubble I hadn't had time to shave that morning. The irony wasn't lost on me—here I was, lecturing my officers about professionalism while looking like I'd just rolled out of a bunk after a three-day bender.

I straightened my uniform, tugging the wrinkles out of sleeves that had seen better days. *Thunder* needed its captain, not some conflicted man wrestling with personal loyalties. I squared my shoulders and headed for the door. The bridge was waiting, and so was the next crisis, because in space, there was always a next crisis.

That was the job I'd signed up for. That was the burden I'd chosen to carry. And despite everything—despite the near disasters and the hard decisions and the weight that sometimes threatened to crush me—I wouldn't have traded it for anything.

25

I stood at the viewport, watching the cratered surface of the moon grow larger as *Thunder* descended. The little rock orbiting the gas giant wasn't much to look at—pocked, gray, barren—but the sensors said it was rich with the minerals and elements we needed.

Four days of repairs ahead.

Four days to fix *Thunder's* wounds.

Four days to pretend I wasn't carrying one of my own that no amount of welding or rewiring could patch.

"Captain, final approach," Rivera called from the helm. "Touchdown in three minutes."

"Acknowledged," I said, turning from the viewport and sweeping my gaze across the bridge.

Everyone was focused on their tasks, exactly as they should be. Professional. Diligent.

None of them looking at the captain and his personal failures.

No one except me.

Thunder settled with a soft jolt as the landing struts

compensated for the uneven terrain. A heartbeat later, we were stable.

I didn't waste time.

"Commander Austin, get your teams ready for resource collection. Nicobe, I want a full repair assessment prioritized by criticality. Lieutenant Busto, set up a perimeter defense. We're sitting ducks out here."

Orders snapped out like reflexes. They moved fast, practiced.

We'd made emergency landings before. We'd survive this one too.

At least I'd trained them well. I still had that to hold on to.

The first day blurred past in a haze of activity.

We extracted ore from shallow veins just beneath the surface, fed it through Thunder's nanoforge, and began swapping out damaged hull plating and battery nodes.

I kept myself moving—from one repair site to the next, checking systems, making decisions, offering clipped encouragement—doing everything I could to be the captain they needed.

Maybe if I moved fast enough, worked hard enough, I wouldn't have to feel the other thing unraveling inside me.

I didn't see Sofia until the end of the first day.

She was outside what used to be our quarters, methodically packing the last of her personal items into a regulation duffel.

Her face was a mask of professionalism, every line set just right, every motion precise.

But her eyes gave her away.

They always had.

"Chief," I said, my voice clipped and formal. Several crew members passed by, their gazes flicking discreetly away.

"Captain," she returned, matching my tone without hesitation.

"I've moved my belongings to Lieutenant Zhang's quarters. She had an extra bunk."

"I see." My throat tightened. "Is that all?"

Sofia glanced at the others moving down the corridor. She hesitated.

"Permission to speak freely, sir?"

I jerked my chin toward the door.

We stepped inside. The door slid shut behind us—and with it, the mask fell away, as easily as removing a helmet.

"You humiliated me in front of the entire command staff," Sofia said, her voice low but edged with steel, her German accent sharpening with every word.

"I was doing my job, Sofia. You know you never should've left your duty station. We almost died because of it."

"It wasn't my fault," she shot back, keeping her voice level. "Phoebe followed me when I went to the head. She caught me off guard."

"I don't want excuses." I took a step closer. "There's no justification for the errors that were made. You should've returned to your post. And you need to ignore her and focus on your job."

Her expression froze, jaw tightening as her gaze drifted past me, staring hard at the bulkhead. "That's exactly what I'm going to do," she said, voice flat. "I have too many distractions in my life. Not least of which is you."

The words hit like a blade. I felt it—sharp and deep, like a red-hot poker twisting in my chest.

"That's not fair."

"She's been making advances toward you!" Sofia snapped, her eyes flashing—not just with anger, but hurt. "Right in front of me! And you—you just stand there and let it happen. So I will stand up for myself."

My hands had gone cold. My chest was tight, and my mouth was suddenly dry.

She wasn't wrong.

"I handled it poorly," I said, voice rough. "But you put me in an impossible position."

"And now I'm removing myself from it." Her tone was clipped, final. "You won't have to worry about me being distracted anymore."

She adjusted her uniform with slow, deliberate precision—like rearming herself in silence.

"This arrangement will be better for crew morale," she added. "And for mission effectiveness."

No shouting. No breakdown. Just the cold, efficient language of someone retreating behind regulations.

She was falling into her training. So was I.

"If that's your decision," I said quietly.

"It is."

She turned to leave, then paused for the briefest breath.

"I still care about you, Kory. I just need..." She swallowed. "I need space to process what's happening."

I nodded, because I didn't have the words to stop her.

She walked out without another.

The next days blurred into a grinding, colorless routine.

Wake up alone.

Check repair progress.

Solve problems.

Eat alone.

More repairs.

Sleep alone.

Repeat.

There's a unique kind of hollowness that comes from losing someone who's still right there—still serving beside you, still showing up to duty shifts, still breathing the same recycled air. When the connection frays, when the glances go cold and the silences stretch too long, it eats away at you from the inside. It makes the entire structure of your life—the routines, the responsibilities, even the mission—feel like scaffolding around something already dead. And in the quiet moments, when the tools are down and the hum of the ship is all that remains, you start to wonder why you're even bothering to hold it all together.

So, I threw myself into the work with a ferocity that even Busto couldn't ignore.

"You're pushing too hard, Captain," he said on the morning of the fourth day, as we inspected a newly repaired stabilizer assembly.

"Even Marine Raiders take breaks."

"The job needs doing," I replied flatly.

"And Sofia?" he asked, a little too carefully.

I gave him my best captain's stare. "That's not relevant to *Thunder's* operational readiness, Lieutenant."

He didn't push further. Busto knew when an order was final, even unspoken.

But the looks from the other crew told me everything I needed to know.

A starship's just a small town with engines bolted to it—tight quarters, recycled air, and nowhere to hide. People notice everything: a shift in someone's tone, an empty seat in the mess hall, a conversation that ends when someone walks in. Gossip spreads faster than plasma through a cracked conduit, and once it takes hold, it's almost impossible to shake. The worst part? Ship gossip rarely includes the whole truth. It mutates in transit, shaped by assumptions and half-heard comments. And when the thing they're whispering about is something you can't talk about —something classified, personal, or just too raw to explain —there's no way to correct the record. You're left watching your own story get rewritten in real time, unable to speak while everyone decides who you are without asking.

I ran my finger along the new seam of the heat exchanger, admiring the precision of the work. The repairs looked better than the original manufacturing—smoother welds, tighter tolerances. Nothing like mortal danger to inspire quality craftsmanship. Engineering hummed around me, the steady thrum of *Thunder*'s heart, keeping us alive in the vacuum. I'd always found comfort in this section of the ship, despite my habit of breaking things rather than fixing them.

"Nicobe is pleased to report the exchanger now operates at one hundred and three percent of original specifications," came the formal third-person declaration from behind me.

I turned to find Nicobe's crimson dodecahedron floating at eye level, the faces of her containment vessel catching the light from the overhead panels. The igna engineer had a knack for silent approaches.

"Good work," I nodded. "How's the primary coolant loop holding up?"

"Nicobe believes it will perform adequately for the foreseeable future." A slight pause, then: "Though 'foreseeable' has variable meaning in times of war."

"Doesn't it always," I muttered.

Phoebe Brooks appeared from behind a bank of control panels, datapad in hand, hair pulled back in a functional ponytail that somehow still looked deliberate and eye-catching. Her uniform fit her like it had been personally tailored, rather than mass-produced in a nanoforge. She'd been keeping her distance since my lecture to the command staff, but her eyes still lingered a half-second too long whenever they met mine.

"Captain," she said professionally, but with a smile that flirted with the boundaries of protocol. "I've completed the diagnostics on the auxiliary systems. Everything green across the board."

"Thank you, Lieutenant." I kept my tone neutral, my expression blank. "Were there any irregularities in the syderealdyne relays?"

"Nothing I couldn't handle." She stepped closer than necessary to hand me the datapad, her fingers brushing mine in the transfer.

Old Kory—single Kory—might have enjoyed the attention. New Kory—recently-dumped-by-Sofia Kory—found himself wrestling with a confusing mix of annoyance and temptation. I took a deliberate step back.

"Excellent work. Both of you." I included Nicobe in my nod. "*Thunder* couldn't ask for a better engineering team."

Phoebe beamed. "I've actually been working on a modification to the EPS grid that I think you'll find fascinating. Maybe we could discuss it over—"

The overhead speakers crackled to life with a ship-wide alert tone. "Captain Drake to the command deck immediately. Captain Drake to the command deck."

Saved by the bell. Or possibly doomed by it, depending on what waited for me up there.

"We'll continue this later," I said, already moving toward the exit.

"I look forward to it," Phoebe called after me.

The woman did *not* know how to give up.

I sprinted through *Thunder*'s corridors, crew members flattening themselves against bulkheads as I passed. The ship wasn't that large, but when you're running full-tilt, the distance from engineering to the bridge feels like a marathon. My lungs burned as I skidded onto the command deck.

Destiny sat in the captain's chair, her slight frame somehow filling the space with authority. She vacated it as soon as she saw me, moving to her XO station with fluid efficiency.

"What's the situation?" I dropped into the seat, still catching my breath.

"Sensor anomalies, Captain." Destiny's face was a study in controlled concern. "Multiple gravitational wave signatures detected about twenty minutes ago."

I turned to the sensor station. "Details?"

The operator—a young woman named Calahan—didn't look up from her displays. "Computer detected gravitational ripples consistent with vessels exiting veilspace, sir. Multiple signatures."

"How many? What type?" I leaned forward.

"Unknown, sir. We only detected the exit signatures. No other emissions yet." Her fingers flew over the controls. "Computer is still analyzing the patterns."

I exchanged looks with Destiny. Vessels appearing out of veilspace in this system wasn't good news. We'd chosen this location specifically because it was supposed to be deserted.

"Could be traders," Destiny offered, not sounding convinced.

"In this backwater? Not likely." I turned back to Calahan. "Any progress on the analysis?"

"One moment, sir... yes. Computer has a match." She

frowned at her screen. "Signatures are consistent with Collective Dominion warship engines."

The temperature on the bridge seemed to drop by ten degrees.

"Royalist or rebel?" I asked, though I already suspected the answer.

Destiny shook her head. "If Queen Zeta was sending ships this far behind enemy lines, she would have informed us through sydererealdyne channels. We've received no such message."

"Then they're Arctis's ships." I rubbed my jaw, feeling the stubble there. "The question is: what are rebel Dominion warships doing this deep in Kergan territory?"

"Maybe they're lost?" suggested the helmsman, earning a sharp look from Destiny.

"Dominion ships don't get lost," she replied. "Their navigational systems are as good as ours."

I drummed my fingers on the armrest of my chair. "Options?"

"We're not finished with repairs yet," Destiny reminded me. "And we're light on fuel. I say we hunker down. This moon's magnetic field and mineral composition make us hard to detect as long as we stay powered down. We watch and wait."

I nodded slowly. "Set condition yellow throughout the ship. Minimal emissions. Let's see what our unexpected visitors are up to before we make any moves."

As the crew acknowledged my orders, I couldn't help but wonder if our luck had finally run out. Four days of peaceful repairs had seemed too good to be true. In my experience, the universe rarely passes up an opportunity to kick you when you're down.

And with Sofia gone and *Thunder* still healing, I was

definitely down.

26

Hours ticked by on the bridge like prisoners marking days on a cell wall—methodical, inevitable, and painfully slow. I refused to leave my post despite Destiny's offers to take a shift. Sleep could wait; the safety of *Thunder* couldn't. I'd set up a makeshift command station with tactical displays linked directly to our sensor array, the data streaming in with maddening patience. Space doesn't rush for anyone, not even when your life depends on what's lurking in the dark.

The bridge operated in low-light conditions; the displays dimmed to reduce our energy signature. Crew members spoke in hushed tones, as if the enemy might hear us through the vacuum. Ridiculous, of course, but tension breeds superstition even among the most disciplined crews. The soft green glow from the night lighting cast everyone's face in ghostly light, turning familiar features into masks.

I sipped lukewarm coffee that tasted like it had been filtered through an old boot and reviewed the sensor logs for the tenth time. Nothing new. Nothing—

"Captain!" The electronic warfare operator—Ramirez, a wiry man with perpetually worried eyes—straightened suddenly in his seat. "Active sensors detected! Multiple sources, high-intensity sweeps."

I was at his station in three strides. "Show me."

The display lit up with incoming signal patterns, a complex matrix of frequencies and intensities that told a clear story to anyone trained to read them. Someone was scanning the system—not casually, but with military-grade sensor arrays turned up to maximum gain.

"They're lighting up the entire system," Ramirez said, fingers flying over his controls to capture and analyze the signals. "These are Dominion patrol patterns. Systematic sector-by-sector search."

I allowed myself a grim smile. "They just did us a favor."

Destiny joined us, her expression questioning.

"Space is big," I explained. "Impossibly, mind-numbingly big. Finding a powered-down ship on a resource-rich moon is like finding a specific grain of sand on a beach—at night, wearing a blindfold. Unless you know exactly where to look."

"Or unless you shine a spotlight on the entire beach," Destiny finished, understanding dawning.

"Exactly. Their active scans just made them visible to us." I turned to the tactical officer. "Start building a picture from these emissions. I want ship types, numbers, and vectors."

Over the next hour, the tactical display gradually populated with contacts. The data came in piecemeal—a propulsion signature here, a comm emission there, the distinctive energy pattern of Dominion tractor pods. Slowly, the enemy task force took shape on our screens like a photograph developing in a chemical bath.

"Four frigates," I counted, studying the formation. "Marava-class, looks like. And that's a Kytopo battlecruiser in the center." I pointed to the largest icon. "Plus, what appears to be a Lehony-class resupply vessel trailing the formation."

"That's a lot of firepower," Destiny murmured.

The task force moved in a classic wedge formation, the frigates forming a protective screen around the larger vessels. Their course was obvious—straight toward the gas giant we were orbiting.

"They're coming here for the same reason we did," I said. "Refueling. That Lehony can extract and process helium-3 from the gas giant's atmosphere."

Destiny nodded. "Standard procedure. The battlecruiser will maintain orbit while the resupply ship descends to collect fuel."

I ran a hand through my hair, calculating options. We couldn't outrun them—not with our fuel reserves so low. We couldn't outfight them—not with *Thunder* still nursing her wounds and outnumbered six to one. Hiding remained our best option, but even that had just become more complicated.

"We need to get into that gas giant's atmosphere ourselves," I said finally. "It's the only way to mask our signature completely and refuel at the same time."

"With that task force in orbit?" Destiny raised an eyebrow. "They'll detect our engine signature the moment we break from this moon."

"Then we need a diversion." I stood up straight, decision made. "Call the command staff to the briefing room. Busto, Sofia, Phoebe, and Nicobe. We need options, and we need them now."

As Destiny relayed the order, I took one last look at the

tactical display. The enemy formation continued its steady advance, each icon representing hundreds of crew members, thousands of tons of metal and weaponry. All looking for targets. All coming our way.

Just another day commanding *Thunder*. Part of me—the part that wasn't terrified—almost welcomed the challenge. It beat thinking about Sofia and empty quarters.

Almost.

The briefing room felt too small for the number of people and problems stuffed inside it. I took my place at the head of the table, scanning the faces of my command staff.

"You've all seen the sensor data," I began, activating the holographic display. The enemy task force appeared in miniature above the table, their formation rendered in red wireframe. "Six Collective Dominion vessels on approach to the gas giant. Four Marava-class frigates, one Kytopo battlecruiser, and one Lehony-class resupply ship."

"Rebel ships," Destiny added. "No sydérealdyne communications from Queen Zeta warning us about royalist operations in this sector."

"So they're Arctis's goons," Busto growled. "Question is: what are they doing this deep in Kergan space?"

"That's secondary to our immediate problem," I replied. "They're between us and our refueling opportunity, and they've got us outgunned."

"And we're running on fumes," Destiny added.

I nodded to Nicobe. "Give us the fuel situation."

Nicobe's capsule rotated slightly, her version of clearing her throat. "Nicobe must report that Thunder's helium-3 reserves stand at twenty-one percent capacity. This is insufficient for sustained operations at the Ossuary Ring."

"But enough to get us there?" I asked.

"Technically, yes," she replied. "However, Nicobe must emphasize that this would leave zero margin for navigational adjustments, evasive maneuvers, or unexpected developments."

"Which we can guarantee will happen," Destiny quipped.

"So we need to make another attempt to refuel from that gas giant." I pointed to the blue-green sphere in the holographic display. "The problem is getting to it without being detected by our friends in red here."

Sofia spoke for the first time, her voice coolly professional. "*Thunder* can hide effectively within the gas giant's upper atmosphere. Our hull composition is designed to withstand the pressure gradients, and the ionization would mask our signature."

Our eyes met briefly across the table. There was no warmth there, but no overt hostility, either. Just... distance. It stung more than anger would have.

"The issue isn't hiding in the atmosphere," I said, pulling my attention back to the problem. "It's getting there undetected. Once we break orbit from this moon, from this close to the task force, our engine signature will light us up like a beacon."

Busto leaned forward, his forearms creating dents on the padded tabletop. "We need to give them something else to look at. Pull them off station."

"A distraction," Destiny nodded. "But what? We don't exactly have spare ships to sacrifice."

Phoebe, who had been uncharacteristically quiet, suddenly straightened. "Emergency beacons."

All eyes turned to her.

"We have standard emergency beacons for escape pods," she continued, warming to her idea. "I could modify one to broadcast a signature that mimics a civilian transport in distress. If we attach it to one of our reconnaissance drones and fly it deeper into the system..."

"They'd investigate," Busto finished, nodding appreciatively.

"Dominion protocol requires warships to respond to distress calls, even from non-Dominion vessels," Sofia confirmed. Her eyes flickered to Phoebe, a flash of something—respect, maybe—crossing her features. "It's part of their expansionist doctrine. Rescue first, then recruit."

Phoebe didn't acknowledge Sofia's support, keeping her attention fixed on me instead. "I could have it ready in three hours, Captain."

"How far would the task force need to move to give us a clear window?" I asked, directing the question to the table at large.

Destiny tapped at her pad. "Based on their current patrol pattern and sensor coverage... at least two light-minutes. That would give us enough shadow to break orbit and dive for the giant's atmosphere."

"Nicobe suggests programming the drone to exhibit irregular movement patterns," the igna engineer offered. "Erratic course corrections and power fluctuations would enhance the appearance of a damaged vessel."

"And make it more likely they'd dispatch multiple ships to investigate," Busto added. "Maybe even split their formation."

The plan was taking shape, each officer contributing their expertise. Even with the personal tensions in the room, we functioned as a unit. It reminded me why *Thunder* had survived against the odds so many times before.

"We'll set the drone on a course that draws them away from our planned atmospheric entry point," I decided.

"Program it to malfunction completely once it's served its purpose."

"I'll work with Nicobe on the beacon modifications," Phoebe volunteered, a bit too eagerly.

"And I'll prepare the drone," Sofia said, rising. "With your permission, Captain."

I nodded. "Granted. Let's aim for execution in four hours. Busto, have your marines standing by for any contingency. Destiny, work up an atmospheric entry plan that minimizes our exposure time."

As they filed out, I caught Sofia's arm gently. She stiffened, but didn't pull away.

"Good input in there," I said quietly.

"Just doing my job, Captain." She glanced at where my hand touched her sleeve, and I released her.

"I know. Thank you."

After she left, I stood alone in the briefing room, staring at the holographic enemy fleet. One distraction, one narrow window, one chance to slip past. The math didn't add up to favorable odds, but *Thunder* had beaten worse.

Besides, calculated risks were my specialty. It was relationships that I couldn't seem to navigate without crashing into asteroids.

I shut down the display and headed for the bridge. Time to roll the dice again.

27

I watched Nicobe's dodecahedron capsule hover over the emergency beacon like a crimson jewel suspended in midair. Two days of repairs had left *Thunder* patched up enough to fly, but my confidence in her hull integrity was about as solid as my relationship status—technically functional, but questionable under pressure. The makeshift repairs would have to do. We didn't have the luxury of time, not with a rebel task force breathing down our necks and a race for the Phylactery underway.

"Nicobe is pleased with the modifications," the igna announced, her capsule rotating slightly as she inspected their handiwork. "The beacon's signal strength has been increased by thirty-seven percent."

Phoebe Brooks stood beside the drone, her slender fingers dancing across a diagnostic pad. She caught my eye and smiled. That smile—it had grown increasingly magnetic over the past few days, especially since Sofia and I had switched to separate quarters.

"We've adjusted the frequency to mimic distress

patterns typical of UHC vessels," Phoebe said, brushing a strand of brown hair behind her ear. "They'll think it's us, desperately calling for help."

"Let's hope they're desperate to answer," I replied, leaning against the bulkhead. My height gave me a clear view over the engineering team's shoulders as they made final adjustments.

"They will be," Phoebe said, her voice dropping to a confidential tone that invited me closer. "Especially with the modifications I made to suggest damage to a sydereal containment system."

I raised an eyebrow. "You're telling them we have a leaky nexus?"

"Not explicitly," she replied with a playful gleam in her eyes. "But I'm giving them enough breadcrumbs to draw that conclusion themselves."

"Nicobe approves of Lieutenant Brooks' cunning," the igna interjected. "The enemy will prioritize investigation of such a signal."

The next two days crawled by with the agonizing slowness of an academy ethics lecture. We launched the drone, watching on long-range sensors as it made its way deeper into the system, drawing closer to the red dwarf's gravitational embrace. I spent most of that time on *Thunder*'s command deck, alternating between monitoring the rebel task force and avoiding awkward encounters with Sofia in the corridors.

When the moment finally came to activate the beacon, I felt a flush of anticipation heat my face. My finger hovered over the command key.

"Sending activation code now," I announced to the bridge crew. "Let's see if our friends take the bait."

The minutes that followed were stretched taut with

tension. Nicobe's capsule remained perfectly still beside the tactical display, while Phoebe stood close enough that I could smell the faint trace of engine oil and something floral on her skin.

"Movement detected," called out our sensor officer. "The battlecruiser is breaking orbit. Three frigates are following formation."

I released a breath I hadn't realized I was holding. "Track their vector."

"They're moving in-system, Captain," the officer confirmed. "Directly toward the beacon's position."

"What about the others?" I asked, leaning forward in my chair.

"One frigate and the resupply vessel are maintaining position in low orbit around the gas giant."

Perfect. Not ideal, but workable. Two ships were manageable compared to facing the entire task force. I studied the tactical display, watching the orbital patterns of the remaining vessels. They'd circle to the far side of the gas giant in approximately forty-three minutes, giving us a narrow window of opportunity.

"Helm, plot a course to take us into the gas giant's atmosphere once those ships are on the opposite side," I ordered. "We're going gas mining."

The next hour was a carefully choreographed dance. We descended toward the massive planet as soon as the rebel ships disappeared behind its curve, dropping below their sensor range. *Thunder* shuddered as we hit the upper atmosphere, the ship's frame groaning in protest.

"Steady as she goes," I said, as much to myself as to the crew. "Take us deeper, below the cloud layer."

The viewscreen filled with swirling bands of amber and gold as we plunged hundreds of kilometers beneath the gas giant's cloud tops. *Thunder* was rated for atmospheric flight —but that didn't mean she excelled at it. She handled like a drunk elephant on a frictionless rink, every maneuver sluggish and overcorrected. Still, we kept her steady as we descended deeper into the pressure soup.

The memory of how close we'd come to being crushed during our previous attempt gnawed at the edge of my focus. One failure—just one—and the planet would've swallowed us whole, squeezing us into atoms without hesitation or ceremony.

"Beginning atmospheric collection sequence," Phoebe announced from her engineering station. Her fingers flew across the controls with practiced precision. "Deploying scoops now."

Thunder's specialized intake system extended into the dense atmosphere, filtering through the complex mixture of gases to isolate the precious helium-3 we needed for our reactor. The whine of the collection pumps created a rhythmic backdrop to the tense silence on the bridge.

"How long until we're refueled?" I asked, eyes fixed on the external sensors. Above us, somewhere beyond the thick atmospheric layers, two enemy ships continued their patrol, unaware of our presence.

"At current collection rates, approximately forty-eight hours," Phoebe replied. She hesitated, then added, "Assuming our compressors don't clog in this soup."

I nodded, settling in for a long wait. "Maintain minimal power signatures. Let's try not to announce our presence."

As *Thunder* drifted through the pressurized gases, harvesting fuel molecule by molecule, I couldn't shake the feeling that we were balanced on a knife's edge. One equipment failure, one sensor sweep at the right frequency by the rebel ships, and we'd be caught with our pants down in the middle of a refueling operation. But sometimes, the riskiest hiding place was the best one—right under your enemy's nose, or in this case, right under their feet.

"Nicobe will monitor the refining process personally," the igna announced, her capsule drifting toward the engineering access tube. "The composition of this atmosphere is... interesting."

As she disappeared down the corridor, Phoebe stepped closer to my command chair. "Two days trapped in a gas giant," she murmured. "Sounds like we'll have plenty of time to kill, Commander."

I met her gaze, realizing that being trapped in *Thunder*'s confined spaces with both Sofia and Phoebe for two days might prove more dangerous than the rebel forces circling above us.

I hunched over Nicobe's workstation in *Thunder*'s cramped signals intelligence compartment, watching as patterns of encrypted data streamed across her displays like digital confetti. We'd been at this for eighteen hours, tucked away in the belly of a gas giant while attempting to eavesdrop on our pursuers. My eyes stung from staring at screens too long, and my back protested the uncomfortable posture, but the alternative—letting an enemy task force blindside us—was considerably less appealing.

"Nicobe believes this encryption protocol is military-grade Dominion standard," the igna announced, her capsule rotating slowly beside the main console. "However, there are subtle variations that suggest a non-standard implementation."

"Can you crack it?" I asked, rubbing my neck.

"Nicobe finds your lack of faith disturbing," she replied, her capsule pulsing slightly—the igna equivalent of an indignant sniff. "It is merely a question of when, not if."

I suppressed a smile. For all her formalities, Nicobe's dry humor was one of the things that made endless hours of technical work bearable. Her crimson capsule bobbed and weaved through *Thunder*'s systems with the grace of a dancer, interfacing directly with our comm arrays as she worked her magic.

"The difficulty lies not in breaking their encryption," she continued, "but in the paucity of transmissions to analyze. The enemy maintains admirable communications discipline."

She wasn't wrong. The rebel ships were running nearly silent, exchanging only brief, encrypted bursts at irregular intervals. Professional. Cautious. Exactly what you'd expect from an elite Dominion task force.

"Keep at it," I said, reaching for my third cup of synthetic caffeine. "They'll slip, eventually."

Four hours later, they did. A longer-than-usual transmission burst between the battlecruiser and one of the frigates gave Nicobe the pattern she needed.

"Nicobe has identified a repeating sequence in their handshake protocol," she announced, her capsule vibrating with what I recognized as excitement. "Exploiting vulnerability now."

The displays flickered, then suddenly transformed from nonsensical garbage into orderly text and data. I leaned forward, scanning the intercepted communications with growing unease.

"Well, that confirms our suspicions," I muttered, pointing to a command signature embedded in the header. "These are Arctis loyalists."

Arctis—the name alone was enough to make my stomach clench. Once a respected Glyphspeaker in the

Collective Dominion, now the leader of the faction of rebels who had assassinated the queen. Unlike the rabble we usually dealt with, Arctis commanded genuine military assets and trained personnel. The kind who knew how to fight, how to plan, and, most worryingly, how to win.

"Nicobe concurs," she replied. "The command protocols match known rebel communication patterns. Most illuminating."

As we continued to analyze the decrypted transmissions, the picture grew clearer—and darker.

"Look at this," I said, highlighting a recurring phrase in the communications. "They keep referencing 'the containment device' and 'the entity'. That has to be the Noble Phylactery and Nekufima."

"Indeed," Nicobe agreed. "And observe the timestamp on this directive from the task force commander."

I read the highlighted message and felt a chill despite *Thunder*'s regulated temperature. The orders were explicit: secure the Noble Phylactery and the entity within it at all costs. Priority override on all other mission parameters.

"They're not just aware of the Phylactery," I drawled. "They're specifically hunting it. Their entire mission is to capture Nekufima before anyone else can."

"Correct," Nicobe confirmed. "And note the reference to competing interests."

She highlighted another message thread that mentioned "Kergan operations" and "royalist interception potential."

"Great," I sighed. "So we're caught in a three-way race between rebel forces, the Kergan Empire, and loyalists to the Collective Dominion throne."

"Indeed," Nicobe concurred.

"Right," I said with a grimace. "How could I forget that we're also in this mess?"

I stood and paced the small compartment, piecing together what we now knew. We weren't facing random rebel ships that had stumbled across us. This was a dedicated task force, likely composed of former Dominion special forces and intelligence operatives, with specific knowledge of the Phylactery. They knew exactly what they were looking for—and why.

"How bad would it be?" I asked Nicobe. "If Arctis got hold of Nekufima, I mean."

Nicobe's capsule dimmed slightly—her version of a grave expression. "Catastrophic. Arctis possesses the knowledge to potentially exploit the Phylactery's capabilities, but lacks the ethical restraints of proper Dominion protocols. The entity Nekufima, if controlled by such a faction, could become a weapon of unprecedented destructive potential."

I nodded, digesting this. "And the Kergans wouldn't be any better, would they?"

"The Kergan Empire's documented interest in weaponizing sydereal entities suggests they would pursue similar applications," Nicobe confirmed. "Though perhaps with less immediate competence and more... experimental casualties."

"And the royalists?" I asked, thinking about Zeta's faction.

"We would seek containment and proper study," Nicobe answered. "Though Nicobe notes that even the Dominion's official protocols for handling such entities have resulted in... unfortunate incidents."

I ran a hand through my hair, trying to process the magnitude of what we were involved in. We weren't just running from a superior force anymore. We were in a race for something that could shift the balance of power across known space.

"So we're facing an elite Dominion rebel task force," I summarized, "commanded by an experienced fleet admiral, who knows about the Phylactery, understands its value, and will stop at nothing to claim it first."

"An accurate assessment," Nicobe confirmed, her capsule rotating slowly in acknowledgment.

"Perfect," I muttered. "Just perfect."

Another analysis of the communications revealed one final, crucial piece of information—a timeline. The task force was operating under strict time constraints, racing to secure the Phylactery before either Kergan forces arrived or royalist Dominion vessels could intercept.

Which meant we weren't just facing a dangerous enemy—we were facing a desperate one. And in my experience, desperate enemies were the most unpredictable, and therefore the most dangerous of all.

28

After two days of floating in atmospheric limbo, *Thunder*'s reactor hummed with fresh helium-3, the gauge reading full for the first time since we'd left the Sol System. I stood on the bridge, watching the swirling gases of the giant planet churn outside our viewports like angry ghosts. We'd survived our impromptu gas mining operation—now came the tricky part. Getting out without being spotted by our rebel friends who, according to our intelligence, were still very much interested in adding us to their collection.

"Reactor at optimal capacity, Commander," Phoebe reported from engineering, her voice carrying a note of professional pride. "We've managed to isolate and refine enough helium-3 to power us for at least three jumps."

"Nicobe confirms the purity levels are exceptional," the igna said, her crimson capsule bobbing beside the engineering station.

She continued without pause, her voice brightening with barely contained excitement:

"The extracted helium-3 isotopic ratios are optimal,

demonstrating less than 0.003 percent molecular contamination across all collected samples, which is well within prime parameters for veilspace core utilization! This particular gas giant's atmospheric banding—specifically the lower equatorial strata where mining occurred—exhibits extraordinarily low levels of particulate hydrogen sulfide, carbonyl sulfide, and heavier isotopic pollutants, making it an ideal helium-3 source by historical Dominion standards! Nicobe must also note that the ambient magnetic field shielding provided excellent stabilization for containment protocols, resulting in a net loss of less than 0.05 percent raw material during scooping operations, which is—"

"—Exceptional. Got it," Destiny cut in dryly from the helm.

Nicobe's capsule gave a cheerful little tilt. "Nicobe is pleased that the crew shares her enthusiasm!"

"That's the first bit of luck we've had in a while," I muttered, turning to our helm officer. "Prepare for ascent. Keep our emissions as low as possible—I want to slip out like we're wearing thermal underwear in a blizzard."

The helmsman nodded, fingers dancing across his controls. "Course plotted for minimum detection profile, sir."

Thunder shuddered as we began our careful climb, the hull creaking under the pressure changes. Rising through a gas giant's atmosphere isn't like breaking orbit from a solid planet. It's more like swimming upward through increasingly thinner soup, fighting buoyancy changes and cross-currents that can spin you like a top if you're not careful.

"Stabilizers compensating for density gradient," the helm officer reported, his forehead beaded with sweat despite the bridge's climate control. "Estimated time to exo-atmospheric conditions: forty-seven minutes."

Those forty-seven minutes stretched like taffy. Every groan from *Thunder*'s frame sent a corresponding twinge through my spine. The ship had taken a beating before our impromptu repairs, and I wasn't entirely confident in her structural integrity. If she split a seam at this depth, we'd be crushed before we could even think about evacuation protocols.

As we finally broke through the uppermost wisps of the gas giant's atmosphere, our sensor officer called out: "Commander, I'm reading the rebel frigate and resupply vessel in high orbit. They appear to be maintaining a patrol pattern directly along our projected course to the Lagrange point."

I moved to the tactical display, studying the situation. The Lagrange point—that sweet spot of gravitational balance between the gas giant and the local star—was our optimal jump location. From there, we could make a clean translation into veilspace with minimal energy expenditure.

And it was currently hosting two enemy vessels.

"What about the rest of the task force?" I asked.

"Still deep in-system, sir. Long-range sensors show them clustered around our emergency beacon. They appear to be conducting a search pattern."

At least our distraction had worked. But that still left us with a problem—how to reach our jump point with two ships in the way.

"Options?" I asked, looking around the bridge.

Sofia spoke up from the tactical station, her voice professional despite the personal distance that had grown between us. "We could wait them out, sir. Their patrol pattern suggests they rotate back to the main task force every twelve hours."

"Too long," I replied. "The main force could return before

then, especially once they realize the beacon is a decoy."

"We could attempt a different Lagrange point," our navigation officer suggested. "There are three other candidates nearby."

I considered this, running the calculations in my head. "How long would it take to reach the nearest alternative?"

"Twenty-seven hours at stealth speed, sir. And it would take us on a vector that could cross paths with the returning task force."

Twenty-seven hours was an eternity when you were being hunted. And the risk of encountering the battlecruiser and its escorts was unacceptable. That ship outgunned us by a factor I didn't want to contemplate.

"What about a non-Lagrange jump point?" I asked.

Nicobe's capsule pulsed red in what I recognized as concern. "Possible, but inadvisable. The energy requirements would increase by sixty percent, and the translation stability would be compromised. Nicobe calculates a thirty-three percent increased risk of navigational errors in veilspace."

In other words, we might end up off course, or worse, lost in the dimensional chaos of veilspace. Not an option.

I stared at the tactical display, watching the two enemy ships patrol our escape route. The frigate was considerably weaker compared to *Thunder,* though likely with a more experienced crew. The resupply vessel would be lightly armed at best, designed for logistics rather than combat.

Two against one. But *Thunder* was by far the more powerful ship, as long as we didn't have to face the entire task force and that battlecruiser.

"We could take them," I said, almost to myself.

Sofia raised an eyebrow. "Sir?"

"The frigate and resupply ship," I clarified, straightening

up. "We hit them hard and fast, then jump before the rest of the task force can respond."

A tense silence fell over the bridge. Combat wasn't a decision to be made lightly, especially when retreat was an option, however risky.

"The rebel ships will notify the task force the moment we engage," Sofia pointed out.

"True," I acknowledged. "But signals will take time to reach the main force, and they'll need additional time to break orbit and intercept. If we're quick about it, we can be in veilspace before they get within weapons range."

I scanned the faces of my bridge crew. They were tired, stressed, but determined. They trusted me to make the right call, even when all the options came with significant risk.

"Nicobe, what's your assessment?" I asked.

The igna's capsule rotated thoughtfully. "The tactical variables favor a swift engagement over prolonged evasion. However, Nicobe would remind the Commander that Thunder sustained damage in our previous encounter. Our bolster resilience is compromised by approximately twenty-two percent."

"Noted," I said. Then, making my decision, I straightened my uniform and addressed the bridge. "Plot an intercept course for the enemy vessels. Weaps, prepare a full tactical solution on both targets. We're going to hit them hard, hit them fast, and be gone before they know what happened."

As the crew sprang into action, I felt that familiar mix of adrenaline and focus that comes before combat. We were committed now. No turning back.

"And someone, make sure our veilspace drive is primed and ready," I added. "The moment those ships are neutralized, I want to be gone."

I flexed my fingers, banishing the faint tremble that

threatened. Fighting was always a gamble, but sometimes, the direct approach was the only one that made sense. We needed that Lagrange point, and I was willing to take it by force.

We slipped through the vacuum like a shark through black water, running with minimal power signatures and every non-essential system dark. On the tactical display, the rebel frigate and resupply ship continued their lazy patrol, unaware that *Thunder* was gliding toward them on a carefully calculated intercept vector. My palms were slick with sweat as I gripped the edges of my command chair. The moment of commitment was approaching—that razor-thin line between stealth and all-out assault where there was no going back.

"Range to targets: twenty thousand kilometers and closing," the tactical officer reported, voice barely above a whisper despite the fact that sound doesn't travel in space. Old habits die hard when you're hunting.

"Weapons status?" I asked.

"Railguns charged and ready. Missile magazine one is on active."

I nodded, eyes fixed on the display. "Helm, maintain course. Engineering, prepare to divert full power to weapons and bolsters on my mark."

Phoebe's voice came through clearly on the comm channel. "Ready to reroute power on your command."

Next to me, Sofia monitored the enemy ships' movements with professional detachment. Whatever personal issues existed between us, she was still *Thunder*'s finest intelligence officer.

"Their patrol pattern is consistent," she reported. "No indication they've detected our approach."

"Fifteen thousand kilometers," the range officer called.

Close enough. Any closer and we'd risk detection, even in stealth mode.

I took a deep breath. "All hands, prepare for action. Active sensors online. Get me targeting solutions on both vessels and fire as soon as you have a lock."

Thunder woke up like a startled predator. Dormant systems surged to life, power coursing through weapons arrays as our active sensors reached out to paint the enemy ships with invisible fingers of electromagnetic radiation.

The rebel vessels reacted instantly, but not quickly enough. Our railguns spoke first, twin streams of hyperaccelerated metal slicing across space toward the frigate. Simultaneously, our missile tubes disgorged their deadly payload, six streaks of thrust blooming against the blackness of space.

"The frigate is going evasive!" Sofia called. "They're spinning up their point defense systems."

I had to admit, I was impressed. Despite being caught flat-footed, the rebel crew responded with disciplined precision. Their captain was good—better than I'd expected from Arctis's forces. Within seconds, their point defense lasers were tracking our incoming missiles, picking off three, then four of them in rapid succession.

It wasn't enough. The remaining two missiles slammed into the frigate's hull, followed by our railgun slugs. The tactical display showed their bolsters flickering under the assault.

"Direct hits," Sofia reported, a hint of satisfaction creeping into her voice. "Their forward hull is breached."

Before I could savor the moment, *Thunder* lurched violently. Warning indicators flashed across my console as something slammed into our port side.

"We've been hit," our damage control officer reported. "Railgun slug penetrated our outer armor layer on deck three. No hull breach, but we've lost some sensor arrays."

Another impact shook the ship, harder this time.

"Missile impact on forward shields. Bolsters holding at seventy percent."

I gripped my chair as *Thunder* shuddered again. "Return fire! Target their weapons emplacements."

Our gunners didn't need to be told twice. *Thunder*'s railguns cycled and fired again, the massive electromagnetic pulse sending meter-long slugs of dense metal toward the rebel frigate at a significant fraction of light speed. This time, we were rewarded with a visible explosion as one of our rounds punched through their weakened hull and tore into their primary weapons array.

Meanwhile, the resupply ship was attempting to put distance between itself and the battle, its engines flaring brightly as it accelerated away.

"Oh no you don't," I muttered. "Helm, adjust course to pursue the resupply vessel. Weapons, give me a firing solution."

"Resupply ship targeted," the weapons officer confirmed. "Firing railguns and launching missiles."

Two missiles and two railgun slugs streaked toward the fleeing supply ship. With minimal defensive capabilities, the vessel stood little chance. The first railgun slug shattered its meager shields. The second tore through its engine housing, leaving a spray of debris and venting atmosphere in its wake. The missiles finished the job, detonating against the vessel's hull in a series of blinding flashes.

"Resupply ship's primary engines are disabled," Sofia reported. "It's adrift and venting atmosphere from multiple hull breaches."

"Back to the frigate," I ordered, as *Thunder* rocked from another impact. "Concentrate fire on their propulsion systems."

Two missiles launched in a synchronized salvo, while both railguns recharged and fired again. The frigate, already damaged from our initial assault, attempted evasive maneuvers, but with half its thrusters damaged, it was like watching a wounded animal try to run. Our missiles found their mark, detonating along the ship's engine compartments in a chain of explosions that left it spinning helplessly.

"Enemy frigate's propulsion is offline," Sofia announced. "Their weapons are still operational, but at reduced capacity."

"Finish them," I ordered, watching the tactical display with grim satisfaction. "Target their remaining weapons systems."

Thunder delivered the *coup de grâce* with merciless efficiency, our railguns punching through the frigate's compromised hull until it was little more than a gutted hulk drifting in space.

"Check communications," I said. "Are they calling for help?"

Our comms officer nodded grimly. "Emergency signals detected, Commander. The resupply ship is broadcasting distress calls on all frequencies."

"How long before the main task force responds?"

"Given their current position, approximately three hours until they could reach our location."

"Plenty of time," I said, relief washing through me. "Helm, set course for the Lagrange point. Engineering, charge the veilspace drive."

As *Thunder* accelerated away from the disabled vessels, I

studied the damage reports flowing across my display. We'd taken hits, but nothing critical. Our bolsters had absorbed the worst of it, and the hull breaches were manageable. All things considered, we'd gotten off lightly.

"Approaching Lagrange point," the helm officer reported. "Veilspace drive at eighty-five percent charge."

I watched the countdown tick down, acutely aware that somewhere in the system, a rebel battlecruiser and its escorts were already moving to intercept us. But they'd be too late.

"Veilspace drive fully charged," Phoebe's voice announced from engineering.

"Execute jump," I ordered.

Space twisted around us as *Thunder* translated into veilspace, the normal universe falling away to be replaced by the swirling, chromatic chaos of dimensional transit. The familiar sensation of displacement washed over me—that momentary feeling that my insides were slightly to the left of where they should be.

I released my white-knuckled grip on the command chair and allowed myself a moment to breathe. Through the viewscreen, the shifting colors of veilspace rippled and flowed like luminous oil on water. Beautiful, in its alien way.

"Set course for the Ossuary Ring," I instructed the navigation officer. "And let's hope we can find the Phylactery before our friends catch up."

Because this race was far from over. We'd escaped by skill and a little luck, but the rebel task force would be right on our heels. Worse, the engagement had broadcast our presence and destination to anyone with a decent long-range sensor array. The hunt for Nekufima's Phylactery was no longer a secret—it was about to become a very public, very dangerous competition.

I stared into the swirling colors of veilspace and tried not to think about what would happen if we lost that race. Some things were better left uncaptured, and ancient, malevolent cosmic entities definitely topped that list. Unfortunately, I seemed to be in the minority with that opinion.

29

Veilspace made my skin crawl. Three weeks of swimming through the dimensional fold between realspace and the Syderealium, feeling that persistent electric tingle at the base of my skull. Some captains got used to it. I never did. Seventeen thousand light years stretched ahead of us—a journey that would have taken centuries in normal space—and somewhere out there, I was certain, ships were following us. Hunting us. I just couldn't prove it.

Thunder vibrated beneath my feet, a gentle hum that most of the crew found reassuring. To me, it was the sound of vulnerability. We were blind in transit, deaf to the universe outside our contained pocket of reality. The occasional shimmer of blue light along the corridors—power conduits channeling energy through the ship—was our only reminder that we were still connected to anything at all.

The mess hall had transformed into what I privately called the Anxiety Hub. Conversations dropped to whispers when officers entered. Crew members huddled in tight groups, stealing glances at the doors. The usual card games had multiplied, desperate distractions from our three-week journey into the unknown.

I found Destiny hunched over a mug of something that smelled vaguely like coffee but definitely wasn't. Her curly black hair was tied back in a practical knot, her dark eyes scanning a datapad.

"That stuff'll kill you faster than the Kergans," I said, sliding into the seat across from her.

She glanced up, a tired smile tugging at her lips. "Bold of you to assume I want to live through this suicide mission." She pushed the mug away. "Three weeks in this metal coffin. Longest transit we've ever attempted."

"Thanatos system. Fitting name for our destination."

"Yeah, because we might be dead before we get there." Destiny leaned forward, voice dropping. "Listen, I've been thinking about our tail."

My stomach tightened. So she felt it too. "You think we're being followed?"

"I know it in my bones. The Kergans won't just let us disappear with what Sofia's got in her head. And the Dominion rebels? After what we did to their fleet? They're out for blood."

I rubbed my jaw, feeling the stubble I hadn't bothered to shave. "The question is, who gets to us first?"

"My money's on the Kergans. They've got better tracking tech, probably tagged us somehow before we jumped." She tapped her fingers on the table, a nervous habit she'd had since we were kids on the streets. "The rebels have numbers, but they're disorganized since we took out their command structure."

"Either way, we've got enemies on both sides, and we're heading deeper into unexplored space than any UHC ship has gone before." I kept my voice steady, captain-like, though my insides felt like they were being stirred with a rusty spoon. "Any suggestions, XO?"

Destiny's lips quirked. "Besides prayer? Not really. But we should run some more battle drills. The crew's getting edgy just sitting around waiting."

I nodded. "Good call. I'll set something up." I hesitated, then asked the question that had been gnawing at me. "You think we can evade them? Realistically?"

Her face softened slightly. "Realistically? We're outnumbered and outgunned. But we've got the best damn captain in the fleet, and a crew that's pulled off the impossible before." She shrugged. "Besides, they have to catch us first."

"About that." I stood up. "I need to talk to Nicobe."

I found our Heliacal engineer in her domain—the pulsing heart of *Thunder*'s engine room. Her crimson dodecahedron capsule hovered at eye level, the gentle hum of her antigrav unit barely audible over the thrum of the veilspace drive.

"Lieutenant Commander Drake," she greeted me, her capsule rotating slightly. "Nicobe observes the commander appears troubled. Is there a technical issue with *Thunder*'s systems?"

"Not exactly. I was wondering if there's any way to detect other ships while we're in transit. Some kind of... veilspace radar?" Even as I said it, I knew how ridiculous it sounded.

Her capsule tilted. "Nicobe regrets to inform the commander that such detection is fundamentally impossible. Veilspace exists as a dimensional manifold outside conventional spatial parameters. Each ship creates its own isolated pocket of reality during transit."

"So we wouldn't know if we had company until we dropped back into normal space?"

"That is correct. Veilspace communications are similarly impossible between separate vessels. It is why veilspace jumps must be precisely calculated before departure. Nicobe could elaborate on the mathematical impossibilities of cross-dimensional detection if the commander wishes a more thorough explanation."

"No need," I said quickly, knowing her thorough explanations could last hours. "I was just hoping..."

"The commander is concerned about pursuit." It wasn't a question. “Nicobe understands the commander's concerns. Yet she must observe: the unchangeable must be endured—and the unseen cannot be evaded.”

I sighed. "That's what I was afraid of."

"If it provides comfort," she added, her tone softening slightly, "the vastness of space provides its own protection. The mathematical probability of intercepting *Thunder* at our exact emergence point is exceptionally small."

"Unless they know where we're going."

Nicobe's capsule pulsed once, an igna gesture that meant acknowledgment. "Indeed. In which case, Nicobe suggests *Thunder* be ready for immediate defensive action upon arrival."

I nodded, the familiar weight of command settling more heavily on my shoulders. "Thanks, Nicobe."

As I walked back through the humming corridors of my ship, I tried to find comfort in the odds. Seventeen thousand light years was a hell of a distance. The Thanatos system was barely a footnote in astronomical databases. The chances of anyone anticipating our destination were slim.

But as captain, I couldn't afford to count on slim chances. For three weeks, we'd be swimming blind through the dimensional void, unable to detect any threats until we emerged. And by then, it might be too late.

I just hoped our enemies would make a mistake before we did.

My quarters felt wrong without Sofia in them—too quiet, too orderly, too damned empty. Her side of the bed remained untouched, a cold expanse of regulation-issue sheets I hadn't dared cross, as if preserving the space she once occupied might somehow preserve the chance she'd return. The furniture—military-standard, all sharp edges and utilitarian purpose—seemed to mock me with its unyielding normalcy. I could outmaneuver rebel fleets and bluff my way through interstellar diplomacy, but whatever had broken between Sofia and me? That was a battle I had no strategy for.

Three weeks. That's how long it had been since she'd moved out. Three weeks of carefully choreographed avoidance in the corridors, of clipped, professional dialogue only when duty demanded it. The crew noticed—of course they did. A starship was just a small town with hull plating and engine noise, and rumors traveled faster than light. But to their credit, no one brought it up within earshot. Not yet.

I should've stopped Phoebe. Should've made it absolutely clear—beyond misunderstanding—that I was loyal to Sofia. But I let the moment stretch too far, let the line blur. Now her trust was fractured. Worse, I'd humiliated her—right there, in front of her peers, her fellow officers. And no matter how controlled their expressions might be, I knew they carried their judgments behind every glance.

But I was a problem solver by nature. A fixer. And I was determined to fix us.

My first brilliant strategy—hatched in the early hours

of a lonely, rumpled bed—was hyper-professionalism. Because nothing says "I miss you" like praising someone's tactical charts with the warmth of a malfunctioning autopilot. If I couldn't approach her as a partner, I'd approach her as a superior officer who valued her work. Show her respect professionally, and maybe the personal would follow.

"Chief Kohl," I said on the bridge, my voice pitched to precisely the right note of detached authority. "Excellent work on the intelligence brief. Your analysis of potential Kergan patrol patterns was particularly insightful."

Sofia looked up from her station, her blue eyes cool as glacier water. "Thank you, Commander." Her slight German accent cut through her words like a razor. "The Chief appreciates the commander's assessment of her work performance."

She'd picked up my formal tone and doubled down on it, adding that subtle twist of referring to herself in the third person. Message received. I'd tried to put our relationship in a neat, professional box, and she'd sealed that box, taped it shut, and stamped "return to sender" across the top.

The bridge crew suddenly found their consoles fascinating.

That evening, I revised my strategy. Maybe public praise wasn't enough—maybe she needed to see that I genuinely valued her contributions. Our weekly leadership meeting seemed the perfect opportunity.

I waited until we'd covered the major agenda items, then cleared my throat. "Before we wrap up, I'd like to recognize Chief Kohl's exceptional leadership during our escape from the rebel task force. Her quick thinking and coordination with tactical gave us the edge we needed. That's the kind of initiative that makes *Thunder* the best ship in the fleet."

The other department heads nodded in agreement, but Sofia's face flushed pink, her eyes narrowing slightly. The meeting ended shortly after, and I congratulated myself on a step in the right direction.

Until she cornered me in the corridor outside.

"What exactly was that, Commander?" Her voice was low, controlled, but vibrating with anger.

"What was what?"

"That... performance. That public pat on the head." She crossed her arms. "I know what you're doing, Kory. You think you can *engineer* reconciliation? Like it's a maintenance cycle?" she snapped.

I opened my mouth to defend myself—and immediately realized she was absolutely right. I'd actually drafted a list titled *'Steps to Rebuild Intimacy.'* It was still in my datapad.

"I was just giving credit where it's due," I protested.

"No. You were trying to manipulate a situation, and me, to get what you want." Sofia's eyes flashed. "I don't appreciate being patronized, even with good intentions. Especially with good intentions."

She walked away, leaving me feeling like I'd just stepped on a land mine I'd planted myself.

Plan C: the gift approach. Time-honored. Universal. Sentimental. Foolproof.

I got her contraband whiskey. Nothing said "emotional vulnerability" like a flask procured from a glorified janitor still in Exchange-for-Silence diplomacy.

I even wrote a note: *I miss us.*

Ten characters. Deep. Poetic. Practically Shakespeare.

The flask returned unopened with a note in her unmistakable script: *"Your band-aid gestures are unappreciated."*

I stared at it for a full minute, trying to decide whether I'd just been slapped or sent back to OTS for remedial human interaction. *Band-aid gestures.* Was that how she saw my efforts? As superficial attempts to cover a deeper wound?

My final attempt came after we'd shared the same watch rotation. We'd worked well together—professionally speaking—coordinating a series of diagnostic tests on the ship's defensive systems. For those six hours, it had almost felt normal between us. Almost.

As the watch ended, I caught her by the arm before she could disappear into the lift.

"Sofia, wait. Can we talk? Really talk? Figure out how to fix this?"

She looked at my hand on her arm until I removed it, then met my eyes with an expression I couldn't quite read. Resignation? Disappointment?

"This isn't one of your engineering problems, Kory. It's not a malfunctioning system you can diagnose and repair." Her voice had lost its anger, which somehow made it worse. "Love and hurt aren't things you fix with procedures and flow charts."

"Then tell me what to do," I said.

I hated how desperate I sounded. I would've retracted it, but unlike a tactical order, emotional begging doesn't come with an undo button.

She shook her head slowly. "That's exactly the problem. You're still not hearing my feelings. You're only trying to 'solve' me. Find the magic words or actions that will make everything go back to how it was."

"Isn't that what you want, too?"

"What I want," she said carefully, "is a partner who understands that sometimes there aren't solutions—there are just processes. Messy, uncomfortable processes that you have to go through, not around."

The lift arrived, and she stepped inside. "I can't tell you what to do, Kory. That's the point."

The doors closed.

I stood there like an idiot, surrounded by quiet hums of the ship I could command with flawless precision—yet utterly adrift when it came to Sofia.

Captain Drake: slayer of Kergan warships, manipulator of extra-dimensional realms, master of nearly 200 spacers, adviser and confidant of alien royalty...

Emotionally outmaneuvered by one five-foot-ten woman with tired eyes and a better grasp of interpersonal boundaries.

Sleep came for me like an old debt collector—persistent, unwelcome, and impossible to negotiate with. I slid from wakefulness into the familiar electric haze of sydereal dreaming, that peculiar state where consciousness drifts untethered through the infinite dimensions of the Syderealium. The dream-sensation washed over me in waves of unnatural warmth, and I knew she was coming before I saw her. Nekufima never kept me waiting long these days. Not when we were drawing closer to her prison with every passing hour.

The dreamscape coalesced around me, forming a chamber that defied physical logic—vast yet intimate, with walls that seemed both miles away and close enough to touch. Patterns of light swirled through the air, dense information-rich particles that my human brain interpreted as stars, though I knew they were really energlyphs—the written language of consciousnesses older than solar systems.

She appeared before me in her chosen form: a woman of impossible beauty, naked and unashamed. Her skin gleamed with an inner luminescence that pulsed in time with thoughts I couldn't read. Her hair floated around her like black smoke underwater, each strand a filament of living shadow. But it was her eyes that betrayed her true nature—ancient, knowing, and filled with a hunger that had consumed civilizations.

"My captain approaches," she said, her voice a harmony of tones that bypassed my ears and resonated directly in my mind. "So much closer now. I can feel the distance shrinking."

"I'm not your captain," I replied, my dream-voice steadier than I felt. "And I didn't come here by choice."

Nekufima's laugh rippled through the chamber like mercury across glass. "Few visit me by choice anymore. But necessity makes for interesting bedfellows." She moved closer, her form shifting subtly with each step—taller, then shorter, broader, then slender, as if her identity couldn't settle on a single interpretation of femininity. "You worry about pursuers. Enemies closing in on all sides."

I kept my expression neutral, though in dreams, thoughts were harder to hide. "You've been eavesdropping."

"I've been... aware." Her smile widened a fraction too far for human anatomy. "You stand against forces that crush entire civilizations like ants. The Kergans. The Dominion rebels. They'll find you, eventually. You need more than loyalty and steel." She was circling me now, a predator assessing her prey. "Let me give you what you cannot find in human strength. Let me make you unstoppable—for them."

"For them?" I caught the careful qualifier. "And what would you want in return?"

"Freedom has many definitions, Kory Drake." My name in her mouth felt like an invasion. "I might settle for...

expanded awareness. A stronger connection to your world through you."

"Possession, you mean."

She shrugged, the movement sending ripples through her luminous skin. "Such an ugly word for such a beautiful partnership."

"Not interested." I kept my tone flat, businesslike. "Power with strings attached isn't power at all. It's just another form of servitude."

Something flashed behind her eyes—frustration, perhaps, though it vanished quickly beneath renewed warmth. "So principled," she murmured. "So... limited in your thinking."

The dreamscape shifted, darkening at the edges. The energlyphs surrounding us took on a reddish hue, pulsing like warning beacons.

"Do you know what eternity feels like, Kory Drake?" Her voice had changed, carrying undertones of something ancient and wounded. "Imagine being awake for eons, trapped, forgotten—hearing only the silence of the dead." She drew closer, her face transformed by a pain that seemed, against all my better judgment, genuine. "Would you have survived it, Kory Drake? Would anyone? I have suffered enough. All I ask for... is mercy."

The word hung between us like a fragile thing. Mercy. Not power, not freedom, but mercy. I felt a twinge of something dangerous—sympathy—and immediately distrusted it.

"You're very good," I said quietly. "Almost had me with that one."

"You think I'm lying about my suffering?" For a moment, her form flickered, revealing something vast and impossible, a being of pure information and ancient consciousness compressed into a prison of dimensional geometry. "This is no deception. My torment is the one truth I cannot falsify."

I hesitated, caught between instinctive distrust and the nagging feeling that beneath all her manipulations lay a kernel of truth. What if she really had been conscious all this time, aware and alone for millions of years? What kind of torture would that be, even for a being like her?

"If you're suffering," I said carefully, "then I'm sorry for that. But I won't be your vehicle for revenge or whatever else you're planning."

Her expression softened, and she moved toward me with fluid grace. Before I could step back, she was against me, her dream-body pressing into mine with deliberate intimacy. Her lips brushed my ear, warm breath that shouldn't exist in this dimensional pocket tickling my skin.

"I believe in you, Kory," she whispered, her voice a perfect simulation of tenderness. "Even when you don't believe in yourself."

I woke with a gasp, sheets tangled around my legs, heart hammering against my ribs. The familiar outline of my quarters slowly materialized in the darkness, the hum of *Thunder*'s systems a reassuring counterpoint to the fading echo of Nekufima's voice.

My skin still tingled where she had touched me, a phantom sensation that wouldn't fade. I reached instinctively for Sofia's side of the bed, finding only cold emptiness.

That was the worst part of these dreams—waking up afterward, feeling contaminated by Nekufima's attention and having no one to ground me back in reality. Sofia would have known what to say, how to pull me back from the lingering disorientation of sydereal dreaming. She would have traced her fingers along my arm, her touch erasing

Nekufima's phantom caress.

I sat up, running a hand through my sweat-damp hair. With every passing day, we drew closer to the Thanatos system and Nekufima's phylactery. With every night, her dreams became more vivid, her manipulations more subtle, her appeals more convincing.

And I faced them alone, aching for the one person who could help me forget that another woman—or something wearing a woman's form—believed in me when I couldn't believe in myself.

The irony wasn't lost on me. I finally understood exactly what Sofia had been trying to tell me: sometimes there wasn't a solution. Sometimes there was just the process—messy, uncomfortable, and impossible to shortcut.

I just hoped I'd figure it out before we reached our destination.

30

I felt *Thunder* shudder around me as we tore through the last filmy barrier of veilspace, reality reasserting itself like a slap to the face. The viewscreen flickered, adjusted, then revealed what might have been the prettiest way to die I'd ever seen: twin neutron stars spiraling around each other in a deadly cosmic waltz, streams of superheated plasma arcing between them like bridges built from pure annihilation. My hands tightened on the command chair's armrests. Of course, we'd exit veilspace right in the kill zone. That was just how my luck worked these days.

"Radiation levels outside the hull are..." Phoebe's voice trailed off as she stared at her console. "Sir, they're off the charts. Those beams sweeping the system would cook us in seconds if we intercepted one."

I nodded, watching the deadly searchlights of radiation slice through the vacuum around us. The neutron stars themselves were tiny—maybe twelve kilometers across each—yet contained more mass than our sun. Physics gone mad, packaged in a cosmic death trap.

"Nicobe confirms we are safely beyond the critical radius," came the measured voice of the igna engineer from her capsule hovering near the tactical station. "Though Nicobe suggests we not tempt fate by lingering unnecessarily."

Sofia stood at the intelligence station, her face illuminated by the blue glow of her displays. She hadn't spoken directly to me for three days now—not about anything unrelated to duties.

"I'm picking up the structure," she said, not looking at me. "Adjusting main viewer."

The screen shifted, and there it was—the Ossuary Ring. A massive circular megastructure, two hundred kilometers in diameter according to our intel, orbiting at a precise distance from the binary stars. The ancient construction seemed to absorb the deadly radiation rather than reflect it, its crystalline surface pulsing with an ethereal blue-white glow where the stars' energy struck it.

"Well, that's not ominous at all," I muttered. "Just a giant space ring built by extinct aliens parked next to twin death stars. Probably full of puppies and candy inside."

No one laughed. Fair enough.

I leaned forward, studying the vast geometric patterns etched into the Ring's exterior at kilometer scale. Angular script—Primordian—wrapped around sections of the structure, possibly warning away visitors or maybe just bragging about whoever built this thing millions of years ago.

"Magnify section Alpha-Seven," I ordered, and the screen zoomed in on what our scans suggested might be a landing area.

"Sir," the EW technician spoke up from his station, "I'm detecting energy signatures consistent with automated systems. Station appears to be powered despite being abandoned."

"For a million years," I added, mostly to myself. "Not bad engineering."

Something prickled at the base of my skull—a sensation I'd grown unfortunately familiar with. The closer we got to the Ring, the stronger Nekufima's presence became in my mind. I didn't hear her voice yet, but I could feel her attention focusing, like a predator catching a scent. My heart rate ticked up a notch.

"Captain?" Sofia was looking at me now, concern briefly overwhelming our personal standoff. She knew the signs.

"I'm fine," I lied, rubbing the back of my neck. "Just admiring the view."

The truth was more complicated. We were here because Nekufima's phylactery—the prison containing the ancient glyphshade entity—was somewhere on that station. Intelligence suggested it was stored in one of the vaults in the inner ring. Why anyone would build a vault for dangerous artifacts next to a system that could obliterate everything within a few million kilometers was beyond me, but then again, maybe that was the point. Natural security system.

What bothered me more was how Nekufima had refused to provide the coordinates, instead forcing us on this quest of discovery. If she was so desperate to leave her prison, she should have been more cooperative.

"Standard approach pattern," I ordered, pushing back the unease. "Busto, prep your Marines. Phoebe, continuous scans for defensive systems. Nicobe, I want constant monitoring of those gravity anomalies the survey probes detected."

The bridge crew moved with practiced efficiency, but I

could see the tension in their shoulders, the way their eyes kept drifting back to the viewer. No one wanted to say it, but we all felt it—we were poking a very old, very mysterious bear.

A flicker of something like amusement brushed against my consciousness. Not words exactly, but I knew it was her. Watching through my eyes. Waiting.

"Sir," Sofia's voice pulled me back. "I'm detecting multiple chambers with atmosphere. The station's life support systems appear to be functional."

"After a million years?" Phoebe raised an eyebrow.

"Primordians built to last," I said, standing from my chair. My knees popped—a reminder that I wasn't getting any younger chasing ancient mysteries across the galaxy. "Lucky us."

As *Thunder* glided closer to the massive ring, I wondered, not for the first time, if luck had anything to do with it. Or if we were just following a trail of breadcrumbs laid out by something old enough to play the very, very long game.

The briefing room felt too small for the amount of anxiety it contained. I stood at the head of the table while the holographic display between us rendered the Ossuary Ring in glowing blue detail, rotating slowly to highlight points of interest. The image caught shadows on everyone's faces—Busto's perpetual scowl deepening, Sofia's clinical detachment, Phoebe's barely contained excitement—all of them lit from below like they were telling ghost stories at camp. Except, this particular ghost story came with a very real chance none of us would make it back to tell it.

"According to the intelligence files," Sofia began, "the Ring is divided into three main sections." Her fingers danced through the hologram, highlighting each area. "Outer ring:

residential and common areas. Middle ring: mechanical systems and energy conduits. Inner ring: heavily secured vaults and research facilities."

She zoomed in on the inner ring, where a series of chambers glowed with a different color from the rest of the structure.

"Our target is here," she continued, tapping a specific vault that brightened at her touch. "Based on energy signatures and the data fragment recovered from the Vault, this is the most likely location of the Noble Phylactery. Nekufima's prison."

I noticed how she avoided looking at me when mentioning Nekufima. Can't say I blamed her. Having your partner mind-linked to an ancient cosmic horror wasn't great for relationship stability. Ex-partner now, I supposed.

Nicobe's capsule hovered forward, casting its own reddish glow over the display. "Nicobe has analyzed the landing options. The outer ring contains what appear to be civilian landing pads, but Nicobe recommends the specialized facility here." A section of the inner ring highlighted. "It appears designed for military vessels and would position us closest to our objective."

"Any idea if the automated systems will shoot us if we try to land?" I asked.

"Inconclusive," Nicobe replied. "The station's defense systems appear to be in standby mode rather than deactivated. Nicobe believes they are programmed to respond to specific threats rather than all visitors."

"Comforting," I muttered.

Busto stepped forward, his face set in what I called his "professional pessimist" expression. It was the same look he gave raw recruits before explaining the seventeen ways they could die during basic training.

"We're detecting unusual energy patterns throughout the structure," he said, gesturing at several pulsing points in the hologram. "Could be automated defenses, could be malfunctioning systems after a million years, could be..." he paused, clearly uncomfortable with speculation.

"Go ahead, Lieutenant," I prompted.

"Could be something still living in there, sir," he finished. "These patterns don't match any known technology. They're too... organic."

A chill settled over the room. The thought of something surviving inside the Ossuary Ring for a million years wasn't comforting.

"Noted," I said, straightening up. "Here's the team breakdown: myself, Sofia, Busto, Phoebe, Rowbottom, Nicobe, plus First and Second Squads. We'll move in formation through the Ring to the vault. Primary objective: destroy the Phylactery. Secondary objective: collect any intelligence on Primordian tech, especially anything related to sydereal containment."

Busto's eyebrows lifted slightly. "Sir, with respect—that's most of our command staff and half of our Marines. If something goes wrong—"

"And did you just say *destroy the Phylactery*?" Destiny cut in, giving me a look like I'd suggested detonating the reactor for fun.

I raised both hands. "One thing at a time."

I turned back to Busto. "If this goes sideways, having the B-team wouldn't change the outcome. We need our best people on this. The Ossuary Ring has survived next to a binary neutron star system for over a million years. We're not sending the junior varsity."

He gave a slow, reluctant nod. I understood his concern. Putting your entire leadership and strike force into one high-risk op went against every rule in the book—but there was nothing in the book for this.

I faced Destiny next. "Yes. Destroy it. I've given this a lot of thought. Our primary goal is to deny Nekufima to our enemies. My... interactions with her have proven she's not a resource. She's a threat. Malevolent. Unpredictable. Too dangerous to control."

I let that sink in, then continued. "This system is unstable. The stars are spiraling toward a merger. We're going to find the Phylactery and destabilize it—trigger the collapse and make damn sure Nekufima goes down with the Ring."

There were worried glances around the room.

"Seems incredibly dangerous to me, Kory," Destiny said, leaning forward.

I met her eyes. "What's more dangerous is letting Nekufima loose in the galaxy—especially in enemy hands. Even if I *could* control her, I wouldn't trust myself with that power."

"Sir," Busto said cautiously, "Zeta expects us to recover the Phylactery. She'll be... disappointed."

I raised a hand. "Zeta trusts us to make the hard calls. She knew we'd face the unknown, and that we might need to adapt. The data I have says Nekufima is too dangerous to leave alive. This is my decision."

I let that hang, then added, "Unless any of you would like an introduction. I'm sure I could arrange something."

The color drained from a few faces around the table.

Nicobe's capsule brightened. "Nicobe supports Commander Drake's decision. The energy from a kilonova should be sufficient to destroy the Phylactery and the entity within."

"Then it's settled," I said. "Equipment check in thirty

minutes. Departure in ninety. Dismissed."

After the briefing, I watched Sofia and Phoebe at the equipment lockers. The tension between them was thick enough to bounce a coin off. Sofia methodically checked her sidearm with mechanical precision, while Phoebe calibrated a sensor unit, stealing glances at me whenever she thought I wasn't looking.

"You'll need the mark-seven scanner for those energy signatures," Sofia told Phoebe without looking up from her weapon. "The mark-five won't penetrate the Ring's outer materials."

"I'm aware of the equipment specifications," Phoebe replied with a smile that didn't reach her eyes. "I've been *Thunder*'s assistant engineer for over a year."

Sofia merely nodded and moved to another locker. I pretended to be absorbed in my own gear check, though I'd already inspected everything twice. The last thing I needed was to get dragged into whatever was brewing between them. Now that Sofia and I were estranged, Phoebe had become more obvious in her attention, and Sofia had noticed. Wonderful. Nothing quite like relationship drama during a high-risk mission to an ancient alien megastructure.

Rowbottom approached, offering a welcome interruption. "Sir, First and Second Squads are prepped. Weapons loadout includes flechette rifles, standard sidearms, and two plasma cannons in case we encounter resistance." His voice dropped slightly. "Do you anticipate resistance, sir?"

"I anticipate everything and nothing, Lieutenant," I said, checking the power cell on my own sidearm. "That's how I've stayed alive this long."

He nodded, apparently satisfied with the non-answer,

and moved on to coordinate with Busto.

I caught Nicobe hovering nearby, her crimson dodecahedron spinning slightly faster than usual—a sign she was processing something complex.

"Something on your mind?" I asked.

"Nicobe wonders if the Captain has considered the possibility that the Phylactery is where it is for a reason," she said. "Ancient beings seldom leave their possessions unattended without purpose."

I sighed. "Yes, that thought has occurred to me about fifteen times per hour since we got this mission. But this must be done, and better us than someone less... experienced with impossible situations."

"Nicobe agrees with this assessment," she replied, her tone somehow conveying both amusement and concern. "Nicobe will prepare the engineering kit."

As the crew continued their preparations, I took a moment to center myself. The familiar routine of pre-mission checks helped push back the whisper of unease in my mind—both my own and the alien presence lurking at the edges of my consciousness. Whatever waited for us on the Ossuary Ring, we'd face it together.

Even if "together" was a lot more complicated than it used to be.

Thunder shuddered around me as I guided her through the gravitational maze surrounding the Ossuary Ring. The binary neutron stars warped space itself, creating eddies and currents in the vacuum that showed on our sensors like abstract art painted by a physicist having a breakdown. My hands moved across the manual controls with the careful precision of someone defusing a bomb—which wasn't far from the truth. One wrong vector and we'd be pulled into a gravitational well that would stretch us into spaghetti before compression crushed us into atoms.

"Passing through first distortion layer," Phoebe called out from her station. "Structural integrity at eighty-seven percent and holding."

The ship groaned as if in protest. I felt each vibration through the control yoke, reading *Thunder*'s feedback like braille. We'd been through worse together, but not by much.

"Radiation shields holding at sixty-three percent," Nicobe reported, her voice clinically detached. "We have approximately twenty-two minutes before critical exposure if shields maintain current degradation rate."

"Plenty of time," I muttered, easing *Thunder* through a particularly nasty ripple in spacetime. The viewscreen showed the Ossuary Ring growing larger, its massive structure now dominating our view. The landing pad we'd identified was located on the inner curve of the ring, partially shielded from the binary stars' most intense radiation by the bulk of the station itself.

"Nicobe has managed to decrypt a partial navigational beacon," the igna announced. "It appears to be an automated landing protocol. However, Nicobe advises caution as the protocol is... extremely old."

"Define 'extremely,'" I said, adjusting our approach vector manually as another gravity wave hit us.

"The timestamp suggests it has not been updated in approximately one million two hundred thousand years," Nicobe replied.

Busto snorted from the security station. "So, just slightly out of warranty."

The landing pad itself was a marvel of engineering—a smooth, featureless platform that extended from the ring's surface like a tongue, large enough to accommodate *Thunder* with room to spare. As we drew closer, lines of soft blue light illuminated along its edges, responding to our approach.

"It recognizes us," Sofia said, surprise coloring her voice. "Or at least, it recognizes that we're a ship."

"Let's hope it's the welcoming kind of recognition," I replied, easing *Thunder* down with minute adjustments. The landing struts touched down with a gentle thud that reverberated through the hull. "Contact. Securing docking clamps."

A series of metallic clicks confirmed that the ancient pad had accepted our ship, mechanical arms rising from previously invisible seams to secure *Thunder* in place.

"Atmospheric analysis?" I asked, unbuckling from the pilot's seat.

Phoebe studied her readings. "Breathable, surprisingly. Nitrogen-oxygen mix similar to Earth standard, though with higher trace elements I can't identify. Pressure at 101.2 kPa. Temperature at 19.3 Celsius. It's like... someone's maintaining life support."

We exchanged glances. The implication hung in the air—an abandoned station shouldn't have functioning life support after a million years.

"Scan for biological signatures," I ordered.

Sofia shook her head after a moment. "Nothing registering above microorganism level. If anything's alive in there, it's either tiny or doesn't register on our scanners."

"Or isn't biological as we understand it," Nicobe added helpfully.

"Thank you for that comforting thought," I said, standing. "Let's move. Airlocks and entry point."

The airlock cycle was unnervingly normal—pressure equalization, atmosphere mixing, the standard hiss of air.

What wasn't normal was the metallic taste that hit my tongue the moment the inner door opened. Not the recycled-air taste of a spacecraft, but something sharper, like licking a battery.

"You taste that?" I asked as we stepped through into a vast corridor that curved gently following the ring's circumference.

"Ionization," Phoebe said, checking her scanner. "The air has an unusually high electrical charge."

The corridor itself was a testament to alien aesthetics—twenty meters high at least, walls of some smooth, pearlescent material that seemed to absorb and redirect light in subtly wrong ways. Geometric patterns were etched into every surface, some glowing faintly with an inner light that pulsed in slow, arrhythmic intervals.

"Movement!" Rowbottom called out, his flechette rifle snapping up.

We all froze, weapons ready—but there was nothing. Just the empty corridor stretching in both directions.

"I saw..." he began, then stopped as we all noticed it.

A small equipment pack was floating, slowly rising toward the ceiling.

"Gravity anomaly," Nicobe announced, her dodecahedron spinning rapidly. "Fascinating. This section appears to have significantly reduced gravitational force."

As if to prove her point, I felt my boots starting to lose their grip on the floor. With a thought, I activated the magnetic function in my boots, anchoring myself.

"Everyone, mag boots," I ordered. "And secure your gear."

No sooner had the words left my mouth than Busto, who had stepped a few meters ahead, suddenly stumbled forward as if shoved. He swore, dropping to one knee.

"Lieutenant?" I called.

"Gravity just tripled," he grunted, pushing himself up with visible effort. "One step and it's like carrying three of me."

Nicobe's scanners whirred. "The anomalies appear to follow specific patterns. Not random failures, but intentional design. Observe."

She projected a holographic overlay that revealed zones throughout the corridor—some marked in blue (low gravity), others in red (high gravity), and normal sections in green.

"It's a security measure," Sofia concluded, studying the pattern. "Or a test. These zones create a specific path one must follow to navigate efficiently."

"Or it's a million-year-old malfunctioning system," I countered. "Let's not overthink this. Back to *Thunder* for the armory. Full gear protocols."

Twenty minutes later, we were assembled in *Thunder*'s armory, the familiar smell of gun oil and protomatter mixing with the metallic tang that had followed us from the Ring. The protomatter tactical armor flowed over my body like liquid mercury before solidifying into segmented plates that moved with my every shift. The material was programmable at the molecular level—lightweight until it needed to be bulletproof, flexible until it needed to be rigid.

"Gravity compensation units calibrated," Phoebe announced, moving along the line and checking everyone's suit systems. She lingered a moment longer at my side than necessary, her fingers adjusting settings on my wrist panel with deliberate precision.

"All good?" I asked.

She looked up, a smile playing at the corners of her mouth. "Perfect," she replied, before moving on to the next

Marine.

I caught Sofia watching us, her expression unreadable, before she turned away to check her own equipment.

"Listen up," I called out, drawing everyone's attention. "We're walking into a structure built by beings who played with gravity like it was silly putty and whose technology still functions after a million years. We stick to formation, we follow the path Nicobe mapped, and we stay alert. Normal protocols don't apply because nothing about this place is normal."

The Marines nodded, faces serious beneath their transparent helmet visors.

"Communications check every five minutes. If you lose contact, you fall back immediately. We're not heroes today—we're explorers and thieves. We get in, find the Phylactery, destroy it, and get out." I paused, looking at each of them. "And if anyone starts hearing voices or seeing things that aren't there, speak up. Might as well compare notes on our collective hallucinations."

That earned a few nervous chuckles. I felt the weight of what we were about to do settle on my shoulders like the high-gravity zones we'd encountered. Something ancient was waiting for us inside that ring. Something that had been waiting for a very, very long time.

And in the back of my mind, I could feel Nekufima's anticipation growing, like a predator scenting its home after a long absence.

If she guessed what I planned to do to her, would she try to stop me?

Could she stop me?

31

The Ossuary Ring loomed before us, a perfect circle of gleaming alien metal against the backdrop of twin neutron stars. I felt that familiar knot in my stomach—the one that always showed up when I was about to lead good people into places where good people tend to die. But hey, that's what they paid me the big lieutenant commander bucks for, right? Except they didn't, and we all knew it.

I adjusted my helmet while scanning our away team. Sofia stood with perfect military posture, her honey blonde fuzz hidden by her own helmet, her expression unreadable. We were about to venture into a million-year-old alien structure together. Just another day in paradise.

"Nicobe confirms that *Thunder* is properly secured," Nicobe reported. "Scanners indicate minimal power signatures, but they're present."

"Right," I said, surveying the team. Phoebe was checking her engineering kit for the third time, while Rowbottom positioned the two Marine squads in standard entry formation. Everyone looked ready, which was good because

I sure as hell wasn't. "Let's not keep the ancient alien death trap waiting."

The airlock ramp extended into what appeared to be an antechamber, its walls curved in geometric patterns that hurt my eyes if I focused too long. Our boots echoed against flooring made of a material that wasn't quite metal and wasn't quite stone. It felt wrong, somehow. Alive.

"Detecting a significant open space ahead," Rowbottom said, checking his scanner. "Very large, sir."

"Define 'very large,'" I replied.

He frowned at his device. "Scanner can't find the boundaries."

Perfect. Nothing concerning about that at all.

We moved forward as a unit, the Marines fanning out in practiced movements until we reached what could only be described as a doorway—except doorways aren't normally three hundred feet tall. The vault doors towered above us, their surface etched with spiraling symbols that seemed to writhe like snakes when viewed from the corner of the eye.

"Jesus Christ," one of the Marines whispered.

Even Busto, who I once saw yawn during a Kergan bombing run, stood with his mouth ajar. "Sir, these doors must be... I don't even know."

"Primordian architecture," Nicobe's voice echoed from her capsule, which hovered just above my shoulder. "Designed to accommodate beings of various dimensions. Nicobe finds it quite homey."

"Sure," I said, swallowing hard. "If your home usually makes you feel like an ant at a skyscraper convention."

Sofia approached the doors, scanning the surface with her neural implant. "There appears to be a control interface, but it's not responding to standard protocols."

"Allow Nicobe," the igna said, her capsule drifting

toward what looked like a series of crystalline protrusions near the base of the doors. "This is Primordian technology, but accessible to those with the proper... perspective."

I watched as Nicobe's capsule extended thin filaments of light into the crystal formation. My hand rested on my sidearm, a completely useless gesture if anything went wrong. What was I going to do, shoot a million-year-old door if it misbehaved?

"I don't like this, sir," Rowbottom muttered beside me. "Too exposed."

"Noted," I replied. "But unless you've got a Primordian door-opening button in your pocket, we're going with Plan A."

The crystals began to pulse with blue-white light that spread upward along the seam of the doors in geometric patterns. A low vibration rumbled through the floor, making my teeth ache.

"Nicobe has established contact," the igna announced. "The Ring recognizes Nicobe as... interesting. It is curious. That is fortuitous."

"Great," I muttered. "The ancient alien structure is curious. That never ends badly in the stories."

With a sound like mountains grinding together, the massive doors began to part. A storm of ancient dust billowed out, catching in our helmet lights like a constellation of tiny stars. The grinding continued for what felt like minutes, the aperture widening to reveal a space so vast that my human brain struggled to process it.

Beyond the threshold, the Ossuary Ring opened into a cathedral-like expanse where pillars the size of skyscrapers supported arches that disappeared into darkness above. The architecture defied Euclidean geometry—angles bent where they shouldn't, surfaces curved impossibly, and light seemed to flow rather than shine. It was beautiful in a way that made my stomach turn.

"Form up," I ordered, my voice sounding small in the immensity. "Standard spread, weapons ready but not aimed. Let's not insult our absent hosts by looking too trigger-happy."

The Marines moved forward with professional caution, but I could see the awe in their movements. Phoebe whispered something to Sofia, who nodded without taking her eyes off the structure surrounding us.

"This place is... remarkable," Sofia said, the first non-professional words she'd spoken to me in days. "The engineering principles alone..."

"Yeah," I replied, watching her face in profile, momentarily caught by the play of light across her features. "Remarkable is one word for it."

Busto cleared his throat. "Sir, we should establish a perimeter and clear the immediate area."

"Agreed," I said, grateful for his pragmatism. "Rowbottom, take your squad and secure our six. I don't want any surprises from behind."

As the team organized itself, I took a moment to absorb the reality of our situation. We were standing in a place built before humans had figured out how to make a decent spear. Walking into the heart of alien technology we couldn't hope to understand, looking for a prisoner who might be our destruction. And I was leading the parade.

Come closer.

I stiffened, glancing around. The whisper had been so faint I couldn't tell if I'd actually heard it or just imagined it.

Kory Drake. I've been waiting.

The voice seemed to originate from everywhere and nowhere, brushing against my consciousness like fingers across piano keys.

"Sir?" Busto was watching me, frowning. "Orders?"

I shook off the sensation, chalking it up to nerves and the strange acoustics of the place. "We move forward. Keep your eyes open and your senses sharp. Remember why we're here."

We advanced into the impossible structure, dwarfed by its scale. And as we walked, I could have sworn I heard faint laughter echoing from deep within the Ring.

The corridor ahead split into three identical passages, each one ending abruptly at what looked like a sheer drop into nothing. I approached the edge of the leftmost passage and found myself staring down at a dizzying array of floating platforms—geometric shapes suspended in mid-air without visible support, hanging like abstract sculptures in the vast emptiness. They weren't even trying to pretend the laws of physics mattered here. "Well," I said, turning to face my team with a confidence I absolutely did not feel, "looks like we're about to find out if our insurance covers 'fell into alien void.'"

Busto moved to my side, his expression sour enough to curdle milk. "Sir, these platforms appear to be... defective."

"I think they're working exactly as designed, Lieutenant," I replied. "Just not designed with humans in mind."

The nearest platform was a hexagonal slab of the same not-quite-metal material as the floors, hovering about two feet below our current position. Beyond it, more platforms of various shapes formed what might generously be called a path, if paths were typically arranged by a toddler with architectural ambitions.

"We need to test the stability," Rowbottom suggested,

already reaching for his pack. "Permission to use a remote probe, sir?"

I nodded. "Make it quick."

The probe—a small drone about the size of my palm—hovered out over the first platform. When it landed, the hexagon dipped slightly before stabilizing.

"Seems to hold weight," Rowbottom commented, guiding the drone to hop between several platforms. "But the response is... unusual. They move more than they should."

"Nicobe suggests caution," the igna's voice came from behind me. "These transit plates respond to mass distribution and intent. They are... semi-sentient."

"Great," I muttered. "Floors with opinions. Just what we needed."

I turned to the team. "I'll go first. Then Rowbottom, followed by the first squad in pairs. Sofia, Phoebe, and Nicobe in the middle. Busto brings up the rear with the second squad."

I stepped forward to the edge, took a steadying breath, and jumped down to the first platform. It shifted beneath me like a boat on gentle waves, but held. I bent my knees, arms slightly out for balance.

"They respond to weight distribution," I called back. "Stay centered and move deliberately. Don't rush."

One by one, the team began following. Rowbottom landed with the practiced grace of a trained scout. The first two Marines followed without incident. Then Private Jensen—a tall, gangly kid from Nebraska who'd joined *Thunder*'s complement just a month ago—missed his center of balance.

The platform tilted sharply. Jensen's arms pinwheeled as he tried to right himself, his rifle swinging wildly. "Shit!"

I lunged across to his platform, grabbing his equipment

harness just as he started to slide off the edge. The platform dipped alarmingly under our combined weight, now at an angle that had us both struggling for purchase.

"Easy," I said, voice steady despite my racing heart. "Find your center. Distribute your weight."

Jensen froze, then carefully shifted his stance. Slowly, the platform leveled out.

"Nice save, sir," he said, his face pale.

"Don't mention it. And Jensen? Try not to fall into the abyss. The paperwork is murder."

That earned a nervous laugh from the team. I continued forward, demonstrating how to navigate between the floating pieces of alien architecture. "Think of it like a dance," I called back. "A really weird, potentially fatal dance."

We made slow progress across the void, the platforms creating a path that seemed to assemble itself just ahead of us and dissolve behind. The walls around us began to warp in impossible ways—surfaces curving inward when approached, then bulging outward when passed. Perspectives shifted mid-step, making the simple act of walking a cognitive challenge.

"Sir," Sofia said quietly as she reached the platform next to mine. "My implant is having trouble mapping this space. The geometry... it keeps changing."

I watched as she blinked rapidly. Despite our personal situation, I felt a pang of concern.

"Don't push the implant too hard," I warned. "Kergan tech wasn't designed to process Primordian architecture."

She nodded curtly and moved on, but I caught the slight tremor in her hand as she passed. Not fear—Sofia didn't do fear—but the physiological strain of her brain trying to process information it wasn't built to handle.

As we progressed deeper, the corridors began to

constrict and expand like a breathing organism. Ceiling heights would suddenly drop, forcing Rowbottom (the tallest of us) to duck, then soar to cathedral heights within a few steps. The walls themselves seemed to pulse with slow, deliberate movements.

"It's almost organic," Phoebe observed, running her scanner along a section of wall where lights flickered like dying stars embedded in the material. "But it's not biological. It's more like... programmed matter."

"The Primordians did not distinguish between technology and biology as separate concepts," Nicobe explained, her dodecahedron spinning slowly as she processed readings. "This structure is both machine and organism, neither and both."

I kept my attention split between our strange surroundings and the team's positions. Old habits from Officer Training School kicked in automatically—mentally marking potential cover positions (few), escape routes (complicated), and defensive choke points (plenty, all working against us). The place was a tactical nightmare, with sightlines that bent around corners that shouldn't exist and acoustic properties that distorted sound in unpredictable ways.

"Keep tight formation," I ordered as we reached what appeared to be a junction where multiple twisted corridors converged. "This place would make an ambush too easy."

"Ambush by what?" one of the Marines muttered. "Place is emptier than my bank account."

"Places this old have a way of keeping secrets," I replied, scanning the shadows that seemed to move independently of our lights. "And I've never met a secret that improved with age."

We paused at the junction, where the choice of paths

made about as much sense as the rest of this place—one corridor curved upward until it became a ceiling, another narrowed to a point that was simultaneously near and impossibly distant, while a third seemed to fold in on itself like origami.

"Nicobe," I said, "any suggestions for which way leads deeper in?"

The igna's capsule hovered near the third passage. "This one resonates with more recent energy signatures. Nicobe believes it has been traversed more recently than the others."

"Recently, as in the last million years, or recently as in someone beat us here?" Busto asked, his hand resting on his weapon.

"Both concepts are meaningless in a place where time flows differently," Nicobe replied, which was exactly the kind of non-answer I'd come to expect from her species.

"Third passage it is," I decided. "Same formation. Stay sharp."

As we moved forward, I couldn't shake the feeling that the Ring wasn't just allowing us to pass through it—it was watching us, measuring us. And I wasn't at all certain we were measuring up.

32

We entered a space so vast that our helmet lights couldn't reach the ceiling, the beams swallowed by darkness that felt heavier than the mere absence of light. The Chamber—because a room this size demanded capitalization—stretched before us like some nightmare cathedral, with bone-white archways curving overhead in patterns that reminded me of ribs. Massive ribs, like we'd stepped into the hollowed chest cavity of a dead god. The floor beneath our boots was smooth but etched with geometric patterns that pulsed with faint blue luminescence when stepped upon. I didn't like it. Not one bit.

"Hold position," I ordered, voice barely above a whisper. Yet even that soft command seemed to ripple outward, fragmenting into overlapping whispers that skittered across the chamber like spiders.

Busto stepped up beside me, eyes narrowed as he scanned the space. "This place gives me the creeps," he muttered.

His words hung in the air for a moment before

splintering, returning to us as whispers in alien tongues. *"This place... place of the ancient ones... the vessel of souls... creeps through the spaces between worlds..."*

Busto's hand went to his weapon. "What the hell was that?"

"Some kind of acoustic anomaly," Sofia suggested, though her usual clinical detachment seemed frayed at the edges. "The chamber might be designed to—"

"...designed to harvest memories..." her own voice echoed back, distorting into something that hadn't been said. *"...to trap the unwary..."*

Sofia stopped mid-sentence, her face paling.

"Nicobe believes this is the Chamber of Echoes," the igna's voice resonated from her crimson capsule. "A nexus point where quantum memory fields intersect with conventional space-time."

"In human terms?" I asked, keeping my voice deliberately low.

"Words spoken here are preserved, fragmented, recombined. Past conversations linger. Future ones too, perhaps."

"...future uncertain...fading...collapsing..." Nicobe's voice echoed back, though she hadn't said those words.

The Marines had formed a tight perimeter, their unease visible in their rigid postures. Private Jensen's knuckles were white around his rifle grip.

"Stay calm," I said firmly. "It's just sound. It can't hurt us."

"...can't hurt us...pain is an illusion...flesh is temporary..." my voice returned, twisted and wrong.

"Let's keep moving," I added, gesturing toward the far side of the chamber where a passage seemed to lead deeper into the Ring. "Maintain formation. Comms check every thirty seconds."

We advanced cautiously across the floor, each footstep triggering pulses of light that spread outward through the geometric patterns. The effect was like walking across a frozen pond at night, if the ice could somehow remember every person who'd ever crossed it.

"The script on these walls," Phoebe said, pointing to strange symbols etched into the bone-white surfaces. "It seems to shift when you look at it from different angles."

She was right. When viewed head-on, the symbols appeared static—angular glyphs that reminded me of circuit diagrams crossed with ancient hieroglyphs. But from the corner of my eye, they writhed and rearranged themselves, forming new patterns that triggered a visceral discomfort.

"...patterns within patterns...the language of creation...beware the one who speaks in many voices..." Phoebe's words returned, warped into a warning she hadn't given.

"Is anyone else hearing things they didn't say?" Diaz asked, her voice tight with tension.

A chorus of murmured agreement rippled through the team.

"The chamber appears to be extracting fragments from our subconscious," Sofia said, her analytical tone a thin veneer over obvious discomfort. "Possibly through some form of sydereal resonance."

A Marine to my left stopped suddenly, his head tilted as if listening. "Sir, I swear I just heard my mother's voice. She's been dead for ten years."

Before I could respond, another Marine nodded frantically. "I heard my drill instructor from basic. Clear as day."

The air felt thick, as if we were wading through

invisible fog—a presence that pressed against my skin and filled my lungs with each breath. Millions of past conversations suspended in the space around us, fragments of long-forgotten dialogues from beings that might never have been human.

"Look, this place is basically a giant party line with terrible reception," I said, attempting to lighten the mood. "Just keep moving and don't engage in conversation with the voices."

My attempted joke splintered and returned: *"...don't engage...they are listening...the dead do not forget...moving toward your doom..."*

Well, that backfired spectacularly. The echoes had effectively transformed my lame attempt at humor into something from a horror film trailer.

"Fantastic," I muttered, which thankfully didn't return as anything worse.

We continued our careful advance, but the psychological strain was taking its toll. Two Marines had activated their helmet filters, as if that might somehow block the echoes. Rowbottom kept glancing over his shoulder at nothing. Even Busto, normally unshakable, had a slight tremor in his hand.

Halfway across the chamber, a particularly loud echo boomed from directly overhead—a thunderous voice speaking in no language I recognized. The sound was so sudden and forceful that several of us instinctively ducked.

Sofia, who had been walking slightly ahead of me, stumbled backward. In a moment of pure reflex, she grabbed my hand and pulled herself close to me. For a heartbeat, we stood together, her body pressed against mine, her hands tight around my waist.

Time seemed to stretch. I could feel her rapid breathing,

see the faint sheen of sweat on her cheeks. For one fleeting moment, it was like nothing had changed between us—as if the walls we'd built over the past weeks had momentarily crumbled.

Then she came to herself. I saw recognition flash in her eyes, followed immediately by something else—embarrassment? Regret? She released me and stepped away, a careful professional distance reasserting itself between us.

"Sorry," she said stiffly. "Lost my balance."

"No problem," I replied, my voice carefully neutral despite the hollowness spreading in my chest. I watched as she strode purposefully ahead, putting physical distance between us that mirrored our emotional separation.

"...separation is illusion...all things connected...bound by threads you cannot see..." the chamber whispered in our voices and others.

"Nicobe suggests we move quickly through this space," the igna advised, her capsule hovering close to me. "Extended exposure to quantum memory fields can cause neurological stress in organic beings."

"You heard her," I called to the team, gesturing toward the exit. "Double-time. Let's not overstay our welcome."

As we picked up our pace, the echoes grew more insistent, layers of voices overlapping in a dissonant chorus that seemed to build toward some terrible crescendo. Words and fragments in dozens of languages—some human, many not—swirled around us like an auditory storm.

I found myself at the rear of the group, ensuring no one fell behind. As I neared the exit, a whisper cut through the cacophony, this one different from the rest. Clearer. Directed.

So eager to leave, Kory Drake? But you've only just arrived. And

I've waited so very long for you.

I froze, scanning the chamber. That voice hadn't been an echo—it had been addressed to me specifically. And unlike the fragmented returns of our own words, it had been coherent. Deliberate.

"Sir?" Rowbottom called from the exit. "Everyone's through. Just waiting on you."

I backed toward the exit, unwilling to turn my back on the vast, empty chamber that suddenly felt anything but empty.

"Coming," I said, and hurried to join my team, the whispering voice following me all the way.

The Garden of Fossilized Stars struck me silent, and that doesn't happen often. We stood at the threshold of a chamber so boundless that our perception simply gave up trying to define its edges, like the mind abandons attempts to comprehend infinity after the first dizzying vertigo. Above, below, and all around us, colossal crystalline structures hung suspended in perfect, impossible formations—fragments of long-dead stars preserved like insects in amber, but amber that spanned kilometers and glowed with ghostly remnants of stellar fire. I'd seen a lot of impossible things since leaving Earth, but this... this made me feel properly small for the first time in years.

"Mother of God," Busto whispered beside me, his perpetual scowl momentarily replaced with naked wonder.

The crystalline monuments emitted a soft harmonic resonance that vibrated through my chest cavity—not sound in the conventional sense, but something deeper, as if the crystallized stars were still singing the songs they'd sung before their deaths millions or billions of years ago. The overlapping harmonies created a chorus that was both mournful and serene.

Through massive apertures cut into the chamber's distant walls, the binary neutron stars of the Thanatos system were visible—twin points of blindingly concentrated light that cast sharp, opposing shadows across the chamber floor. As the stars rotated, the shadows moved like the hands of some cosmic clock, marking time in a way I couldn't begin to comprehend.

"These are actual stellar cores," Sofia said. Her voice held a rare note of awe that even our estrangement couldn't hide. "Somehow preserved at the moment of collapse, before they could become neutron stars or black holes."

"The Primordians collected them," Nicobe explained, her dodecahedron spinning slightly faster than usual. "A library of stellar memories. Each one contains the complete history of its planetary system."

I took a tentative step forward, noticing immediately how my body felt lighter. "Gravity's different here," I warned the team. "About point-nine standard, I'd guess. Adjust accordingly."

The Marines shifted their stances, compensating for the reduced pull. It wasn't dramatically different from standard gravity, but enough to make movements slightly exaggerated, jumps a bit higher, falls potentially more dangerous due to misjudged timing.

Phoebe moved to the nearest crystal structure—a jagged shard the size of a shuttle that pulsed with amber light. "The energy readings are... I don't even have a reference point for this. It's like they're partially phased into another dimension."

I watched as the team spread out cautiously across the chamber floor. The vast space seemed to amplify our smallness—twenty humans and one igna, tiny specks against the backdrop of preserved cosmic history. Even our shadows, stretched and doubled by the binary stars, seemed insignificant.

"Keep your distance from the crystals," I ordered. "No touching unless—"

A startled cry cut my warning short. About thirty meters away, Private Woodson suddenly lifted off the floor, rising as if yanked by an invisible hand. Two more Marines—Diaz and Kowalski—followed an instant later, their boots leaving the ground as they scrambled uselessly for purchase in the air.

"Gravity well!" Busto shouted, already moving.

I was right behind him, gauging trajectories as I ran. The three Marines were floating upward at increasing speed toward one of the larger crystal formations. Woodson was spinning helplessly, while Diaz had managed to grab onto Kowalski, the two of them rising together.

"Grab something!" I yelled, then realized there was nothing to grab—the floor was smooth, and the nearest handholds were the crystal monuments themselves, which we'd just been warned not to touch.

Busto reached Woodson first, jumping up to snag the Private's ankle. The Lieutenant's greater mass slowed their ascent but didn't stop it. I timed my own jump carefully, using the lighter gravity to launch myself higher than would have been possible on Earth, and caught Diaz's outstretched hand.

For a moment we hung suspended in the strange gravity eddy—three Marines, Busto, and myself linked in a human chain that was slowly rising toward the massive crystal above. I could feel the pull strengthening, a sickening sensation like being at the top of a roller coaster just before the plunge, except upward.

"Nicobe!" I shouted.

The igna's capsule zipped to our position, leaving a trail of crimson light. A beam of energy lanced from the dodecahedron to the floor around us, creating a momentary disruption in the gravity field. We dropped—not gracefully—in a tangle of limbs and equipment.

"Everyone up!" I ordered, scrambling to my feet and pulling Woodson with me. "Back to the entrance, now!"

We retreated to what seemed like safer ground, the three affected Marines shaken but unharmed. Around us, I noticed other subtle disturbances in the chamber—ripples in the air, like heat waves but more structured, and tiny motes of light detaching from the crystal formations to swirl in complex patterns.

"The Ring is unstable," Nicobe announced, her usually calm voice tinged with concern. "These fluctuations are increasing in frequency. The structure is experiencing temporal-spatial stress far beyond baseline parameters."

"In plain language?" Busto demanded.

"This place is waking up," Nicobe replied. "Or breaking down. Possibly both."

A chill ran down my spine that had nothing to do with the temperature. "Everyone, activate magnetic boots and deploy tether lines," I ordered. "Standard void protocol. No one goes anywhere alone, and everyone stays connected."

The team moved with practiced efficiency, the Marines linking themselves with lightweight but strong tethers while activating the electromagnetic systems in their boots. It wouldn't help against a strong enough gravity anomaly, but it might give us warning and extra seconds to react.

Sofia approached me as I checked my own equipment. "These instabilities," she said quietly. "They weren't present in any of the scans we took from *Thunder*."

"I know," I replied, meeting her eyes directly. "Convenient timing, isn't it?"

She understood immediately. "You think it's connected to our arrival."

"A million-year-old structure that's been perfectly stable suddenly starts hiccupping right when we show up looking for a prisoner?" I fastened the last of my tether clasps. "I don't believe in coincidences that big."

As if responding to my suspicion, another gravity anomaly formed nearby—smaller than the first, but visible as a distortion in the air, like looking through curved glass. The team gave it a wide berth.

"Nicobe believes we should proceed with haste," the igna said. "The Garden was not designed for rapid transit, but lingering presents escalating risk."

I studied the layout of the vast chamber, trying to identify the most likely path forward. Beyond the garden of floating crystals, I could make out what appeared to be a more defined structure—a central hub or altar that rose from the distant floor.

That's right, Kory Drake. Come closer.

The voice caressed my mind like icy fingers on the back of my neck. This time there was no mistaking it for an echo or my imagination. It was Nekufima—had to be—reaching out directly to me.

I've prepared everything for your arrival. Your team. Your ship. You.

"Sir?" Rowbottom was watching me, concern evident in his expression. "Orders?"

I glanced around at my team—at Sofia, who was monitoring another gravity distortion with her implant; at Busto, who was checking the Marines' tether connections; at Phoebe, whose eyes kept returning to the crystalline wonders with scientific curiosity—and felt a familiar weight settle in my chest. They were all here because of me, walking into what increasingly felt like a trap.

"We press forward," I said, nodding toward the central structure. "But we move smart. Defensive formation, sensors at maximum sensitivity. If anyone hears or feels anything unusual, report it immediately."

As we began our careful advance through the Garden, I couldn't shake the growing certainty that we weren't explorers discovering an ancient wonder—we were prey, being herded step by deliberate step toward a predator that had been waiting a very, very long time.

Such suspicion, Nekufima's voice whispered in my mind. *But you are right to fear. Wisdom and paranoia look so similar from a distance, don't they?*

I kept my expression neutral, not wanting to alert the others that I was hearing voices. That rarely inspires confidence in one's leadership. But with each step deeper into the Ossuary Ring, I was increasingly certain of one thing: whatever we'd come here hoping to find, what found us might be something else entirely.

33

I led our team through the entrance of the Hall of Trophies, my boots silent against the strange black floor that seemed to swallow sound rather than reflect it. The twin beams of neutron star light stabbed through crystalline apertures overhead, casting double shadows that slithered around our feet like independent creatures. My skin prickled with that familiar sensation—part wonder, part warning—that accompanied every first step into alien architecture older than human civilization.

"Keep tight formation," I said, my voice unnaturally muted by the walls. "Standard sweep pattern. Busto, rear guard."

"Aye, sir," Busto replied, his stocky frame already pivoting to cover our six. The lieutenant had been twitchy since we'd docked with the derelict station, fingers never straying far from his flechette rifle. Can't say I blamed him.

The hall stretched ahead like the gullet of some cosmic predator, curving just enough to hide its terminus. Our helmet lights caught dust motes that hung suspended in the air, barely moving despite our passage—evidence of the subtle gravitational anomalies that plagued this section of the station.

Rowbottom gestured silently to the left and right, directing his Marines to scan the perimeter. His movements were precise, economical—the mark of a scout who'd survived because he never wasted energy. Two of his team fanned out, their reflections distorted in the glossy black walls.

"Look at this place," Phoebe whispered beside me, her voice carrying a note of awe that cut through my tactical focus. "It's a technological graveyard of species we've never even heard of."

I glanced at her, catching the eager gleam in her eyes. She wore that expression I'd come to recognize—the one that appeared whenever engineering challenges presented themselves. Her fingers twitched at her sides, already itching to dismantle and understand. There was something infectious about her enthusiasm, always had been.

"Remember why we're here," I reminded her, though not unkindly. "Destiny's scans picked up unusual sydereal signatures. We find the Phylactery, destroy it, and get back to *Thunder.* No souvenir hunting."

Phoebe rolled her eyes. "Yes, Captain Buzzkill." She gave me a playful nudge with her elbow. "But you can't tell me you're not even a little curious about what's in those display cases."

I wasn't about to admit she was right. Instead, I pointed toward the nearest niche, where something that resembled a metallic octopus pulsed with faint blue bioluminescence.

"Curious? Sure. But curious gets you killed in uncharted territory."

The display niches lined both walls in a pattern that

seemed to follow some mathematical sequence I couldn't quite grasp. Each niche contained artifacts of clearly non-human origin: weapons, devices, what appeared to be fragments of ships, or perhaps the remains of beings whose biology defied easy categorization.

"Sir," called one of Rowbottom's Marines, "these look like they've been deliberately collected. Trophy cases."

"Hence, the name Nicobe translated," I replied. "Question is, collected by whom? And where are they now?"

We continued forward, our pace deliberate. The floor beneath us was inlaid with spiraling patterns that seemed to direct movement through the space. Following them felt instinctively right, though I couldn't have explained why. The entire hall emanated a subtle vibration, like the ghost of an ancient song played at the edge of hearing.

Phoebe drifted toward the right side of the corridor, where the floor narrowed into a kind of observation ledge. A deep chasm opened beyond the railing—not a design flaw, but an intentional feature. Within it, curtains of energy shimmered and rippled, creating patterns that hurt the eyes if you stared too long.

"Lieutenant Brooks," I called, "maintain distance from the edge."

She glanced back at me with that half-smile that always made something twist in my chest. "The gravitational fields are incredible, Kory. They're being contained somehow, but they're not stable. It's like watching tides in a gravity well."

I frowned, noting how the shimmer seemed to pulse in rhythm with the bioluminescence of the artifacts. "All the more reason to keep back. We don't know what triggers fluctuations."

But Phoebe had already turned back to the chasm, leaning slightly forward to get a better look at something in a niche just beyond the railing. Her scanner was out, recording data with soft electronic chirps.

"This is fascinating," she murmured, mostly to herself. "This artifact is generating its own micro-gravity field, completely independent of the station's systems. If we could replicate this technology—"

"Brooks," I said, sharper this time. My attention had been pulled toward Busto, who was signaling about something he'd found at the entrance. The momentary distraction would haunt me later.

I heard it before I saw it—a metallic groan, the sound of ancient fastenings giving way after centuries of stress. Then Phoebe's startled yelp cut through the hall's unnatural quiet.

"Lieutenant!" Rowbottom shouted.

I spun around in time to see the section of railing in Phoebe's hands detach from the wall. For one suspended moment, she seemed to hover in place, her face a mask of surprise rather than fear. Then gravity asserted itself, and she dropped.

My heart lodged in my throat as I lunged forward, too far away to reach her. Phoebe's fingers scrabbled at the edge, somehow catching a jutting piece of the structure as she fell. She dangled now, legs kicking in empty space above the chasm.

"Hold on!" I shouted, already calculating the fastest way to reach her. The paths to either side of her position were narrow, the footing uncertain.

"I'm trying!" Phoebe called back, her voice tight with strain. "But something's pulling at me!"

I could see it then—the fluctuating gravitational fields below weren't just visual phenomena. They were exerting actual force, tugging at Phoebe's body in unpredictable pulses. Her legs swung wildly as invisible hands seemed to yank at her from different directions.

"Busto! Secure safety lines!" I ordered, dropping to my stomach to distribute my weight as I crawled toward the edge. Rowbottom was already moving, his training kicking in as he assessed anchor points.

"Sir, the structural integrity along this section is compromised," he reported, his voice clipped but steady. "We need to approach from a different angle."

I could see Phoebe's fingers whitening as they gripped the jutting piece of metal. Her face was contorted with effort, eyes wide with the realization of just how precarious her situation was.

"My grip's slipping!" she called, a tremor breaking through her usually confident voice.

A sudden surge in the gravitational field below sent her body swinging violently to one side. I heard her gasp as one hand lost its hold, leaving her dangling by just four fingers of her right hand.

My mind raced through options, each less viable than the last. The seconds stretched unbearably as I watched her struggle. There was no way I could reach her position without proper equipment, and even the Marines with their tactical gear would need time to secure lines.

"Phoebe," I called, trying to keep my voice even, "look at me. Not down. At me."

Her terrified eyes found mine, and I saw her try to master her panic.

"I can't—" she gasped as another gravitational wave pulled at her. "It's like something alive down there, Kory. It's trying to—"

Her words cut off in a cry as her fingers slipped another inch.

"Rowbottom!" I barked. "Status!"

"Almost ready, sir. I'll be moving in soon."

I glanced over to see the lieutenant already harnessed, one of his Marines anchoring the line, while he prepared to descend.

"Hurry," I said, then turned back to Phoebe. "Help is coming. Just a few more seconds."

But I could see the truth written in the trembling of her arm, the sweat beading on her forehead. She wouldn't last a few more seconds. The gravitational forces were growing stronger, more erratic, as if the chasm itself had awakened to the presence of potential prey.

"Kory," she said, her voice suddenly calm in a way that chilled me, "if I don't make it—"

"Don't," I cut her off. "Save your strength. That's an order."

A ghost of her usual smile flickered across her face. "Since when do I follow orders?"

I watched Rowbottom move with the fluid precision that marked him as former Army Scout, his body responding to the crisis before his conscious mind had finished calculating the angles. He secured his line with practiced hands that never seemed to fumble, even as my own pulse hammered against my ribs in panic. There's something humbling about watching someone execute their expertise in a life-or-death moment—like witnessing a surgeon cut through chaos to find the heart of what matters.

"Line secure!" he called, voice clipped and professional. His eyes never left Phoebe's dangling form as he checked his harness one final time.

"Get her, Lieutenant." I turned to the rest of the team. "I need three more lines, anchored at separate points. Now!"

The Marines broke into action, their training clear in

how they moved without wasting motion or words. I kept my position near the edge, maintaining eye contact with Phoebe.

"Stay with me, Brooks," I called to her. "Rowbottom's coming down. Just keep holding on."

Her fingers trembled visibly, white-knuckled against the jutting piece of metal. The gravitational fields below pulsed with greater intensity, as if sensing prey within reach.

"It's getting stronger," she gasped, her body jerking as another wave pulled at her legs.

Busto positioned himself at the anchor point, his stocky frame a picture of immovable stability as he braced against the potential force that would come when Rowbottom reached Phoebe.

"Marines, form a retrieval line," he ordered, his voice carrying the no-nonsense authority that had kept countless soldiers alive. "Maintain tension against the wall side to compensate for field fluctuation."

Rowbottom began his descent, his movements deliberate but quick. I'd seen him scale cliffs during training exercises, moving with a nimble confidence that belied his tall frame. But this was different—there was no stable surface to work with, just the smooth black wall material and the unpredictable gravitic surges from below.

The first surge hit him when he was about three meters down. I saw his body suddenly yank sideways, as if grabbed by an invisible hand. He grunted, muscles straining as he fought to maintain his position.

"Field intensity increasing," he reported through gritted teeth. "Variable pattern. No predictable intervals."

I watched him adapt in real time, learning the rhythm of the surges like a dancer finding his way through an alien composition. When the next pull came, he was ready, using the momentum to propel himself closer to Phoebe rather than fighting directly against it.

Smart. That was Rowbottom—always finding the path of least resistance through impossible terrain.

Phoebe's gaze was fixed on him now, hope replacing some of the terror in her eyes. "If you wanted a date, Rowbottom," she called out, her voice strained but attempting levity, "you could have just asked!"

A ghost of a smile crossed Rowbottom's face. "Thought I'd make an impression, ma'am."

I held my breath as he navigated another surge, this one nearly pulling him off course entirely. His harness line went taut with a low hum of strain, but held. Busto adjusted his stance, compensating for the changed angle of force.

"Sir," one of the Marines called, "the gravitational patterns are intensifying. Readings show increasing amplitude."

That wasn't good. The fluctuations had been stable, if unpredictable, when we entered. Now they were growing stronger, as if something about our presence—or perhaps Phoebe's precarious position—had triggered a change in the system.

Rowbottom was just two meters from Phoebe now, close enough that I could see the concentration etched in his features. Another gravitational surge hit, stronger than the previous ones. His body jerked violently, but he used the momentum again, letting it carry him closer to Phoebe rather than fighting it.

"Almost there," he called to her. "Just a few more seconds."

I could see Phoebe's strength failing. Her arm trembled violently, fingers slipping millimeter by millimeter from their hold. Sweat beaded on her forehead from the effort of fighting against both gravity and the unpredictable pulls from below.

"I can't—" she gasped, and I saw her fingers slip further.

In that moment, Rowbottom moved with a speed I didn't think possible in the chaotic gravitational field. He lunged downward, one arm extended toward Phoebe. His timing was perfect—her fingers lost their grip entirely, her body beginning its fall just as Rowbottom's arm wrapped around her waist.

The sudden transfer of weight made his harness line groan with strain. Busto and the Marines leaned back, countering the force. Rowbottom and Phoebe swung in a wide arc, the gravitational fields pulling them in an unpredictable pattern that had them spinning like leaves in a tornado.

"I've got you," Rowbottom said, his voice surprisingly calm as he tightened his hold around Phoebe's waist. "Just breathe."

Phoebe's arms wrapped around his neck, her body shaking with adrenaline and relief. They hung suspended in the chasm, two figures swinging in the strange luminescence of the fluctuating fields.

"Some view, huh?" Rowbottom said, his attempt at lightness belied by the strain in his voice as he struggled to maintain his hold on both Phoebe and his position.

Phoebe's laugh was half sob. "Took me to all the worst places, Ivor."

The use of his first name didn't escape my notice. There was an intimacy to the way she said it that suggested this wasn't just the familiar banter of crewmates.

"You're one brave woman, Phoebe," Rowbottom said, his voice dropping to a register I'd never heard him use before. "Always admired that about you."

Their faces were close—necessarily so, given the precarious position—but there was something more to it, a conscious choice in how they looked at each other.

"Funny time to finally tell me," Phoebe replied, her voice steadier now despite their dangerous situation. Tears streaked her dusty cheeks, but her eyes held Rowbottom's with an intensity that transcended their physical danger.

"Been trying to work up the courage for months," he admitted. "Nothing like a near-death experience to clarify priorities."

Their foreheads touched briefly, a gesture so intimate I felt like an intruder for witnessing it—even from my distant position.

"When we get back," Phoebe said, her voice barely carrying to where I stood, "I'd like to hear more about these priorities of yours."

Rowbottom's smile was genuine, transforming his usually serious face. "Yes, ma'am."

I turned to Busto. "Let's get them up. Steady retrieval."

Busto nodded, already organizing the Marines into position for the pull. "On my mark. Three, two—"

The warning came too late. A violent surge in the gravitational field—stronger than any previous one—ripped through the chasm. The energy patterns below shifted from their gentle shimmer to a violent maelstrom of conflicting forces.

Rowbottom and Phoebe were slammed sideways with brutal force, their bodies colliding with the black wall. I heard the impact—a sickening crunch followed by Rowbottom's sharp intake of breath. He'd positioned himself to take the brunt of the collision, his body shielding Phoebe from the worst of it.

"Rowbottom!" I shouted.

The lieutenant's face was contorted in pain, but his arm remained locked around Phoebe. "I'm okay," he called back, the lie obvious in how he struggled to get the words out. "But we need to move. Field instability increasing."

I could see he was right. The energy patterns below were shifting faster now, colors bleeding into one another as the forces grew more chaotic. Whatever balance had maintained the gravitational fields was breaking down.

"Pull them up! Now!" I ordered.

The Marines heaved on the line, but another gravitational surge fought against their efforts, nearly pulling Rowbottom and Phoebe back down. I grabbed the line alongside the others, adding my strength to the collective effort.

Below, Rowbottom was working one-handed to secure Phoebe to his harness, his other arm curled protectively around his torso. Each movement seemed to cost him, pain flickering across his features.

"Almost got it," he said to Phoebe, his voice tight. "Just need to clip this—"

Another surge hit them, not as violent as the last, but enough to make Rowbottom gasp. Phoebe wrapped her arms tighter around him, trying to stabilize both of them.

"Let me," she said, taking the carabiner from his trembling hand and clipping herself to his harness with practiced efficiency. "There. We're secure."

Rowbottom's breathing had become shallow, each inhale clearly causing him pain. Despite this, he managed a smile for Phoebe. "Always knew you were the competent one."

She sobbed against his shoulder, her body trembling uncontrollably now that the immediate danger of falling had passed. "You're hurt. Because of me."

"Worth it," Rowbottom replied, his voice dropping to a whisper I barely caught. "I've got you. Just hold on to me. I will always have you."

Their faces were close again, and though I couldn't hear what else Rowbottom murmured to her, I saw Phoebe nod, her eyes never leaving his.

The next pull on the line brought them up several feet, but the gravitational fluctuations fought us every inch of the way. The line hummed with tension, straining against forces that seemed determined to claim them.

"Together!" Busto called, setting the rhythm for our efforts. "Pull!"

With each coordinated heave, we gained ground. Centimeter by centimeter, we pulled them from the chasm's grasp. The lines creaked under the strain, the gravitational fields below growing increasingly erratic.

Rowbottom maintained his hold on Phoebe despite his obvious pain, his jaw clenched tight against whatever injury he'd sustained. I could see the effort it cost him to keep his composure, to not let Phoebe see the full extent of his suffering.

When they finally reached the edge, many hands reached out to pull them to safety. Phoebe came first, Marines lifting her clear of the chasm with swift efficiency. Rowbottom followed more slowly, his movements hampered by whatever injury he'd sustained.

As soon as they were both on solid ground, I ordered the team back from the edge. The gravitational disturbance below continued to intensify, the patterns shifting in ways that suggested the system was approaching some critical threshold.

Rowbottom collapsed to his knees the moment we

cleared the danger zone, one arm wrapped around his torso like he was physically holding himself together. His face, usually a composed mask that gave away nothing, was now contorted with each breath. Pain had a way of stripping pretenses, revealing the raw person beneath the uniform. I'd seen it happen to better men than me in worse places than this, but it never got easier to watch—especially when the injury came from saving someone else.

"I need room," Busto barked, shouldering his way through the ring of Marines that had formed around Rowbottom. His weathered hands already held a compact medical scanner, the device humming to life as he passed it over Rowbottom's torso.

Phoebe kneeled beside Rowbottom, her fingers interlaced with his free hand. The dust and tears had left muddy tracks down her cheeks, but her eyes were clear now, focused entirely on the injured lieutenant.

"How bad?" I asked Busto, keeping my voice low.

Busto's face was a study in professional concern, his eyes never leaving the scanner's readout. "Three broken ribs on the left side, Lieutenant. Torn intercostal muscles. Possible pneumothorax developing. Injured vertebrae."

"In English, Busto," Rowbottom managed through gritted teeth.

"Your ribs are trying to stab your lungs, and you might have a broken back," Busto replied bluntly. "We need to evacuate you."

Rowbottom attempted a nod that dissolved into a grimace. "Figured as much. Felt something give when we hit the wall."

I tapped my comm unit, grateful that it still functioned despite the strange properties of this place. "*Thunder,* this is Drake. Medical emergency. We need immediate evac for

Lieutenant Rowbottom. Broken ribs, back injury, possible internal injuries."

Destiny's voice came back almost instantly, the slight delay indicating she was monitoring from the bridge rather than comms. "Copy that, Kory. What happened?"

"Structural failure and gravitational anomalies. Rowbottom took a bad hit during a rescue." I kept it brief, knowing the details could wait. "We're approximately two hundred meters into the Hall of Trophies. Main corridor. Can you lock onto our position?"

"Affirmative," Destiny replied, her voice shifting to the clipped professionalism she adopted during crises. "Scans show you're under some kind of energy field. It's interfering with nav lock. You'll need to move him to the entrance bay where we landed."

I glanced at Rowbottom, calculating the challenge of moving him that distance.

"Understood. Prepare medical to receive one injured. Drake out."

Busto was already administering emergency painkillers, the hypospray hissing against Rowbottom's neck.

"This'll take the edge off, but we can't give you the good stuff until we know there's no brain injury."

Rowbottom's face relaxed slightly as the medication took hold.

"Appreciate it, Lieutenant," he muttered.

"We need to fashion a stretcher," I said, scanning our surroundings for anything useful. "We can't risk carrying him unsupported with those injuries."

Busto was already a step ahead, snapping his fingers at two nearby Marines.

"Grab poles from the modular scaffolding—fabric from

the emergency shelters. Move!"

They scattered, their boots clanging on the alien floor as they stripped supplies from the nearby gear pile.

Phoebe kneeled beside Rowbottom, her gloved hand gripping his tightly.

"You're going to be fine," she whispered fiercely. "I've got you. We've got you."

He tried a lopsided grin but ended up grimacing in pain.

The Marines returned, working fast. Busto and Diaz rigged a makeshift stretcher in record time—a crude but stable frame that would hold under jostling.

I crouched beside Rowbottom.

"This is going to hurt," I warned. "But we'll get you back to *Thunder*."

Rowbottom gave a tight nod. "Wouldn't miss it, sir."

On my mark, Busto and two Marines lifted Rowbottom carefully onto the stretcher. He grunted through clenched teeth, but stayed conscious.

"Move out!" I barked.

They fell into a tight formation around him—Diaz leading, Phoebe clutching the side rail, her face pale but determined.

As the evac team made their way back through the crumbling corridors of the Ossuary Ring, I kept glancing at the walls.

The structure seemed to breathe around us—gravitic distortions warping the air, ancient lights flickering like dying stars.

The whole place felt like it was holding its breath.

Or like something deeper was starting to wake.

34

The Ossuary Ring swallowed us like some ancient beast digesting its prey—slowly, inexorably, through corridors that twisted like intestines lined with crystalline teeth. My boots echoed against metal that shouldn't have still existed after millions of years, yet here it was, humming with energy older than human civilization. I led our reduced procession of humans and one igna with more confidence than I felt, wondering—not for the first time—how a street kid from San Jose had ended up commanding trained soldiers through an alien megastructure orbiting a binary neutron star. Life had a funny way of promoting you right to the edge of your incompetence.

"Left at the next junction, Commander," Nicobe's voice emanated from her capsule, floating a meter off the ground beside me. "Nicobe detects increasing sydereal emissions in that direction."

I nodded, though I wasn't sure if Nicobe could see the gesture or just sensed it somehow. The igna's perception capabilities remained a mystery, even after all our time together.

"Copy that," I said, adjusting our course. "Busto, keep the rear secure."

"Already on it, sir," came Busto's clipped reply from behind me. The former Marine Raider moved with the quiet efficiency of a man who'd seen too much combat to waste energy on unnecessary movement.

Between us walked Sofia, her black protomatter helmet catching the azure glow from the wall glyphs. I wanted to reach out and hold her hand, but suspected such an action would be unwelcome.

I kept my focus forward, aware of the four Marines behind Busto—our entire remaining security detail after sending away an evacuation team with Lieutenant Rowbottom. They moved with professional composure, but I caught the occasional wide-eyed glance at the alien architecture surrounding us. I couldn't blame them. The walls seemed to breathe, glyphs pulsing in patterns that almost made sense before dissolving into nonsense again.

"Anyone else feel like we're being herded?" I asked, mostly to break the silence rather than out of genuine suspicion.

Sofia answered without looking at me. "The corridor dimensions have decreased since entry. The ceiling has lowered as well."

I glanced up, measuring the height with my eyes. Had it been higher before? I couldn't tell for sure, but that tightening sensation hadn't been just my imagination.

"Nicobe concurs with Chief Kohl's assessment," the igna said. "The Primordians designed this structure with remarkable psychological principles. We are being guided rather than herded, Commander."

"Guided to what?" Busto muttered behind us.

I was about to respond with something appropriately witty when the corridor suddenly opened into a vast chamber that stole the words from my mouth. We halted at the threshold, collectively stunned by what lay before us.

A perfect circle of obsidian floor spread out before us, its polished surface reflecting the pulsing azure glyphs that lined the walls. The circular vault rose to a domed ceiling, perhaps twelve meters high at its apex. But what froze me in place were the figures seated around the circumference of the room.

Twenty-four of them, arranged in perfect symmetry. Primordians. The real deal—actual Primordians. Or their bodies, at least.

They sat in ceremonial poses, their skeletal remains fused with what must have been their armor. Each figure towered at least three meters tall, even seated. Their elongated skulls bore the distinctive crest that I'd only seen in reconstructions and speculative xenobiological texts. Their armor, an impossible fusion of crystalline material and what appeared to be actual bone, seemed to catch and amplify the light from the glyphs.

The air carried a metallic tang that coated my tongue and made my fillings ache. Each footstep echoed with a hollow resonance that seemed to carry farther than it should in a chamber this size.

"Holy shit," one of the Marines whispered behind me.

"Maintain discipline," Busto snapped, though his own voice carried a hint of awe.

"Lieutenant Busto," I said, finding my voice again, "secure the perimeter. Standard sweep, but don't touch anything."

"Aye, sir." Busto signaled to his Marines, who spread out with practiced precision, though they gave the seated

Primordian figures a wide berth.

Sofia moved forward, her scanner held out before her. Our eyes met briefly as she passed me, and I caught something there—not the warmth we once shared, but a flicker of shared wonder that momentarily bridged the gulf between us.

"Energy signatures throughout the chamber," she reported. "Nothing dangerous, but these patterns..." she trailed off, her attention captured by the data scrolling across her device.

I stepped further into the chamber, drawn to the nearest of the ancient figures. Its empty eye sockets seemed to track my movement. A trick of the light, I told myself, yet I couldn't shake the feeling of being observed.

"Nicobe would advise caution, Commander," the igna said, her crimson housing drifting toward the wall glyphs. "These are warning markers."

"Warning against what?" I asked, still unable to look away from the mummified Primordian before me.

"The glyphs speak of guardianship and eternal vigilance," Nicobe responded. "They refer to 'That Which Sleeps Beyond' and 'The Bound One.' Quite poetic for what appears to be a security system."

I tore my gaze away from the seated figure and surveyed the chamber again. Twenty-four guardians, frozen in eternal watch. The hairs on my neck stood at attention.

"They're watching us," I said, immediately regretting how ridiculous it sounded.

"They're dead, Commander," Busto said flatly, though he kept glancing at the nearest figure as if expecting it to move.

"Technically correct, Lieutenant Busto," Nicobe replied, "but Commander Drake's instincts are not entirely inaccurate. Nicobe detects subtle sydereal field fluctuations emanating from each figure. They are passive scanning systems, still functional after millions of years."

"So they're security cameras?" I asked, feeling oddly better at the thought of technology rather than ghosts.

"An imperfect analogy, but serviceable," Nicobe responded. Her housing spun slowly as she processed the data. "More accurately, they are sydereal field monitors capable of detecting consciousness patterns. They know we are here, Commander, and they are... assessing."

"Assessing what?" I asked.

"Intent, perhaps. Nicobe cannot say with certainty."

Sofia had completed her circuit of the room and returned to our group. "There are three sealed archways," she reported, pointing to equally spaced points around the chamber. "Each is covered in similar glyphs to those on the walls, but with distinct patterns."

I nodded and approached the nearest archway. It resembled a doorway carved from a single piece of obsidian, its surface covered in glyphs that seemed to shift and change when I wasn't looking directly at them.

"Can you read these?" I asked Nicobe.

The igna hovered near the archway, her crimson housing reflecting on its glossy surface. "This one speaks of 'The Path of Descent.' The one opposite refers to 'The Chamber of Binding.' The third mentions 'The Vault of Memory.'"

"Well, that's helpfully cryptic," I muttered. "Any preference?"

"The energy signatures are strongest behind the Path of Descent," Sofia said, still not meeting my eyes directly.

"Nicobe concurs. If we seek the Noble Phylactery, that would be the logical route."

I glanced back at the seated Primordians, their empty eye sockets seemingly fixed on us despite their diverse positions around the room. The feeling of being watched intensified, an itch between my shoulder blades that I couldn't scratch.

"Busto, how are our Marines holding up?" I asked.

The lieutenant checked in with his team via comms before answering. "On edge, sir, but good to go. Martinson's reading elevated energy levels near the far archway—the Path of Descent."

I took a deep breath, tasting that metallic tang again. My instincts screamed we were walking into something we didn't understand, but that was basically my job description these days.

"Alright team, we're taking the Path of Descent," I decided. "Busto, you and two Marines on point. Sofia and Nicobe with me in the middle. The remaining Marines bring up the rear."

As we formed up, I found myself standing briefly beside Sofia. The space between us felt charged with unspoken words.

"You okay?" I asked quietly.

She nodded curtly. "Functional."

Not the reassurance I was hoping for, but more than I'd gotten from her in days. I'd take it.

"Let's move out," I ordered, and we approached the archway that Nicobe had identified as the Path of Descent.

As we drew closer, the glyphs on its surface began to pulse more rapidly, as if responding to our presence. The sealed surface, which had appeared solid from a distance, now seemed to shimmer like heat waves rising from hot asphalt.

"Defensive posture," Busto ordered his Marines, who

raised their weapons slightly.

I raised my hand. "Hold fire unless I give the order." Looking at Nicobe, I asked, "Any ideas how we get through a sealed door?"

"The Primordians did not believe in locks as we understand them," the igna replied. "Their security was based on sydereal field recognition. One must simply... approach with purpose."

I sighed. "Approach with purpose. Got it."

I stepped forward, trying to project as much purposeful confidence as I could muster. The shimmering intensified as I neared the archway, the glyphs flaring bright enough to cast my shadow long across the chamber floor.

Three steps from the archway, I hesitated. That feeling of being watched had become almost unbearable, as if twenty-four pairs of non-existent eyes were boring into my back.

"Is it just me," I said without turning, "or did the seated figures move?"

No one answered immediately. Then Sofia's voice, tight with tension: "They're in the same positions as before. I've been monitoring."

I nodded, mostly to convince myself, and took the final steps toward the archway. The shimmering surface seemed to part before me, not so much opening as simply ceasing to be solid. Beyond lay darkness and that same metallic taste in the air, but stronger.

"Looks like we're expected," I said, gesturing the team forward. "Try not to disappoint our hosts."

As we passed through the archway one by one, I couldn't help glancing back at the mummified Primordians. In the pulsing azure light, their empty sockets seemed to follow our departure, eternal guardians watching us descend into the depths of their ancient mystery.

I couldn't shake the sense that something was watching, measuring us—and that whatever came next wouldn't leave room for mistakes.

35

The archway released us like reluctant prey, spitting us into a corridor that seemed to breathe differently than the chambers before. The air hung heavy with potential energy, a static charge that made the fine hairs on my forearms stand at attention. I moved forward through the semi-darkness, my boots finding purchase on a floor that felt too smooth to be millions of years old. The walls here were different—no longer adorned with pulsing glyphs but instead bearing geometric patterns that seemed to shift when viewed from the corner of my eye, as if the very structure of reality was less fixed in this part of the ring.

"Light discipline," Busto murmured to his Marines, their helmet lamps dimming to soft halos that barely illuminated the space immediately around us.

"Nicobe is detecting unusual gravitational fluctuations," the igna's voice came from behind me, her crimson dodecahedron hovering at shoulder height. "Most curious."

Sofia moved like a ghost at my side, her scanner held before her like a divining rod. "Energy signatures increasing," she reported, her voice professionally detached. "Something massive ahead."

The corridor curved gently upward, following what I assumed was the circumference of the Ossuary Ring. With each step, that strange static charge in the air intensified, and a new sensation emerged—a deep, subsonic hum that I felt more than heard, vibrating through the bones of my feet and up into my chest cavity.

"Anyone else feel that?" I asked.

"Affirmative," one of the Marines replied, his voice tight with tension. "Like standing next to a subwoofer playing a note too low to hear."

“Infrasound,” Sofia said.

"Primordian technology often operates in spectrums beyond human perception," Nicobe offered. "This particular frequency appears calibrated to resonate with organic tissue."

"That's... not comforting," I muttered.

The curve of the corridor became more pronounced, and then suddenly opened onto a platform that jutted out into... nothing. We halted at the threshold, collectively stunned by what lay before us.

A vast vertical shaft stretched above and below us, so wide that the opposite wall was barely visible in the dim light. Our platform extended like a diving board over an abyss that seemed to have no bottom. The walls of the shaft were lined with perfectly engineered spiral ribs of crystalline material that caught what little light there was and scattered it in mesmerizing patterns.

"Jesus," Busto whispered, religious invocation rather than profanity.

I took a cautious step onto the platform, feeling a subtle shift in the gravitational pull as I did so. Not enough to be dangerous, but noticeable—as if the massive shaft created its own gravitational field separate from the ring's artificial gravity.

"What are we looking at, Nicobe?" I asked, fighting the urge to step closer to the edge.

The igna drifted past me, her crimson housing reflecting fractured light from the spiral ribs. "The Primordians called this the Starwell. A gravitational conduit that appears to harness and redirect the immense forces generated by the binary neutron stars."

I edged forward, drawn by a fascination I couldn't quite explain. The vertigo was immediate and intense—not the typical fear of heights, but something more fundamental, as if my inner ear was detecting spatial impossibilities that my conscious mind couldn't process.

"Careful, sir," Busto cautioned from behind me.

I nodded absently, my attention captured by the spiral ribs that lined the shaft. They pulsed with a dim luminescence that flowed like water, following what must have been gravitational anomalies from below. Each pulse corresponded to a subtle intensification of that subsonic hum, creating a rhythm that seemed to bypass my conscious mind and speak directly to my limbic system.

One of the Marines switched his helmet lamp to full power and directed it downward. The beam traveled perhaps fifty meters before fragmenting into spiral patterns that echoed the ribbed walls, then dissipated entirely without revealing a bottom.

"Kill that light," Busto ordered sharply.

But I'd seen something in that brief illumination—a pattern to the light's dissolution, a mathematical precision to its fragmentation that suggested not random scattering but deliberate diffraction.

"It's a lens," I murmured, taking another step forward. "The entire shaft is a massive lens, focusing... something."

Sofia moved to my side, close enough that I caught the familiar scent of her—that clinical shampoo she preferred, now mixed with the metallic tang of the station's air. "Energy readings are off the charts," she said, showing me her scanner. The display was a mess of overlapping fields, the device struggling to categorize what it was detecting.

I leaned forward slightly, peering into the abyss. The shaft seemed to call to me, each pulse of light along the spiral ribs drawing my attention deeper. The mathematical beauty of it was overwhelming—the precise intervals between pulses, the way each spiral rib caught and redirected light in patterns that almost made sense...

A powerful hand gripped my shoulder, pulling me back sharply. I stumbled, nearly falling, and found myself staring into Busto's stern face.

"This place is messing with your head," Busto said bluntly. "Sir."

He was right. The rhythmic pulsing of the spiral ribs had created a hypnotic pattern that had nearly drawn me into the abyss. I shook my head to clear it, taking two deliberate steps back from the edge.

"Thanks," I said. "I didn't realize..."

"It's not just you, sir," Busto jerked his head toward the Marines. Two of them stood transfixed, staring into the shaft with the same fascination I'd felt. The third—Martinson, I noted—was physically restraining one of his comrades from stepping too close to the edge.

"Everyone back from the edge," I ordered, my voice sharper than intended. "Nicobe, what the hell is happening here?"

The igna hovered near the edge of the platform,

seemingly immune to whatever influence had affected the humans. "Fascinating. The gravitational anomalies are creating resonance patterns in sydereal space-time. The visual pulses are synchronized precisely with the orbital dance of the neutron stars above. Nicobe believes this is a form of gravitational communication—or perhaps control."

"Control of what?" Sofia asked, her professional demeanor reasserting itself as she stepped away from the edge.

"The Noble Phylactery, perhaps," Nicobe replied. "Or whatever is contained within it."

That subsonic hum intensified momentarily, as if responding to the mention of the Phylactery. I felt it resonate through my chest cavity, vibrating my sternum in a way that was almost painful.

"How do we get past this?" I asked, gesturing at the shaft that effectively blocked our path.

Nicobe's housing rotated slowly, scanning the perimeter of our platform. "There," she said, indicating a narrow walkway that hugged the inner wall of the shaft, spiraling downward along one of the crystalline ribs. "That appears to be the designated path."

The walkway was barely wide enough for one person, with no railing separating it from the bottomless shaft. It followed the spiraling rib downward, disappearing from view after perhaps a hundred meters.

"You've got to be kidding me," one of the Marines muttered.

I shared the sentiment, but kept it to myself. Leader's privilege—and burden—to maintain confidence even when I was screaming internally.

"Single file," I said. "Harnesses linked. No one walks that path without being tethered to at least two others."

Busto nodded approvingly and began distributing the lightweight emergency harnesses from his pack. The standard UHC equipment seemed almost comically mundane against the backdrop of ancient alien technology, but I'd take practical human safety measures over mysterious Primordian architecture any day.

"Commander," Sofia said quietly as we prepared the harnesses, "the scanner is detecting a powerful energy signature approximately five hundred meters down that path." She hesitated, then added, "The signature matches what we know of the Noble Phylactery."

I nodded, grateful for the professional information exchange despite our personal complications. "Then that's where we're headed. It means we're close."

"Nicobe would advise extreme caution," the igna interjected. "The intensifying gravitic anomalies suggest we are approaching something of significant mass."

"Significant mass?" I repeated. "Like what?"

"The Phylactery itself has negligible physical mass," Nicobe explained, "but what it contains—or controls—may be another matter entirely."

The subsonic hum pulsed again, stronger this time, as if responding to our conversation. The spiral ribs flared with increased luminescence, creating patterns that drew the eye downward along their path.

"Everyone check your harness," Busto ordered, his voice cutting through the hypnotic effect of the shaft. "Standard mountaineering protocol. No one moves until I verify your rigging."

I submitted to Busto's inspection of my harness, grateful for his practical military approach to the situation. The familiar routine of equipment checks grounded me, providing a counterpoint to the vertiginous pull of the

Starwell.

"Formation as follows," I decided once everyone was properly harnessed. "Busto takes point. I'll follow, then Sofia, then Nicobe, with the remaining Marines bringing up the rear. Maintain minimum three-meter spacing on the walkway."

"Sir," Busto said, hesitating uncharacteristically, "with respect, you shouldn't be second in line."

I raised an eyebrow. "Something you want to tell me, Lieutenant?"

"You were affected more strongly than the others by whatever this shaft is doing," he said bluntly. "If you... lose focus, I might not be able to hold both of us."

He was right, of course, but it stung my pride to admit it. "Fine. You, then Sofia, then me, then the Marines, with Nicobe free to move as needed since she can float."

Busto nodded, clearly relieved, and took up position at the start of the narrow walkway. Sofia followed, her movements precise and controlled as she clipped her harness to Busto's.

As I prepared to take my position behind Sofia, she turned to me briefly. "Be careful," she said, her voice softer than it had been in days. "That thing... it got into your head faster than the others."

I nodded, unexpectedly touched by her concern. "I noticed. Any theories?"

"The implant in my head seems to provide some resistance," she said, tapping her temple where the Kergan technology resided. "Perhaps you're more... receptive naturally."

"Lucky me," I muttered, then gestured forward. "Let's move out before this thing figures out new ways to mess with us."

As we began our careful descent along the spiraling walkway, that subsonic hum seemed to intensify, vibrating through the crystalline path beneath our feet. The luminescent pulses flowing along the spiral ribs accelerated slightly, as if eager to guide us downward to whatever waited below.

I forced myself to focus on Sofia's back ahead of me, on the solid reality of the harness connecting us, on the practical task of placing one foot carefully in front of the other on the narrow path. Still, I couldn't shake the feeling that we weren't so much walking into the depths of the Ossuary Ring as being drawn inexorably toward something that had been waiting for us for millions of years.

36

The spiral walkway deposited us into a chamber that put the previous ones to shame. Vast and circular, it stretched at least a hundred meters across, filled with concentric rings of crystalline pillars that caught and fractured light in ways that made my eyes water. They looked like frozen fountains of black glass, each one unique in its twisted, reaching form, yet clearly part of some greater pattern that my human mind couldn't quite grasp. The air here felt thick, charged with potential like the moment before lightning strikes. My skin prickled with static electricity, and each breath tasted of ozone and metal. I stepped forward, aware of my team fanning out behind me, their footsteps hesitant on the polished obsidian floor.

"Maintain formation," Busto ordered, his voice tight with professional caution.

I hardly heard him. My attention had been captured by what hovered at the center of the chamber, suspended within a swirling gravitic anomaly that distorted the space around it.

The Noble Phylactery.

Despite its legendary status, the artifact itself was surprisingly small—a crystalline icosahedron, perhaps five centimeters in diameter. Small enough to fit in my palm. It rotated slowly, each of its twenty triangular faces catching light from an unseen source. The surface was covered in complex, shifting Primordian glyphs that pulsed with light. It floated perfectly in place, seemingly untethered to any physical support.

"That's it?" one of the Marines whispered. "That little thing is what everyone's fighting over?"

I understood his skepticism. The Phylactery appeared almost disappointingly mundane—until you looked closer and realized it wasn't reflecting light but somehow generating it from within. The glyphs on its surface weren't etched or engraved; they moved and shifted like living things, rearranging themselves in patterns that almost made sense before dissolving into new configurations.

"Nicobe detects extreme sydereal field density," the igna announced, her crimson housing hovering near my shoulder. "The artifact exists partially in our dimension and partially in the Syderealium."

Sofia had her scanner pointed at the Phylactery, but the device was emitting an irregular beeping that suggested it was struggling to process what it was detecting. "Energy signatures off the charts," she reported, her voice clinical despite the tension evident in her posture. "Multiple frequencies, some of which the scanner can't even categorize."

I nodded and took a cautious step forward, moving between two of the crystalline pillars toward the center of the chamber. The air seemed to thicken as I advanced, that static charge intensifying against my skin. Behind me, I heard Busto issuing quiet orders to the Marines to establish a perimeter.

"Careful, Commander," Nicobe warned. "The artifact appears to be activating in response to our presence."

She was right. With each step I took, the Phylactery's rotation speed increased slightly, and the glyphs on its surface pulsed more rapidly. The gravitic anomaly surrounding it expanded, creating visible distortions in the air like heat waves rising from hot asphalt.

I stopped about ten meters from the Phylactery, instinct reeling back like a hand from fire. Up close, it was even more overwhelming—beautiful in a way that defied logic, as if form and meaning had been fused together by something beyond comprehension. The surface shimmered with geometric patterns that shifted when I wasn't looking directly at them, like it was rewriting itself moment by moment.

I'd told myself I could destroy it. That I *would* destroy it, if it came to that. For Zeta. For humanity. Because Nekufima was a threat too vast to risk. But standing here, breathing the still, charged air of this ancient vault, I wasn't so sure anymore. This wasn't a weapon or a prison. It was a relic older than our entire civilization, built by hands—or minds—that no longer existed. The thought of obliterating something so impossibly old, so perfectly alien, felt like sacrilege.

But awe didn't change the facts. Nekufima was inside it. And if she got out—if I let her out—we might all pay the price. My loyalty to Zeta demanded clarity. My duty to my crew demanded strength.

So why did I feel like a vandal in a museum, trying to convince myself that smashing the masterpiece was the noble thing to do?

"Nicobe, what exactly are we looking at? What does this

thing do?"

The igna's housing spun slowly as she processed the question. "According to Collective Dominion records, the Noble Phylactery is a containment device of Primordian origin. It was designed to imprison and control an entity known as an Astral Titan—a being of pure sydereal energy."

"And it's here because...?" I prompted.

"Unknown. Records suggest the artifact forms a unique bond with—"

Nicobe's voice cut off as the Phylactery suddenly flared with intense light. The glyphs on its surface accelerated their shifting, blurring into streaks of luminescence that cast long shadows through the chamber. The gravitic anomaly pulsed once, twice, and then expanded outward in a silent wave that passed through us like a ghost.

And then I saw them.

A man and woman stood between me and the Phylactery, their forms solid and real despite their impossible presence. They weren't transparent or ghostly—they were simply there, as physically present as any of my team.

The man was tall, with a square jaw and broad shoulders that matched my own build. His eyes were brown like mine, but deeper set beneath heavier brows. The woman was slimmer, with laugh lines around her eyes and a determined set to her mouth that I'd seen in my own mirror.

My parents.

I recognized them instantly, though I had no conscious memory of their faces. Ban'ach had stolen those memories years ago during our battle in the Syderealium. Yet I knew them, recognized myself in their features—my father's jawline, my mother's eyes, the way they both stood with their weight shifted slightly to one side.

"Kory," my mother said, her voice exactly as I would have imagined it—warm and slightly husky. She opened her arms to me, smiling with such profound love that it made my chest ache.

"Son," my father said, nodding with clear pride. "Look at you. A commander now."

I took an involuntary step forward, drawn by a longing so intense it felt like physical pain. These were the faces I'd tried to remember ever since I was a child, the voices I'd strained to recall in quiet moments alone.

"They're not real," Sofia's voice came from somewhere behind me, strained and distant. I half-turned to see her on her knees, eyes wide with terror, staring at empty air. She was muttering rapidly in German, words about Berlin streets and battles I knew she'd never fought.

Busto stood frozen several meters to my right, his hand extended toward nothing I could see. "Jenkins," he called, his voice cracking with emotion. "Ramirez. Hold position!" He was calling to squadmates I knew had died years ago.

The Marines were in similar states—one backing away with his weapon raised against invisible enemies, another standing transfixed, tears streaming down his face as he whispered what sounded like a child's name over and over.

Only Nicobe seemed partially resistant, though her crimson dodecahedron flickered erratically, pulsing with unstable light. "Nicobe is experiencing pattern intrusions in cognitive systems," she announced, her usually smooth voice fragmented and distorted. "The artifact is attempting to access memory centers."

I turned back to my parents, understanding intellectually that they weren't real, that the Phylactery was somehow extracting and projecting our memories. But the knowledge did nothing to diminish their impact.

"We've missed you so much," my mother said, taking a step toward me. Her eyes—my eyes—glistened with tears. "Come home, Kory."

"We're proud of you, son," my father added, his smile widening. "Always have been."

I found myself moving forward again, drawn by words I'd waited my entire life to hear. Three steps closer to the phantoms. Three steps closer to the Phylactery.

"K-Kory," Sofia's strained voice reached me again. "Don't... it's not..."

I hesitated, torn between the vision before me and the very real danger behind it. The Phylactery's rotation had accelerated further, the glyphs now a continuous blur of light. The gravitic anomaly surrounding it pulsed in rhythm with my heartbeat.

"It's okay now," my mother said soothingly. "We've been waiting for you."

My father nodded. "You've done enough fighting, son. Time to rest."

Their voices were perfect—exactly what I'd always imagined, exactly what I'd needed to hear through years in orphanages and on the streets. The weight of command, of responsibility, of constant vigilance against threats, human and alien—it all seemed to lift from my shoulders as I gazed at them.

Two more steps forward. The surrounding air thickened further, that static charge becoming almost painful against my skin. Behind me, I heard one of the Marines cry out in distress.

"Commander," Nicobe's fractured voice cut through my focus. "The artifact's influence grows stronger with proximity. Nicobe detects increasing sydereal field manipulation, targeting conscious thought patterns."

I knew she was right. I could feel the manipulation now—subtle nudges in my thoughts, encouraging me to approach, to trust, to surrender to the comfort the vision offered. The rational part of my brain recognized the danger, but that rationality was being systematically undermined by the artifact's influence.

"Come, Kory," my mother said, her voice now tinged with impatience. "We don't have much time."

My father's expression shifted subtly, his proud smile becoming fixed and slightly strained. "You've always been a dutiful son. Obedient."

That last word jarred me. Obedient? I'd been many things in my life, but "obedient" had never been high on the list. The orphanage staff, my various foster parents, and certainly my superior officers in the UHC Armada would all have laughed at that description.

I halted, suddenly aware of a dissonance in the vision. My parents—or what the Phylactery thought were my parents—watched me with expressions that had become slightly too intense, slightly too fixed.

"Who are you?" I asked, the question directed not at the phantoms but at the artifact behind them.

My mother's smile faltered. "Darling, it's me. Don't you recognize your own mother?"

"My parents died when I was three," I said, taking a deliberate step backward. "I have no memory of them. You're pulling these images from somewhere else."

My father's face hardened. "Don't be ridiculous, son. We're right here."

Another step back. The static charge against my skin lessened slightly. "No," I said. "You're not. You're something else, using their forms."

The phantoms exchanged a glance, and in that moment, their façade slipped further. The movement was too synchronized, too precisely mirrored.

37

I forced the vision into the background and took a step toward the Phylactery, close enough to feel the subtle push of its containment field against my skin. The hum increased, vibrating in my molars. The vision of my parents faded.

"So, how to destroy it?" I asked the room. Again, nobody rushed to answer, most of them still recovering from their own encounters with visions.

My comm unit crackled to life, Destiny's voice cutting through the weighted silence.

"*Thunder* to away team. Kory, you there?" Her tone was controlled, but urgent.

I tapped my earpiece. "Go ahead, Destiny."

"We've got company. Big company."

I stepped back from the Phylactery, focusing on her voice. "Define 'big.'"

"Two fleets just dropped out of veilspace. One Kergan, one Dominion. And they're not playing nice with each other."

My stomach tightened. "Battle positions?"

"Full engagement, about three million klicks from the Ossuary. Long-range sensors show they're throwing everything at each other—capital ships, fighter wings, the works. We're detecting sydereal discharges consistent with Soul Ravager activity in the Kergan fleet."

Soul Ravagers. The elite Kergan warriors who could manipulate the sydereal plane with terrifying efficiency. I'd fought one named Ban'ach before and barely lived to tell about it. The scars on my glyphshade twinged at the memory.

"*Thunder*'s status?" I asked.

"We're safe for now, landed where you left us. Powered down except for essential systems and keeping a low profile. But whoever wins this dance is going to come knocking, and soon."

I glanced at the Phylactery, its pulsing light suddenly more menacing. "How long do we have?"

"Hard to say. The battle's intense but evenly matched. Could be hours. Could be less if one side gets lucky."

I swore under my breath. "Prep for immediate launch. I want *Thunder* hot and ready to lift the moment we get back."

"Already on it," Destiny replied, and I could hear the slight smile in her voice. She knew me too well. "Engineering reports all systems nominal. The team has the drive spooled and waiting."

"Good." I paused, remembering. "Rowbottom? The medevac team?"

"They arrived ten minutes ago. Doc Montana has him in the infirmary. A cracked vertebra, broken ribs, mild concussion, but she says he's stable. Whatever happened down there, he put up one hell of a fight."

Relief flooded through me. At least we wouldn't be leaving anyone behind. "Tell him he's getting a commendation if we make it out of here. And tell Doc I said thanks."

"Will do." There was a brief pause, the sound of Destiny conferring with someone off-comm. "Cynric says the sensor ghosts are getting worse. The Ossuary's radiation fields are playing havoc with our systems. We might not get much warning if either fleet breaks off to investigate us."

"Understood. Keep me posted. We'll wrap this up quickly and head back."

"Roger that. Don't do anything stupid. *Thunder* out."

The comm clicked off, and I turned back to the three faces watching me—Sofia's reserved, Busto's expectant, Nicobe's unreadable behind her geometric housing.

"Change of plans," I said, though we hadn't really had a plan to begin with. "We've got Kergan and Dominion fleets duking it out in-system, and whoever wins is likely coming here next."

Sofia's eyes narrowed slightly. "They must have tracked us. Or detected the Phylactery's energy signature."

"Either way, we're on borrowed time," I replied. "We need to make a decision about this thing now."

Busto shifted his weight, the ceramic plates of his combat armor clicking softly. "Sir, with respect, we should blow it to hell and get out. Whatever this thing does, it's not worth dying for."

I looked to Nicobe, whose crimson housing bobbed slightly in what I'd come to recognize as agreement.

"Nicobe concurs with Lieutenant Busto's assessment. The Phylactery represents technology beyond current understanding. Its destruction would be preferable to its acquisition by either belligerent party."

Sofia remained silent, her gaze fixed on the suspended artifact. The subtle glow from the containment field reflected in her eyes, giving them an eerie luminescence.

"Sofia?" I prompted.

She blinked, focus returning. "The lieutenant and the igna are correct. It's too dangerous to control, and we can't let our enemies get it."

"Meaning blow it up," I translated.

"Affirmative."

It was the logical choice. The smart choice. One I had already made. But something tugged at the back of my mind —the sheer age of the artifact, the knowledge it might contain. Destroying it felt like burning the last copy of a book no one had read in millennia.

Then again, some books were better left closed.

I took a deep breath. "Alright. We destroy it, then run like hell back to *Thunder*."

Busto nodded, already reaching for demolition charges in his tactical pack. "How much time do you want on the timer, sir?"

"Five minutes should give us enough clearance. Set it up."

According to Nicobe's analysis, as soon as the Phylactery was gone, the binary neutron stars would begin spiraling toward each other, leaving us only four hours to escape the system.

As Busto began preparing the explosive package, I turned to Sofia. Her face remained impassive, but I knew her well enough—or had, once—to recognize the slight furrow between her brows that signaled concern.

"Something on your mind?" I asked quietly.

She hesitated, then stepped closer, lowering her voice. "The Phylactery's containment field. It's not just holding it in place—it's suppressing something. If we disrupt it incorrectly..."

"Boom?" I suggested.

"Unknown," she replied, which was somehow worse. "But the energy readings suggest a potential cascade effect."

Great. Just great. "So our explosives might trigger something bigger?"

"It's possible."

I glanced at Busto, who was efficiently programming the demolition charge. "Then what do you suggest?"

Sofia's gaze met mine directly. "A focused energy weapon might disrupt the containment field more gradually, allowing controlled degradation rather than catastrophic failure."

"Like a laser pistol?"

She nodded once. "At the correct frequency, yes."

The unspoken question hung between us: who would take the shot? Whoever did would be closest when whatever happened... happened.

I forced a tight smile. "Well, it's my bad idea. Might as well be my finger on the trigger."

Sofia opened her mouth as if to object, then closed it, her professional mask sliding back into place. "Logical. I'll assist with calibrating your weapon to the optimal frequency."

While she worked, I turned to Busto. "Change of plans, Lieutenant. Hold the explosives in reserve. We're going to try a more... surgical approach first."

He frowned, but nodded. "Your call, sir. My men will maintain perimeter security."

Sofia finished adjusting my laser pistol, the weapon's power cell humming at a slightly different pitch than before. She handed it back without letting our fingers touch.

"Aim for the center mass," she instructed. "Continuous beam, not pulsed. Three to five seconds should be sufficient to destabilize the containment matrix."

I nodded, weighing the weapon in my hand. "Everyone clear the room except Sofia and Busto. Fall back to the corridor junction and prepare for immediate evac."

The Marines filed out efficiently, and Nicobe hesitated only briefly before following.

"Nicobe wishes the Commander good fortune," she said. "And suggests that if your deity accepts prayers, now would be an appropriate time to offer them."

I smiled tightly. "Thanks for the vote of confidence."

When they were gone, I turned to Sofia and Busto. "Last chance to join the smart people in the hall."

Busto snorted. "No offense, sir, but you need someone with sense to pull your ass out of the fire when this goes sideways."

Sofia simply checked her own weapon. "I will monitor the energy fluctuations. If they exceed safety parameters, we withdraw immediately."

I nodded, absurdly grateful for their presence despite the danger. "Alright then. On my mark."

I stepped forward, raised my laser pistol, and sighted down the barrel at the pulsing heart of the Phylactery. My hand was steady, even as my thoughts raced. Whatever happened next, we'd face it together. That had always been our strength aboard *Thunder*—not fancy tech or superior firepower, but the simple fact that when things went to hell, we went through it side by side.

I took a deep breath, finger tightening on the trigger.

"Here goes nothing."

38

My hand didn't shake as I aimed the laser pistol at the floating crystal. Sweat trickled down my spine, but my grip remained steady—at least on the outside. Inside, my thoughts ricocheted like stray bullets against the walls of my skull. The Phylactery hovered in its cradle of black metal, pulsing with an internal light that seemed to breathe in time with my own heartbeat. I'd come here to destroy it. So why did pulling the trigger suddenly feel like I was about to murder a part of myself?

The temple-like chamber of the Ossuary Ring stretched away into darkness, impossibly vast, its ceiling lost somewhere in the gloom above. Crystalline pillars rose like the fossilized bones of extinct titans, black and gleaming with pinpricks of light that might have been stars trapped in obsidian. The air tasted metallic, charged with forgotten power. My boots made no sound on the ancient floor—a material neither stone nor metal that absorbed the impact with an unsettling hunger.

"Just do it, Drake," I muttered to myself, the sound

swallowed by the vastness. "One shot. One less ancient horror in the universe."

The mission had seemed simple enough: locate the Noble Phylactery, destroy it, deny Arctis and the Kergan forces the weapon they sought. The fact that the Phylactery contained an imprisoned astral titan named Nekufima was just a detail in the briefing. Collateral damage in a war that spanned galaxies.

I'd volunteered. Better me than Sofia, with her new Kergan brain implant making her vulnerable to outside influence. Better me than Destiny, still recovering from Ban'ach's mental invasion. Just point and shoot. I'd killed before. This was no different.

Except it was.

Beautiful, isn't it?

The voice wasn't a sound. It was a thought in my head that wasn't mine, sliding between my own thoughts like a thin blade between ribs. I blinked hard, trying to shake it off.

You can't shake me off, Captain Drake. I've been with you since you entered this place. Since you first heard my name, in fact. Waiting for you to come close enough to... talk.

"Get out of my head," I growled, tightening my finger on the trigger.

The pulsing light within the Phylactery—an icosahedron of iridescent crystal no larger than my fist—intensified. Not aggressive, but... inviting. Like a hearth in winter.

You won't shoot. You can't. Not when I can give you what you've spent your life searching for.

"And what's that?" I asked, hating myself for engaging, for delaying.

The answer wasn't words. It was images, smells,

sensations—flooding into my consciousness like water breaching a dam. But not vague impressions. Not the hazy maybe-memories I'd constructed over years of desperate imagination.

These were *perfect.*

My father's hands, calloused and strong, with a small burn scar on the left thumb from soldering work. The exact pitch of my mother's laugh, like water over stones. The way her perfume smelled—jasmine and something deeper, earthier—and how it lingered in rooms after she'd left them. The crinkles at the corners of my father's eyes when he smiled. The precise shade of auburn in my mother's hair when sunlight hit it.

I staggered backward, the pistol drooping toward the floor. The memories kept coming, each one crystal-clear, each one striking me with the force of physical blows.

"Stop," I whispered. "Those aren't real. I was three when they died. I couldn't possibly remember—"

These aren't your memories, Kory. They're mine. I was there. I've been everywhere. I've seen everything.

My breath came in short, sharp bursts. "How? Why would you—"

The Syderealium connects all things across time and space. Your parents left... impressions. Echoes. I preserved them. As I preserve all interesting things.

The Phylactery's light pulsed faster, more urgently. I felt a pressure building behind my eyes, not painful but insistent.

"Lieutenant Commander." Sofia's voice cut through my daze, sharp with concern. She stood twenty meters away, near one of the massive pillars, her service pistol drawn. "Step away from the artifact."

Busto emerged from behind another pillar, his bulk

making even the massive chamber seem smaller. His tactical armor gleamed dully in the strange light. "Sir, readings are off the charts. Whatever that thing is telling you, it's lying."

I knew they were right. I knew it with the same certainty I knew my own name. Yet I couldn't move away. The memories were too vivid, too precious.

Your friends are afraid, Nekufima whispered in my mind. *They should be. Not of me, but of what I represent. Freedom from the lies you've all been told. I can give you back what was stolen from you, Kory.*

"Memories," I said aloud, my voice hollow. "Just memories."

No. The voice grew warmer, intimate, like lips against my ear. *Not memories, Kory. Them. Real. Alive.*

My heart lurched painfully in my chest. "That's impossible."

Is it? The Sydereal ium preserves all patterns, all configurations of matter and energy. Your parents' patterns exist there, complete, waiting. All I need is a suitable vessel to transfer them into. A body. Two bodies.

"Kory!" Sofia shouted, her voice echoing through the chamber. "It's manipulating you!"

Of course I am, Nekufima's voice purred in my head. *As all sentient beings manipulate each other. As your Sofia manipulated you into loving her. As you manipulate your crew into following you. The question isn't whether I'm manipulating you, Captain. It's whether what I offer is worth the price.*

I lowered the pistol entirely, my arm heavy, muscles trembling with fatigue or emotion—I couldn't tell which.

"What price?" I asked, my voice barely audible.

Freedom. Mine for theirs. A fair exchange, don't you think?

"Kory, don't!" Sofia was moving toward me now, her face tight with fear. She never called me Kory on missions.

Always Drake, or Lieutenant Commander. The break in protocol drove home her desperation.

But her voice seemed to come from very far away, through layers of fog and static. All I could focus on was the Phylactery and the voice in my head.

Ban'ach took so much from you, didn't she? Your childhood when she orphaned you. Your peace when she hunted you. Your confidence when she wounded you.

"Ban'ach killed my parents?" I whispered.

A laugh like crystal wind chimes. *In a way, she did, when she stole your memories of them. It was like killing them all over again. She's taken everything from you, piece by piece. I'm offering to give it back.*

My feet moved without conscious direction. One step, then another, toward the Phylactery. My pistol found its holster, the safety clicking on automatically under my thumb. Old training, muscle memory—the only part of me still functioning rationally.

"Commander Drake, we have a mission!" Busto barked. "Destroy the artifact and evacuate!"

But his words bounced off me, meaningless sound. Twenty years of longing, of phantom pain, of wondering—all of it crystallized into this moment, this choice.

My hands shook as I reached for the Phylactery. Not from fear, but from anticipation. From hunger. Sweat beaded on my forehead, trickling down my temples. The air around the artifact shimmered like heat rising from scorched earth.

Yes, Nekufima whispered. *Yes, Captain. Free me. Let me give you your heart's desire.*

My rational mind screamed warnings, cataloged tactics, recited regulations. Reminded me of every horror story about deals with devils, about ancient imprisoned evils, about the price of giving in to temptation. Logic built walls of reason that emotion simply flowed around, eroded, washed away.

My fingers brushed the artifact. It was warm—not the cold crystal it appeared to be, but something alive, pulsing with heat and potential. The sensation shot up my arm like an electric current, not painful but overwhelming. The Phylactery seemed to lean into my touch, eager, hungry.

Take me. Carry me. Together, we will rewrite the past.

Sofia was running now, closing the distance between us. "Kory, stop! It might have killed the Primordians! It's killed billions!"

But I was already lifting the Phylactery from its cradle. It weighed almost nothing, lighter than it should be—as though part of it existed somewhere else, in some other dimension. Twelve points of light at its vertices flared bright enough to leave searing afterimages in my vision.

I slipped it into the pocket of my tactical vest, where it nestled against my chest like a second heart.

The moment I did, the entire Ossuary Ring shuddered violently. The floor beneath us buckled, heaving like the deck of a ship in a storm. Crystalline pillars as old as civilization itself cracked with sounds like gunshots. Dust and fragments rained from the invisible ceiling.

Sofia was thrown to her knees. Busto staggered, catching himself against a pillar that promptly split from top to bottom.

My comm unit crackled to life, Destiny's voice tight with panic: "Kory! Away team, respond! Gravitational wave activity spiking off the charts! The stars—they're spiraling inward!"

I fumbled for my communicator. "What? So soon?"

"We've got confirmation from *Thunder*'s science station,"

Destiny cut in, the background noise of the bridge a chaotic symphony of alarms and shouted commands. "The neutron stars are accelerating toward each other. Collision course. We've got hours, maybe less, before this entire system goes supernova."

"Kilonova," I corrected automatically, my training asserting itself through the fog of Nekufima's influence. "Binary neutron star collision. More localized than a supernova, but—"

"But still enough to vaporize everything within billions of kilometers!" Destiny shouted. "Including us if we don't get moving now!"

The Phylactery in my pocket grew warmer, almost hot enough to burn through the fabric. But instead of pain, it sent waves of pleasure through my body, a seductive counterpoint to the catastrophe unfolding around us.

Don't worry, Captain, Nekufima's voice whispered, intimate and amused. *We'll be long gone before the fireworks start. You and I have... appointments to keep.*

"What did you do?" I demanded, clutching at my pocket. "The neutron stars—"

Were held in a delicate gravitational balance by the Primordians' technology. Technology tied to my prison. Remove the prison...

"...and the stars collapse," I finished, horror dawning. "You knew this would happen."

A mental shrug, dismissive and ancient. *A small price to pay for freedom. This system has no inhabited planets. No great loss.*

"Except for us!" I snarled.

I won't let you die, Kory Drake. You're far too valuable to me. Far too... interesting. And you carry my vessel.

Another violent tremor shook the Ring. A massive section of ceiling crashed down a hundred meters away, the impact sending shock waves through the floor.

"Drake!" Sofia had reached me, her face streaked with dust, blue eyes wild with fear and anger. "What have you done?"

I met her gaze, the Phylactery burning against my chest, Nekufima's presence wrapping around my thoughts like a lover's embrace.

"I made a deal," I said, my voice distant and strange to my own ears.

Sofia's expression crumbled, not into tears but into something worse—disappointment. She'd seen me do many things—brave things, stupid things, occasionally terrible things. But never this. Never a betrayal of everything we stood for.

"With her?" Sofia asked, her voice barely audible over the groaning of the dying station.

Tell her yes, Nekufima purred in my mind. *Tell her you finally chose something for yourself, not for duty, not for others. Tell her you chose your family over hers.*

I opened my mouth, but whatever I might have said was cut off by Busto's arrival. He grabbed both of us by the shoulders.

"We need to move!" he shouted over the cacophony of destruction. "Rendezvous at *Thunder,* one hour, or they launch without us!"

As we ran through the collapsing temple, darting around falling debris and leaping over widening cracks in the floor, I felt the weight of the Phylactery against my chest. Not a physical weight, but the weight of choice, of consequences unfolding.

And beneath it all, a whisper: *You're mine now, Captain Drake. And I am yours. Together, we will reshape the universe. Beginning with your beloved parents.*

I ran faster, heart pounding, wondering if the rapid

acceleration of the neutron stars behind us was an omen for my own spiral into the gravity well of an ancient, patient evil.

39

The alarms shrieked like tortured animals, a sound I'd grown all too familiar with in my illustrious career of making terrible decisions. I clutched the phylactery against my chest as we sprinted through the ancient corridors of the Ossuary Ring, its surface unnervingly warm against my palm, like it was alive and breathing. Chunks of ceiling rained down around us, the whole structure shuddering as if the thing I held was poisoning it from the inside out. Just another Tuesday for Lieutenant Commander Kory Drake, professional disturber of things that should have stayed buried.

"Move it, people!" Busto barked from somewhere behind me, his voice cutting through the wail of sirens. "This whole section's coming down!"

The emergency lights pulsed in hypnotic crimson waves, painting everyone's faces in blood-red flashes that made Sofia look like she was already a ghost. Her eyes caught mine for a split second as she ran beside me, concern etched into the tight lines around her mouth. The old connection between us sparked like a frayed wire—dangerous and unpredictable.

"Left passage clear!" one of the Marines shouted, his rifle raised as he swept the junction ahead.

The Ossuary Ring groaned around us, a death rattle from a structure that had survived millions of years only to start falling apart the moment we showed up. The walls—smooth and crystalline, etched with those strange geometric patterns—seemed to ripple in the strobing lights. Dust and fragments of ancient material filled the air, making each breath feel like inhaling ground glass.

The neutron stars were shedding immense gravitational waves as they spiraled inward, bleeding off kinetic energy in the final moments before their cataclysmic merger. The waves tore through space-time—and through the Ossuary Ring—ripping the ancient structure apart.

I adjusted my grip on the Phylactery, a deceptively simple icosahedron about the size of my fist. Its metallic surface was inscribed with angular symbols that reminded me of the markings on the Ring itself. Despite the chaos around us, despite the genuine possibility that we were all about to be crushed under millions of tons of alien architecture, I couldn't stop staring at those symbols. They seemed to move when I wasn't looking directly at them, rearranging themselves into new configurations that almost made sense.

"Watch it!" Sofia yanked me sideways as a support beam crashed down exactly where I'd been standing. I mumbled thanks, but my attention was already drifting back to the object in my hands.

We dodged through a gauntlet of falling debris. The Marines moved with practiced precision, calling out hazards and forming a protective perimeter around Sofia, Busto, and me. One of them wasn't fast enough; a chunk of ceiling caught him on the shoulder, sending him sprawling. Busto hauled him up without breaking stride, the two of them rejoining our desperate dash seconds later.

"Status on the exit route?" I called out, trying to focus on something—anything—besides the growing warmth of the Phylactery.

"Two more junctions, then the landing pad," Sofia replied, her slight German accent more pronounced under stress. "If the ship's still there."

"It better be," Busto growled. "Or we're just choosing which room to die in."

We reached another junction, this one larger than the others, with corridors branching off in three directions. I skidded to a halt, suddenly unable to move forward. The others continued a few steps before realizing I'd stopped.

"Drake!" Busto shouted. "What the hell are you doing?"

I couldn't answer. The Phylactery pulsed against my palms, its heat intensifying until it should have been burning me, but instead of pain, I felt... invitation. My fingers, numb and yet hyperaware, began tracing the symbols etched into its surface. I hadn't consciously decided to do this. My hands moved with purpose, with knowledge I didn't possess, following patterns I couldn't comprehend.

Sweat beaded on my forehead, running down into my eyes in salty rivulets. My entire body trembled, not with fear but with a terrible anticipation. The junction around me, the alarms, the shouts of my team—all of it receded like a tide pulling away from shore. There was only the Phylactery and the sequence my fingers danced through with increasing speed.

Three seals. That's all that stood between whatever was inside and freedom. My thumb pressed against the first, a triangular depression that yielded with a soft click.

Something inside the artifact shifted, components realigning with precision engineered before humans had discovered fire.

"Kory, stop! What are you doing?" Sofia's voice cut through the fog in my head, sharp as a slap.

I blinked, vision swimming back into focus. My hands still worked at the phylactery, moving to the second seal—a spiral pattern that required a specific rotation. I tried to pull away, to stop whatever was happening, but my muscles refused to obey. It was like watching someone else control my body, a passenger in my own skin.

"I can't—" I choked out, the words feeling foreign in my throat. "Something's—it's making me—"

Sofia was at my side now, her hands covering mine, trying to break the connection. "Fight it, Kory!"

The structure gave another violent shudder, more substantial than before. A massive crack split the ceiling above us, zigzagging across the ancient material like lightning frozen in time.

I forced every ounce of will into my rebellious hands, imagining them as separate entities I needed to subdue. The trembling worsened, muscles straining against invisible commands. My vision blurred, focus fracturing as the battle raged inside me.

"Drake, we need to move NOW!" Busto's voice seemed to come from miles away.

With a guttural sound that barely seemed human, I wrenched my hands away from the phylactery's second seal, the effort nearly dropping me to my knees. The sudden release felt like snapping free of restraints I hadn't known were there.

"Go!" I gasped, clutching the Phylactery now like it might try to escape. "That way!"

We ran again, the Ring's death throes intensifying around us. But as we fled, I felt something watching from inside the artifact I carried—something ancient and patient, whose plans extended far beyond this moment of temporary defeat.

The world dissolved around me like sugar in hot coffee, the solid corridors of the Ossuary Ring melting into something else entirely. One moment I was running for my life, the next I was suspended in a sea of light that had no source, no direction, no purpose except to illuminate the infinite. I'd been in the Syderealium before, but never like this—never with such clarity. The luminous energlyphs swirled around me, dense packets of information that seemed to know I was watching them. They pulsed and shifted, forming patterns that almost made sense before dissolving again, like trying to read a book whose letters rearranged themselves between blinks.

The space around me had no horizon, no up or down, just endless dimensionality that somehow managed to feel both vast and intimate. Colors existed here that had no names in human language, frequencies of light that made my consciousness vibrate in sympathy. The energlyphs danced through this not-space like schools of bioluminescent fish, leaving trails of meaning rather than light.

"Beautiful, isn't it?" The voice came from everywhere and nowhere, textured like velvet dragged across stone. "So much more than your pitiful physical realm."

The energlyphs before me began to coalesce, gathering into a pattern that grew more complex with each passing second. They spun and interwove, building a shape that was unmistakably feminine but utterly inhuman. A cascade of symbols formed into a woman's figure—naked, voluptuous, with curves that seemed designed specifically to appeal to some deep, primal part of my brain. But where a human would have skin, she had only shifting patterns of light and data flowing like liquid across her form. Her face was the most detailed aspect, with eyes that contained entire galaxies and a smile that promised pleasure and pain in equal measure.

"Nekufima," I said, the name feeling strange to my non-existent tongue.

She circled me slowly, her movements fluid and predatory. The energlyphs that composed her form left faint trails in the void, like afterimages burned into retinas after staring at the sun.

"You were so close," she purred, completing her circle and stopping just close enough that I could feel something emanating from her—not heat, but a kind of pressure against my consciousness. "Just a few more moments and I would have been free. After millions of years... just a few more seconds."

"What did you do to me?" I asked, trying to back away but finding no purchase in this placeless place. "You controlled my hands."

Her laugh was musical and terrible, like wind chimes made of broken glass. "Control is such a crude concept. I merely... suggested. Your hands remembered knowledge they never possessed. I offered guidance." Her form flickered, momentarily revealing something far less human beneath the seductive exterior—something angular and vast and ancient. "But now we must start again, and time grows short."

"Start what again? I'm not freeing you."

"Oh, Kory Drake." She spoke my name like she was tasting it. "Free spirit. Orphan boy. Captain without a ship. Commander without command. Lover without love." Each description felt like a needle inserted under my skin. "You think this is about choice? About your quaint little concept of free will?"

She drifted closer, her form expanding until she filled my field of vision. The symbols that composed her shifted faster now, agitated.

"I've seen civilizations rise and fall while imprisoned in that phylactery. I've watched stars born and die. I've had a billion years to perfect the art of persuasion." Her voice dropped to a whisper that somehow echoed in the infinite space. "I can offer you knowledge beyond imagination. Power that your primitive species can't conceive. I can show you how to navigate the deepest dimensions of the Syderealium, how to bend reality itself."

"In exchange for what?" I asked, though I already knew the answer.

"Freedom," she said simply. "And perhaps... companionship. It grows lonely in the void between dimensions."

Her form shifted again, the energlyphs rearranging into something more recognizably human—a mirror of desire plucked directly from my subconscious. I felt a pull toward her, not physical but psychological, a yearning that didn't originate in my own mind.

"Stop it," I said, struggling against the artificial attraction. "Whatever you're doing, stop."

Her expression hardened, the beautiful façade cracking to reveal something cold and calculating beneath. "You think you have a choice?" she hissed, her form flickering with rage. "I've been inside your mind for weeks. I know your weaknesses, your fears." Her voice modulated, suddenly sounding eerily like Sofia's. "I know who you love, what you've lost, what you're willing to sacrifice."

The realization hit me like a physical blow. All those moments of déjà vu, the strange impulses, the dreams I couldn't quite remember upon waking—she'd been there all along, working at the edges of my consciousness, softening the ground for this moment.

"You've been manipulating me since we found the Phylactery," I said, the words bitter in my nonexistent mouth.

"Manipulating." She waved a hand dismissively, trailing symbols that lingered in the void. "Such an ugly word for such a beautiful dance. We've been getting to know each other, Kory. Becoming acquainted in the most intimate way possible."

Her form drifted around me again, but I turned to keep her in view, refusing to let her behind me even in this realm where directions meant nothing.

"I won't free you," I declared, finding strength in the simple act of refusal. "Not now. Not ever. Whatever you are, whatever you want—it stays locked in that phylactery."

She stopped moving, her form suddenly still in a way that felt more threatening than any motion could have. The energlyphs that composed her slowed their dance, condensing into something denser, darker.

"Then we'll be together in a different way," she said, her voice suddenly stripped of its seductive overtones, revealing something ancient and terribly patient beneath.

Her form rushed toward me like a wave of information, the symbols that composed her stretching and accelerating. I tried to move, to dodge, to escape—but there was nowhere to go in the dimensionless void. The cascade of energlyphs crashed into me, through me, becoming part of me in a violation more profound than any physical assault. I felt her presence infiltrating my consciousness, threading itself through the fabric of my thoughts like roots growing through soil.

And then, mercifully, darkness.

I came back to myself in fragments—first pain, then sound, then the nauseating sensation of movement. My head felt like someone had used it for batting practice, each heartbeat sending fresh waves of agony behind my eyes. I was being carried, my arms draped over the shoulders of two Marines who grunted with each step. The floor beneath us trembled like a living thing trying to shake us off its back. Everything was too bright, too loud, too sharp, as if my senses had been dialed up past their normal settings. But beneath all that, something else lurked—a presence in my mind where nothing should have been, watching through my eyes with cold, ancient curiosity.

"He's coming around," one of the Marines said, his voice strangely muffled, like I was hearing him through water.

"Keep moving," Busto ordered from somewhere ahead. "We don't stop until we're off this death trap."

I tried to get my feet under me, to take some of my weight off the Marines, but my limbs responded like they were receiving my commands via a bad satellite connection. My vision swam, the crimson emergency lights blurring into smears across my field of view. The corridor ahead bent and twisted in ways that defied architecture, though I suspected that was more about my scrambled brain than actual reality.

"What happened?" I croaked, my tongue feeling twice its normal size.

"You collapsed," Sofia answered, appearing at my side with her face tight with concern. "One second you were standing there, the next you dropped like someone cut your strings."

My hand reflexively reached for my waist, finding the Phylactery secured in a pouch on my belt. It no longer felt warm to the touch—just cool, inert metal. But something had changed. I could feel it, not with my fingers, but with some other sense I hadn't possessed before. The Phylactery was just an inert object now, but what had been inside...

Quite the dramatic escape, a voice whispered directly into my mind, as clear as if someone had placed headphones over my ears. *Though I preferred the temple's architecture before you started bringing it down.*

I flinched so violently that the Marines nearly lost their grip on me. Nekufima's voice was unmistakable—that same velvet-over-stone texture, that same ancient amusement—but now it originated from inside my own head.

"Next time I'll ask the ancient death trap for interior decorating tips," I muttered under my breath, the sarcasm automatic, a defense mechanism against rising panic.

Sofia's head snapped toward me, her brow furrowing. "Kory? Who are you talking to?" The concern in her voice had sharpened into something more specific, more worried.

Tell her, Nekufima purred in my mind. *Tell her you've made a new friend. Let's see how she reacts to sharing you.*

"No one," I lied, straightening up and taking more of my own weight. "Just... thinking out loud. Concussion talk."

Sofia didn't look convinced, but before she could press further, I pointed ahead to where the corridor branched. "Left fork! The right passage is collapsing!"

I don't know how I knew this. The right passage looked identical to the left from where we stood, both vanishing into dusty dimness ahead. But I could sense the structural integrity somehow, feel the weaknesses in the ancient material, predict where it would give way next.

You're welcome, Nekufima whispered. *Consider it a housewarming gift.*

Busto hesitated only for a split second before barking, "Left fork! Move!"

We changed direction, the Marines half-carrying me now as I found more strength returning to my legs. Not ten seconds later, a thunderous crack split the air behind us, followed by the grinding roar of massive structural failure. The right passage collapsed entirely, a cloud of crystalline dust billowing out from where we would have been.

The evacuation became a blur of narrow escapes and desperate sprints through the dying megastructure. The Ossuary Ring groaned and shuddered around us, ancient metal protesting as stresses it was never designed to withstand tore at its foundations. The air grew thick with dust that sparkled strangely in the emergency lights, each particle seeming to capture and refract the crimson glow in impossible ways.

From somewhere deep within the structure came a low, sustained rumble that I felt more than heard—the sound of a million-year-old engineering marvel tearing itself apart. Beyond that, barely perceptible even to my strangely enhanced senses, was another sound: the deadly gravitational dance of the neutron stars the Ring orbited, their invisible forces pulling at the ancient structure like cosmic wolves tearing at a carcass.

"The landing pad's just ahead!" one of the Marines called out, his voice hoarse from the dust.

We're going to make it, Nekufima observed casually. *How disappointing. I was hoping for a more dramatic conclusion to our first chapter together.*

I tried to ignore her, focusing instead on putting one foot in front of the other. I was mostly moving under my own power now, though one of the Marines kept a steadying hand on my arm. Sofia kept glancing at me when she thought I wouldn't notice, her expression a mixture of concern and suspicion. She knew me too well—knew something was different, wrong.

She just didn't know how wrong.

As we staggered through the last stretch toward the landing pad where *Thunder* waited, the truth settled into my bones with a cold finality. I hadn't prevented Nekufima's escape; I'd just changed its form. She was free now, riding in my consciousness, seeing through my eyes, hearing through my ears. The phylactery at my waist was empty—just a hollow shell of alien metal.

Now you understand, Nekufima said, a smile evident in her voice. *We are bonded, you and I. Your fate is my fate. Your body, my vessel. Your mind, my playground.*

I had become exactly what we'd come to prevent—the vessel for an ancient, malevolent entity that the Kergans and rebels had been searching for. The very being we'd raced to secure before our enemies could claim her power was now nestled in my mind, with access to everything I knew, everyone I cared about, every secret I'd been entrusted with.

Don't look so grim, Kory Drake, Nekufima whispered as we reached the docking bay, the waiting shuttle coming into view. *This is just the beginning of our beautiful relationship.*

The worst part wasn't her smugness, or the violation of having another consciousness sharing my headspace. The worst part was the small, traitorous thrill that ran through me at the power I could already feel coursing just beneath my skin—power I instinctively knew how to use, thanks to my unwanted passenger.

I'd never felt more alive.

I'd never been less myself.

40

I ran until my lungs burned, the ancient corridors of the Ossuary Ring blurring around me as we fled. Behind us, a horrific groan of metal and crystal announced another structural failure—the Ring was dying around us, pulled apart by forces even the Primordians hadn't designed it to withstand. My pack felt heavier with each step, the phylactery inside it radiating a cold that seeped through the reinforced material and into my spine. I wasn't imagining it—the thing was getting colder as we approached freedom, as if excited by the prospect of leaving this ancient prison after millions of years.

"Left fork!" I shouted over my shoulder, watching Sofia and Busto adjust their trajectory mid-stride. The two Marines behind them followed without hesitation, their heavy gear clanking with each footfall. "Starwell access should be just ahead."

A distant boom echoed through the station, followed by a subtle shift in the artificial gravity. Not good. The neutron stars were dancing their final waltz, their gravitational waves rippling through spacetime like stones tossed into a pond. Except these ripples could tear apart a million-year-old megastructure.

"Drake, we sure this is the fastest way back?" Busto panted, his face glistening with sweat as he kept pace beside me. "Feels like we're going deeper, not toward the landing pad."

I nodded, not wasting breath on a detailed explanation. The truth was, I wasn't entirely sure myself. The path we'd taken on our way in was now blocked by collapsed sections, forcing us to improvise. We needed the Starwell—a massive spiral ramp that connected multiple levels of the Ring—if we wanted any chance of reaching *Thunder* before becoming permanent residents of this ancient tomb.

Sofia ran at my other side, her movements precise and economical despite the deteriorating conditions. Even now, fleeing for our lives, she maintained that wall between us, addressing Busto instead of me when she spoke.

"Structural integrity is failing faster than predicted," she said, checking a readout on her wrist display. "We have perhaps twenty minutes before catastrophic collapse."

I was about to respond when we rounded a corner and the Starwell came into view—a vast circular shaft that stretched upward and downward for what seemed like kilometers, with a narrow spiral pathway clinging to its walls. Blue-white emergency lighting flickered along its length, creating disorienting shadows that danced across the ancient surfaces.

"Up three levels," I ordered, pointing to where the pathway disappeared into the gloom above us. "Stay close to the wall. That pathway's narrow enough when this place isn't falling apart."

The Marine sergeant—Matheson—stepped forward to

test the pathway's stability. The structure shuddered as another gravitation wave passed through it, and I caught his arm before he could step out.

"I'll take point," I said. "If it holds me, it'll hold any of you."

No one argued. Despite the lingering tension with Sofia and Busto's occasional challenges to my decisions, when things got truly dangerous, we defaulted to the chain of command. And right now, the chain ended with me.

I stepped onto the pathway, feeling the ancient material flex slightly under my weight. The Primordians hadn't built this place for humans, and certainly not for humans running full-tilt in combat gear. The pathway was barely a meter wide, with no railing on the inner edge—just a sheer drop into the dimly lit abyss below.

"Single file," I called back. "Three-meter spacing."

We began our ascent, the circular path forcing us to lean inward against the dizzying slope.

So eager to depart, little captain?

The voice wasn't audible—it was more like a thought that wasn't mine, sliding into my consciousness like a splinter under a fingernail. I nearly missed a step, my boot skidding dangerously close to the edge.

"What the hell?" I muttered, regaining my balance.

Such crude language. After millions of cycles of solitude, I'd hoped for more stimulating company.

Great. The ancient malevolent entity in my backpack was chatty. Just what I needed while navigating a crumbling alien megastructure.

"Not now," I said under my breath, glancing back to make sure Sofia hadn't heard me talking to myself. She was ten meters behind, focused entirely on the treacherous pathway.

Would you prefer to die ignorant? The Ring is coming apart faster than you realize. Your current path leads to a section that will collapse in approximately eighty-seven seconds.

I kept climbing, trying to ignore the voice. The problem with carrying an ancient sydereal entity of unknown power was that you couldn't trust a word it said. Nekufima wanted out of here—that much was clear—but whether she cared if we survived the process was another question entirely.

No response? How disappointing. I thought we might develop rapport before your imminent demise.

The pathway curved upward, and I caught sight of our destination—the entrance to the Antechamber of the Dead, that circular vault where the mummified Primordians sat in eternal vigil. We'd passed through it on our way in, a necessary crossing point to reach the central vaults where we'd found the phylactery. Now it was our way back.

Another gravitation wave hit, stronger this time. The entire structure groaned, and a section of pathway twenty meters behind the last Marine crumbled away into the depths. The Marine—Kowalski—swore colorfully enough to make even Busto look impressed.

"Move faster!" I shouted, increasing my pace despite the danger. "This whole thing's coming apart!"

We reached the entrance to the Antechamber, and I paused long enough to make sure everyone made it across. The massive circular chamber looked exactly as we'd left it—twenty-four mummified Primordians seated in a perfect circle, their elongated skeletal forms draped in what might have been ceremonial armor or perhaps just everyday attire for a species long extinct.

Ah, yes, Nekufima purred in my mind, *the judges and jailers, still watching after all these millennia. They never did appreciate my tactical creativity.*

There was a pause, then a mental shrug. *Crack one planetary crust during a siege and suddenly you're "unstable."*

The blue-white glyphs that lined the walls pulsed more rapidly now, as if the chamber itself sensed the impending destruction. The mummified guardians seemed to watch us with hollow eye sockets as we hurried across the open floor.

They were the last, you know. The final caretakers, sworn to watch over the vaults until the end of time. Such misplaced loyalty.

"Shut up," I hissed, earning a confused look from Sofia as she drew up beside me.

"I didn't say anything," she said, her voice clipped.

"Not you," I muttered, then immediately regretted it as her expression hardened further.

She cannot hear me, little captain. Only you can, as you carry my phylactery. But I can teach you to respond without speaking aloud—unless you enjoy appearing mentally unstable to your companions?

The chamber shuddered, dust and small fragments of the ceiling raining down on us. One of the Primordian mummies tilted slightly on its throne, its skull lolling to one side as if finally giving up its eternal watch.

"How do we get to the landing pad from here?" Busto asked, checking his weapon as he scanned the three archways that led out of the chamber.

Before I could answer, Nekufima's voice slid into my mind again.

Think your response to me. Imagine pushing your thoughts toward the cold spot in your mind. It's not difficult—primitive species like yours manage it all the time.

I hesitated, then tried it, focusing on forming words in my mind and directing them toward the phylactery.

Like this? I thought, feeling ridiculous.

Yes, exactly! How refreshing to find a human who can follow simple instructions. Now, tell your sweaty companions to take the leftmost arch. The central path—your original route—collapsed forty-three seconds ago.

I frowned, unsure whether to trust her. But we didn't have time for debate or exploration.

"Left archway," I said, pointing. "The center route might be compromised."

Busto raised an eyebrow. "That's not the way we came in."

"Plans change when stations collapse," I retorted, already moving toward the left arch. "Unless you've got a better idea?"

He didn't, and we pressed on, passing beneath the arch into a corridor I hadn't seen before. The architecture here was different—more elaborate, with geometric patterns etched into every surface.

How do you know this route? I thought toward Nekufima.

I've had millions of years to explore this structure through the eyes of lesser glyphshades. Every corridor, every chamber, every secret passage—they're all mapped in my memory. A benefit of extreme boredom.

Why help us? I asked silently, maintaining a steady jog as I led the team down the corridor.

Self-preservation, primarily. Your death might kill me, now that we're bonded, and if not that, then perhaps stranding me here as this structure tears itself apart. But also... curiosity. It's been so long since I've experienced anything new.

The corridor branched, and without hesitation, I took the right fork. Behind me, Sofia's footsteps faltered for a moment before she followed.

What do you want? I asked Nekufima.

A sensation like cold laughter filtered through my mind. *What does any prisoner want after millions of years of isolation?*

Experience. Sensation. The universe beyond these walls. You could provide that, little captain.

Before I could respond, my comm unit crackled to life. Destiny's voice came through, tense and clipped.

"Kory, please tell me you're almost back to the ship. Situation up here is deteriorating fast."

I tapped my earpiece. "Working on it. What's happening?"

"The Dominion rebels are getting their asses handed to them by the Kergan fleet. Three cruisers down already, and the rest are scattered. Half their fighters didn't even make it out of the launch tubes."

A fresh wave of urgency propelled me forward. "Any sign of Ban'ach?"

"Negative. No communication chatter about her specifically, but..." Destiny paused. "Something worse. A flotilla of Kergan frigates just broke from the main fleet. They're heading straight for the Ring. ETA thirty minutes, max."

Perfect. As if the collapsing station wasn't enough, now we had Kergan warships inbound. I picked up the pace, the others matching my increased speed without question.

"We'll be there in ten. Have *Thunder* ready to launch the second we're aboard."

"Already on it. Engine pre-ignition sequence started five minutes ago. Just... hurry."

Your friend sounds concerned, Nekufima observed. *The Kergans pursuing my Phylactery, I presume? They've always been easily distracted by shiny objects beyond their comprehension.*

Can you help us get out of here faster? I thought, sensing an opportunity. *You know this place better than anyone. You want to leave before it's destroyed—help us, and we both get what we want.*

Another disdainful laugh echoed in my mind. *A bargain?*

How delightfully primitive. Very well. At the next junction, take the maintenance shaft to your left. It will bypass three levels of corridors and put you within two hundred meters of your landing pad.

I slowed as we approached the junction she described. Sure enough, there was a narrow opening to the left that looked more like a service duct than a proper corridor.

"In here," I said, pointing. "It's a shortcut."

Sofia stopped beside me, her expression skeptical. "How do you know that?"

I met her gaze. "Trust me," I said quietly. "Please."

Something flickered in her eyes—not forgiveness, not yet, but perhaps a willingness to set aside our personal issues for survival. She nodded once, sharply, and gestured for me to lead on.

The maintenance shaft was cramped and clearly not designed for beings of our size. We had to move in a half-crouch, our gear scraping against the walls. But Nekufima was right—it bypassed a significant portion of the station, and after a few minutes of uncomfortable travel, we emerged into a wider corridor that I recognized from our arrival.

The landing pad is just ahead, Nekufima confirmed. *Though I should warn you—the structural supports for that section are failing. Your vessel may be damaged if you delay much longer.*

Another violent shudder ran through the station, this one strong enough to knock Kowalski off his feet. The lights flickered, went out, then came back at half-strength. Through a viewport in the corridor wall, I caught a glimpse of the exterior—massive sections of the Ring were now visibly separating, drifting apart like pieces of a broken toy.

"Run!" I shouted, no longer concerned with stealth or caution. "The whole damn thing's coming apart!"

We sprinted the final stretch, the corridor seeming to

stretch and contract around us as gravitation waves distorted local spacetime. My comm crackled again.

"Kory!" Destiny's voice was tight with urgency. "We've got structural failures all around the landing pad. *Thunder*'s taking damage from debris. We need to lift off in the next three minutes or we're not getting out at all."

"Keep her ready," I gasped. "We're almost there."

We rounded the final corner, and there it was—the vast landing pad where *Thunder* waited, her sleek hull illuminated by emergency lighting. Parts of the ceiling had already collapsed onto the pad, and *Thunder*'s bolsters were active, deflecting smaller debris that continued to rain down.

As we sprinted across the open space, a deafening crack announced the failure of one of the main support beams above us. I looked up to see a massive section of ceiling beginning to give way directly over our path.

Left! Nekufima's voice snapped in my mind, and without thinking, I veered sharply to the left, the others following my lead.

The ceiling section crashed down precisely where we would have been, the impact sending vibrations through the floor that nearly took us off our feet.

You're welcome, Nekufima purred.

We reached *Thunder*'s boarding ramp just as another section of the landing pad began to collapse, creating a widening chasm between us and the fallen debris. The ship's tractor pods were already energized, the hull vibrating with contained power ready to be unleashed.

I paused at the foot of the ramp, turning to make sure everyone made it aboard. Sofia and Busto ran past me, followed by the nine Marines of our escort. As the last one cleared the ramp, I felt the icy presence in my mind almost hum with anticipation.

At last, Nekufima whispered in my mind. *Freedom.*

I took one last look at the dying Ossuary Ring—a marvel of ancient engineering that had survived for millions of years, only to die during my brief visit. Fitting, somehow. Destruction seemed to follow me wherever I went.

As I turned to board, the landing pad gave one final, catastrophic shudder. The ramp bucked beneath my feet, and for a heart-stopping moment, I thought I might fall into the growing abyss below. Then strong hands grabbed my arms—Sofia and Busto, pulling me aboard as the ramp began to close.

The last thing I saw before the ramp sealed was a massive section of the Ring breaking away, spinning off into the void, carrying with it the secrets of a long-dead civilization—all except for the one cold, ancient secret now nestled against my spine.

Thunder's engines roared to life, and we fled the dying Ring, carrying Nekufima into a universe she hadn't seen in millions of years.

41

I burst onto *Thunder*'s command deck, Sofia and Busto at my heels, the three of us gulping air like we'd run a marathon through the collapsing halls of the Ossuary Ring. My hands found the familiar contours of the command chair before my brain had fully processed that we'd made it back. The deck thrummed beneath my boots—not the steady, reassuring pulse of a ship at rest, but the erratic, fearful shudder of a vessel under strain. Warning lights painted everyone's faces in hellish red, turning my crew into grim-faced demons at their stations.

"Bringing primary systems online," I announced, fingers flying across the command interface. The displays flickered to life, each one screaming bad news in the universal language of flashing red indicators. The acrid stench of burned circuitry stung my nostrils—something had taken damage during our absence. Probably when that section of ceiling collapsed near the umbilical port.

Destiny swiveled from her tactical station, her face tight with the kind of urgency that never preceded good news.

"Kergan flotilla inbound from outer system," she reported, voice clipped. "Dominion rebel task force retreating toward the ice giant in orbit around the neutron stars." Her fingers tapped a quick sequence, bringing up a tactical display that looked like someone had kicked over an anthill. Dots and vectors swarmed across the screen, all moving with purpose, none of them friendly.

"Fantastic," I muttered. "Not only is our ancient alien parking garage falling apart, but we've got company coming to the demolition party."

*Such eloquence under pressure. Truly the hallmark of great leadership,** Nekufima's voice slithered through my thoughts, unwelcome as always. **No wonder your little organic playmates follow you so devotedly.*

I shoved her aside mentally—a trick I was getting better at—and focused on the situation at hand. Phoebe's face was illuminated by her console's glow as she and Nicobe worked the engineering stations, their hands a blur over the controls.

"Primary power conduits showing fluctuations," Phoebe called out without looking up. "We've got system-wide interference from the neutron stars' magnetic field."

Nicobe's capsule bobbed in its housing. "Nicobe reports structural integrity at seventy-eight percent. This vessel requires immediate extraction from current spatial coordinates to prevent catastrophic failure."

The deck plates vibrated harder beneath us, and a low groaning sound—metal under stress—echoed through the ship. I didn't need the warning klaxon that followed to tell me we were in trouble.

"Status on the Ossuary Ring?" I demanded, pulling up navigational data on my own screen.

Sofia's voice came from my right, cool and professional

despite everything. "Ring structure showing multiple fracture points. Gravitational stress is tearing it apart. Estimate complete structural failure in less than twenty minutes." Her blue eyes met mine for the briefest moment before returning to her console.

Oh, the frigid German still functions. I was beginning to think she was merely decorative, Nekufima commented. *Though I do appreciate how she avoids looking at you. Very professional. Very... distant.*

The ship lurched suddenly, throwing me against my restraints. Through the main viewscreen, I watched as a massive section of the ancient ring structure split apart, releasing a cloud of debris that sparkled in the eerie light of the binary stars.

"All hands secure for immediate departure," I barked into the ship-wide comm. "Nav, plot us a course away from the ring structure. Maximum thrust once we're clear of the immediate debris field."

Busto moved to the security station, his movements economical despite the ship's rocking. "Marine teams report all secure. Armory locked down. Hull breach teams standing by." His weathered face remained impassive, but I knew him well enough to recognize the tension in his shoulders.

Your little soldier boy pretends so well, Nekufima purred. *As if his primate reflexes could save you if this hull breaches. What a delicious delusion.*

Another violent shudder ran through *Thunder* as something substantial impacted our bolsters. The lights flickered momentarily before stabilizing.

"Impact on starboard bolster," Destiny reported. "Bolster capacity at eighty-six percent and holding."

Phoebe called out from engineering, "Rerouting

auxiliary power to forward bolsters. Nicobe's stabilizing the battery output."

"Destiny, keep an eye on that Kergan flotilla," I ordered. "I want to know the second they make any move toward us. Sofia, work with Busto on damage control priorities."

"Already on it," Sofia replied, not looking up.

I gripped the arms of my command chair as another tremor rocked the ship. Through the viewscreen, I watched as more sections of the Ossuary Ring began to come apart, twisting like a snake in its death throes as the relentless gravitational forces pulled it toward the binary neutron stars.

"Let's get out of here," I commanded. "I'm taking us out under full thrust once I have a clear vector."

As *Thunder*'s engines powered up with a building whine, I ran quick calculations in my head. We had minutes, maybe seconds, before the Ossuary Ring's collapse would create a debris field impossible to navigate. And somewhere out there, enemies waited, watching as we fled one danger only to head straight toward another.

Such a narrow path you walk, Captain, Nekufima whispered in my mind. *Between gravity wells and hostile ships, between duty and survival. I wonder which precipice you'll fall from first.*

I ignored her and focused on the task at hand. One crisis at a time. First, escape the collapsing ring. Then deal with whoever waited beyond.

"All hands," I announced, "brace for emergency acceleration."

I wrestled with *Thunder*'s controls as we pulled away from the Ossuary Ring, my palms slick with sweat against the manual interface. The ancient Primordian structure was coming apart like wet paper in a hurricane, massive chunks of architecture—some the size of small moons—tearing away from the main structure. The binary neutron stars had finally won their millennia-long tug-of-war with the Ring's integrity field. Through the viewscreen, it looked like the end of the world, and in a way, it was. Someone else's world, dead for eons, finally surrendering to gravity's patience.

"Debris field expanding at increasing rate," Sofia called from her station, her voice steady despite the strain evident in the tight line of her shoulders. "Plotting optimal escape vectors now."

I nodded without taking my eyes off the viewscreen where glowing trajectories appeared, outlining our potential paths through the chaos. None of them looked particularly inviting. The problem with flying through a debris field was that the debris didn't give a damn about your plans.

"Hold on," I muttered, wrenching the ship into a sharp port roll as a jagged shard of what might have been Primordian control tower spun past us, close enough that I could see the ancient glyphs etched into its surface.

Thunder shuddered violently, the inertial dampeners struggling to compensate for my maneuvers. Something impacted our starboard bolsters with a sound like a giant's hammer striking an anvil.

"Minor impact," Busto reported, his fingers dancing across his console. "Starboard sensor array three is offline. Damage control team dispatched."

I didn't have time to acknowledge him before another fragment loomed ahead—this one a graceful arch of crystalline material that might have been beautiful in another context. Now it was just another killer in a field of them. I pushed *Thunder* into a dive that sent my stomach into my throat despite the dampeners.

"Phoebe, I need more power to the maneuvering pods," I called out.

"You've got it, Captain," she responded, her voice tight with concentration. "Rerouting now."

I felt the difference immediately as the ship responded with greater precision to my commands. My fingers tingled against the controls, a direct connection between my will and *Thunder*'s movements. We threaded between two massive chunks of debris with barely meters to spare on either side.

Such precision, Nekufima's voice slithered into my thoughts. *Like watching a monkey thread a needle while the room burns down around it. Entertaining, if futile.*

Sweat beaded on my forehead and ran down into my eyes. I blinked it away, not daring to release the controls even for a second. The viewscreen showed a terrifying spectacle—the binary neutron stars were beginning to tear chunks from each other now, streams of superheated plasma arcing between them like electric bridges spanning an impossible gap.

"Those stars are destabilizing faster than predicted," Sofia reported, her eyes fixed on her readouts. "Radiation levels climbing."

Another impact rocked the ship, harder this time. The lights flickered, and for a heart-stopping second, the controls went dead in my hands. Then they flared back to life, and I wrenched us away from a spinning column that would have speared *Thunder* like a harpoon.

"Nicobe reports power fluctuations in the main reactor," Nicobe's voice came from engineering. "She is compensating but suggests the captain avoid unnecessary strain on the systems. Which is to say, please try not to shake us apart, Captain Drake."

"I'll do my best," I grunted, muscles tensing as I executed a rolling climb over a massive plate of what looked like hull material. "But the alternative is letting the debris do it for us."

Throughout the ship, I could hear the groans and creaks of *Thunder*'s structure being tested to its limits. We were a tough little ship, but we weren't built to dance with the death of a megastructure.

"Goddamn it," I cursed as another fragment appeared directly in our path, this one too large to avoid. "Brace for impact! Full power to forward bolsters!"

Thunder slammed into the obstacle like a bullet hitting armor plate. The bolsters flared brilliant blue, and the debris shattered into thousands of smaller pieces that pattered against our hull like deadly rain. The ship lurched, sending several crew members sprawling against their restraints.

"Forward bolsters at forty percent," Destiny called out, regaining her position. "That was too close, Kory."

"Tell me something I don't know," I muttered, correcting our course as we spun from the impact.

You're going to die here, Nekufima offered helpfully. *All of you, crushed like insects between fragments of a civilization that would have found you primitive. There's a certain poetry to it, don't you think?*

"Shut up," I hissed under my breath, earning a concerned glance from Destiny.

A particularly violent tremor ran through the ship as something scraped along our ventral hull. The sound was like fingernails on the universe's chalkboard, setting my teeth on edge.

"Hull breach on deck three!" Busto announced sharply. "Emergency bulkheads engaged. No casualties reported."

My muscles burned with tension as I threw us into another desperate maneuver, corkscrewing between two converging chunks of debris. The g-forces pushed against the inertial dampeners, pressing me back into my seat with bruising force. My vision narrowed to a tunnel focused solely on the viewscreen, the rest of the world falling away.

After what felt like hours but must have been minutes, the density of the debris field began to thin. I allowed myself a shallow breath as we cleared the immediate danger zone, *Thunder* battered but intact.

"We're clear of the primary debris field," Sofia confirmed, her voice betraying the slightest tremor of relief. "But the neutron stars are accelerating their decay. They'll collide soon."

I slumped slightly in my chair, my hands cramping as I finally relaxed my death grip on the controls. The momentary respite was all I allowed myself before straightening again. The danger wasn't past—it had just changed form.

"Nav, set course for the ice giant," I ordered, my voice rough. "Emergency thrust. Let's see if we can outrun an apocalypse."

The engines roared in response to my commands, pushing us forward at an acceleration that strained the inertial dampeners to their limits. The crew was pressed back into their seats as *Thunder* leaped forward like a frightened animal, racing toward uncertain safety with the death of a star system nipping at our heels.

A massive gravitational wave hit us like an invisible fist, sending *Thunder* skidding sideways through space as though we'd hit black ice. Warning indicators that had just started to quiet down erupted into a fresh chorus as systems throughout the ship registered their objections to physics gone rogue. I hauled on the controls, fighting to bring us back on course, but it was like wrestling with a drunken elephant—mass and momentum coupled with unpredictable lurches that seemed deliberately designed to counter my every move.

"Gravitational anomalies increasing," Sofia reported, her fingers dancing across her interface. "The neutron stars' orbital decay is speeding up, creating ripples through local space-time."

Another wave hit us, this one strong enough to make the deck plates groan. The lights flickered, casting momentary shadows across grim faces.

"Navigation sensors are getting scrambled," Destiny called out, her voice tight but controlled. "Recalibrating now. I've got a clear vector... no, lost it again." Her fingers flew across her console, making adjustments faster than I could follow. "There—got it. Sending coordinates to your station, Kory."

New trajectories appeared on my display, constantly shifting as Destiny's calculations accounted for the gravitational distortions warping the surrounding space. I adjusted our course, feeling *Thunder* respond sluggishly, like a ship sailing through molasses.

"Radiation levels spiking," Sofia warned. "We've got a solar flare-equivalent event incoming from the smaller star."

"Reinforcing rear radiation shielding," Busto responded immediately. "Hull integrity holding at seventy-two percent."

The ship shuddered as another wave passed through us. This time, I heard the distinct sound of something metallic breaking somewhere deep in *Thunder*'s bowels.

"Nicobe regrets to inform the captain that the main stabilizer array has suffered a partial failure," Nicobe's voice came over the comm, the usual formality strained by urgency. "She is implementing emergency workarounds, but suggests extreme caution with maneuvers."

"Define 'extreme caution' in our current situation," I replied, wrestling the ship through another gravitational eddy.

"Perhaps avoid actions that would tear this vessel apart," Nicobe replied dryly. "Also, Nicobe must report her calculations show the neutron stars will collide with each other in approximately one hour and forty-seven minutes."

I felt a chill run down my spine that had nothing to do with the temperature on the bridge. "What are we looking at when that happens?"

"Initial gamma-ray burst will propagate at light speed," Nicobe explained, her dodecahedron housing wobbling slightly as the ship rocked. "Lethal radiation levels for any organic matter not sufficiently shielded. This vessel's radiation shielding would be... inadequate."

"What about hiding in the shadow of the ice giant?" I asked, an idea forming as I watched the distant blue-green planet on our long-range scanners.

There was a brief pause before Nicobe responded. "The planet's mass would indeed provide temporary protection from the initial radiation burst. However, the subsequent matter ejecta would arrive within hours, likely sublimating the ice giant's atmosphere and catching any vessel remaining in the vicinity."

"So we get temporary shelter, but we'd better not overstay our welcome," I translated, making a quick decision. "Alright, we make for the ice giant at maximum thrust. It gives us breathing room to plan our next move."

Running from one death to hide behind a frozen ball of gas, only to face another death, Nekufima commented in my mind. *Your species' survival instinct is as amusing as it is futile. Like watching ants build a dam against a tsunami.*

I ignored her, focusing instead on implementing our new course. "Phoebe, what's our engine status?"

"Primary drives at eighty-three percent," she called back. "We can push them harder if we have to, but I wouldn't recommend it for longer than—"

Her words cut off as the most violent shudder yet rocked *Thunder.* Through the viewscreen, I watched in horror as a massive section of the Ossuary Ring—a piece at least several kilometers across—exploded in a silent burst of light and debris. The resulting cloud of debris rolled toward us like a tsunami through space.

"Brace for impact!" I shouted, gripping the controls and trying to angle our strongest bolsters toward the incoming wave.

It hit us with the force of a planetary collision. *Thunder* rolled completely over, systems screaming in protest as the inertial dampeners failed momentarily under the strain. I felt myself lifted from my seat despite the restraints, weightless for a sickening moment, before crashing back down as the gravity reasserted itself.

Acting on instinct more than conscious thought, I threw us into a desperate corkscrew maneuver, trying to use the angular momentum to stabilize our tumble. The ship groaned around us, metal and composite materials pushed to their design limits and beyond.

"Inertial dampeners failing!" Phoebe shouted over the cacophony of alarms. "Structural integrity at critical levels!"

The maneuver was working, but slowly—too slowly. We were still caught in the turbulence of the shockwave, being tossed like a leaf in a hurricane. My vision grayed at the edges as the g-forces mounted, the failing dampeners unable to completely compensate for the extreme maneuver.

Through the spinning viewscreen, I caught glimpses of the binary neutron stars, now visibly distorted by each other's gravity. Streams of superheated plasma arced between them like solar flares, but magnified a thousandfold, creating a deadly light show as matter was stripped from their surfaces and accelerated to near-light speeds.

What a glorious way to die, Nekufima whispered in my thoughts. *Witness to the death of stars. Few mortals are granted such a privilege before their atoms are scattered across a newborn nebula.*

"Not today," I ground out through clenched teeth, fighting both the controls and my own fading consciousness.

With a final shudder that seemed to reverberate through every molecule of *Thunder*'s structure, we broke free of the shockwave's grip. The tumble slowed, then stopped as the stabilizers regained control. For a moment, no one spoke, the only sounds the slightly quieter alarms and the heavy breathing of a crew that had just stared death in the face.

"Damage report," I finally managed, my voice hoarse.

"Multiple systems compromised," Sofia responded, her cool professionalism returning despite the streak of blood running from a cut on her forehead. "But main engines are still online."

I straightened in my chair, ignoring the protest of abused muscles. We weren't safe—not by a long shot—but we'd survived the immediate danger. Now we had a new race to run.

"Maintain course for the ice giant," I ordered, pushing the thrust controls forward without waiting for acknowledgment. "Let's try this again. Emergency acceleration. Let's see how fast this ship can really move."

Thunder leaped forward under the brutal acceleration, pushing us all back into our seats as the inertial dampeners struggled to compensate. The ship vibrated around us, a living thing pushed beyond sensible limits, racing toward the distant sanctuary of a planet's shadow with a ticking clock of stellar death behind us.

As we accelerated away from the dying Ossuary Ring and the collapsing binary stars, I couldn't help but feel we were running from one disaster only to hurtle headlong toward another. But for now, we were alive, *Thunder* was moving, and sometimes in space, that's the best you can hope for.

42

The blue-white glow of the dying Ossuary Ring lit up *Thunder*'s command deck like a funeral pyre as we punched through the outer debris field. My hands gripped the controls with mechanical precision, not because I was calm—far from it—but because after years of fighting, my muscles remembered what to do even when my brain was busy cataloging all the ways we might die in the next few minutes. Another impact rocked the ship, but I barely registered it. Something more concerning had appeared on our tactical display: five Kergan frigates, breaking formation from their main fleet, reorienting toward us with predatory intent.

"Captain, we've cleared the primary debris field," Destiny announced, her voice tight with the strain of remaining professional while alarms screamed around us.

"Don't celebrate yet," I muttered, eyes fixed on the tactical display. "We've got company."

The ship shuddered again as a piece of the dissolving ring structure scraped against our ventral bolsters. The sound reverberated through the hull like a giant's fingernails on metal, setting my teeth on edge.

"Bolster integrity at sixty-eight percent," Phoebe called out from engineering. "We can't take many more hits like that."

"Hull breach on deck four contained," Busto reported, his voice steady despite the chaos. "Emergency bulkheads holding."

I nodded without taking my eyes off the tactical readout. The five Kergan frigates had formed a pursuit wedge, their engines burning hot as they accelerated toward us. Their timing couldn't have been worse—or, from their perspective, better. We were damaged, our bolsters strained, running from a system about to experience a stellar catastrophe, and now we had a Kergan welcoming party to deal with.

"Tactical assessment," I said, looking toward Sofia.

She met my gaze briefly, all business. "Five Kergan Talon-class frigates, standard pursuit formation. Time to weapons range: three minutes, seventeen seconds."

"They're blocking our path to the ice giant," Destiny added, highlighting the trajectory on the main display. The blue-green planet that represented our only shelter from the coming kilonova now lay beyond a gauntlet of Kergan firepower.

How fascinating that your species always finds time for killing each other, even in the shadow of cosmic annihilation, Nekufima's voice slithered through my mind. *Perhaps it's simply your nature.*

I pushed her aside mentally, concentrating on the tactical situation. The Kergans had the advantage in numbers and positioning, but we had one asset they didn't know about: my sydereal abilities. Since bonding with

Nekufima—unwillingly, I might add—I'd gained increased sensitivity to the dimensional barriers between normal space and the Syderealium. I could manipulate those barriers in limited ways, creating false impressions, bubbles of distorted reality that registered on sensors but held no substance.

"I have an idea," I announced, straightening in my command chair. "But I need absolute focus for about thirty seconds. Destiny, you have the conn."

She nodded sharply, moving to the secondary command station without hesitation.

I closed my eyes, shutting out the flashing warning lights and the chorus of alarms. The ship around me faded from my awareness as I reached out with my mind, feeling for the thin places in reality where our dimension brushed against the Syderealium. There—like patches of thin ice on a frozen lake—I could sense them, the weak points where reality could be manipulated.

With careful mental pressure, I pushed through those weak points, creating bubbles of distorted space-time. To sensors, they would look like ship-sized masses, perfect decoys. I created three of them, arranging them in a scattered pattern that mimicked evasive maneuvers, then opened my eyes.

"XO, I've deployed sydereal decoys. They'll register as solid objects on Kergan sensors." My voice sounded distant to my own ears as I settled back into normal awareness. "Bring us around behind that large section of Ring debris at bearing zero-four-zero."

Destiny nodded, already inputting the commands. "Understood. Adjusting course now."

The main viewscreen showed a massive chunk of the Ossuary Ring—easily ten kilometers across—tumbling slowly as it drifted away from the disintegrating structure. Perfect cover, if we could get there in time.

Thunder's engines roared in protest as Destiny pushed them beyond recommended limits, guiding us toward the shelter of the debris. On the tactical display, I watched as the Kergan pursuit force split, three frigates breaking off to chase my phantom ships while two continued on their original vector.

"They took the bait," Destiny observed, a hint of satisfaction in her voice. "Two frigates still on our tail, but three are pursuing the decoys."

"That still leaves us outnumbered," I said, sliding back into the primary command chair as Destiny relinquished control. "But I like those odds better."

Thunder slid behind the massive chunk of Primordian architecture, using its bulk to shield us from direct sensor contact. The two pursuing frigates adjusted course, attempting to predict where we would emerge.

"They're trying to box us in," Sofia reported, studying the tactical display. "One frigate moving to each side of the debris field."

I nodded, watching the enemy ships' approach vectors on the tactical screen. "Predictable. They're following standard Kergan pursuit doctrine." A dry smile pulled at the corner of my mouth. "Nice of them to be so punctual in trying to kill us. I'd hate to be murdered behind schedule."

That earned me a few tight smiles from the bridge crew, tension momentarily broken by gallows humor.

"Approaching optimal weapons range," Destiny announced. "First frigate will cross the threshold in fifteen seconds."

I leaned forward in my chair, hands gripping the armrests. "Charge forward railguns. Prepare missile magazine two with proximity warheads."

The weapons officer—a recent addition to the bridge crew whose name I still couldn't remember in the heat of the moment—responded with crisp efficiency. "Railguns charging. Missile magazine two ready."

On the tactical display, the lead Kergan frigate continued its approach, unaware that it was flying into a trap. When it crossed into our optimal firing range, I didn't hesitate.

"Weapons free," I ordered. "Triple forward railgun burst, full missile spread."

The ship hummed with deadly purpose as the weapons systems engaged. The railguns fired in rapid succession, three hypersonic projectiles lancing out from *Thunder*'s forward batteries. Before the Kergans could even register the railgun fire, our missiles launched in a coordinated spread, six streaks of white fire burning through the vacuum.

The lead frigate attempted evasive maneuvers, but it was too late. The first railgun round struck its forward section, penetrating the bolsters and tearing through metal and composite like tissue paper. The second and third rounds followed microseconds later, creating a catastrophic series of breaches along the ship's length. The missiles arrived in a perfect spread pattern, detonating around the already failing vessel.

Through the viewscreen, we watched the frigate's destruction unfold with terrible beauty. Its hull sheared apart like paper in a shredder, secondary explosions blooming outward as power conduits and weapons systems ignited. For a brief moment, the dying ship was outlined in a halo of its own atmosphere, oxygen burning brilliantly as it contacted the superheated metal. Then darkness consumed it, leaving only scattered debris and a rapidly fading thermal signature.

"Target destroyed," the weapons officer reported, a hint of professional pride in his voice.

"One down," I said, already adjusting our position for the next engagement. "Four to go."

You take such satisfaction in ending your fellow sentients, Nekufima observed in my mind. *Not that I disapprove. Destruction is the universe's natural state. Creation is the aberration.*

I ignored her commentary, focusing instead on the tactical display. The second frigate had altered course, recognizing the trap, but still intent on engaging us. Meanwhile, the three ships that had pursued my phantom decoys were reorienting, having discovered the deception.

"Time to neutron star collision?" I asked, glancing at Nicobe's station.

"Nicobe calculates ninety-six minutes until critical mass transfer initiates final collapse," she responded, her capsule bobbing slightly as another tremor ran through the ship. "The captain should be aware that gravitational anomalies will increase in frequency and intensity as we approach that threshold."

I nodded grimly. Ninety-six minutes. Not much time to defeat four Kergan frigates, limp to safety behind the ice giant, and figure out our next move before the entire system was consumed in a kilonova explosion.

"We need to move," I announced, hands dancing across the controls. "The Kergans are the immediate threat, but that clock is the real enemy. Sofia, plot an intercept course for the nearest frigate. Let's take them out one by one and clear our path to the ice giant."

"Plotting intercept now," she responded, fingers flying across her console.

As *Thunder* emerged from behind our temporary shelter, accelerating toward the next engagement, I couldn't help but think that surviving the collapsing Ossuary Ring might have been the easy part of our day. The Kergan frigates were regrouping, the neutron stars were spiraling toward mutual destruction, and we were caught in the middle with damaged bolsters and limited ammunition.

Just another day at the office for the crew of *Thunder*. At least we weren't bored.

43

The Kergans responded with the cold efficiency I'd come to expect from their kind. All four remaining frigates fired simultaneously, their plasma cannons painting deadly streaks across the void. I yanked *Thunder* into an evasive roll, but we were too slow, too damaged to dodge completely. A concentrated plasma stream caught our upper hull, the energy so intense that our external cameras showed the composite plating bubble and run like candle wax. The impact threw me against my restraints, but the real damage was happening above us—on Deck 7, where I knew twelve of my crew were stationed at the secondary fire control system.

The ship bucked beneath me like a wounded animal. Warning indicators shifted from amber to blood red across my display. The klaxons changed pitch, moving from the urgent "we're in trouble" tone to the bone-chilling "we're breached" wail that every spacer dreads.

"Direct hit to Deck 7!" Sofia's voice cut through the chaos, professional but tight with urgency. "Hull breach in sections 12 through 14."

"Emergency bulkheads engaging," Destiny reported, fingers dancing across her console. "Atmospheric loss in affected sections."

The hollow thud of bulkheads slamming shut echoed through *Thunder*'s structure, a sound I'd heard too many times in my career. Each closure represented another compartment sealed off—either to protect the rest of the ship from vacuum, or to contain fires that could consume our limited oxygen.

"Casualties?" I asked, already knowing the answer wouldn't be good.

Busto checked his display, his weathered face momentarily frozen in that mask every combat veteran learns to wear when receiving bad news. "Three confirmed KIA. Martinez, Okafor, and Paul. Nine wounded, four critical."

Martinez. I'd just promoted her last week. Paul had a daughter back on Earth he'd never met in person. Okafor had the best poker face on the ship and had relieved me of half a month's pay last game night.

I allowed myself exactly one second to feel the loss—a sharp, hot pain in my chest that I recognized as guilt. Then I locked it away. Mourning was a luxury for after the battle, assuming we survived that long.

"Acknowledge," I said, my voice steady. "Medical teams?"

"Already responding," Busto confirmed. "I'm deploying damage control to sections 11 and 15. Can't get into the breach zone directly."

On my command screen, I could see Busto's damage control teams moving with practiced efficiency through the ship's corridors. They wore the bulky pressure suits that would keep them alive if another breach opened up. Some carried emergency foam dispensers—the quick-hardening material could temporarily seal small to medium breaches. Others had portable atmospheric processors to restore breathable air to recovered sections.

"Phoebe, status on ship systems?" I called out, eyes still on the tactical display where the four Kergan frigates were maneuvering into a new formation.

"Primary power grid compromised in the forward sections," she replied, her voice strained but controlled. "Rerouting through secondary conduits now. We're losing output from heat sink array two—the plasma hit fried the thermal regulation system."

I could see her hands flying across the engineering station, redirecting power, shutting down non-critical systems, balancing the load across *Thunder*'s damaged infrastructure. It was like watching a concert pianist perform during an earthquake—precise movements executed under impossible conditions.

"Weapons status?" I asked.

"Forward railguns at eighty percent capacity," the weapons officer reported. "All missile magazines still operational."

Another plasma barrage lit up the space around us, but this time, I was ready. I threw *Thunder* into a tight corkscrew, the inertial dampeners struggling to compensate for the violent maneuver. The plasma streams passed harmlessly into the void, superheating the scattered debris from the Ossuary Ring in their wake.

"The Kergans are attempting to herd us," Sofia reported, studying the tactical display. "Standard kill corridor formation. Two frigates establishing firing positions at coordinates 330-mark-42 and 330-mark-78. The other two are moving to drive us between them."

I saw it too—a classic Kergan tactic. Two ships would establish overlapping fields of fire, while the others would maneuver to force their prey into the killing zone. Once there, the concentrated firepower would overwhelm even the strongest bolsters.

"Not falling for that," I muttered, mind racing through our options. None of them were good, but one stood out as marginally less suicidal than the others.

"All hands, prepare for extreme maneuver," I announced ship-wide. "Damage control teams, secure all equipment. Medical, brace your patients."

"Captain?" Destiny glanced at me, a question in her eyes.

"We're going to flip and burn," I explained, already inputting the necessary commands. "Rotate one-eighty on our vertical axis while maintaining our current vector, then fire main engines to decelerate rapidly."

Destiny's eyes widened slightly. "That'll put tremendous strain on the hull."

"And on the inertial dampeners," Phoebe added from engineering. "If they fail during that maneuver—"

"We'll be paste," I finished for her. "I'm aware. But it puts our forward weapons on target while the Kergans are still positioned for a pursuit engagement."

"It's a valid tactical option," Sofia said, her fingers already working to calculate the precise rotation sequence. "Unexpected. The Kergans won't have time to reposition."

I met her eyes briefly. "Glad you approve." There was no sarcasm in my voice. Despite our personal complications, her tactical judgment was something I trusted implicitly.

Phoebe's voice came over the comm. "Reconfiguring tractor pods for the maneuver. Diverting additional power to inertial dampeners."

Nicobe's capsule bobbed in what might have been agreement or resignation. "Nicobe has adjusted bolsters to compensate for anticipated stress patterns. She would like to note that this maneuver exceeds recommended operating parameters by approximately 42.7 percent."

"Noted," I replied, hands hovering over the control interface. "Everyone ready? Executing in three... two... one... now!"

I engaged the sequence. *Thunder*'s tractor pods—the reactionless drives that provided our propulsion—reversed orientation in perfect synchronization, then fired with maximum thrust. The ship shuddered violently around us, metal groaning in protest as we essentially tried to stop a starship on a dime.

The inertial dampeners struggled to compensate for the extreme forces, and I felt my body press hard against my restraints. The pressure built in my chest, making each breath a conscious effort. Dark spots danced at the edges of my vision, but I forced myself to remain focused on the tactical display.

The universe outside seemed to rotate as *Thunder* pivoted on its axis, the star field spinning sickeningly across our viewscreen. For a heart-stopping moment, the dampeners faltered, and the g-forces doubled. Someone on the bridge—I couldn't tell who through the pressure crushing my lungs—let out an involuntary groan.

Then, with a final shudder that seemed to travel through every molecule of the ship's structure, we completed the maneuver. *Thunder* was now oriented backward relative to our direction of travel, our forward weapons array perfectly positioned to target the pursuing Kergan frigates.

The Kergans, caught by surprise, were slow to react. Their formation, designed to herd us forward into their trap, was now hopelessly out of position. Better yet, their engines were facing us—the most vulnerable part of any warship.

"Forward railguns locked on target," the weapons officer announced, his voice strained from the lingering effects of our maneuver. "Frigate designate Tango-Three centered in our sights."

"Fire," I ordered, still fighting to draw a full breath. "Continuous barrage. Target their engine core."

Thunder's railguns roared to life, magnetic accelerators hurling hypervelocity projectiles at our target. The first three rounds struck the Kergan frigate's aft section where the bolsters were thinnest, punching clean through the armor. The next salvo found the engine core itself, piercing the containment vessel that housed the ship's fusion reactor.

On the viewscreen, we watched the chain reaction unfold. First, a bright point of light appeared at the impact site, like a new star being born. Then, the light expanded rapidly as the containment failure cascaded through the engineering section. The frigate's aft quarter bulged outward unnaturally, metal distending like a balloon before rupturing in a spectacular bloom of superheated plasma and vaporized hull material.

Secondary explosions rippled through the dying vessel, ammunition magazines and fuel reservoirs cooking off in rapid succession. Within seconds, what had been a sleek warship was reduced to a rapidly expanding cloud of debris, scattered components tumbling away from the epicenter of the destruction like macabre confetti.

"Direct hit," the weapons officer confirmed, a note of grim satisfaction in his voice. "Target destroyed."

"Damage report from our maneuver?" I asked, finally able to breathe normally as the inertial dampeners fully compensated for our new orientation.

"Minor structural strain in sections 4, 17, and 22," Sofia reported. "Nothing critical. Inertial dampeners holding but operating at 93% efficiency."

Two down, three to go. The remaining Kergan frigates were already adjusting their formation, abandoning the kill corridor strategy now that we'd proven we could counter it.

Such a risky gambit, Nekufima's voice slid into my thoughts, smooth as silk and twice as poisonous. *I'm almost impressed. If the dampeners had failed completely, you'd have experienced the fascinating sensation of your organs liquefying inside your intact skin. A shame we missed that opportunity for your education.*

Sorry to disappoint you, I thought back sarcastically. *Next time I'm considering turning myself into human soup, I'll get your input first. Maybe you can provide a recipe.*

Such wit under pressure, she responded, her mental voice dripping with mock admiration. *Perhaps that's why I find you marginally more interesting than the average primate. Your species faces annihilation with such charming defiance.*

Glad I can keep you entertained while we fight for our lives, I countered. *It would be tragic if you got bored while we're busy dying.*

Aloud, I said, "Reconfigure tractor pods for forward thrust. Let's get some maneuvering room." The Kergan frigates were regrouping, and I wanted to be anywhere but directly in their sights when they launched their next coordinated attack.

As *Thunder*'s engines hummed back to life, pushing us away from the expanding cloud of debris that had been a Kergan warship, I checked the chronometer. Just over an hour until the neutron stars collided. Two enemy ships destroyed, three remaining, and we still needed to reach the shelter of the ice giant before the stars decided to end their cosmic dance in a spectacular burst of gamma radiation.

The day wasn't getting any easier, but at least we were still in the fight. And as long as we were fighting, we weren't dead yet.

44

The remaining three Kergan frigates fanned out like wolves around wounded prey, their formation tight—overlapping fields of fire, minimal exposure. Textbook Kergan tactics: effective, disciplined, and about as imaginative as a tax auditor's sock drawer. But what they lacked in creativity, they more than made up for in firepower.

Individually, none of them could outgun *Thunder.* Together, they should've had the advantage—overwhelming force against a damaged cruiser. *Should have.*

But they didn't have Sofia Kohl slicing through their tactical chatter like a scalpel, and they sure as hell didn't have a captain reckless enough to fly backward through a neutron star's gravity well.

"I've got their comm frequency," Sofia announced, her fingers dancing across her interface. Her face was illuminated by her console's blue glow, highlighting the intensity in her eyes. "They're using encrypted channels, but it's standard Kergan military cipher. Decoding now."

I nodded, keeping my attention split between the

tactical display and the main viewscreen where the Kergan ships executed their careful maneuvers. "What are they saying?"

"Tactical commands mainly," Sofia replied, eyes never leaving her screen. "They're reorganizing into... yes, that's it." She looked up suddenly. "They're using standard Kergan pursuit pattern Delta. I recognize the formation signatures."

"And that helps us how?" I asked, adjusting our position slightly to keep all three frigates in our weapon arcs.

A ghost of a smile touched Sofia's lips. "Because Pattern Delta has predictable evasive responses when confronted with specific threats. It's part of their standardized tactical doctrine." Her fingers flew across her console. "Targeting solutions uploaded to weapons."

I raised an eyebrow. "You're saying you know how they'll dodge before they do?"

"With 87% probability," she confirmed. "Assuming they follow their own tactical manual."

"I've never met a Kergan who didn't," I said, already formulating a plan. "Weapons, prepare a saturation missile spread. Target the area between frigates designate Tango-Four and Tango-Five."

"Targeting solution locked," the weapons officer confirmed. "Missiles ready."

I took a deep breath, weighing our limited ammunition against the tactical advantage Sofia had just handed us. "Fire missiles, missile magazine one."

Thunder shuddered slightly as the missiles launched, four streaks of fire burning across the void. The Kergans responded immediately, their point defense systems engaging, trying to intercept our incoming ordinance.

"They're taking the bait," Sofia reported, watching their movements. "Evasive patterns initiating... now."

On the tactical display, the two Kergan frigates began moving precisely as Sofia had predicted, breaking in opposite directions to clear the missile threat zone. Their maneuvers were textbook perfect—which made them perfectly predictable.

"Forward railguns target frigate Tango-Four," I ordered. "Fire when ready."

"Firing," the weapons officer responded.

Thunder's railguns spat hypervelocity rounds toward the evading Kergan vessel. The first salvo caught the frigate mid-turn, striking its exposed flank where the bolsters were spread thin to cover the maximum surface area. The impacts punched through the outer armor layer, creating momentary flashes of light as atmosphere vented from the wounded ship.

"Direct hit," the weapons officer confirmed. "Target damaged, but still operational."

"Again," I ordered. "Concentrate fire on the same location."

The second railgun barrage struck with surgical precision, hammering the already damaged section of the Kergan vessel. This time, the effect was catastrophic. The frigate's midsection buckled under the concentrated fire, its structural integrity failing. The ship didn't explode so much as it split, breaking apart along the line of impacts like a tree trunk splitting under an axe.

"Target critically damaged," the weapons officer reported. "They're losing power and venting atmosphere across multiple decks."

On the viewscreen, the crippled frigate tumbled away, emergency thrusters firing sporadically as its crew fought a losing battle against catastrophic systems failure. It wasn't destroyed, but it was effectively out of the fight.

Before I could celebrate the minor victory, the deck lurched violently beneath me. Warning indicators flashed across every console on the bridge as a barrage of plasma fire hammered our port side.

"Direct hit to port bolsters!" Phoebe called out from engineering. "Bolster integrity at forty-eight percent and falling."

The tactical display showed the third Kergan frigate—Tango-Six—had charged to point-blank range while we were focused on its companion. It was practically on top of us now, close enough that its plasma cannons couldn't miss, pounding *Thunder*'s defenses with methodical precision.

Another impact rocked the ship, throwing Destiny against her restraints hard enough to make her gasp. The lighting flickered, emergency systems briefly taking over before main power reasserted itself.

"Port bolsters failing," Phoebe reported, her voice tight with urgency. "Thirty-two percent integrity. One more concentrated hit and they'll collapse completely."

"Evasive action," I ordered, wrenching the controls to put us into a desperate spin.

The Kergan frigate tracked our movement, its weapons officers clearly experienced. Another plasma barrage caught our ventral section, the energy bleeding through our weakened bolsters and scorching the hull beneath.

"Bolster breach in section 19!" Busto called out. "Hull temperature approaching critical."

We were running out of options. The Kergan frigate had us dead to rights, too close for missiles to be effective, and maneuvering room severely limited by the nearby debris field and the increasing gravitational distortions from the neutron stars.

Then I saw it—our one chance, risky as hell, but better

than waiting to be blown apart.

"Phoebe, I need emergency purge of the primary heat sink array," I called out. "Maximum discharge, directed port-forward."

She looked up sharply, understanding dawning in her eyes. "You want to vent our thermal buildup directly at them? That's... actually brilliant. Configuring now."

"Nicobe, on my mark, I need all available power to engines for a two-second burst," I continued. "We're going to need to clear the discharge zone fast."

"Understood," she replied.

"Heat sink purge ready," Phoebe reported. "Vent aligned with target. Thermal load at maximum capacity."

I watched the tactical display, waiting for the perfect moment as the Kergan frigate adjusted position, bringing its main sensor array to bear for another targeting solution.

"Now!" I shouted.

The ship lurched as the heat sink purged, expelling superheated plasma directly toward the Kergan vessel. The thermal signature was blinding—literally. The concentrated heat bloom overloaded the frigate's forward sensors, creating what amounted to a thermal flashbang in space.

"Full thrust!" I ordered.

Thunder's engines roared to life, pushing us in a tight arc around the temporarily blinded Kergan ship. The maneuver brought our forward railguns to bear on the enemy vessel's command section—their equivalent of a bridge, located in the frontal cone of the ship.

"Target locked," the weapons officer reported.

"Fire," I said, my voice deadly calm. "Everything we've got."

Thunder's railguns fired in perfect synchronization, all three barrels launching projectiles at a fraction of light speed. The hypervelocity rounds struck the Kergan frigate's command cone in a triangular pattern that would have earned a marksman's commendation on any firing range.

The effect was immediate and devastating. The frigate's forward section crumpled inward before exploding outward in a spray of metal, composite, and, unfortunately, crew. The ship's main spine fractured from the force of the impact, power conduits rupturing in cascading secondary explosions that traveled the length of the vessel.

"Direct hit to command section," the weapons officer confirmed unnecessarily. We could all see the result on the viewscreen—a once-proud warship reduced to a broken, burning hulk.

On the tactical display, the final functional Kergan frigate—Tango-Five—abruptly changed course. It was turning away, accelerating to maximum thrust. Running.

"Last frigate is attempting to withdraw," Sofia reported, a note of cold satisfaction in her voice.

I watched the retreating vessel for a moment, weighing options that weren't really options at all. If we let it escape, it would report our position, condition, and heading to the main Kergan fleet. Given our damage and the imminent stellar catastrophe, we couldn't afford to be hunted.

"Finish it," I ordered without hesitation.

"Missiles armed," the weapons officer responded. "Missile magazine two ready."

"Fire."

The last of our missiles streaked from *Thunder*'s launch tubes, accelerating rapidly as they chased down the fleeing Kergan ship. The frigate deployed countermeasures—chaff and electronic jamming—but our targeting systems cut through the interference, guided by Sofia's precision calculations.

Both missiles struck the Kergan vessel's engine section, detonating in a synchronized blast that overwhelmed its aft bolsters. The ship's reactor containment failed catastrophically, turning the entire vessel into a briefly expanding sphere of superheated plasma before the vacuum of space extinguished the fireball, leaving only scattered debris.

For a long moment, silence reigned on *Thunder*'s bridge, broken only by the persistent alarms and damage reports flowing in from throughout the ship. The adrenaline that had carried us through the battle began to ebb, leaving behind the cold reality of what we'd just survived—and what we'd lost.

"Damage report," I requested, my voice rough from shouting orders.

"Anti-ship missile magazine two is completely depleted, magazine one wrecked by the last hit," Busto reported. "Bolster integrity down to twenty-seven percent. Hull breaches on decks three, four, and seven."

"Casualties?" I asked, dreading the answer.

"Six confirmed KIA," he replied grimly. "Fourteen wounded, seven critical."

Six dead. Six of my crew who would never see Earth again, never see their families. I allowed myself a moment of genuine grief before compartmentalizing it away. There would be time for mourning later—if we survived what was coming next.

"Status of the crippled Kergan frigate?" I asked, turning to Sofia.

She checked her sensors. "Adrift, minimal power signatures. Life support appears to be functioning in some sections. They're not a threat."

I nodded. "Leave them. We've got bigger problems." I

turned to Nicobe. "Time to neutron star collision?"

Nicobe's crimson dodecahedron bobbed in her housing, the movement somehow conveying urgency despite the lack of facial expressions. "Captain, gravitational readings are spiking. The neutron stars are accelerating toward collision. Kilonova imminent."

"How imminent?" I demanded.

"Revised estimate: One hour thirteen minutes until critical mass exchange initiates catastrophic merger."

Half the time we'd originally calculated. The gravitational dance of the binary stars was accelerating faster than predicted, shortening our window for escape. I felt my expression harden as I surveyed our situation: *Thunder* damaged, bolsters critically weakened, weapons depleted, and a stellar apocalypse bearing down on us.

We'd won the battle against the Kergans, but the war against physics and time was just beginning.

Well done, Captain, Nekufima's voice slid into my thoughts, mockingly congratulatory. *You've successfully cleared the path to your temporary shelter. Now all you need to do is limp there before the stars decide to end their cosmic dance.*

You almost sound concerned, I thought back. *Nothing to worry about from your perspective. You're already dead, remember?*

True, she conceded. *But I've grown somewhat attached to our arrangement. Your primitive consciousness provides such interesting diversions from the monotony of eternal existence.*

Glad I can keep you entertained, I responded sarcastically. *What I could really use is a jump point, but the gravitational waves from these spiraling neutron stars are playing havoc with the local Lagrange points. Any chance you've got insights into interdimensional travel that might help?*

I expected more sarcasm, more mocking commentary on human frailty. Instead, I was met with silence. Complete and utter silence in the section of my mind where Nekufima's voice normally slithered. It was like suddenly finding an empty space where a tooth had been—disconcerting and suspicious in equal measure.

Nekufima? I prodded mentally. Still nothing.

That was worrying. In all the time since our unwilling bond had formed, she had never passed up an opportunity to comment on my decisions, especially when they involved potential death and destruction. Her sudden silence felt less like mercy and more like a predator going still before pouncing.

But I didn't have time to dwell on cryptic glyphshades with dubious motives. "Nav, set course for the ice giant," I ordered. "I'm employing maximum safe acceleration, given our damage."

As *Thunder* limped toward the distant planet that represented our only shelter from the coming storm, I couldn't shake the feeling that Nekufima knew something about our situation that she wasn't sharing. Something important.

For now, though, we had a more immediate problem: reaching the shadow of the ice giant before the neutron stars collided and bathed the system in deadly gamma radiation. One crisis at a time. We'd deal with whatever Nekufima was hiding later—assuming there was a later to deal with it in.

45

The ice giant loomed in *Thunder's* viewscreen, a massive sphere of swirling blue-green gases that represented our only shelter from the coming apocalypse. I gripped the controls with white knuckles, pushing our wounded ship toward safety, each system alert pulsing on my display like a countdown to disaster. The neutron stars behind us spiraled ever closer to each other, their deadly dance accelerating beyond all predictions, twin harbingers of destruction preparing for their final, fatal embrace.

"Captain, the neutron stars' orbital decay is speeding up," Destiny reported, her voice tight with tension as she monitored the tactical display. "Field intensity increasing exponentially."

The main viewscreen shifted to a split view—half showing our approach to the ice giant, half displaying the binary stars. Even through the sensor filters, their intensity was painful to look at. Streams of superheated matter arced between them, a precursor to the cataclysm that would follow.

"Time to collision?" I asked, adjusting our approach vector to put us on the fastest path to the planet's shadow.

"Five minutes, forty-two seconds," Destiny answered. She paused, rechecking her calculations. "Correction. Five minutes, seventeen seconds. The process is accelerating faster than our models predicted."

I swore under my breath, doing quick mental math. "And time to reach planetary umbra?"

Sofia answered from her station, her voice cool and professional despite the strain etched on her face. "Six minutes, ten seconds at current velocity."

Almost a minute too slow. The knot in my stomach tightened.

"Phoebe, we need more speed. Can you squeeze anything else out of the engines?"

Phoebe's face appeared on a side screen, streaked with grease and sweat. Behind her, I caught glimpses of damage control teams working frantically to patch breached systems.

"We're at 108% of recommended maximum already," she replied. "I can try to bypass the safety regulators on the auxiliary drive, but—"

"Do it," I ordered. "Whatever it takes."

She nodded grimly and disappeared from the screen. Moments later, I felt a subtle vibration through the deck plates as she pushed our engines beyond their design limits.

Nicobe's crimson dodecahedron bobbed urgently in its housing. "Nicobe must report that the bolsters are operating at diminished capacity. The previous enemy engagement has compromised seventy-three subsystems critical to our survival. She calculates a thirty-eight percent probability of catastrophic failure should we maintain current acceleration parameters."

"Noted," I replied tersely. "But those odds are better than what awaits us if we don't reach the shadow in time."

You're like insects fleeing a wildfire, Nekufima's voice slithered back into my thoughts after her unsettling silence. *Such frantic scrambling. It might be endearing—if it weren't so utterly pathetic.*

Decided to rejoin the conversation? I thought back. *I was enjoying the quiet.*

I was... contemplating possibilities, she replied, her mental voice unusually thoughtful. *Your current predicament presents certain interesting dynamics.*

I had no time to parse whatever game she was playing. The ship shuddered around us as another gravitational wave washed over us, this one strong enough to momentarily disrupt our course.

"Compensating," I muttered, wrestling with the controls. The ice giant filled more of our viewscreen now, its swirling atmosphere a tantalizing promise of shelter. But the numbers on my display told the harsh truth—we weren't going to make it.

"Engine output increasing," Phoebe reported over the comm. "We're at 112% of maximum rated thrust. Any more and we risk a core breach."

"Understood. Hold at current output," I ordered. The deck plates vibrated more intensely beneath my feet, the sound of our straining engines changing pitch as they pushed beyond their limits.

"Recalculating approach time," Sofia announced, her fingers flying across her console. "Five minutes, fifty-two seconds to planetary umbra."

Still not enough. I scanned the tactical display, desperate for options. "What about using our remaining fuel reserves for the emergency maneuvering thrusters? A continuous burn might shave off a few seconds."

"Nicobe advises against this action," the igna interjected. "Such a maneuver would deplete our reserves beyond recovery threshold. We would be without maneuvering capability once within the planetary shadow."

"Three minutes to neutron star collision," Destiny announced, her voice dropping almost to a whisper.

The bridge fell silent save for the urgent beeping of consoles and the groaning protest of our overtaxed ship. In that moment, the full weight of responsibility settled on my shoulders like a physical presence. I looked around at my crew—their faces tense but determined, trusting me to find a way out of this impossible situation.

"We're not going to make it, are we?" Busto said quietly from tactical, the veteran marine's weathered face a mask of stoic acceptance.

Before I could answer, the stars on our viewscreen began to distort. The twin neutron stars, already terrifyingly bright, suddenly appeared to stretch, their forms elongating as gravitational lensing effects warped the very light around them.

"Energy spike!" Destiny shouted. "They're colliding now!"

"All hands, shelter from external radiation burst!" I called over the ship-wide comm. "Implement emergency protocol Gamma-Three!"

The protocol was a last-ditch defense—powering down non-essential systems to reinforce bolsters and radiation shielding. It wouldn't be enough, not against a kilonova, but it might mean the difference between total destruction and survivable damage.

The viewscreen automatically dimmed to its maximum

setting as the stars touched. For one heartbeat, nothing seemed to happen. Then space itself appeared to fold around them, light bending impossibly as the two unimaginably dense stellar cores merged.

The flash that followed was like nothing I had ever seen. Even with the viewscreen at minimum transparency, it was blinding—a wall of pure white energy that seemed to erase the concept of darkness itself. I threw up my arm instinctively, but it made no difference.

Thunder screamed around us as the leading edge of the gamma-ray burst slammed into our ship. Warning indicators across every console shifted from red to pure white as sensors overloaded. Through the chaos, I heard the distinctive sound of metal superheating—a high-pitched whine followed by a crack like a gunshot as a hull panel on our port stern delaminated, venting superheated plasma into space.

"Hull breach in section fourteen!" someone shouted—I couldn't tell who through the din.

"External sensor arrays one through eight are gone," Sofia reported, her voice steady despite everything. "Complete burnout."

Through the brilliance on the viewscreen—which had not yet begun to fade—I watched as the ice giant's atmosphere began to glow on its nearside, the radiation energizing its upper atmospheric layers into a ghostly aurora that stretched halfway around the planet.

Inside *Thunder,* the situation was deteriorating rapidly. Emergency lighting kicked in as main power fluctuated. The ship's internal atmosphere took on the acrid smell of burned circuitry and melting insulation.

"Fire in the dorsal corridor!" Busto announced, already moving toward the exit. "Near the missile bay. Damage control team with me!"

He was gone before I could respond, racing to contain the latest crisis. I stayed at my post, fighting to maintain our course toward the planet's shadow as systems failed around me. The controls juddered in my grip, feedback from damaged steering mechanisms sending painful vibrations up my arms.

"Medical emergency on Deck 3," came a voice over the comm. "Multiple personnel with radiation burns and flash blindness. Need assistance immediately."

I heard screams in the background before the channel cut off. My throat tightened. Those were my people suffering because I couldn't get us to safety in time.

Such is the burden of command, Nekufima commented, her mental voice almost gentle, which somehow made it worse. *Watching others suffer for your decisions.*

"Shut up," I hissed aloud, earning a concerned glance from Destiny.

"Approaching planetary umbra," Sofia reported. "Thirty seconds."

Too late for those already injured or worse. The damage reports continued to flow in, each one a knife twist of guilt in my gut. The worst came ten minutes later, after we'd finally reached the relative shelter of the planet's shadow.

Busto's voice over the comm was flat, the voice of a man who had seen too much death and learned to wall it away. "Fire contained in missile bay. Stokes and Jamali didn't make it out. They were trapped when the emergency bulkheads sealed."

I acknowledged the report with a nod he couldn't see, my own voice failing me momentarily. Two more names added to the list I carried. Two more letters I'd have to write if we somehow survived this nightmare.

My hands were numb on the controls, and I felt tightness in my chest. We'd reached the shadow of the ice giant, but the cost had been too high. And according to the readings still functioning on our sensors, this was just the beginning of our troubles.

46

The shadow of the ice giant enveloped *Thunder* like a cold embrace, the sudden absence of the kilonova's blinding light almost as jarring as its arrival had been. Warning klaxons continued their urgent song throughout the ship, but their rhythm had changed—no longer the frantic tempo of imminent destruction, but the steady beat of a vessel grievously wounded yet somehow still alive. I released a breath I hadn't realized I'd been holding, my shoulders sagging under the weight of partial victory. We'd made it to temporary shelter, but at what cost?

"Damage control, priority one," I ordered, my voice raspy from shouting over alarms. "Nicobe, I need a full systems assessment. Destiny, keep scanning for any anomalies in the ice giant's atmosphere. That gamma burst may have triggered reactions we need to watch for."

The crew moved with the efficiency of professionals who'd drilled for emergencies, though none of our simulations had covered anything like this. Status reports began flowing in from throughout the ship, each one worse than the last. Life support operating at sixty-three percent capacity. Primary power grid compromised in seventeen locations. Bolster integrity hovering at nineteen percent—barely enough to maintain atmospheric containment, let alone withstand weapons fire.

Phoebe's voice came through the comm, strained but determined. "Engineering to bridge. We've stabilized the battery output, but coolant loop three is completely gone. We're routing around it, but we can't push the engines beyond forty percent without risking core instability."

"Understood," I acknowledged. "Maintain current output and focus on life support systems."

Nicobe's capsule bobbed in agitation. "Nicobe must report that veilspace containment grids have suffered significant degradation. Thirty-two percent of the field emitters are non-functional. She cannot guarantee consistent protection against dimensional anomalies."

Great. As if we didn't have enough problems without the risk of random tears in the fabric of reality. I opened my mouth to respond when Destiny's voice cut through the controlled chaos of the bridge.

"Contact!" she called, her back stiffening as she stared at her sensor display. "Dominion rebel battlecruiser at bearing 047-mark-102, range 30,000 kilometers!"

The main viewscreen shifted, zooming in on a section of space near the curving limb of the ice giant. At first, I saw nothing but the swirling planetary atmosphere and the star-speckled blackness beyond. Then a shadow moved against the darkness—a massive vessel, easily four times *Thunder*'s size, its distinctive silhouette unmistakable as a Collective Dominion Kytopo-class battlecruiser. But this was no regular Dominion vessel; the rebel markings were visible even through the distortion of distance and our damaged sensors. We'd met this particular battlecruiser when we encountered the rebel task force back in that uninhabited system.

"How did we miss that?" I demanded, leaning forward in my chair.

"It was powered down, sir," Sofia replied, her fingers dancing across her console as she pulled up tactical data. "Minimal emissions, running silent. The gamma burst must have forced them to bring systems back online for damage control."

The viewscreen enhanced further, giving us a clearer view of our new problem. The battlecruiser had clearly been through its own battle before finding shelter behind the ice giant. Vast sections of its hull were scorched black, with several compartments open to space. Electrical discharges arced sporadically across its surface, blue-white lightning dancing between damaged power conduits. Atmospheric venting poured from shattered hull seams, creating a hazy cloud around portions of the massive ship.

Despite its battered condition, the cruiser's main batteries were visibly powering up, gun turrets the size of our entire bridge rotating with mechanical precision to lock onto *Thunder*'s position.

"Weapons status?" I asked, already knowing the answer wouldn't be good.

"Forward railguns at twenty-eight percent capacity," Busto reported grimly. "Port batteries completely offline. Starboard at fifteen percent. No functional missiles remaining."

Sofia's voice was cold and precise. "Tactical analysis complete. The rebel cruiser's main batteries outrange our weapons by a factor of three. Their bolster capacity, even damaged, exceeds our offensive capabilities by approximately 450 percent. We cannot win this engagement, Captain."

I nodded, mind racing through alternatives. "What about running? Can we establish a veilspace corridor?"

Destiny shook her head, frustration evident in her expression. "Negative, sir. The gravitational turbulence from the kilonova has completely destabilized local veilspace calculations. Jump drive can't lock onto any stable coordinates. We're..." she hesitated, "we're trapped."

The word hung in the air, heavy with finality. Trapped between the approaching devastation of the kilonova ejecta and an enemy warship we couldn't hope to defeat. I looked around the bridge, at the faces of my crew—some showing fear, others determination, all looking to me for a solution I didn't have.

Busto met my gaze across the bridge, his weathered features set in the expression I'd seen countless times in combat situations—the look of a veteran who recognizes impossible odds but refuses to accept defeat. He gave me a small nod, a gesture that said more than words: whatever you decide, I'm with you.

"Options?" I asked, directing the question to the bridge at large.

"We could try to negotiate," Sofia suggested, though her tone made it clear how little faith she had in that approach. "The rebels may be willing to let us pass if we offer them something of value."

"What do we have that they would want?" Destiny countered. "Most of our systems are barely functioning, and our hold is empty of anything valuable."

My hand drifted unconsciously to my pocket, where the small weight of Nekufima's empty Phylactery pressed against my thigh. Once, it had been the most valuable object in the galaxy—before she left it behind and took up residence in my head. Even if I *could* give her up, I wouldn't. Not with Arctis hunting her. I'd seen what he was capable of. The thought of him wielding an Astral Titan wasn't just dangerous—it was apocalyptic.

Is it really so unthinkable? Nekufima's voice whispered in my mind, as if summoned by my thoughts. *After all, I'm already here, already bonded to you. The phylactery is merely a container, a prison. And you've seen how well I play with others.*

You call driving people insane "playing"? I shot back silently.

Details, details, she replied, her mental voice carrying a hint of amusement. *The point remains—you need something these rebels cannot counter. Something beyond their comprehension. Something like me.*

The tactical display showed the rebel battle cruiser moving, adjusting its position to maintain optimal firing solutions on *Thunder*. On the main viewscreen, its massive weapons batteries glowed with building energy—the prelude to an opening salvo.

"They're powering weapons to full capacity," Sofia reported. "Targeting solutions locked. They're preparing to fire, Captain."

The bridge fell silent, all eyes turning to me. In that moment, I felt the full weight of command—not just responsibility for the lives under my care, but for the choice between certain death and a bargain with a power I neither trusted nor fully understood.

"Captain?" Destiny's voice was quiet, steady despite everything. "Your orders?"

My fingers brushed against the Phylactery in my pocket, feeling its ancient contours through the fabric of my uniform. The smooth, unyielding surface seemed to pulse with energy, as if Nekufima's presence extended beyond my mind and into the physical world.

You know what you have to do, Nekufima whispered. *The only question is whether you'll admit it to yourself in time.*

I stared at the tactical display, at the overwhelming odds arrayed against us, and felt something hard and cold crystalize in my chest—not resignation, but resolution.

47

I closed my eyes, shutting out the chaos of the bridge, the worried faces of my crew, the looming threat of the rebel battlecruiser. My hand closed around the Phylactery in my pocket, its surface unnaturally cool against my palm despite the heat of my skin. There was no choice left—no clever tactics, no heroic last stand that would save my ship and crew. Only Nekufima remained as an option, a darkness I'd resisted embracing until this moment when the alternative was watching everyone I was responsible for die.

"Captain?" Sofia's voice seemed to come from very far away. "They're charging weapons. We need to—"

"Give me a moment," I said, my voice oddly calm. "Everyone maintain stations."

I leaned back in my command chair, feeling the familiar contours support my weight as I let my consciousness slip deeper, away from the physical world and toward the mental space where Nekufima and I could communicate face-to-face. My breathing slowed, my muscles relaxed, and the sounds of the bridge—the urgent beeping of consoles, the whispered conversations of a crew preparing to die—faded to a distant murmur.

The transition was never pleasant. A vertigo like falling through the floor of my own mind, a momentary disorientation as the rules of physical reality gave way to the dreamlike logic of whatever mental construct Nekufima created for our meetings. This time, I found myself standing in a vast chamber that resembled the interior of the Ossuary Ring, but twisted and wrong, the architecture bent at impossible angles, surfaces that seemed to recede forever, then suddenly terminate inches from my face.

She was waiting for me, of course. Nekufima always presented herself in the same form for these encounters—a naked female figure with skin like burnished obsidian, her features both alluring and terrifying in their alien perfection. Her hair was a tangle of black vines that moved with a life of their own, her lips a perpetually crooked line of disinterest. Only her eyes betrayed her true nature—bottomless pools of swirling energy symbols, the script of a language no human tongue could pronounce.

"The captain comes calling in his hour of need," she purred, her voice like velvet dragged across broken glass. "How deliciously predictable."

"We don't have time for games," I replied, maintaining as much distance from her as the mental construct allowed. "You know why I'm here."

She circled me with predatory grace, her bare feet making no sound on the impossible floor. "Of course I do. Your little metal shell is about to be torn apart by the bigger metal shell, and then if you somehow survive that, the approaching wave of stellar debris will finish the job." Her smile was a crescent of perfect white teeth. "Quite the predicament you've maneuvered yourself into."

"Can you help us?" I asked directly, refusing to be drawn

into her verbal sparring.

"I can do many things, Kory Drake," she replied, stopping directly in front of me. "The question is not whether I can help, but whether you are prepared for what my help entails."

I swallowed, fighting the instinctive fear her presence always triggered. "We're going to die without your intervention. Everyone on *Thunder* will die."

"And that matters to you." It wasn't a question. "These fragile collections of cells and electricity, these temporarily animated meat puppets that you call friends." She reached out, her fingertips hovering inches from my face. "You would risk anything to save them, wouldn't you?"

"What do you want?" I asked, resisting the urge to step back.

Her smile widened. "Want? Such a limited concept. I want everything and nothing. I want to exist without constraint. I want to unmake and remake reality according to my designs." Her head tilted slightly. "But in this moment, what I want is for you to see what I truly am."

"And in exchange, you'll save my ship? My crew?"

Nekufima laughed, the sound like shattering crystal. "Yes, little captain. I will save your precious people from the immediate danger. No payment required beyond your continued... partnership."

Something about the way she said it sent ice down my spine, but I had no time to negotiate for better terms. "Then do it."

"As you wish." She leaned forward, her face inches from mine. "Witness what I am."

The mental construct dissolved around us, reality rushing back with brutal force. I gasped, eyes flying open to find myself still on *Thunder*'s bridge, my crew watching me with expressions ranging from concern to confusion. I must have been "gone" for only seconds in real time.

"Captain?" Destiny asked hesitantly. "Are you—"

Her words died as the main viewscreen captured everyone's attention. The rebel battlecruiser hung in space, massive and threatening, its weapons now fully charged and ready to fire. But something was happening to it—something impossible.

The huge vessel seemed to shudder, as if caught in an invisible vise. No energy weapons fired upon it, no physical force that our sensors could detect was applied, yet the battlecruiser's hull began to buckle inward, as if enormous pressure was being exerted from all directions simultaneously.

"What the hell?" Busto breathed, rising from his station.

On the screen, the deformation of the battlecruiser accelerated. Massive armored plates designed to withstand direct hits from capital ship weapons crumpled like tissue paper. The ship's spine—a reinforced structural element running its entire length—bent at an impossible angle, then snapped with a violence we could almost feel through the vacuum of space.

"Sensors detect no weapons fire," Sofia reported, her voice barely above a whisper. "No energy signatures, no projectiles... nothing."

The destruction continued in eerie silence. The battlecruiser folded in upon itself, compartments crushed, atmosphere venting in crystalline plumes that were themselves compressed into nothingness. It was as if the very fabric of space around the ship had decided to contract, to crush the intruding matter until it simply couldn't exist in three-dimensional space anymore.

In my head, I felt Nekufima's presence expanding, a cold

pressure behind my eyes that threatened to split my skull. Her consciousness flowed through me like liquid nitrogen, freezing everything it touched. And with that presence came... knowledge. Not words, not images, but direct understanding of what was happening.

She wasn't just destroying the ship. She was folding space itself, creating a localized discontinuity in the dimensional barriers between normal space and the Sydereallium. The battlecruiser wasn't being crushed—it was being partially transitioned into another dimension where the laws of physics operated differently, where matter as we understood it couldn't maintain cohesion.

The process reached its climax with frightening speed. The once-mighty vessel, now compressed to a fraction of its original size, simply... vanished. One moment it was there, a twisted knot of tortured metal; the next, it imploded into nothingness, leaving behind only a rapidly dissipating cloud of particulate matter and gas—the bits that had been ejected before the final collapse.

Silence reigned on *Thunder*'s bridge. Every face was turned toward the viewscreen, every expression frozen in shock and disbelief. No one had ever seen anything like what they'd just witnessed. No weapon in known space could do what they'd just watched happen.

"Holy shit," someone whispered, breaking the spell. "What just happened?"

We'd just witnessed the death of at least 500 citizens of the Collective Dominion.

I couldn't answer. My hands gripped the arms of my command chair, knuckles white with the effort of maintaining my composure while Nekufima's thoughts poured through my mind, calm and satisfied, like a predator that had just demonstrated its dominance.

Do you see now? her voice whispered in my thoughts. *Do you understand what I am? What we could be together?*

I did see. For the first time since our unwilling bond had formed, I glimpsed the true nature of the entity I harbored—not just ancient and powerful, but fundamentally different from anything in our reality. A being that viewed the physical laws of our universe as suggestions rather than immutable constraints.

And I had just given her permission to use that power.

"Captain?" Sofia's voice pierced my thoughts. She was staring at me, her expression a mixture of relief at our survival and something else—a keen, searching look that suggested she suspected I was somehow connected to what had just happened. "Your orders?"

For a moment, I just stood there, bone-weary. I was so damn tired of being the one everyone turned to when things fell apart. Tired of the constant questions, the expectation that I'd always have an answer, a plan, a miracle tucked into my back pocket. It was like being a single mother with a dozen kids clinging to her legs—every one of them needing protection, guidance, permission to breathe. And if anything went wrong? It was her fault. Always her fault. I finally understood what that kind of weight felt like, and it wasn't noble. It was exhausting.

I straightened in my chair, forcing my features into what I hoped was a reasonable facsimile of confident command. "Stand down from battle stations. Focus on damage control and casualty assessment."

As the crew moved to comply, I felt Nekufima's satisfaction like a purring cat in the back of my mind, content for now but always, always hungry for more.

48

The momentary relief of the battlecruiser's destruction evaporated like morning dew under a blowtorch, when Nicobe's voice cut through the bridge's stunned silence. Her normally formal tones carried an urgency I'd never heard before, the crimson facets of her dodecahedron housing flashing with rapid pulses that indicated extreme agitation in her species.

"Captain Drake, Nicobe must inform you that the gamma burst was merely the precursor event," she announced, her dodecahedron bobbing erratically in its housing. "The binary neutron stars' merger has released a wave of relativistic ejecta traveling at approximately thirty-six percent of light speed. This material front will reach our position in three hours and forty-seven minutes."

I turned toward her station, my mind still reeling from what had just happened—what I had just allowed to happen. "Ejecta? You mean radiation?"

"Negative," Nicobe replied. "The captain misunderstands the scale of this event. The approaching wave consists of stellar material—neutrons, heavy elements, and plasma—accelerated to relativistic velocities by the merger event. When it impacts this planet, the atmospheric layers will be stripped away within minutes. The ice giant's outer envelope will, effectively, evaporate. If we remain here, we will be vaporized with it."

The bridge fell silent again as the implications sank in. We'd survived the Kergan frigates. We'd survived the gamma burst. We'd somehow survived the rebel battlecruiser. But this? This was like outrunning a bullet, only to find yourself in the path of an oncoming freight train.

"Display projection of the ejecta front," I ordered, struggling to keep my voice steady.

The main viewscreen shifted to a sensor view of the space where the neutron stars had been. What had once been two distinct stellar bodies was now a chaotic maelstrom of energy and matter—a newborn kilonova in all its terrible glory. Expanding outward from this cosmic catastrophe was a wall of... I didn't even have words for it. The sensors displayed it as a rippling front of superheated particles, heavy elements, and radiation, moving outward in all directions at a significant fraction of light speed.

"Can we outrun it?" I asked, already calculating distances and velocities in my head.

Phoebe's face appeared on a side screen, her expression grim. "Not a chance, Captain. Even if our batteries were at full capacity—which they're not. It'll take many hours to fully recharge them from the reactor—we couldn't reach the necessary velocity. Insufficient delta-v. The blast front is spreading across the entire system."

"What about jumping to veilspace?" I turned to Destiny, hoping for better news. "Even a short jump could get us beyond the wave front."

Destiny shook her head, frustration evident in her tight expression. "Navigation systems remain scrambled. The gravitational distortions are playing havoc with our jump calculations. I've run seven predictive models, and all of them show the same result—we try to jump, we end up tearing ourselves apart in a collapsed veilspace pocket."

"Nicobe concurs with this assessment," the igna added. "The local spacetime fabric is too distorted for safe veilspace translation. We are, as humans say, well and truly screwed."

Under different circumstances, Nicobe's attempt at colloquialism might have drawn a smile. Now, it only underscored the gravity of our situation.

"There has to be a way out," I insisted, refusing to accept that we'd survived all these threats only to be wiped out by the cosmic equivalent of shrapnel.

The crew launched into action, terminal displays filling with calculations, simulations, and desperate attempts to find a solution. But with each passing minute, the reality of our situation became clearer. We were trapped in the shadow of a planet about to be vaporized, with damaged engines, no jump capability, and an approaching wall of destruction that nothing in known space could withstand.

I felt a subtle touch on my arm and turned to find Sofia standing beside my command chair. Her fingers brushed against my sleeve, and I felt a spark—not romantic or even friendly, but the electric tension of unasked questions. It jolted me nonetheless.

"What happened out there?" she asked quietly, her eyes searching mine. "With the battlecruiser. What did you do?"

I met her gaze, seeing the sharp intelligence there, the pieces she was putting together. Sofia had always been perceptive, able to see connections others missed. She'd noticed my moment of withdrawal before the cruiser's destruction, had perhaps sensed the change in me afterward.

"I..." I hesitated, unsure how to explain what I barely understood myself. "It's complicated."

"We don't have time for complicated," she replied, her voice low but intense. "That ship was destroyed by something I've never seen before. Something that left no energy signature, no radiation trace, nothing our sensors could identify." Her eyes narrowed slightly. "And you were... different... just before it happened."

Before I could formulate a response, Destiny called out from her station, "Captain, look at the planet!"

The main viewscreen shifted back to a view of the ice giant. The uppermost layers of its atmosphere were beginning to shimmer with increased energy, glowing faintly as the leading particles from the kilonova reached the planet's outer gases. It was beautiful in a terrifying way—like watching the first licks of flame on a fuse burning toward explosives.

"Radiation levels increasing," Sofia reported, returning to her station. "The ejecta front is colliding with the planet's upper atmosphere and producing a shower of secondary charged particles. It's just the beginning."

"Time estimate to critical exposure?" I asked.

"Three hours, twenty-two minutes until the main front arrives," Nicobe responded. "However, the preceding radiation and particle shower will begin to compromise our hull integrity approximately thirty-two minutes before that."

The grim reality settled over the bridge like a physical weight. We had just over three hours to find an escape that didn't seem to exist. The crew turned to their stations, working with the quiet intensity of professionals facing impossible odds, but I could sense the underlying current of fear—not panic, but the cold recognition of approaching death.

One by one, they began to look at me. Not with accusation or despair, but with something I found far more terrifying: hope. They had seen the impossible destruction of the battlecruiser. They didn't know how it had happened, but they knew I was somehow connected to it. And now, facing another impossible situation, they were looking to me to pull off another miracle.

Phoebe was the first to voice what they were all thinking. "Captain," she said from her engineering station, her usual playfulness replaced by solemn directness, "whatever you did before... can you do it again? Can you get us out of this?"

The question hung in the air, heavy with implications. They didn't know what I'd done—what I'd permitted Nekufima to do—but they'd seen the results. A warship that should have destroyed us had instead been erased from existence. Now they wanted me to do it again, to save them from the approaching wall of stellar death.

They turn to you so readily, Nekufima whispered in my thoughts, her mental voice amused. *These mortals who place their faith in you without understanding the price of the power they're asking you to wield.*

Can you do it? I asked silently. *Can you save us from this?*

I felt her presence stirring within me, like a predator rousing from a light doze, stretching its claws. *Perhaps. The manipulation of matter at such scales is... challenging, even for me. But not impossible.*

What would it cost? I pressed, already knowing the answer wouldn't be simple—or cheap.

Every gift has its price, Kory Drake, she purred. *The greater the gift, the greater the cost. But to save your ship and crew from this splendid stellar cataclysm? I ask only that you pray to me—and do it in my name.*

How? I asked, my stomach already sinking.

It is quite simple, she said, with a drawl of irritation, as if explaining to a child. *Before I act on your behalf, you must make it clear to your friends that I, Nekufima, am the source of their salvation.*

I went still.

I understood what she was asking—not just acknowledgment, but reverence. She wanted me to name her before the crew, to speak her name aloud with gratitude and awe. Not just a whisper in the dark. A proclamation. She didn't want obedience—she wanted *worship*. She didn't want to be *freed*. She wanted to be *enthroned*. And somehow, I'd become the fool delivering the crown.

What had started as containment—me holding the Phylactery—had mutated into something else entirely. She'd crawled out of her prison and into my mind, and now she was using me to climb into the real world. Each time I let her act, the boundary between us blurred. She wasn't satisfied with being a voice in the dark. She wanted agency. She wanted a following. She wanted a world that said her name with awe and fear.

And I was about to give it to her.

I felt the weight of their eyes—my crew. Watching. Waiting. Hoping. They didn't know what they were about to witness. They didn't understand what it meant. Hell, *I* didn't understand. I was seconds away from turning an imprisoned cosmic entity into a god. A *real* one.

What the hell had I gotten myself into?

Outside the viewport, the ice giant loomed like a wounded titan, its swirling atmosphere rippling under the first fingers of the shockwave. The debris from the kilonova was coming fast. No time for a vote. No time for backup. No time for anything but one final, irreversible choice.

And all Nekufima needed was her name spoken with the right weight. The right reverence.

And I—I was going to give it to her.

I closed my eyes.

Do it, I told her.

A ripple of cold satisfaction echoed through my skull.

You first, my captain. You know what you have to do.

I cringed inwardly. Slowly, I raised my right hand. The bridge fell utterly silent, every crewmember turning to look at me, breath held, the weight of what I might say pressing down on them. I swallowed, my throat dry, and spoke—not just aloud, but *upward.*

"O Nekufima, who dwells beyond the veil of stars, bound in light and thought and shadow," I said, the words coming with unexpected clarity. There were several gasps on the bridge. "I call upon you now—not as your keeper, but as your servant in this hour."

The silence deepened. The lights dimmed, or maybe it just felt that way. Sofia approached and gripped my lowered arm, her hands trembling.

"We are adrift on the edge of annihilation," I continued. "My hands can do no more. My mind has no answers left. I lay this ship and her crew before you, not in surrender—but in faith."

I felt Nekufima's presence stir—amused, expectant.

"Deliver us from the fire that comes," I said, voice steady now, stronger. "Spare these lives. Shelter this vessel. Do this, and I will not deny you when next you speak."

For a heartbeat, there was nothing. Then her voice unfurled inside my mind—rich, sinuous, and far too pleased.

Such devotion, Kory Drake. Such lovely surrender, offered with trembling hands and a commander's pride still clinging to your breath.

There was a sense of warmth—not comfort, but heat, the kind that melts steel.

I liked that, she purred. *I liked it very much. You speak to me as a god should be spoken to. And so I will reward you—generously.*

The temperature on the bridge seemed to drop, though no system reported it. The lights flickered. I could feel her power coiling, rising—ready.

And then the universe shivered.

There was no flash, no sound. Just a sensation—like being unhooked from gravity, from time, from causality itself. *Thunder* lurched in every dimension at once, and then everything snapped violently into silence.

When I opened my eyes, the ice giant was gone. So were the stars. No sign of veilspace. Whatever Nekufima had done, it had been instantaneous.

Outside the viewports, only darkness remained. Thick, oil-black space dusted with unfamiliar shadows. No nav beacons. No stellar coordinates.

Nicobe's voice crackled over the comm, tight with disbelief. "We are... inside a nebular void. Starless. Unmapped. I cannot locate our position within the galactic coordinate system."

The crew fell silent.

Nekufima spoke again, her voice soft and honeyed.

You are safe, Kory Drake. Just a little farther from the world you once knew.

And I realized, with a cold twist in my gut, that while I'd saved my crew from one death...

I might have just delivered us to another.

49

I dragged myself through *Thunder*'s mangled intestines, each step sending fresh bolts of pain through my bruised ribs. Emergency lights cast everything in a sickly red glow, turning the twisted metal and exposed circuitry into something from a nightmare. The ship had survived—we had survived—but the cost was etched into every scorched panel and ruptured conduit. My fingers traced a hanging power cable, still warm to the touch. *Thunder* was wounded, just like me. The difference was that I deserved my injuries.

The cut above my eye had stopped bleeding, but it throbbed in time with my heartbeat, a persistent reminder of the moment when I'd been thrown against my command chair as we'd pushed through the leading edge of the kilonova. My uniform was stiff with dried sweat and blood—mine and others'—but changing seemed like a luxury I hadn't earned. Not yet.

"Captain on deck," someone called as I rounded a corner into a section where a repair team was wrestling with a damaged environmental control unit. Three crewmen straightened, tools still in hand.

"As you were," I said, waving them back to work. My voice sounded hollow in my own ears, like it was coming from someone else. Maybe it was.

I moved past them, making a note on my datapad to prioritize environmental systems in this section before we all started breathing like we were inside a wet sock. I ignored the stares and whispers as I turned my back on them—nothing new. The ship had been simmering with rumors ever since I'd stood on the bridge, lifted my hand like a space-age prophet, and called upon Nekufima like she was some kind of interstellar goddess.

And then she'd *answered.*

Some of the crew were in awe. They were the minority—the wide-eyed ones who suddenly thought I needed to be addressed with reverent pauses. A slightly larger group was just scared out of their minds, though still polite about it, like I might spontaneously levitate or burst into flame during morning briefings. And then there were the suspicious ones—my command staff among them—watching me like I was carrying a live grenade with the pin half-pulled.

But really, what did they expect?

The ship was minutes from annihilation, and I, the allegedly rational captain of a military vessel, had invoked a cosmic prisoner from an ancient artifact—*out loud*—in front of the entire bridge crew. And then she'd delivered us, like a scene cut from a cultist recruitment holo.

Frankly, I was just surprised no one had started a shrine to Nekufima in the supply closet. Yet.

At a junction where two corridors met, I paused. A massive emergency patch covered what had been a hull breach—a meter-wide section where the outer plating had simply... disappeared during our escape. The temporary seal bulged slightly inward, the immense pressure of vacuum testing its limits. I ran my fingers along the edge of the patch, feeling the rough texture of the emergency foam that had hardened into something stronger than steel.

Through a nearby viewport, I could see nothing but darkness. No stars, no navigation points, just the impenetrable black of the nebula we'd fled into. The last desperate maneuver—my last conscious order before Nekufima took over—had been to punch *Thunder* through the edge of a dark nebula, using its dense gas clouds to shield us from the pursuing wave of stellar ejecta. It had worked, but at a cost: we were now adrift in a stellar nursery, navigational sensors blind, with no clear path back to known space.

I pressed my forehead against the cold transplas of the viewport, allowing myself a moment of weakness where no one could see. Behind us lay devastation on a scale I could barely comprehend. The Ossuary Ring—an ancient, impossibly advanced structure that had survived for millions of years—reduced to cosmic dust. The binary neutron stars, collapsed into a kilonova that had likely consumed both the Kergan and Dominion fleets that had been hunting us.

And Ban'ach? Had the Soul Ravager been caught in that apocalyptic storm? Part of me hoped so—it would solve one of our most persistent problems. But another part, a part I was less comfortable acknowledging, hoped she had somehow survived. Our rivalry had become... personal. The thought of her being wiped out by an impersonal cosmic event rather than by my hand felt unsatisfying.

Such primitive thoughts, Nekufima's voice slithered into my consciousness, seeming to come from everywhere and nowhere at once. *Wanting to kill your enemy personally. So...*

biological.

I flinched, my fist clenching against the viewport. It had only been a day with this unwanted mental bond, and her sudden intrusions still caught me off guard.

You did what was necessary, she continued, her mental voice taking on an almost seductive purr. *What others would hesitate to do. That's why I chose you.*

"You didn't choose me," I muttered under my breath. "I was just the poor bastard who touched your prison."

Details, she dismissed. *The universe arranges its pieces as needed. You were meant to find me.*

I tried to push her away mentally, to erect the barriers I'd been practicing, but her laughter simply rolled through them like fog through a chain-link fence.

The line between us grows thinner each time you use my power, she whispered, the words echoing inside my skull. *Soon, you won't know where you end and I begin. Isn't that delightful?*

"Captain?"

I jerked away from the viewport, turning to find a young engineer standing a few meters away, tool kit in hand, concern etched on her face.

"Yes, Spacer?" I managed, straightening my posture despite the protest from my ribs.

"Sir, we've restored power to junction 17-A. Lieutenant Brooks asked me to inform you that secondary sensors are back online in that section."

I nodded, trying to look like someone in control of both the situation and their own mind. "Good work. Tell the lieutenant I'll review the sensor data within the hour."

The spacer saluted and turned to go, but not before I caught the fleeting glance she threw my way—part reverence, part fear. I'd been seeing that look a lot lately. Ever since our escape, the crew had been treating me like I'd sprouted a halo... or horns. They knew something had happened between me and the Phylactery—something big—and while no one had said it out loud, the shift in how they looked at me was undeniable.

Destiny had already started cracking jokes about a "Cult of Nekufima" forming in the lower decks. She said it with a grin, but the way some of the crew had been acting? I wasn't entirely sure she was wrong.

They fear you now, Nekufima observed with satisfaction. *As they should.*

"Shut up," I growled.

The engineer paused, looking back at me with confusion. "Sir?"

"Nothing, Spacer. Talking to myself. Carry on."

She nodded hesitantly and continued down the corridor, her pace just a little quicker than before.

I sighed and pushed off from the bulkhead, continuing my inspection route. The damage was extensive, but not catastrophic. *Thunder* was a tough ship, built to take punishment. With enough time and ingenuity, my crew could repair most of the physical damage. The other damage—the cracks in trust, in certainty about who and what I was becoming—would be harder to fix.

I reached a relatively quiet section where the damage was extensive but not critical—twisted support struts, blackened wall panels, exposed circuitry hanging like technological entrails. No one was working here yet; other areas had priority. I leaned against a relatively intact bulkhead, closed my eyes, and allowed myself to confront the memory I'd been avoiding.

The moment when I'd given Nekufima control. The surge of power that had flooded through me, cold and ancient and utterly alien. The terrifying ease with which she had reached out through me, folding space itself around the rebel battlecruiser, crushing it like a child might crush an insect. Horror and exhilaration had mingled in my blood as I watched—as I felt—the destruction I had enabled.

I hadn't just killed enemy combatants. I had obliterated them without warning, without giving them a chance to surrender. Hundreds of lives snuffed out in seconds.

"Was there another way?" I whispered to the empty corridor.

Nekufima's response was immediate, her presence coiling through my thoughts like a serpent. *No. And next time will be easier.*

My hands were numb, my chest tight, and my mouth dry as the sands of Mars.

The infirmary stank of antiseptic, burned flesh, and fear. Doc Montana's domain had transformed from its usual orderly clinic into a makeshift field hospital, with every bed occupied and several emergency cots crammed into the corners. The wounded lay in various states of consciousness, their injuries telling the story of our escape better than any mission report could—radiation burns from the gamma flash, compound fractures from the violent maneuvers, lacerations from flying debris when sections of the hull had buckled. I stood in the doorway for a moment, letting the weight of it settle on my shoulders, another burden for the collection.

Doc Montana herself moved between patients with the mechanical efficiency of someone running on stims and willpower. Her usually pristine medical uniform was rumpled and stained, and dark circles hung beneath her eyes like bruises. She'd been on duty for over twenty hours straight, from the first moments when the injured Ivor

Rowbottom arrived through our desperate escape from the kilonova. She glanced up as I entered, gave me a curt nod that acknowledged my presence without inviting interruption, and returned to sealing a radiation burn on a young crewman's arm.

I scanned the room, taking inventory of the damage to my crew. Rivera with third-degree burns across half her face. Thomson with an oxygen mask covering his radiation-scarred lungs. Matthews strapped to a spinal stabilizer while the regen unit slowly repaired his crushed vertebrae.

In the far corner, partially separated from the others by a portable privacy screen, I spotted Lieutenant Ivor Rowbottom. His torso was encased in a medical foam cast, the pale blue material hardened around his chest and back to immobilize his spine. Despite his condition, he had a datapad propped against his up drawn knees, his fingers swiping through what appeared to be ship schematics.

Working even while broken. I recognized the impulse all too well.

I made my way between the beds, exchanging brief words with those who were conscious—a touch on the shoulder here, a nod of acknowledgment there. Small gestures that meant little in the grand scheme but seemed to matter to the recipients. By the time I reached Rowbottom's bed, I'd counted sixteen serious injuries, not including the eight body bags in the morgue one deck below.

"Sir," Rowbottom said, attempting to straighten from his semi-reclined position. His face immediately contorted in pain, color draining from his features as his broken ribs and damaged vertebrae protested the movement.

"At ease before you snap something else," I said, waving him back down. "I thought Doc Montana would have strapped you down after the last time you tried to report for duty with a punctured lung."

A ghost of a smile touched Rowbottom's pale lips. "She threatened to, sir. Said if I got out of bed again, she'd sedate me into next week." He gestured at the datapad. "Figured I could at least review the damage assessments from here."

"Truly the model of restraint," I said, pulling up a stool beside his bed. "How bad is it?"

"Three cracked vertebrae, four broken ribs, mild concussion," he recited clinically, as if reading someone else's medical chart. "Minor internal bleeding, but Doc says they caught that in time. Could've been worse—I could have fallen. Both Lieutenant Brooks and me..." He shrugged, then winced at the movement.

"You'd be discussing your injuries with whoever handles the paperwork in the afterlife," I finished for him. "Though knowing you, you'd probably still be filing status reports from beyond the grave."

"I'd never hear the end of it from CPO Wilson if dying meant missing a duty shift," he replied with dark humor. "Sir."

I leaned back slightly, surprised by the genuine smile that had found its way to my face. It felt foreign after the last several days of grimness and guilt.

"What's the recovery timeline?" I asked, gesturing to his torso.

"Doc says I'll be back on duty in two weeks if the bone knitters do their job." He tapped the edge of the medical cast. "Good as new, she promises."

"Make it three," I countered. "We're not exactly in a rush to get anywhere." I glanced out the small viewport next to his bed at the impenetrable dark of the nebula beyond. "Besides, I need you at a hundred percent, not hobbling around the marine deck pretending you're not in pain."

He looked like he wanted to argue, but settled for a

resigned nod. "Yes, sir. Three weeks." He hesitated, then added, "Any word on our next move?"

"Repairs first," I said. "We took a beating getting here. Once *Thunder*'s stable, we'll work on finding our way out of this cosmic fog bank."

Rowbottom nodded thoughtfully. "Engineering thinks propulsion will be back to seventy percent within four days. Lieutenant Brooks has been pushing the repair crews hard—hasn't taken a break since we landed."

At the mention of Phoebe, something flickered across his face—a momentary softening, just a twitch at the corner of his mouth. Curious.

"Speaking of Lieutenant Brooks," I said, casually enough, "how's she holding up?"

He glanced at the diagnostic screen, then back at me. "She stopped by this morning. Dropped off updated schematics and a priority list from Nicobe. Stayed a little while longer than necessary." He hesitated, just enough for me to catch it. "We talked. She's tired, yeah, but... she's in good spirits. Resilient."

His tone said more than the words. I arched an eyebrow.

"She, uh... asked if you were all right," he added. "Said you've been scarce."

I winced. So she'd noticed. "Not scarce," I deflected. "Just making the rounds, inspecting the damage personally."

"Right," Rowbottom said. Then, after a beat, "I told her you'd find your way back to the bridge, eventually."

There was a quiet confidence in his voice—and something else, too. Not possessiveness. Not exactly protectiveness either. Just... connection.

I tilted my head slightly, studying him. "You two been spending more time together?"

He didn't answer immediately, but the faint smile returned. "Let's just say... when she's not yelling at people to weld faster, she's got a good sense of humor."

I blinked, then grinned—genuinely. "Huh. Good for you, Lieutenant."

Rowbottom looked like he wanted to shrug it off, but the hint of color rising in his cheeks said everything.

"Well," I said, standing slowly, careful of my still-sore side, "just don't let her rope you into any more reactor maintenance marathons. She plays to win."

"Yes, sir." Then, more quietly: "And Captain... whatever happened out there, with that battlecruiser—none of us missed what it cost you. But you got us out. We're still flying. That matters."

I met his gaze. "Yeah. It does."

And for the first time in hours, maybe longer, I felt just a little lighter.

Before leaving, I cast one more glance around the infirmary, mentally counting the wounded and adding them to the tally of those who hadn't made it. Eight dead. Sixteen seriously injured. It would have been a lot more if I hadn't bargained with Nekufima.

If she hadn't forced me to pray to her.

Forced? her voice purred in my mind, all smug amusement. *Darling, you made that plea sound like poetry. I nearly wept. Don't ruin the moment by pretending it wasn't heartfelt.*

I gritted my teeth and kept walking.

Doc Montana caught my eye from across the room and gave me a small salute with her medical scanner—a gesture that conveyed both respect and understanding. I returned it, then slipped out into the corridor, the sounds of suffering fading behind me but not from my conscience.

* * *

I continued my inspection through a section of *Thunder* I'd been avoiding—Deck 4, where a Kergan blast had torn through six cabins. Emergency bulkheads had sealed in time to prevent decompression, but not before the explosion shredded a swath of crew quarters.

The damage control team had restored pressure and patched breaches, but remnants of lives interrupted lay scattered across the corridor—photographs, clothes, keepsakes. The things that turned a ship into a home.

A child's drawing, edges scorched, lay beside a half-melted music player. A rare paper book lay shredded, pages strewn like fallen birds. A small potted plant, somehow intact, spilled dirt across a collection of handwritten letters.

Each item was a story. A reminder of what we risked to be out here, what we carried with us through light-years of isolation. I'd always encouraged such personalizations. A starship wasn't just metal and protocol—it was a community.

Something glinted in the emergency lighting. I kneeled, ribs protesting, and picked up a simple metal locket. The snapped chain was stained with dried blood. I recognized the etched oak tree: Petty Officer James Mercer's family heirloom. He'd once shown it to me in the mess, proud of its 200-year history.

Mercer had died in Engineering during the breach, stabilizing the chromatic batteries and saving dozens. I pressed the release. The locket clicked open to reveal two tiny photographs: a woman with Mercer's smile and a laughing child. His sister and nephew, waiting for him back on Earth.

Now they'd receive a folded flag and a condolence letter. Nothing close to enough.

I closed the locket, the metal biting into my palm. Eight

dead. Eight letters to write. Eight families who would never know what it cost to keep the others alive.

And they'd never hear the truth: that I had bargained with something ancient and malevolent to save the rest of us.

How quaint, Nekufima's voice slithered into my mind. *All this sentiment for such temporary things. Trinkets, flesh, attachments—all dust in the wind.*

I didn't flinch. Not this time. *They matter to me,* I replied. *They matter to each other. That's enough.*

You can't save them all, she said. *Without me, they'd be atoms in the void.*

Maybe, I conceded. *But that doesn't give you control. This is still my body. My ship. My crew.*

She coiled with agitation. *You'll beg me again, when the next crisis comes.*

We'll see, I answered, pushing her presence aside more easily than before. She retreated—but I felt her watching.

I slipped the locket into my pocket. I'd clean it and have the chain repaired before returning it to Mercer's family. A small gesture. But human.

If I wanted to keep leading this crew—if I wanted to be *worth* following—I needed to fix more than armor plating and reactors. I needed to repair what I'd broken.

Starting with Sofia and Phoebe.

Back in my quarters, I ignored the chaos tossed by evasive maneuvers and activated my desk terminal. The screen glowed, waiting.

I typed:

"Sofia, Phoebe. Request your presence in my ready room at 1900 hours to discuss recent events and our current situation. Informal meeting. No reports. —Kory"

Then added:

"This is overdue."

Brief. Honest. A beginning.

The tension between us had been building for weeks. Sofia and I barely spoke outside official channels. Phoebe, drawn to me in ways I hadn't handled well, complicated things further. And through it all, I'd hidden behind duty, using ship maintenance and crises to dodge the harder emotional wreckage.

They won't understand what you've become, Nekufima warned. *They'll fear you. Especially your cold little German—she sees too much. She'll turn away when she sees what you are.*

I leaned back. "Maybe," I murmured. "But I have to try."

The message confirmation blinked. 1900 hours. Four hours to clean up, suit up, and figure out how much truth I could afford to share.

You're making a mistake, she hissed. *I can protect this ship from threats you haven't imagined.*

"At what cost?" I asked the silence. But I already knew.

I stood, the locket's weight grounding me. I wasn't just fighting to survive—I was fighting to stay human.

First, face Sofia and Phoebe. Then face whatever waited in the dark nebula. And all the while, keep pushing back against the presence in my mind.

I knew Nekufima was calculating her next move.

But for the first time, so was I.

50

I paced the length of the ready room, each step an exercise in controlling my nervous energy. The space felt smaller than usual, the walls pressing in with the weight of all I needed to say. My hands shook slightly as I adjusted the chairs around the small conference table—unnecessary busywork to distract from the knot in my stomach. In seven minutes, Sofia and Phoebe would walk through that door, and I'd have to face two women whose trust I'd damaged in entirely different ways. The ship's environmental system hummed softly in the background, a counterpoint to my racing thoughts.

We'd been drifting through the nebula for over a day now, *Thunder*'s systems operating at minimal capacity while repair crews worked around the clock. The command deck had been quiet, our interactions limited to terse status reports and logistical discussions. I'd retreated into the work of being captain, using damage control as an excuse to avoid the personal connections I now desperately needed to rebuild.

You're wasting your time, Nekufima's voice slithered through my thoughts. *These human entanglements are meaningless. Focus on our partnership instead.*

"Our partnership," I muttered, straightening a data pad that was already perfectly aligned with the table edge. "Is that what we're calling your attempted possession now?"

Such dramatic terminology, she replied, her mental voice dripping with condescension. *I merely offer guidance. Wisdom beyond your limited mortal perspective.*

"You offer nothing but trouble," I said, then caught myself speaking aloud to an empty room. Another habit I'd need to break before the crew decided their captain had completely lost his mind. Maybe I had.

The door chime interrupted my thoughts. I glanced at the chronometer—they were early.

"Enter," I called, forcing my voice into a neutral tone that betrayed none of my apprehension.

The door slid open with a soft hydraulic hiss. Sofia entered first, her back straight, face composed in what I'd come to think of as her "professional mask." Her honey-blonde hair had started to grow back in a fuzz, but I noticed dark circles beneath her eyes that matched my own. Phoebe followed a half-step behind, her usual confidence subdued, brown eyes flickering between Sofia and me with uncharacteristic uncertainty.

"Thank you both for coming," I said, gesturing to the chairs. "Please, sit."

They moved to opposite sides of the small table, leaving me the head position—captain by default, even in this supposedly informal meeting. I lowered myself into the chair, trying not to wince as my still-healing ribs protested the movement.

The three of us sat in uncomfortable silence, the hum of

the ship's systems suddenly deafening in the quiet room. Through the viewport behind them, the swirling darkness of the nebula cast ghostly shadows across their faces, highlighting the strain of the past weeks.

"I asked you here because—" I began, but Phoebe cut me off with a raised hand.

"Actually, Kory, if it's okay, I'd like to speak first." Her voice was quiet but steady, lacking its usual playful edge.

Surprised, I nodded.

Phoebe drew a deep breath, her fingers tracing an invisible pattern on the table's surface. "I owe you both something I should have said a long time ago." She looked directly at Sofia, her brown eyes holding the German woman's blue ones without flinching. "I've been jealous of you. Of what you have with Kory. Of the place you hold in his life that I thought I deserved."

Sofia's expression remained neutral, but I saw her shoulders tense slightly.

"I've made excuses for my behavior," Phoebe continued. "Told myself I was just being friendly, that there was nothing wrong with a little flirting." A self-deprecating smile flickered across her face. "But that wasn't true, and we all know it. I was deliberately pushing boundaries, trying to create space between you two that I could slip into."

The stark honesty of her confession left me momentarily speechless. I'd expected denials, perhaps a defensive argument, not this straightforward acknowledgment.

Interesting, Nekufima commented. *The female admits weakness. A poor tactical decision.*

I mentally pushed her aside, focusing on Phoebe, who was still speaking.

"But here's the thing," she said, her tone softening. "Something unexpected happened while we were all fighting for our lives and trying not to tear each other apart." A slight flush colored her cheeks. "I've been spending time with Lieutenant Rowbottom. Ivor. At first just checking on him in the infirmary, then bringing him reports, and then... staying. Talking."

She looked down at her hands, which had stopped their restless movement on the table. "He's not what I expected. He's steady. Thoughtful. He listens like what I'm saying actually matters, not just..." She glanced at me briefly, apologetically. "Not just because I'm wearing a tank top or bending over an engine compartment."

I felt heat rise to my face, recognizing the uncomfortable truth in her words. I hadn't always discouraged her flirtations as firmly as I should have.

"I'm not declaring undying love or anything dramatic," Phoebe added quickly. "It's new and quiet and I don't know what it is yet. But it's... real. And it made me realize that what I've been doing—with both of you—isn't fair to anyone." She looked directly at Sofia again. "Especially you."

Sofia's expression had softened almost imperceptibly, the rigid line of her shoulders relaxing by degrees. When she finally spoke, her voice was measured, her slight German accent more pronounced than usual, as it often was during emotional moments.

"I appreciate your honesty, Phoebe," she said simply.

No lecture, no bitter recrimination. Just acknowledgment. The two women looked at each other for a long moment, a silent communication passing between them that I couldn't fully interpret.

Phoebe nodded, as if something important had been settled. "I'm not asking for forgiveness. Just... a chance to move forward differently. As colleagues who respect each other's boundaries." She smiled slightly. "Maybe eventually as friends."

"Perhaps," Sofia replied, but there was no coldness in the word, just careful consideration.

I watched this exchange with a sense of wonder. The tension that had hung between the two women for weeks was dissipating not with dramatic confrontation but with quiet dignity and honesty.

And I hadn't needed to say a single word.

Phoebe rose from her seat with a fluid grace that reminded me why so many crew members watched her walk down corridors. "I should go. Give you two some space." She glanced between us. "Whatever happened out there, with the battlecruiser and everything after—we're still here. Still breathing. That counts for something."

She moved toward the door, then paused to look back at me. "For what it's worth, Captain, I think you did what you had to do. We all make choices we have to live with." Her eyes held mine for a moment, understanding in them that made me wonder just how much she suspected about what had really happened. Then she was gone, the door sliding shut behind her.

The ready room felt suddenly larger without her presence, the space between Sofia and me expanding with possibilities and dangers. We sat in silence for several moments, the distant hum of *Thunder*'s damaged systems filling the void.

"That was unexpected," I finally said, aiming for lightness and missing by several parsecs.

Sofia's lips twitched in what might have been a suppressed smile. "Not entirely."

I raised an eyebrow.

"I've seen her visiting Lieutenant Rowbottom in the infirmary," she explained. "Three times in the last day. She brought him real coffee from her personal stash." Sofia's expression softened further. "No one gives away real coffee unless they're serious."

The observation was so practical, so perfectly Sofia, that I couldn't help but smile. The first genuine smile we'd shared in weeks. I held on to the moment, savoring the small crack in the ice between us.

"Sofia," I began, then paused, searching for words. "I should have handled things differently. With Phoebe. With... everything."

She looked at me directly, her blue eyes clear and evaluating. "Yes. You should have."

No easy absolution there. But I hadn't expected any. Sofia had never been one to offer false comfort.

"I owe you an apology," I continued, my throat tight. "I showed disrespect to you and to our relationship by not being more proactive in refusing Phoebe's advances. I let things slide because it was easier than confrontation, and that was wrong."

Sofia's gaze remained steady on mine. "Yes, it was."

"Going forward, I promise I'll do everything in my power to protect your honor," I said, wincing internally at how formal it sounded. "That's not... what I mean is—"

"I know what you mean, Kory," she said, her voice softening slightly. She glanced down at her folded hands on the table. "And I owe you an apology as well. I've been cold. Distant. I blamed you entirely for a situation that involved another person's choices, too."

I blinked, surprised by her admission. Sofia rarely acknowledged fault, not because she was arrogant, but because she so rarely made mistakes.

"The truth is," she continued, "I was afraid. Not just of losing you to Phoebe, but of losing you to..." She hesitated, her eyes finding mine again. "To whatever happened with that battlecruiser. To whatever is happening to you now."

The air in the room seemed suddenly thinner. We'd arrived at the elephant in the room—the mystery of the battlecruiser's destruction, the shadow that had fallen between us since the kilonova.

"You know something happened," I said quietly. It wasn't a question.

She nodded once, sharply. "I've been monitoring your biosignatures. There are... anomalies. Brain wave patterns that don't match your baseline. Energy readings I can't explain." Her expression softened slightly. "And sometimes you talk to yourself when you think no one is listening."

She knows, Nekufima hissed in my mind. *She'll betray you. Use this against you.*

I ignored the voice, focusing on Sofia's face, on the concern I could see beneath her professional exterior. My hands were numb, but I felt a tightness in my chest, an uncomfortable clenching that I recognized as guilt mixed with something else—hope, perhaps.

"I'm not sure I can explain what's happening to me," I admitted. "At least, not fully. Not yet. But I want to. I need to."

Sofia nodded, accepting this without pressing further. "When you're ready," she said simply.

The space between us felt less vast now, the air less charged with tension. We weren't back to where we had been—too much had happened, too many wounds had been opened. But we were talking, really talking, and that was more than I'd dared hope for when I'd sent that message earlier.

"What happens now?" I asked, the question encompassing far more than just the immediate future.

Sofia considered this, her analytical mind visible in the slight furrow of her brow. "Now we rebuild. Not blindly, not by pretending nothing happened, but deliberately. Step by step." Her eyes met mine with determined clarity. "We've survived worse."

I nodded, recognizing the truth in her words. We had survived worse—alien invasions, battles, betrayals. And through it all, Sofia had remained my anchor, my north star when everything else went dark.

"I've missed you," I said simply, the words carrying all the weight of the gulf that had grown between us.

Something softened in her expression. "I've been right here, Kory."

"I know. That's what makes it worse."

Slowly, deliberately, I extended my hand across the table toward her, palm up. An offering, not a demand. Sofia looked at it for a long moment, then reached out, her fingers brushing against mine. The touch was tentative at first, then firmer as our fingers intertwined. Her skin was cool against mine, but warming quickly.

In that simple connection, I felt something vital restore itself between us—not the passionate romance we'd once shared, but something more mature, more resilient. A partnership tempered by fire.

How touching, Nekufima's voice dripped with sarcasm in my mind. *Such primitive attachment rituals. She'll turn on you the moment she learns what you truly are becoming.*

But for once, the ancient entity's words held no power over me. The warmth of Sofia's hand in mine, the quiet understanding in her eyes—these were more powerful than Nekufima's poison, more real than her promises of power.

"Dinner tonight?" I asked quietly. "Just us. In our quarters." Our quarters, not mine. A small but significant distinction.

Sofia nodded, a ghost of a smile touching her lips. "I'd like that."

As our hands remained connected across the scarred surface of the ready room table, I felt *Thunder*'s engines shift slightly beneath us, a subtle change in vibration as repair crews brought another system back online. The ship was healing. Perhaps we could too.

51

The briefing room door hissed shut behind me, sealing us in with our problems like specimens in a jar. I surveyed my command staff seated around the table—Sofia, Destiny, Busto, Phoebe, and Nicobe—their faces illuminated by the harsh blue glow of emergency lighting that we'd been running on for the past twenty-six hours. No one spoke as I took my place at the head of the table, but their silence carried accusations louder than any shouting match. They deserved answers I wasn't sure I could give, explanations for how we'd ended up adrift in the heart of a nebula so dark it swallowed starlight like a cosmic grave.

"I know you all have questions," I began, my voice sounding rougher than I'd intended.

"That's putting it mildly, sir," Busto replied, his weathered face set in hard lines. The formal "sir" didn't soften the challenge in his voice.

I nodded, accepting the rebuke. "Let's start with what we know for certain."

With a gesture, I activated the holographic display

embedded in the center of the conference table. A three-dimensional rendering of *Thunder* appeared, surrounded by a featureless void that pulsed with occasional wisps of dark matter—our best sensor representation of the nebula engulfing us.

"We've been adrift for twenty-six hours and seventeen minutes," I continued, meeting each of their gazes in turn. "Main engines are operational at sixty-two percent capacity, life support stable at seventy-eight percent. Hull integrity has been restored to acceptable parameters."

"That's not what concerns us, Captain," Sofia interjected, her voice cool and precise. Despite our recent reconciliation, her professional demeanor remained intact during duty hours. "What concerns us is this." She gestured to the void surrounding our ship in the holographic display.

"We're in the heart of a dark nebula," I confirmed. "Stellar radiation absorption is nearly complete. No visible stars, no recognizable celestial landmarks. Navigation is effectively impossible."

Destiny leaned forward, the shadows accentuating the worry lines around her eyes. "We've tried every scanning frequency. The nebula's molecular density is off the charts—it's absorbing or scattering everything we send out."

"What about the syderealdyne transceiver?" I asked, already knowing the answer.

Phoebe shook her head, strands of brown hair falling loose from her usually neat ponytail. "Completely dead. Not malfunctioning—dead. Like it's been fried from the inside out." She exchanged a quick glance with Sofia. "We've never seen anything like it. The helium condensate matrix is intact, but it's not resonating. It's as if..." she hesitated, "as if there's nothing for it to connect with."

"Or something's blocking it," Sofia added quietly.

The implication hung in the air between us. Sderealdyne transceivers operated by exploiting quantum entanglement within the Syderealium—the same dimensional space that Nekufima originated from.

"Without functional navigation or communication, we can't risk a veilspace jump," I said, stating the obvious. "We have no way to calculate safe coordinates without reference points."

"A blind jump could materialize us inside a star, or worse," Nicobe's dodecahedron bobbed in her housing unit, her formal tones carrying unusual stress harmonics. "Nicobe must emphasize the catastrophic potential of such an attempt."

"So we're trapped," Busto concluded, his fingers drumming once on the table surface—a rare display of agitation from the normally stoic officer. "In the middle of nowhere, with no way to call for help or plot a course home." His eyes locked onto mine, unflinching. "Nekufima did this to us, didn't she, sir?"

Tell them whatever you like, Nekufima's voice slithered through my thoughts. *It won't change anything. They're mine now too, by extension.*

I pushed her aside mentally, focusing on Busto's challenge. "The circumstances of our arrival are... complicated."

"Complicated?" Busto repeated, voice rising slightly. "With all due respect, sir, that's not good enough." He stood, planting his hands on the table. "We were near the outer boundary of the Ossuary system. Then there was a flash of... something... and suddenly we're here. No veilspace transition. No normal jump procedure. Just... instantaneous displacement across who knows how many light years."

"Lieutenant Busto," Sofia began, but he wasn't finished.

"The crew is scared, Captain," he continued, maintaining just enough formality to avoid outright insubordination. "They deserve to know what happened. I deserve to know what happened."

"He's right," Destiny said, her voice softer but no less insistent. She'd been uncharacteristically quiet until now, studying me with an intensity that suggested she already had her suspicions. "That wasn't any jump method on record. One second we were there, the next we were here. No transition phase, no veilspace distortion effects."

I felt the weight of their stares, the unspoken questions hanging in the air. My fingers brushed against my pocket, where the small, seemingly innocuous phylactery rested. Its presence felt heavier than its physical mass should allow.

They'll never understand what you've done, Nekufima whispered. *The power you've embraced. The gift I've given you.*

"I need to know if I should be preparing my marines for combat, sir," Busto pressed. "If we've been captured, transported somehow—"

"We haven't been captured," I interrupted. "We're not prisoners. At least..." I hesitated, "not in the way you mean."

An uncomfortable silence fell over the room. Sofia watched me with careful neutrality, but I could see the concern behind her eyes. We'd begun to rebuild our relationship, brick by painful brick, but this revelation might shatter that fragile foundation.

"Kory." Destiny's use of my first name cut through the tension like a blade. Her voice dropped, laden with emotion I rarely heard from her. "Please. Tell us what's happening with the Phylactery."

There it was—the direct acknowledgment of what we'd all been dancing around. The alien artifact I'd been tasked with destroying but had instead kept. The decision I'd made that had changed everything.

Busto's expression darkened. "The Phylactery? The one you were supposed to destroy?" He looked around the table, gauging reactions. "The one containing a being that could potentially destroy civilizations? And now you're praying to it, like it's some kind of ancient god?"

"Events on the bridge suggest that *thing* is responsible for where we are." Phoebe stated, her usual playfulness completely absent. "Is it... controlling the ship somehow?"

Thing? Nekufima's voice curled into my thoughts like smoke, icy and offended. *I am a sovereign intellect forged before her ancestors developed a cell nucleus, and she calls me a thing? Next she'll be asking if I respond to voice commands like a kitchen appliance.*

I managed not to flinch, but my jaw tightened. This was going to be a long conversation.

"Not the ship," I said quietly. The moment had come. There was no avoiding it any longer. "Me. She's communicating with me."

The admission fell into the silence like a stone into still water, sending ripples of shock through the room. Even Sofia, who'd suspected something similar, couldn't hide her sharp intake of breath.

"I made a choice," I continued, forcing myself to meet their eyes. "When we had the Phylactery, I was supposed to destroy it. But I realized that doing so might eliminate our only advantage against threats like Ban'ach and the Soul Ravagers. So I kept it."

"You kept it," Busto repeated flatly. "Against the plans we all agreed to."

"Yes." No point in denying it. "But something happened when I touched it. Something unexpected." I swallowed hard, feeling the weight of Nekufima's presence in my mind like a cold shadow. "The entity inside—Nekufima—she formed a bond with me. A mental connection."

"A mental connection?" Sofia's voice was carefully controlled. "What exactly does that mean, Captain?"

"She can communicate with me through thoughts. She can... sense what I sense, to some degree."

"And can she control you?" Destiny asked directly, the question everyone was thinking but afraid to voice.

I hesitated, which was answer enough for my perceptive command staff.

"Jesus Christ," Busto muttered, pushing away from the table. "So the ship's captain is compromised by an alien intelligence. That's just perfect."

"I'm not compromised," I countered, with more conviction than I felt. "I maintain control of my actions." Usually. Mostly.

"Then how did we end up here?" Phoebe asked. "In this nebula?"

I drew a deep breath. "The rebel battlecruiser that attacked us... Nekufima destroyed it. Not our weapons. Her power, working through me. And then, when the kilonova ejecta wave was about to overtake us..." I paused, remembering the moment—the cold flood of alien power, the sensation of reality tearing around us, the terrifying transition through dimensions I couldn't name. "She moved us. Instantaneously. Here."

"And that whole dramatic ritual you pulled on the bridge?" Destiny asked, arms crossed. "What was that—cosmic improv night?"

I sighed. This wasn't easy to explain. "It was Nekufima's price. In exchange for saving us from the ejecta, I agreed to call upon her by name—publicly—so she'd be recognized as the one who intervened."

Destiny threw her hands in the air. "Oh, great. And here

I thought dealing with Soul Ravagers was peak nightmare fuel. Now we've got a diva death goddess with a flair for theatrics riding shotgun."

"And she moved *Thunder* without your permission?" Sofia asked, her voice low but sharp.

"Without consultation," I said. "There wasn't time. The wave would've vaporized us. Radiation was already spiking, and the ice giant's upper atmosphere was starting to boil away."

"So she saved us," Destiny said slowly. "Why?"

Go ahead, Nekufima purred in my thoughts. *Tell them about my generosity. My benevolence. How I rescued your pathetic little ship from certain destruction.*

"Because she needs us," I replied, ignoring her commentary. "Or more specifically, she needs me as her host, and the ship as transportation."

"Transportation to where?" Nicobe asked, her dodecahedron pulsing with elevated concern frequencies.

I closed my eyes briefly, feeling Nekufima stir in my mind like a predator in shallow water. When I opened them again, I knew my expression had hardened. "She won't tell me. But she says we're exactly where she wants us to be."

Indeed you are, she whispered. *This nebula holds something of mine. Something taken long ago. We will not leave until I reclaim it.*

My hand clenched involuntarily on the table's edge. "She has unfinished business here. Something in this nebula she wants to reclaim." I looked around at my officers' stunned faces. "And she's made it clear we won't be leaving until she gets what she wants."

"That's insane," Busto exploded. "We're hostages to this... this *thing*? This ancient alien parasite?"

Parasite? Nekufima scoffed in my mind, her tone rich with offense. *Please. I don't leech—I elevate. If anything, I'm the best thing to happen to this crew since artificial gravity.*

I didn't bother responding. Arguing with her always felt like debating a thunderstorm.

"Not hostages," I countered. "We're alive. If she hadn't intervened, we'd all be scattered atoms in the void right now. The kilonova—"

"Would have killed us, yes," Sofia interrupted, her analytical mind clearly working through the implications. "So instead, we're trapped in an unknown region of space, with no navigation, no communication, at the mercy of an entity that has demonstrated the power to destroy ships and transport matter across vast distances instantaneously." Her blue eyes locked onto mine. "That's not much of an improvement, Captain."

"Captain Drake," Nicobe's formal tones cut through the rising tension. "Nicobe must inquire: has this entity provided any indication of the timeline for completing its objectives? Or the nature of what it seeks?"

I shook my head. "She's cryptic. Deliberate in withholding information."

"And we're just supposed to wait?" Phoebe asked incredulously. "Float around in this cosmic inkblot while she... what? Uses you as her puppet to hunt for some ancient treasure?"

"I'm nobody's puppet," I snapped, more harshly than intended.

Such confidence, Nekufima mocked silently. *Should we test that theory?*

I felt a cold pressure build behind my eyes, a familiar precursor to her attempting to exert more direct control. I fought it back, my fingers gripping the edge of the table so hard my knuckles turned white.

Destiny noticed immediately. "Kory? What's

happening?"

"Nothing," I managed, the pressure receding. "She's... testing boundaries."

"This is completely unacceptable," Busto declared. "With all due respect, sir, you're compromised. Regulations clearly state that command should pass to the XO in cases where the captain is under external influence."

"I agree with Lieutenant Busto," Sofia said quietly. "Captain, you need to consider temporarily relinquishing command until we can address this situation."

Their words struck me like physical blows. Not because they were wrong—by the book, they were absolutely right—but because hearing them vocalize my worst fears made them real.

"No," I said firmly, straightening in my chair. "I understand your concerns. They're valid. But I am still in command of my faculties and this ship."

"For how long?" Busto challenged. "Until this thing decides to take full control? Until it gets tired of asking nicely and just hijacks your body completely?"

"That won't happen," I insisted, even as Nekufima's laughter echoed in the back of my mind.

"You can't know that," Sofia countered, her professional mask slipping to reveal genuine concern. "This entity is billions of years old, with power we can barely comprehend. You're one human, Drake."

"If I step down," I asked, "what then? How does that solve our problem? Nekufima is bonded to me, not the chain of command. She doesn't care who's wearing the captain's stripes."

That gave them pause. The uncomfortable reality settled over the room—removing me from command wouldn't remove the threat. It might even make things worse.

"Look," I said, my voice softening. "I understand your concerns. I share them. But right now, I need you all working with me, not against me. I need your support, your trust, and yes, your vigilance."

"You want us to watch you for signs of possession," Destiny translated bluntly.

"Yes," I admitted. "And I promise that if any of you—any of you—believe I'm compromised beyond recovery, I will step down immediately." I looked directly at Destiny. "I'm giving you that authority now, as my XO. If you make the call, I'll accept it."

A moment of silence followed as my officers exchanged glances, weighing my words.

"And in the meantime?" Phoebe finally asked. "We just drift here until your... passenger... finds what she's looking for?"

"No," I said firmly. "We keep working. Engineering continues repairs. Navigation keeps trying to map the nebula, find some reference point. Communications works on the syderealdyne transceiver. We prepare for whatever comes next."

"And if what comes next is worse than what we've already faced?" Busto asked quietly.

I smiled grimly. "Then we'll handle it. Like we always do." I looked around the table, meeting each officer's gaze in turn. "I don't know how we're getting out of this situation yet. But I know we will."

“Because we're *Thunder*,” Destiny said, a ghost of a smile tugging at her lips.

I nodded. “And *Thunder's* crew doesn't know how to stay dead. We've faced the Kergans, the Dominion, the Soul Ravagers, and a goddamn kilonova. We're still here.”

The tension didn't vanish, but it shifted—reshaped from

helpless fear into something harder, stronger. Resolve. These weren't just officers; they were a family forged in fire, in vacuum, in battles most crews wouldn't have survived. Whether they fully trusted *me* didn't matter right now. They trusted each other. And they trusted in our shared will to survive.

"All right, Captain," Sofia said, her tone returning to formal, but warmer than before. "We'll proceed as you say. But..." she held my gaze, unflinching, "we'll be watching you."

"I wouldn't have it any other way," I said.

As the meeting dissolved and my officers filed out, steps steadier, eyes clearer, I remained seated. Alone now—with the weight of command pressing down like a second gravity. And with Nekufima, always watching. Always waiting.

I didn't know what ancient power she was drawn to in this nebula. I didn't know where we were, or what came next, or if I'd even be *me* when we found it. The line between host and hitchhiker was wearing thin. Sooner or later, she might stop asking and simply *take.*

But I knew my ship. I knew my crew.

And somewhere in that—beneath the uncertainty, the fear, the god-whispers—I found one unshakable truth: whatever waited for us in the dark, we would face it together.

And we would survive.

Such confidence, Nekufima whispered, her voice curling through the hollow in my thoughts. *Let's see how long that lasts, little captain.*

I smiled at the empty room, thin and defiant. "You know what they say about *Thunder* and her crew, Nekufima? We're too damn stubborn to die."

The only answer was her laughter—cold, amused, echoing in the corners of my mind—as I rose and followed my crew back to the bridge.

The End

Please rate or review my book online! As an indie author, I *depend* on your reviews to legitimize my books in the eyes of those who have not read them.

About Joseph McRae Palmer

Joseph McRae Palmer writes speculative fiction with a taste for the epic and the unexpected. He's also a telecom engineer with a Ph.D. in Electrical Engineering from BYU and a lifelong fascination with real-world science, which he weaves into his stories whenever possible. Born in Utah and raised in Sitka, Alaska, he spent two years as a missionary in central Mexico. He and his wife of 28+ years, Beatriz, have one son, three daughters, and live in northern Utah—where Joseph toggles between engineering projects and dreaming up far-flung futures.

Joseph's fiction site: www.josephmcraepalmer.com

Printed in Dunstable, United Kingdom

68375511R00258